THE CHRO[

BOOK FOUR

THE
MAKING
OF A
KING

BENJAMIN SANFORD

STENOX PUBLISHING
Clarksburg, MD

First originally published by Page Publishing 2023

Cover art by Karl Moline

ISBN 979-8-9886249-8-1(pbk)
ISBN 979-8-9886249-9-8 (digital)

Printed in the United States of America

King Lore & Queen Letha Family Tree

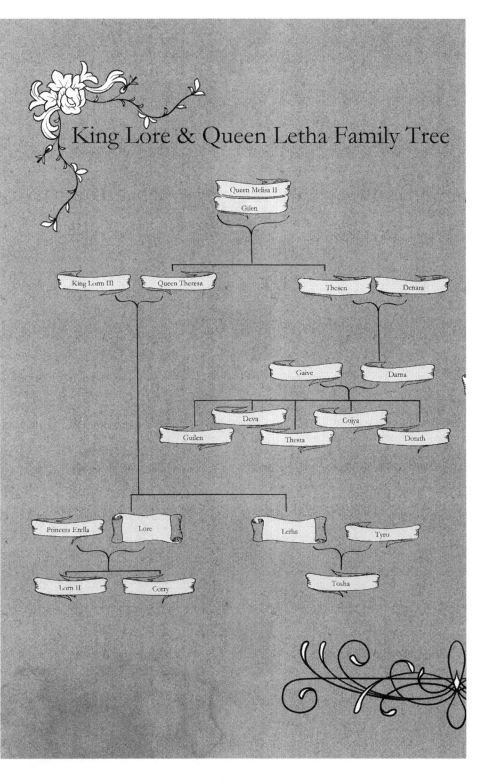

CHAPTER 1

The Casian Sea

"I yield!" Lucas raised his hands in mock surrender as Ular removed the blade pressing his throat. They stood upon the stern of the 1st deck, with the tropic sun glaring overhead.

"Show me that again, Ular," Kendra said, observing the two warriors practicing their martial skills. Grigg and Orlom stood beside her, each staring with childlike wonder, waiting excitedly for their turn.

"As you wish, Mistress Kendra," Ular's voice rippled like water. He smoothly flipped the knife in his hand, offering the hilt to Lucas.

"Ular, I am simply Kendra. I am no mistress," she pointed out, but he was having none of it. The appellation held a different meaning to each of them.

"You are a warrior and female—a mistress of blade, bow, and dagger. I would be remiss to address you without your demonstrated worth," Ular coolly stated, his bulbous eyes blinking hypnotically.

"The terms *master* and *mistress* do not denote ownership or station in Enoructa. They mean proficiency of skill," Brokov said, overlooking them from the stern of the 2nd deck, his elbows resting on the rail above.

"Oh!" She blushed, realizing the compliment Ular paid her, regarding her weapon handling. If she was a mistress of the blade, then Ular was a grand master. Her eyes drew wide as he again dodged

Lucas's measured thrust, disarming him and again pressing the blade to his throat in one fluid motion.

"And I thought Kato's lessons were humiliating." Lucas shook his head, wondering how Ular's hands moved faster than his eyes.

Ular repeated the move, demonstrating the process slow enough for Lucas to follow. He increased speed as Lucas improved his countermeasures before switching roles. The others eventually rotated in, taking turns learning the move. They followed up with Lucas instructing them on grappling holds and throws.

Corry stood beside Brokov watching the activity below. The scene brought back a memory of Terin training under Torg. She lost count of the times she went to see him train, watching from the shadows overlooking the arena. Was she hopelessly smitten even then? She closed her eyes trying to shake the thoughts of him, lest she lose her mind, but it was pointless. She closed her eyes, and he was there, his visage playing cruelly before her, taking shape in the darkness, his countenance alit like a blazing sun. If she opened her eyes, she would find a reminder of him in whatever she saw.

"Your man Lucas is an impressive grappler," Brokov pointed out. He didn't recall sharing many words with Corry during her last voyage on the *Stenox*. Even then, she was overcome with relief and joy after being rescued. Now she looked as if the entire world rested on her shoulders.

"Master Vantel claims Lucas is the finest he has taught, which is high praise coming from him," she said.

"Vantel is your master of arms?" he asked, trying to recall what Lucas and Corry had said earlier.

"Yes, but also the commander of the Tory Elite and guardian of the king."

"If he is the guardian of the king, why wasn't he—"

"At Kregmarin?" she asked, finishing his question. "My father asked Torg to remain at Corell to oversee Terin's instruction. It is fortunate that he did so, or he would have perished with the rest."

"I am sorry for your loss, Corry. Losing a parent is a difficult thing," he said from experience.

And I have lost both. She kept that self-pitying remark to herself.

"Many good men died at Kregmarin. Arsenc was a good friend of ours, and we can count our Araxan friends on the fingers of one hand," Brokov sighed.

"I only met with Arsenc briefly after Molten Isle. He risked desertion in order to rescue Cronus. It speaks to his character that he would do so, and to Cronus's for someone to do so on his behalf. You Earthers choose your friends well."

"We'd like to think so," he said, smiling, though thought she was talking about someone other than Cronus or Arsenc. It was as obvious as the sun above who dominated her thoughts.

"And you would do almost anything for your friends, which validates my decision in seeking your aid."

"I didn't know Terin for very long, Princess, but what I did know, I admired."

"He felt the same about all of you," she sighed.

"Don't worry. If Terin's anywhere near that island, we'll find him. Zem and I are working on a new project that will help with that."

"If it is anything like your other magical tools, I have little doubt of its success."

"As long as Raven doesn't touch it, we'll be fine." He snickered.

"Why is that?"

"He tends to break things."

"Purposely?"

"No, but as often as it happens, I sometimes wonder. He's just a klutz, a *big klutz*. And now we're saddled with two idiots just like him." He regarded Grigg and Orlom, the latter of which nearly fumbled a knife over the side of the ship as soon as the words escaped Brokov's lips.

"Argos was the first ape I ever encountered. I never took him for ungainly." She wondered if all apes were similarly afflicted.

"Argos is a great warrior and highly intelligent. Grigg and Orlom are…" Brokov closed his mouth rather than saying something he'd regret.

"It seems Raven isn't the only Earther who speaks his mind." Corry bit off a smile, finding this side of Brokov rather endearing.

She found most warriors reserved, their faces betraying little of what they were thinking, if they were thinking at all. Many were dullards, trained brutes who thought little beyond their martial craft. Others were simply shrewd, quietly observing their surroundings and taking the measure of others before uttering a word. Most men were similarly afflicted, rarely talkative. It was frustrating at times trying to know where someone stood when all they did was stare in silence. Even Terin, with his childlike innocence, was guardedly observant until she maneuvered him into revealing his thoughts. What she discovered was an intelligent, moral, and kindhearted young man. She scolded herself with her thoughts again leading back to him. Thankfully, Brokov missed the frown briefly crossing her lips.

"When Raven speaks his mind, he isn't really revealing anything." He smiled.

"Why do you disparage your captain?" she asked, noticing the constant aspersions he, Lorken, and even Zem sent in Raven's direction. She couldn't for the life of her wonder how they survived this long with so little discipline.

"Because it's too hard not to when he makes it so easy." He grinned.

She smiled, shaking her head. At least Raven was receiving the same discourtesy from his crew that he gave her at Cagan. Perhaps she shouldn't be offended if this is how they all treat one another.

"If your newest recruits are deficient, then why don't you dismiss them?" she asked, regarding Orlom and Grigg as Ular and Lucas instructed them.

"We don't get rid of our crewmates just because they are idiots. Otherwise, we'd have tossed Raven overboard a long time ago."

She thought he was enjoying himself far too much but couldn't hide her glee at his ridicule of Raven.

"Could you have tossed him overboard?" She raised an eyebrow at that, trying to picture it.

Brokov was a large man, far larger than any Araxan human, but Raven was far larger than him. Brokov had taken off the thick coat that they constantly wore, his unnaturally large arms bulging from the short-sleeved shirt he wore underneath. Lorken was of similar size, and Raven was far larger. They looked almost inhuman.

Were all Earthers this large? she wondered. *No, Kato was not.* She wondered what he was doing right now. *Probably lamenting Terin's loss.* She couldn't help but think of how different all the Earthers were. They were more diverse in their appearance and character than all the peoples of Arax. How did they ever come together to build such an advanced civilization?

"Only Zem could toss him overboard without any help, maybe Argos too," he said.

"That would be an impressive sight." She lightly laughed.

"Yes, someday it will be." He smirked.

"Sometimes I don't know when you are jesting or not. You are all so…different."

"We're different all right," he agreed with a shrug.

"You are good-humored. Kato is dutiful…" She began.

"Zem is egotistical. Raven is ornery. Argos is a big bully." He couldn't help himself. Corry caught the intent but not the meaning of most of what he said.

"They are a bit much." She smiled.

"Yes, they are, and I wonder how we put up with them." He laughed.

For all his aspersions, she knew he thought highly of his friends. Their back-and-forth banter proved they didn't take themselves too seriously and, therefore, didn't take anyone else too seriously either. As bad as Raven's behavior was with her in Cagan, she couldn't imagine how he conducted himself at Fera.

"And yet, you are fond of each other. Kato speaks well of each of you, though his demeanor is far different from yours."

"Kato is respectful of traditions and authority. His countrymen are known for it."

"I thought you were of one nation?" she asked.

"We are all from Earth but hail from different nations or realms as you know them. Kato is from Japan, and his true name is Kaito. Kato is only the abbreviated name we call him."

"Kaito?"

"Well, his full name is Kaito Nakumara."

"A lovely name, befitting a great warrior," she said, thinking fondly of him. "And is your true name Brokov?"

"My family name is Borovkov. My given name is Grigory. I've been called Brokov since my days in the academy. It's been a long time since anyone called me Grigory."

"Shall I refer to you as Grigory then?"

"Stick with Brokov, or you'll just confuse Raven." He smiled.

"And I assume his true name is the elongated version of *Raven?*"

"No. Raven and Lorken were their call names. Those are nicknames used by pilots in our flight squadrons. They picked those monikers because they were also their nicknames. If you want their true names, you'll have to ask them."

"I thought you might substitute one of your monikers for their names to belittle them."

"I would've if I thought of it. Maybe you could come up with something witty like *Super Klutz* and *Trigger Happy*. You'll have to start practicing them if you ever want to get the best of Raven in an argument. You'll have to set aside Corry the Princess and become Corry the *Stenox* crewmember, if only for the short while you're with us." He gave her that parting advice before entering the bridge to relieve Raven at the helm.

Set aside being a princess? she reflected. Hadn't she done that by coming here, abandoning duty to save the man she loved? Part of her that held to duty whispered in her ear that saving Terin was her duty. Terin was the champion of the realm, the blood of Kal, the one they desperately needed against the enemy. All of that was theoretically correct but, in truth, was a lie. She didn't come to save the realm. She sought out Raven to save her breaking heart. Her deepest fear was not just Terin dying but to see him bound to another. Most slaves in the Sisterhood were not used intimately, but she couldn't imagine Terin escaping the eye of his mistress in that way. Jonas said there was still time, but how much time did he mean? She wanted nothing more than to hurry along, and the *Stenox* had already sailed seven hundred leagues in little more than a day, coursing over the surface of the sea at speeds unheard of. The ship slowed significantly a short while ago, reducing speed so the crew could safely practice their combat skills on the deck below, without being tossed from their feet. It was only a brief respite before they continued their arduous pace.

Corry was struck by how quickly they responded to her plea. No sooner did she mention Terin needing help that the crew began preparations to depart. She regretted being able to only bring one of her men with her but wisely chose Lucas. The others would remain at Torn Harbor as *honored guests* of the Ape Republic until she returned.

"He could've warned me it was this hot out here!" She heard Raven grumble as he stepped out of the bridge, the tropic heat blasting him in the face. He quickly stripped off his jacket, tossing it through the door of the bridge before it closed behind him.

"It is strangely hot while Corell is in the heart of winter," she opined as he stepped beside her.

"You got five minutes to finish up before we pick up speed!" Raven warned the others gathered below.

"Aye, Boss!" Grigg waved up to him with his toothy grin before Orlom swept his leg, pinning him to the deck.

"Kids." Raven shook his head as Grigg responded to Orlom's victory by putting him in a headlock with his left arm and striking his face with his right. "Would you like to adopt them?" he asked her.

"No, I think it best if they remain with you." She smiled, taken aback by his attempt at humor. They barely spoke a word to each other since the start of this journey.

"I know you are anxious to get to Bansuck—"

"*Bansoch*," she corrected.

"Bansoch, Bansuck, same difference. I know you're in a hurry to get there, but we have to make a port of call at Teris. It will be brief but necessary. While there, I want you and Lucas to remain below deck and out of sight."

"I understand and agree," she said, not wishing to antagonize the Casian Federation toward the Torry Realm, if they saw her in league with their archenemy. It was little secret the Casians held the Earthers responsible for most of their setbacks during the ape revolution.

"Argos will lead the shore party. Ular and I will be going along."

"Each representing your respective peoples," she surmised, making this an official visit of state.

"I'm just going along for extra security. Argos speaks for us, and Ular for Linkortis."

"Argos is an Earther now?" She lifted a curious brow at that revelation.

"Actually, we are part of the Ape Republic. President Matuzak offered each of us a reserve commission in their newly formed navy."

She was taken aback. Did he just say that he pledged his loyalty to an Araxan monarch?

"You look surprised?"

"You've made it very clear that you bow to no one, and yet you bent the knee to a gorilla warlord?"

"Bent the knee?" He made a face. "Apes don't kneel to anyone, even to one another. We helped them establish a *republic*. The only republic on Arax where all apes, men, or sentients of any kind stand equal to one another and before the law. That was why Argos joined us at Central City before we rescued you. General Matuzak needed our help in transforming the Ape Empire into a republic."

"What is a republic?" Her head was spinning from all that he was saying.

"The people or apes, in this case, select their tribal leaders, and their chieftains select an over chieftain to rule as president for a specific period of time. They are still working out the details, but the president will likely serve only a six-year term before they select a replacement. The same goes for each chieftain. Each tribe will have separate representations in the legislative body as well."

"And you formally joined this...republic?"

"Yep, providing our fleet doesn't find us in the meantime. Since we could be stuck here on this planet for the rest of our lives, we might as well settle down somewhere."

"And the apes' lands are your home now?"

"I can't think of a better place to raise a family. The ape tribes are good, honorable, and share our values."

"I wonder how Kato will feel about your new allegiance."

"When he's done playing soldier for your people, I'll ask him."

"Kato is a good, brave man. We are deeply indebted to him for all he has done for our people. After the siege was lifted, I formally named him *friend* of the Torry Realm."

"Friend? Is that an official title?"

"In a way, yes, an honorary appellation granting sanctuary to a non-Torry for their service to the realm. A *friend* may dwell in the Torry Realm until the end of their days, a guest of the royal court."

"Kato is quite a friend," he agreed.

"Very much so."

"And how is he doing? You said he is in Yatin."

"He helped lift the siege of Mosar, and my brother named him to the Torry High Elite, which he accepted."

"Does he intend to come back to us?"

"I am certain but not until the war is over. He took a bride as well."

"A bride?" This was news.

"A healer matron named Ilesa. They were wed by my brother after the siege of Mosar. She is quite lovely if Lucas speaks true."

"Huh, I don't remember ever seeing Kato with anyone before."

"Some men guard their hearts better than others."

"Well, I'm happy for him. This Ilesa girl is lucky to have him. Kato is a good man. I miss the little fella." He smiled.

"A very good man who I count among my dearest friends." She smiled too. If there was one thing that gave them common cause, it was the friends they shared.

"So he's doing fine?"

"When Lucas departed Maeii, Kato was still somewhere inland, making his way to the Yatin port. As far as how he fares, he was in great spirits when he departed Corell. I can ill imagine how he received news of Terin," she reflected sadly.

"You said, as far as your brother knows, Terin is dead. You're going off the vision of Terin's father."

There it was, the hard reality that drove her to beseech his aid. This entire adventure rested on a prophetic vision that only blind faith could justly follow.

"I am," she sighed.

"And we're taking you there on that faith. Don't get me wrong, Corry. If there's a small hope that your story is true, I am willing to chance it. I don't know much about this place we're going to, but I wouldn't leave a dog to their mercy."

"Dog?"

"A small animal, about wee big, four legs, a tail, barks a lot. It's man's best friend," he said, his explanation lost on her. "Never mind," he said. "Look, if Terin's there, we'll find him."

"Thank you." She was grateful.

"But I want you to be honest with me."

"How so?"

"There is more to this than you are saying." His remark caused her to look away, confirming his suspicion.

"You could've sent one of your thousands of underlings to ask for our help, but you came yourself," he said.

"I came so you would know the urgency of our quest. Terin is the champion of the realm, the hero of Corell. We need him when Morac's legions return," she answered, her eyes fixed to the sea.

"I'm not very good at understanding what goes on in a woman's mind, Princess, but even I know that look in your eyes."

"What look?" she asked darkly, her eyes turning sharply to his.

"You like him."

"Like who?"

"What do you mean who? Terin, that's who. You're in love with him."

"How DARE YOU!"

"Hah, you do," he said with a stupid grin that she wanted to hit.

She opened and quickly closed her mouth before looking away.

"Does he feel the same about you?"

She didn't answer right away, looking off the starboard side of the ship, staring longingly to the horizon.

Cursed tears! she thought miserably as one escaped her moistened eyes, trailing freely along her left cheek. She didn't want to show weakness, especially to Raven.

"If it makes you feel any better, I have the same effect on Tosha. I guess pissing off princesses comes naturally to me."

She didn't know the phrase *pissing off* but could guess its meaning. She certainly wasn't going to ask him about it.

"Back to my question. Does he feel the same? I remember how he followed you around when you were on the *Stenox* last time. I know that look a man has when he likes a girl."

"A girl?" she asked darkly.

"You're a girl, aren't you?"

A princess of the realm was not referred to as simply a *girl*. Was he even aware of his insolence? He was hopelessly offensive, and attempting to correct him was pointless.

"Terin's feelings are reciprocal," she answered his original question.

"All right, then we best find him before something happens." He cut to the heart of the matter.

She was taken aback that he not only discovered her true motivation in finding Terin but agreed with her even more so because of it. He would help her find Terin before he fell into the hands of another.

"Now onto another matter. I've never been to Bansuck. What's it like, and what can I expect when we arrive?"

"*Bansoch*"—she again corrected him—"rests at the mouth of the Sova River, on the eastern coast of the isle. You will be received at the court of Queen Letha at her palace, which rests upon Melida Hill, where the Soch king was thrown down and the Sisterhood born."

"Let's talk about the queen's court. What is the layout of the palace? I need to know exit points in case things go bad. What is the palace troop strength? How far from the palace walls to the water? How—"

"Why are you asking for all that? You sound as if you are going to war or planning a raid. Are you not expected? You promised Princess Tosha you would be there. Are you expecting a trap?"

"This is Tosha we're talking about. She's been setting traps for me since the day we met."

"She's carrying your child. The times for foolishness and petty squabbles need to end."

"There's no argument from me. She's the one who's always pulling dirty tricks."

"That was all her effort to bring you with her to Bansoch. You have to understand her precarious position."

"Precarious? She's their spoiled princess who gets what she wants. What's precarious about that?"

"Royal marriages are usually arranged, with a match benefiting the realm, either by strengthening the crown's ties to their vassals or other kingdoms. By choosing you, Tosha gains neither. All the great houses of the Sisterhood have petitioned the queen for a royal match, offering their sons as consorts to bind them to the throne. By choosing you, she risks offending her vassals and subjects. Your absence further compounds the problem."

"I told her I'd be there, so what's the problem?"

"The duties of a royal consort require your presence at *all* times, especially after you are first wed, where you are formally presented to the realm. She has returned without you and with child. Tongues will whisper," Corry explained.

"Maybe she should've asked me before starting all of this!" he growled.

"Yes, that would have been preferable but does not change the problem at hand."

"I don't understand the problem. Is she in trouble for marrying me?"

"Yes. Perhaps you could show her a little understanding for she risks much by wedding a man who is wholly unsuited for that role."

"Unsuited? You think I'm not good enough for her? I'm the one who's settling here. There's plenty of princesses in this world but only one me."

She nearly face-palmed at that utterance. "Unsuited for life at court. There will be expectations of you when we arrive at Bansoch."

"I can handle it. Meeting her mother can't be worse than meeting dear old dad."

"Dear old dad?" She made a face.

"Tyro. Visiting him was no picnic, so how much worse can Queen Lethal be?"

"Queen *Letha*," she corrected him. "She is not one to suffer fools, but there is no monarch in all of Arax who is a greater friend to the Torry throne. She is a powerful and fair queen who deserves your utmost respect."

"Respect goes both ways. If she's not a jerk, I won't be one either."

Jerk? She didn't bother asking him the definition.

"If you enter her court with that attitude, I don't favor the outcome."

"What are they gonna do, beat me up?" He dismissed her concern. To him, the idea of a bunch of girls attacking him was just nonsense.

"For someone who complains about royal arrogance and privilege, you demonstrate a healthy measure of both."

"You don't like me very much, do you?" he asked with an infuriating grin.

"Not particularly."

"I knew it! It must have been difficult asking for my help."

"You're insufferable." She rolled her eyes. *How did Tosha bear his presence?*

"Yep, I'm insufferable, arrogant, loud, and a lot of fun to be around."

"This is going to be a disaster." She put her hands to her face, not sure if she should laugh or cry. How could she expect Raven to enter Letha's court and not offend everyone with his mere presence? And that was before he opens his mouth.

"Don't worry about it. I got this. I'll keep my mother-in-law and wife entertained long enough for you and the boy genius in there to find Terin." He jerked a thumb over his shoulder toward the bridge, where Brokov was.

Mother-in-law? She surmised his meaning, but following his choice of words was a chore unto itself.

"Perhaps I should come with you and act as an intermediary," she sighed.

"I don't need any help talking with Tosha's mom. Besides, I thought you wanted to conceal your presence so no one would know you aren't at Corell?"

"Morac will renew his attack whenever he is ready. I doubt he'll move up his plans just because I am absent. Torg is more than capable of handling the duties of regent. It is best if I address Queen Letha on your behalf, as long as you remain quiet and treat her with the respect befitting a host monarch."

"And what respect is that?"

"You must kneel in her presence unlike your performance with me at Cagan and Tyro at Fera."

"You can forget that. I'm not kneeling to anyone!" he said indignantly.

"It is merely an acknowledgment of respect to her authority. You would insult Queen Letha in her very court? How does that gain you anything that you seek?"

"Not doing it." He shook his head.

"If you care at all for Tosha, you would suffer this for her sake."

"She knew what she was getting when she married me. If she wanted a beaten-down wimp, she could've picked one from her lousy island."

Her jaw nearly fell open with that insult. Did he truly think so little of the menfolk of the Sisterhood? Were they held in less regard than the womenfolk of the Torry Realm? Her great-grandfather Gilen was such a man, a consort to Queen Melisa II. Queen Letha spoke lovingly of the man, telling her stories of his deep intellect and kindness. Raven could see the face she was making, obviously offended by his remark.

"What is it now?"

"Must you insult everyone? The men of the Sisterhood are not less than others. It is unbecoming to say so when you have never known them."

"Why are you defending the Sisterhood?" he asked. "Tosha is the daughter of Tyro and her mother married him. You should want me to go in guns blazing and level the place to the ground."

"The Torry Realm has no greater friend than Queen Letha." She lifted her chin, choosing her words carefully.

"I can think of several greater friends than her off the top of my head. The Jenaii, the Yatins, and Kato are actually fighting beside you against Tyro. What is so special about Queen Lethal?"

"Queen *Letha*," she again corrected him.

"All right, Queen *Letha*. What's so special about her? You are obviously good pals with her, so enlighten me?"

She scolded herself for backing into this corner. There was no lie she could conjure that would appease his curiosity. If she didn't need his help, she would simply refuse to answer, but she did need his help. Terin needs his help, and that took precedence over safely guarded family secrets.

"Queen Letha is my aunt."

"Huh?" he said with a dumb expression on his face.

"My grandfather King Lorm III wed Queen Theresa of the Sisterhood. Their marriage was kept quiet, few in either realm knowing the true identity of their sovereign's consort or queen. Fortunately, they produced an heir for each realm from their blessed union—a king for the Torry Kingdom and a queen for the Sisterhood. My father was that king, and his sister—"

"Is Queen Letha." Raven finished her sentence.

"Yes. And that is why I believe whoever holds Terin captive is doing so without the queen's knowledge. She has forbidden slavers from trading Torry captives to the Sisterhood."

"Well, that explains a lot, but why didn't Tosha mention this to me? Why didn't she advise her father not to go to war with her mother's kin?"

"Tosha doesn't know. The queen will eventually tell her that we are cousins but has not yet done so."

"You know, it's nothing but drama with you people—all these secrets and so and so married to so and so. Since half you royals are related anyway, you'd think you could all get along. This is like the Hatfields and the McCoys."

"Who?" she asked, weary of another reference that only he knew.

"Never mind." He regretted bringing it up. "Are there any other secrets you'd like to share with me? Anything else that you're leaving out that I should know?"

The look she gave him proved there was more.

"Oh, for crying out loud, now what?" He stood fully up with his arms crossed, shaking his head.

And so she told him of Terin's heritage, of Kal, Torg, and finally Tyro, and the significance of his Kalinian blood. She thought at first to safely guard these secrets that only a few were privy, but her instinct proved otherwise. When she finished, Raven just stood there, stupefied.

"Are you going to say anything?" she asked, irritated by his silence.

"What do you want me to say? Terin being Tosha's nephew is the most relevant part as far as it concerns me. I guess I'm his uncle now."

"That is what you gleaned from what I just revealed?" She shook her head. He was impossible, and what he said next made her question the wisdom of her instincts.

"You know, Princess, if you end up marrying Terin, that would make you my niece by marriage. Wouldn't it be something to hear you call me *Uncle Raven*?"

* * *

Teris

They dropped anchor the following morn in the capital of the Casian League, a tropical port resting on the northeastern portion of the isle of Casia. The very sight of the *Stenox* sent the populace in full panic, fearing an attack by the alien vessel, their fears only subsiding when a blue flag of truce was seen waving above its highest deck.

A heavily armed trioar greeted them at the mouth of the inlet, its crew standing proudly at their posts in case the *Stenox* proved hostile. Of course, they would be helpless if they were. Raven decided to set them at ease, standing upon the 3rd deck beside Argos, in full view as they pulled up alongside the Casian warship. The Casian sailors wore uniform steel breastplates, greaves, and vambraces over white tunics with red, blue, or gray feathered plumes running the center of their helms, denoting rank. Their galley was a foreboding weapon of war, built from sturdy timbers native to the isle. Catapults and ballista ran the length of the deck, with a heavy steel ram jutting prominently from the prow, its sharp point cresting the surface like the dorsal fin of a dorun.

"Who seeks entrance to Teris?" a sailor wearing a bright-red cape and matching feathers in the plume of his helm shouted.

"Raven, captain of the *Stenox*!" Raven shouted back, stating the obvious, the vessels stopping some fifty paces apart, resting port to port.

"I am Veril, captain of the *Rising Flame*. For what purpose do you enter our city?"

"I bring a delegation from the Ape Republic and Enoructa, seeking audience with the forum of the Casian League!" Raven shouted back.

The Casian captain stood amidship, weighing his answer briefly before relenting.

They followed the *Rising Flame* to the central docking area, in the center of the city. Argos's dark eyes surveyed the splendor of the tropic port. Stone wharves ran along much of the waterfront, with a series of redoubts and towers resting further back, overlooking the docks. Nearly every dwelling in Teris was crafted in stone, sunlight playing off their white surface. The city ringed the inlet of the bay, surrounded further by lush greenery upon the hilltops overlooking the port, with palatial estates of the ruling families sitting like crowns upon their summits. The mouth of the Teri River bisected the city, spilling into the bay.

"Quite a sight," Raven said as they neared the shore.

"Impressive," Argos snorted grudgingly, his eyes trained on the war galleys moored in circular docking harbors near the mouth of the Teri. He lost count at thirty-nine warships, knowing there were at least a dozen he missed.

"They've rebuilt half the ships they lost at Torn," Raven said, guessing what his friend was thinking. They both remembered well the battle of Torn, where they decimated the Casian Navy during the revolution, reclaiming the apes' ancestral coastal lands from the colonial-minded Casians. Only a few of the galleys lost were from Teris, most were from Milito, the easternmost port of the Casian League.

"Their united fleet could decimate our infant navy." Argos's wide nostrils flared with that summation.

"Teris has sixty war galleys and a garrison of three telnics. Coven can sail one hundred war galleys, and Milito over eighty. Not to mention Port West and a dozen lesser ports. Despite all that, they won't attempt a return to Torn unless it's by peaceful invite," Raven said.

"That's because they know the *Stenox* stands with us." He gave Raven a knowing look.

"We always have your back, Arg. But even without us, the Casians can't defeat a united Ape Republic. They could only defeat your navy right now if they sailed their entire fleet and the *Stenox* wasn't involved. Neither is possible. If they sent everything at you, it would expose their homeports to raiders from Varabis or attacks from the Naybin Empire," Raven pointed out.

The Casian League required a strong navy to unify and protect its far-flung and isolated trade alliance. They were a consortium of city-states, drawing upon their collective strength to protect their home cities and secure their trade routes.

A contingent of the port garrison greeted them along the wharf as they dropped anchor, two units of infantry standing with shields and spears, their eyes trained nervously as the *Stenox* came to rest. The soldiers parted to either side of the wharf as several harbor officials, clad in rich Calnesian robes, stepped forth to receive them.

* * *

"This is outrageous!" Gaven Foris, patriarch of House Foris, protested, his opinion chorused by many of the gathered assembly.

"The terms are just. It is wise to accept through peace what even victory in war could not achieve," Nullis Vacelis, of House

Vacelis, countered, his oratory receiving equal agreement from the assemblage.

Raven stood off to the side as Argos and Ular stood in the center circle of the city forum, the representatives of the Casian League sitting upon stone benches that circled above. Members from Port West to Milito and dozens of smaller port villages in between gathered to receive the terms Matuzak offered.

"Tro has betrayed us!" Davelin Tors of Coven spat in disgust.

"What choice have they with Darkhon's dagger at their throat?" Morlin Galu of Milito said, referring to Tyro with the name he was known in these southern waters.

Argos and Ular sparked the heated debate, presenting Matuzak's terms. All trade with Tro now required permission from the Ape Republic and Enoructa. The Troan Council conceded free access to their port for a military alliance with the Ape Republic, thus forcing the Casian League to meet Matuzak's *generous* terms. The apes and Enoructans would guarantee free passage of all Casian ships to Tro as long as their trading routes were secured through the Casian Sea in return. Such a move would cost them their exclusive control of trade between eastern ports and those to the southwest.

"Granting this upstart republic free access to our western trade routes will only embolden their greedy expansion!" Favel Foris, vice archon of Teris, further protested, his voice carrying the weight of most of the nobles of the capital city.

"I concur. Our dominion of east-west trade must be exclusive," Porlin Galba, vice archon of Port West, said.

"Of course, you would align with Teris, trying to earn their good graces since one of your captains ran off with their archon's daughter!" Nullis Vacelis growled, standing one bench above Porlin Galba.

"How dare you!" Porlin Galba shot back, his face flushed with rage.

Raven shook his head, fully expecting them to go to blows right there in the forum. This was followed by a dozen others joining the argument on either side, all pretense of civility quickly falling away.

"Enough!" Raven shouted, causing everyone to stop, every eye shifting suddenly to the Earther who stepped onto the center circle below, joining his friends.

"You can argue all day and half the night for all I care, gentlemen, but it won't accomplish much other than wasting our time." Raven's eyes swept the assemblage above, many averting his terrible gaze before he continued.

"This is not about what you might lose, which is your exclusive control of this vital shipping lane but what you will gain. You can sit here and cry your eyes out about the good ole days when you controlled access to all shipping lanes from Tro to El-Tova, but you don't control them anymore. Everything north of Milito falls under the dominion of my friends here," he said, jerking a thumb to Argos and Ular.

"The days of bribing ape warlords to enforce your control over Torn and the ape coast are over. The ape tribes are unified under one flag, one nation, one republic. They are all that stands between Tyro and you," Raven said.

"From what we hear, Darkhon is your kin, Earther. Why should we trust anything you say?" Dain Vapus of Coven said.

"And that should tell you everything," Raven shot back. "If he wants me dead, the man he married off his only daughter to, what hope do any of you have of reasoning with him? I know for a fact by the reputation of a number of you that I'm not the only one with a crazy relative. All that matters here is that the Ape Republic controls access to Tro. You control access to all points west. They will grant you full tariff-free access to Tro and all points beyond in return for access to all points west. Your navy will safeguard all ape, Troan, and Enoructan vessels through the Casian Sea. The Ape Republic and Enoructa will do the same for all of your ships sailing the eastern sea. You either vote yes and double your trade routes or vote no and sever all links beyond Milito. One more thing, Matuzak has no tolerance for slavery within his ports. All merchant vessels anchoring at any ape ports must be powered by free oarsmen."

"Outrageous!" Gleb Gortus of Coven protested.

"Matuzak thinks slavery is outrageous, and I agree with him," Raven shot back. "The apes won't interfere with your slave trade. They only ask you not taint their lands with that sin."

"Sin?" Gleb Gortus snarled, his beady mustard eyes staring daggers at Raven. "Don't stand before this esteemed council and cast aspersions upon our honor! You will not use shame to rob us of our property!"

"There will be no slaves in our lands!" Argos growled, his outburst echoing off the walls, shaking the forum members to silence.

"Easy, Arg," Raven said, trying to calm his large friend, watching his big hands balled into fists.

The Casians looked on with ashen faces. Few had served in the fateful campaign at Torn, not able to see the power of the apes when their fury was unleashed. When news reached the home cities of the debacle, most ascribed their defeat to the Earther's interference, but those there were forever haunted by the apes attack.

"Members of this esteemed forum, here are my words of peace." Ular took a step forward, then started circling Raven and Argos while addressing the assemblage, his bulbous dark eyes blinking and voice rippling like running water.

"I, Ular, named champion by my chieftains, stand before you as a friend to your people. My people stand astride the conflict that has brought strife between you and our ape brothers. Let us make peace between us, each offering something of great value to the other. It is reason to which you must rely, not emotions that cause mindless suffering and loss. War among you is illogical. Hundreds of leagues separate your peoples while Enoructa lies between you. The aggressor has little chance to project his strength upon the other. You are unified, and so is the Ape Republic. Neither can impose their will upon the other. The only choice before you is not between war and peace but between more wealth for each of you or less. Should you choose wisely, my chieftains have offered to send one of our dignitaries upon every vessel, ape or Casian, that sails into the other's waters. Thus, any attack upon a merchant vessel is an attack upon Enoructa. This is our guarantee of peace and trade."

"Are you not militarily aligned with the apes?" Davelin Tors of Coven asked.

"Only if the apes are attacked, not if they are the aggressors," Ular said.

"Let us convene!" Pors Vitara, archon of Teris declared.

* * *

"How long will they be?" Lucas asked as Brokov stood at the dining table, manipulating several small discs. He spent the better part of the day fiddling with the strange devices after Raven and the others set ashore.

"Damned if I know. You know how long these political types take discussing things," Brokov said, lifting one of the small discs to his eye, examining it carefully before setting it back down.

"Shouldn't you be watching them? What if some trouble befell them?" Corry asked, visibly irritated by their delay. They were supposed to only visit Teris briefly, but here they remained for nearly half the day. She was struck by a memory of when Raven delivered her to Cagan and was anxious to depart to rescue Cronus and was delayed by the protocols of her court. She thought of him as an uncultured barbarian, and yet was she any different? When the life of one you love or deeply care about is in danger, you will lash out at any delay, especially foolish pomp and ceremony.

"They'll be fine. The Casians are smart enough to know if anything happens to them, we'll flatten the city, and there isn't a thing they can do about it." Brokov shrugged as if it were a trivial thing.

"I never took you to be as arrogant as Raven." Corry shook her head at their sense of omnipotence.

"It's not arrogance but simple fact, Princess. They have no weapons to penetrate our hull, and our weapons can vaporize everything in view."

She tiredly sighed, hating to concede her point, but Brokov was right. The Earthers were dangerous individually, but together with the power of the *Stenox*, they were beyond frightening. She was growing anxious trapped below deck, wanting to do something to hurry things along. Standing here for hours in the dining cabin with Lucas and Brokov was becoming intolerable. Visions of Terin in the clutches of some…woman were driving her insane.

"Should Lorken be alone on the outer deck? Shouldn't one of us be with him in the event the Casians grow hostile?" Lucas asked.

"Lorken will be fine. He's just keeping an eye on the troops gathered along the pier. He's only out there so they can see a presence on the ship. If he came below deck, they might think we aren't watching them," Brokov pointed out.

"Would they be so foolish to attack the *Stenox* if they saw no one visible?" Corry asked.

"Maybe not, but why take the chance with an unpredictable species like humans. Hand me the activator." Brokov pointed to a palm-sized device with a luminous screen resting on the far side of the table.

Lucas handed him the strange oddity as Brokov started tapping it with his fingers.

"If we should remain below deck to conceal our presence, perhaps Grigg and Orlom could stand outside with Lorken to further deter the Casians," Lucas said.

"The last thing we need during a peace negotiation is those two anywhere in public. Zem's keeping them occupied in the engineering room, bless his little heart," Brokov said.

"I apologize for my impatience, Brokov. I fear for Terin and am anxious to depart," Corry sighed.

"Don't worry yourself about our delay. It gave me time to work on this," Brokov said, barely masking his excitement.

"What is it?" Lucas asked.

"This is how we are going to find Terin." Brokov tapped the activator, the small thumb-sized disc lifting in the air, hovering above the table's surface.

* * *

Two days hence
Eighty-five leagues southeast of Cesa

Raven sat the captain's chair, staring out at the endless expanse of ocean, the afternoon sun hidden behind gray overcast. The thoughts of what awaited him at Bansoch clouded his mood, thoughts of Terin suffering, and Tosha…well, whatever reception she was certain to give him. It seemed ages ago that he last saw her on the shore of Lake Veneba, but again it seemed like yesterday. He thought of her constantly, tortured by her golden eyes that stared back at him with the intensity of a thousand suns. He missed her smell. If he closed his eyes, he could clearly recall the enticing scent, so feminine, so alluring, so…

She drives me crazy even when she's not here, he growled to himself. How could he let a woman do this to him? His appetite was off, his mind constantly distracted, and mood souring with every passing day. It suddenly dawned on him that he had no plan after reaching Bansoch. Once the child was born, what next? He couldn't stay there. But then what? If the child was a girl, Tosha would insist she remain at Bansoch in her mother's palace, as heir to the Sisterhood. If it was a boy…

Tyro would claim it. He couldn't trust Tosha not to hand their son over to her father. Raven knew he had to bring his son with him. In that case, Tosha would just have to come with him, her throne be damned.

"Rav, I'm picking up a lot of ship activity to our north," Lorken said, sitting the helm, staring at his radar screen.

"It is a major shipping lane," he pointed out.

"Merchant ships don't usually sail in these kinds of formations." Lorken magnified an image before transferring it to Raven's viewscreen.

Raven sat up straight, the image drawing his attention. Heat sensors indicated ship placements, forming two V-shaped formations skirting the coastline. "Battle formations," Raven said, seeing if the two formations were in conflict or not.

"They look to be heading in the same easterly direction," Lorken determined. "You want to take a closer look?"

"Don't know. We lost a whole day at Teris for nothing," Raven growled.

"They were still voting when we left. It might not have been a waste."

"If they were going to approve Matuzak's trade agreement, they would've done it while we were there. They just didn't want us around when they said no," Raven snorted.

"Or maybe they didn't want to see the satisfaction on our faces when they voted yes," Lorken countered.

"Politicians." Raven shook his head.

"Yeah, those darn arrogant politicians. Why couldn't they be humble like you." Lorken rolled his eyes.

"Like you're a pillar of humility," Raven mumbled before raising Brokov on the comm. "Brokov, I found a good place to test your new toys. Take a look at the radar image I just sent you."

"Aye," Brokov answered, standing over Kendra's shoulder in the engineering room as she sat, monitoring the viewscreen.

"That switch," he instructed, as she brought the image up.

Corry stood over her other shoulder, trying to make sense of the configuration glaring on their screen.

"Interesting," Brokov observed, asking Kendra to clean up the image.

"What is it?" Corry asked. All she could see were hundreds of little dots illuminated on the screen.

"Those dots are human heat signatures, and the shape they are taking indicates a ship. You see the elongated oval patterns here and here and…here?"

"Yes," she said.

"Those are ships," he said.

"Why is that significant?" she asked, not understanding the fuss.

"It's not the ships, but the formations they are taking. Merchant ships don't sail like that."

"Like what?" she asked.

"Battle formation," Kendra answered.

"Battle formation?" she asked.

"Yes. It warrants a closer look," Brokov said, telling Raven to change course.

"Can we do so? Time is against us," Corry asked, anxious in further delaying Terin's rescue.

"You tell me, Princess. Those ships are near the Macon-Torry border, sailing in battle formation. I think it's worth a few hours of our time to investigate." Brokov's summation sent a shudder down her spine. She desperately wanted to proceed to Bansoch but couldn't ignore a possible war with the Macon Empire.

Corry sighed, agreeing with a resigned nod.

* * *

Thirty-five leagues southwest of Cesa

Lorken picked up several more groups of ships as they closed distance to target. Brokov stepped onto the stern as the *Stenox* eased to a stop, setting seven thumb-sized discs on the deck, before tapping the initiate sequence on his device. The discs hummed to life, levitating into the air, hovering briefly before flying off.

Grigg and Orlom hooted excitedly from the 2nd deck, their eyes filled with wonder. Brokov gave them a warning look not to do something stupid, like using the discs for target practice.

"Where did they go?" Orlom asked as the objects sped off.

"I sent them on a scouting mission," Brokov said before heading back inside.

"How are they going to tell you what they see?" Grigg made a face, holding an annoyed Brokov up.

"They are going to take pictures and send the images back to us," he said as both apes leaned dangerously over the rail above, hanging on his every word. The discs would actually give them a live feed, but he thought a picture explained things in terms they could understand.

"What's a picture?" Orlom asked.

"Can we help?" Grigg added, which Orlom quickly nodded in agreement.

"I think I can handle it. You should check with Raven and Lorken. I think they could use your help."

* * *

"Zoom in on that one," Brokov said, indicating the first marker to reach a target. He again stood over Kendra's shoulder as she sat the console in the engineering room, with Corry and Lucas looking on.

Corry gazed with wonder as the detailed map of the area was alit on the viewscreen, depicting the Macon coastline and the Isle of Null in rich detail. Several groups of ships were represented by blinking red dots on the screen while the discs Brokov sent out were spread out across the area, represented by blue blinking dots.

Kendra magnified the image, the map expanding, pushing everything else away until only the area beneath that particular disc remained. Corry and Lucas gasped as a fleet of warships took shape before their eyes through the lens of the disc camera, which hovered several hundred yards off the ships' starboard. They could make out the faces of sailors manning the catapults upon the decks and the ships' banners lifting in the crisp wind.

"You recognize those ships?" Brokov asked

"A broken anchor upon a field of blue," Kendra said, identifying the sigil on the lead ship's banner.

"The Torry 5th Fleet," Corry said, panic taking her heart. She could see two of the vessels trailing the fleet, engulfed in fire, a third vessel remaining with them, collecting survivors.

"Looks like they've seen some action, but I don't see any Macon ships nearby," Brokov observed.

"What's that?" Kendra picked up a heat signature further northeast of the Torry Fleet, shrinking the image, bringing the surrounding area into view.

"Leave disc 1 with the Torry Fleet. Send disc 4 to identify whatever that is," Brokov said.

27

Within minutes, disc 4 sent back images of three magantors flying over the Macon coastline, heading toward the Torry Fleet, fire munitions dangling from their necks.

"Well, that explains the fires," Lucas said, still coming to grips with what he was seeing and how he was seeing it.

"That removes any doubt that you are at war with the Macons. Let's see what the other discs are picking up," Brokov said, reaching over Kendra's shoulder, tapping the screen where disc 3 hovered just east of the Torry 5th Fleet. Not surprisingly, the Macon 4th Fleet came into focus. They seemed to be holding position. Brokov quickly counted the eighteen vessels before switching to disc 2. Disc 2 hovered ten leagues west of Cesa, where twenty galleys of the Macon 1st Fleet were underway, racing to join the 4th Fleet. Disc 5 discovered the Macon 2nd Fleet fifteen leagues northwest of Null, appearing en route to join the others. Several leagues west of the Torry 5th Fleet, disc 7 picked up the fifty galleys of the Torry 2nd Fleet.

"Looks like we have the perfect view to watch a battle," Brokov said, Corry and Lucas sharing a grim look.

"What do we do?" Kendra asked, looking back at him, over her shoulder, her brown eyes meeting his blue.

"Let's run it by the captain."

* * *

"What do you got?" were the first words out of Raven's mouth passing through the door of the dining cabin.

"It appears to be a major fleet action," Brokov answered, sitting at the table's head, a digital map coming to life across its surface. The others were either seated or standing around the table, their eyes following the visual display with keen interest.

"Have my seat, Boss," Grigg offered Raven, the other seats already taken.

"Keep your seat, Junior, I'll stand." Raven patted the young gorilla on the shoulder while standing behind him. He noticed Zem, Orlom, and Lorken standing across from him, the later of them busy eating a sandwich, taking greater interest in his lunch than the information being put out. The sandwich looked pretty good, the more Raven thought about it.

"Our first contact is here, which we can confirm is seventeen galleys of the Torry 5th Fleet," Brokov said, a light blinking on the map forty leagues west of Cesa. "The 5th Fleet appears to be the advance force of a full Torry assault. We discovered the Torry 2nd Fleet trailing further west with fifty warships, including a magantor carrier. Each ship of the 2nd Fleet is laden with infantry."

"Infantry?" That piqued Raven's interest.

"Yes, which means they will disembark along this line," Brokov pointed out a stretch of coastline some leagues west of Cesa. They couldn't risk losing ships laden with infantry in a fleet action. That meant the 5th Fleet and the magantor carrier would clear the way.

"Whaggts at?" Lorken asked with his mouth full, pointing at a small marker between the Torry Fleets while leaning over Brokov's shoulder, sauce dripping from his sandwich.

"Couldn't you wait and eat after we are done?" Brokov growled, wiping sauce off his shoulder.

"I was hungry."

"You're always hungry. That marker is two Torry vessels sinking and another collecting survivors. They were set afire by a land-based Macon magantor strike. We have visuals of at least one magantor corpse in that vicinity, floating in the water," Brokov explained.

"What about Macon forces?" Raven asked, noticing the grim demeanor of Corry and Lucas, who sat either side of Brokov.

"We have three separate fleet contacts. The closest to the Torry 5th Fleet is the Macon 4th Fleet, which is here." Brokov indicated a point ten leagues east of the Torry Fleet. "The Macon 1st and 2nd Fleets appear en route to join the 4th, each coming from Cesa and Null respectively."

"How soon until this thing kicks off?" Raven asked, the Araxans giving him curious looks with the phrase *kicks off*.

"If the Macon 4th Fleet holds position, the Torry 5th Fleet will make contact within the hour, two at most. The Macons could withdraw, consolidating all three fleets before engaging, but that would take the better part of the day and allow the Torry infantry to disembark. My guess is, the Macon 4th Fleet will fight a delaying action, preventing the Torries from landing their troops until the other fleets join them," Brokov explained.

"Why don't the Macons use their own infantry and deny them at the shore? Then they can consolidate their fleets," Raven asked.

"That would be my plan if I were the Macons, but their troops haven't left the Torry border. I sent disc 6 along this line, stopping here." Brokov ran a finger along the line of hills that formed the border of Torry South and Macon, stopping at a point mid distance along that line, where a natural break rested.

"Let me guess. The nearest Macon Army is just sitting there," Raven said, Brokov's nod affirming it.

"And the remaining Macon Armies are apparently busy else-where," Brokov added.

"They are laying siege to Sawyer," Corry said, having received that news shortly before Lucas returned to Corell with the tidings of Terin.

"Didn't you say Cronus was at Sawyer?" Raven growled, won-dering why she hadn't shared that information earlier.

"He escorted Minister Antillius, who journeyed there under the protection of diplomacy," Lucas quickly defended the princess, who stared daggers at Raven.

"But you haven't heard from him since, so for all we know, he might be dead," Raven said, redirecting his ire to Lucas.

"Easy, Rav. They have no way of knowing the condition of any-one so far away. They are at war, in case you forgot, without real-time communications that we enjoy," Brokov rightly pointed out.

"If we want to help Cronus, the best thing we can do is help out the Torry Navy," Lorken said between mouthfuls.

"But it isn't our fight," Kendra said, receiving a heated glare from Corry.

"It might not be our fight, but Kato is out there somewhere fighting this battle, if the Yatin Campaign is finished. Besides, do we really want the Torry southern flank compromised while Tyro looms in the north? We can give them a little help before we continue on our merry way," Raven said, which drew surprised looks from his crew and sighs of relief from Corry and Lucas.

* * *

Minisub Atlantis
Two nautical miles south of the Macon 4th Fleet

"You sure this is a good idea, Rav?" Lorken asked, sitting the pilot seat.

"Which part?" Raven asked, sitting the captain's seat behind him, Brokov sitting the weaponeer's seat to his front right.

"The three of us here, leaving Zem the only Earther aboard the *Stenox*," Brokov said what Lorken was thinking.

"Well, for one thing, we're heading into combat, not a scouting mission or training exercise. It's best we handle it. Second, Zem can take care of things while we're gone. Besides, did you see him perk up when he realized he gets to be captain while we're away?" Raven asked.

"How could we not when he said the *Stenox* will finally operate with superior leadership," Brokov parroted Zem's parting remark.

"I bet he can't wait for us to die of old age so he can be captain for good." Lorken shook his head.

"He'd rather Space Fleet find us so he can continue on with his rapid promotion. He fancies himself an admiral," Brokov said.

"He's still bent over that, blaming our being stranded here for ruining his career," Raven said.

"Can you imagine if Space Fleet never finds us, and we all die of old age, and Zem lives until his battery runs out in a thousand years? Or is it ten thousand years?" Lorken wondered.

"Now that's something I haven't thought about. What will he do? You'd think he'd get bored with the *Stenox* after a while," Raven asked.

"Knowing him, he'll probably start up his own academy dedicated to his favorite subject…himself." Brokov chuckled.

"A course in philosophy on why Zem is so awesome." Raven grinned.

"Or literature, *the greatest Earther who ever lived—the story of Zem*." Lorken laughed.

"How about mathematics, two plus two equals Zem is the best," Brokov added.

"Who would take his classes? The students would die of boredom," Lorken said.

"He wouldn't let them quit without bashing their skulls." Raven laughed.

"Trust me, that's no deterrent after listening to him for a while. Death would be a blessing." Brokov grinned.

"Maybe that's what we should do with Tyro if he loses the war. We can tie him up and make him listen to Zem ramble on for the rest of his life," Raven said in all seriousness.

"That's damn cruel." Lorken cringed thinking about it.

"Murdering and enslaving thousands of people still doesn't warrant that degree of torture." Brokov chuckled.

"Here we go," Lorken said in all seriousness. The *Atlantis* was slowing rapidly, the surprisingly clean ocean water providing a clear view through the front portal. Brokov touched his viewscreen, live feed from disc 1 feeding into it, providing a clear visual of the surface above them. The Torry 5th Fleet was just to their west, their lead vessels hurling fire munitions from their forward catapults. The Macon 4th Fleet was just above them, responding in kind, their expert ballista crews finding purchase on two Torry vessels, fires spreading across their prows. He watched as another struck a forward mast of a Torry bioar, its furled sail awash in flames.

"Let's get to work," Raven said as Lorken guided the *Atlantis* below the keel of the nearest Macon galley, laser slicing into the hull at the bow, gutting the vessel port to starboard, before passing on to the next ship in sight.

Brokov kept the lasers short, their intense beams not punching through the ship's uppermost deck, concealing their presence from everyone except those in the lower hold. All anyone could see on the surface was the bow of the ship dipping severely, before the sea swallowed her whole.

The *Atlantis* sped through the water toward the bow of the next galley, a Macon bioar, its veteran crew working their catapults to great effect on the Torry warships. Lorken swept underneath the keel, laser cutting a sizable chunk from its hull. The Macon crew struggled to keep their feet, the ship dipping suddenly at the bow. One sailor clung to the starboard rail amidship, the *Atlantis*'s large shadow catching his eye as it passed from under the ship, speeding off toward their sistership, the *Setting Sun*, sailing just off their starboard bow. He looked on in horror as the shadow dipped under the stern of the *Setting Sun*, driving the length of the vessel, steam bubbling along the length of the ship, before disappearing from his view. The *Setting Sun* listed severely to port, water flooding the length of its hull, the sound of dying men silenced as they were swallowed by the sea.

* * *

Corry stared at the screen over Kendra's shoulder, regarding the horrific scene with watery eyes. The battle played out before her like a theater, the actors aligned perfectly for her viewing pleasure, but pleasure did not describe what she was feeling. She watched as ship after ship buckled, their bows suddenly dipping into the surf never to come up, their crews struggling to abandon ship before they were swallowed by the sea.

The disc hovered above the carnage, sending the stunning visuals back to the *Stenox*. Corry could make out the *Atlantis* coursing below the surface like a *versk* tearing into a pod of *worken*. She was stunned; the Macon Fleet sunk before her eyes in a matter of moments. The Earther's terrible power ended the battle with pathetic ease. She wiped a tear from her cheek, a tear for the Torry sailors saved and for the Macons who died. She cried for friend and foe alike. She thought of Terin at that moment, of the pain his loss caused her. How many of the dead Macon sailors had wives or lovers who would lament their loss as much as she mourned Terin? Each of them was a son, a husband, a father, a precious soul lost at sea, lost…forever.

She cringed; another vessel listed severely to starboard, rolling fully onto its side before slipping beneath the waves, dozens of sailors struggling through the surf to escape the wreck.

"Oh no!" Kendra groaned as Zem's metallic voice sounded over the ship's comm.

"This is your captain. All crewmembers will standby to receive the *Atlantis* in approximately thirteen minutes, twelve seconds. All crewmembers are expected to carry out their duties with professionalism. Acting 1st Officer Argos will oversee crew inspection. I would like to commend…" Zem droned on, Kendra burying her face in her hands, begging Raven and the others to hurry back.

CHAPTER 2

They made their way through the busy streets of Central City, with the sun shining brightly in the summer sky. They passed under the shadow of Leltic Palace, the massive structure looming powerfully to their south, separating them from the gentle flowing Stlen. The foregrounds of the palace met the open area of the city square, dominated by a great fountain, surrounded by a spacious common area where the good people of Central City gathered as the day grew late.

"You should smile more." Cordi elbowed his elder brother. It was the third girl they passed that shyly smiled at Cronus that caused Cordi to wonder if Cronus was blind or a fool or just a blind fool. Cronus responded to each with polite nods that held all the charm of a cold fish.

"Why?" Cronus asked, barely cognizant of his surroundings, his mind elsewhere.

"The ladies. That was the third attractive maid to smile at you since we left the barracks, and all you can spare her is a nod?"

"She was just being polite. I am sure she has many suitors more ready for courtship than I."

"When exactly shall you be ready? You are now a commander of a unit. You need to find a wife and build a future," Cordi said.

Cronus worked tirelessly since his fourteenth year to earn his rank, a rank of honor that most women would be drawn to.

"A commander of junior rank has little to offer a woman other than years of hardship. It could take years before I can provide her suitable comfort."

"Years? Life is too short to wait so long, brother. If gold is what's needed to win a woman's heart, you should come with me."

"Life as a mercenary?" Cronus asked disapprovingly.

"Don't guilt me with that look, Cronus. There is more to being a free sword than selfish pursuits. There is a whole world out there to explore, and I won't die an old man regretting not seeing it. You are the one that talks constantly of the Sentinel of Tro. You might never see it while serving the crown."

"Our uncle didn't want that kind of life for us, Cordi. We spent our childhood in mercenary camps, following him on one campaign after another. This is where he wanted us to set our roots, serving our Torry homeland."

"Then what point is there in planting roots if you don't find a wife to share it with? You are adorned with the trappings of responsibility. Use them to find a woman worthy of your name, to carry on the Kenti legacy," Cordi goaded him, his cheery smile contrasting Cronus's serious demeanor.

"Perhaps I'll seek a wife after I return from Cagan," Cronus offered, wanting to end the conversation.

"That will be half a year from now. What if you find your true love today?" Cordi asked. As a new commander of unit, Cronus was required to serve a period of time in Torry South, just as commanders there served in the north to familiarize each with the other realm.

"You are a hopeless romantic, Cordi. Good marriages are built of firmer things than such childish notions. Love is earned and nurtured, not won at first glance," Cronus sighed. No sooner had he spoken when fate threw his words back at him, his eyes drawn to the most beautiful woman he had ever seen.

She stood beside the great fountain, dressed in a loose twiln gown that clung invitingly to her womanly form. Long golden hair framed her achingly beautiful face, sunlight playing off her golden locks as if they were lucent. Her deep olive skin contrasted perfectly to her white gown, which swirled about her ankles in the summer breeze.

"You were saying?" Cordi grinned, following what drew Cronus's eyes.

"Beautiful" was all he could say.

"Go talk to her!" Cordi nudged him.

"I...no...I couldn't..."

"Why not?" Cordi urged him on, amused by the terrified look on his brother's face. Cronus faced some of the deadliest swords he had ever seen, with deathly calm, but now was too frightened to talk to a girl?

"I don't have a good reason." Cronus shrugged in all honesty.

"Wait here." Cordi grinned, hurrying across the city square where a vendor was hawking fresh flowers. He quickly returned with a long-stemmed voli, giving his brother the fragrant blue flower.

"Very well," Cronus relented, removing his helm and handing it to his brother before straightening his uniform and venturing forth, like a soldier marching to his death.

"A strong heart wins the fair maid," Cordi reminded him as he stepped away.

Cronus steeled himself as he approached the woman, working out what he would say. The last time he was so forward was his sixteenth year when he asked a girl to dance, which she said yes. He couldn't ask this woman to dance, forcing him to think of what to say. Unfortunately, he stepped too quickly, coming upon her before he was ready. She turned as he drew near, her soft blue eyes meeting his green.

"My lady," Cronus said, offering her the voli, his blood racing as she took the flower.

"Shall this purchase my affection?" she asked dryly, her cold tone taking him aback.

"My lady, if I thought to purchase your affection, I would offer you three hundred and six certras," he calmly said, regaining his senses and tempering his response.

"Three hundred and six certras?" she asked, an odd expression painting her countenance. It was a very specific and minor sum to purchase someone's affection.

"Three hundred and six. The sum of all that I own," he offered in all honesty.

She had been offered much by wealthy men that wished to court her, but never everything. Those men never revealed the extent of their wealth, each secretly guarding their true worth. She believed such men would always place their wealth above all else, including her. She feared *she would be a mere ornament of their fortune, to be set aside and ignored when time stripped away her beauty. Though modest, three hundred certras was not a great sum. This man's pride was not tied to his wealth. He was attractive in his uniform, silver mail over a knee-length gray tunic with double-corded braids adorning each shoulder, signifying his rank. She was intrigued the deeper she looked into his green eyes. He was quite tall, with hair black as a moonless sky. There was a kindness in his eyes that softened his masculine features. She decided to test him further.*

"Three hundred certras is not very much!" she said dismissively.

"No, it's not." He lifted his chin and turned away.

"Wait!" she called after him, taken aback by his abrupt departure.

He stopped, turning back to her with a look that gave her pause.

"You have nothing else to say?" She lifted a curious brow.

"What else is there to say? If all that I have is not enough, there is nothing more to discuss. I may not be a rich man, but I know my worth. You are a beautiful woman, the most beautiful I have ever seen, but if you value a man on the contents of his purse over all else, then I have no desire for your beauty. Good day." He finished, his voice equally sad and kind before turning away.

No man ever spoke so open and direct to her. She misjudged him and insulted him. Instead of screaming his disgust at her, he merely stated his feelings and walked away, with no malice in his tone. She pressed the voli to her nose, its blue petals tickling her nostrils, the sweet fragrance bringing a smile to her lips.

"Wait!" she again called him back.

He stopped midstride, before turning back as she stepped nigh.

"I am sorry." She gave him her prettiest smile, losing herself in his eyes.

"Cronus Kenti." He bowed, introducing himself.

"Leanna Celen." She curtsied.

* * *

Straits of Cesa

The memory faded as the wind pressed his face, drawing him from his melancholy. Cronus eyed the Macon coastline off his left, the rocky shore looming ominously off the portside of the magantor carrier *Plexus*. The grim gray rocky slopes of the distant shore matched his disposition, memories of Leanna bringing joy and sadness in equal measure. The memory of their first meeting played again and again in his mind, recalling the greatest day of his life. And yet the stronger their love, the more torturous her absence, plaguing his spirit with forlorn misery. He wondered what she was doing at this very moment. Was she standing upon the upper battlements of Corell, looking off toward the west, thinking of him as he did her? How he longed to hold her, to take her in his arms, and to never let go. She was the only solace for the pain in his heart. What but love could fill the void of so much loss? Cordi, Arsenc, Kato, and Terin were dear friends, and now were gone.

I have so few friends left, he sadly reflected, thinking of Raven. Raven would not take Kato's loss well. If there was only a way for Cronus to tell him. This was the sort of thing that needed to be said from his own lips, not passed on through fourth-hand rumors. But what other choice had he? They were caught up in the current of war and were captive to wherever it took them, and that current now led to the straits of Cesa.

"Packaww!" a magantor cried out, circling overhead. Cronus gazed skyward, spotting two of the great avian passing over the bow of the ship, their riders scanning the horizon for enemy warbirds.

Behind him, other magantors prepared to take flight while others returned from battle. The *Plexus* trailed the vanguard of the Torry 2nd Fleet, the fleet's heavier trioar galleys surrounding the carrier, protecting the irreplaceable vessel. Cronus narrowed his eyes against the eastern horizon, trying to make out the ships in the distance. He observed billows of smoke drifting above the hulls of a few ships, handiwork of enemy warbirds who were driven off by their own magantors.

"And so it begins," Jentra sighed tiredly, standing at his side, his hand resting on the bulwark.

"Let us hope the 5th Fleet can drive them off," Cronus said, eyeing the crowded decks of the ships surrounding them. The Cagan garrison was crammed onto every ship in the 2nd Fleet. They needed the 5th Fleet to clear a path so they could disembark somewhere west of Cesa. The coastline they were presently passing was impossible to draw near without tearing the hulls of their ships, let alone set ashore.

"They better, or the sea will flow with our blood. If they break through and engage the fleet directly, we'll lose a unit of infantry for every vessel sunk. Our soldiers and their kin will blame Lorn for this," Jentra snorted.

"Is that likely? The scouts claim only one of the Macon Fleets is engaged up ahead. The odds seem even."

"The Macon warships are swift, and their catapult crews devastatingly accurate. Our ships are not nearly as good," Jentra said, looking warily at the serried decks of the surrounding ships, where the Cagan garrison was crammed.

"We should do something." Cronus felt the pull of Terin's sword, urging him to act. He realized how much Terin struggled suppressing the blade's mysterious power. Lorn told him that the call of the blade was far weaker with normal men. Terin's Kalinian blood enhanced the sword's power manyfold. If that was true, he couldn't imagine the restraint Terin exercised in curbing the sword's inclinations.

"Admiral Horikor is adamant that we leave this battle in his hands unless the enemy breaks through Morita's fleet up ahead."

"We are of the Elite. We can pull rank if we choose," Cronus reminded him.

"We can overrule the admiral if we want to, Cronus, but we better be correct in doing so. You are not an expert magantor rider. You barely manage flying your warbird from one place to the next, let alone maneuvering in combat. And what if you lose that sword that Lorn has entrusted in your keeping? Can you fetch it from the bottom of the sea if it somehow slips your grasp?" Jentra asked, as another returning magantor approached the bow of the *Plexus*, its outstretched wings gliding above the lapping waves, before passing overhead, setting down upon the flat deck behind them.

"What news have you?" Commander Tullen, captain of the *Plexus*, called out to the rider guiding his magantor to the side of the deck, where handlers took control of the bird. Captain Tullen strode forth across the deck, along with Admiral Horikor, as the rider and his archer dismounted.

"We counted eight Macon warbirds attacking the 5th Fleet, Captain. Our patrols slew two. Another was brought down by ballista from the *Dorun's Fin*. The others fled back to the coast. They successfully dropped fire munitions on several of our vessels, two of them hopelessly lost," the rider reported, holding his helm in his hand while standing at attention, his dark mane lifting in the warm breeze.

Jentra and Cronus overheard most of the man's utterance as they approached.

"What of the Macon Fleet?" Captain Tullen asked.

"It waits just beyond the 5th Fleet."

"It waits in place or advances upon us?"

"It holds position."

"Very well. See to your mount," the captain ordered, the rider thrusting his fist to his heart. The captain relayed orders to his riders, who hurried off in several directions.

"Admiral, Captain," Jentra hailed as they drew nigh.

"King's Elite Prime, King's Elite Kenti," Admiral Horikor greeted as the four men huddled close, a light breeze sweeping over the flat deck. The admiral was a sturdy-built warrior with silver tainting his once vibrant brown mane. His studious brown eyes regarded both Elite warily. It was little secret that the admiral opposed this operation from the start and knew Prince Lorn ordered Jentra and Cronus to accompany him to stiffen his resolve.

"We are at your disposal, Admiral, if you have need of us," Jentra said, attempting to assuage the admiral's suspicions.

Admiral Horikor's eyes narrowed severely, Jentra's words only reinforcing his misgivings.

"Prince Lorn ordered you to disembark the Cagan garrison at or near Cesa, Admiral. How you achieve this falls under your purview. We will not overrule your orders. We will serve wherever you have need of us." Cronus's attempt to appease Horikor fared little better, but the admiral finally relented after a painfully long silence.

Behind them, the crew was preparing a dozen warbirds for battle; the great avian talons shifting slightly across the wooden planks as the vessel crested the gentle waves.

"Very well. You make yourselves useful by joining our close air patrols. If Macon magantors appear, you will only engage if they manage to defeat our own warbirds," Horikor said.

"We can do that," Jentra agreed.

"Good," Horikor said stiffly. "Captain Tullen, send a message to Admiral Morita. He is to close on the Macon 4th Fleet and give battle. Prepare to launch two magantor strike groups with fire munitions. I want them to strike the enemy fleet once our ships engage. Split your remaining magantors between each of our fleets. I want every bird in the air and on lookout for Macon land-based magantors."

* * *

Wind Racer bore Cronus through the air, skirting the left flank of the Torry fleets, keeping a watchful eye to his north, the Macon coast looming ominously in the distance. His eyes scanned the horizon, looking for any shapes emerging in the distant sky. If the Macons were to contest their advance, it would be now. He pushed east, Jentra's mount drawing up beside him, the grizzled warrior eyeing the vanguard of the 5th Fleet approaching the Macon 4th Fleet. Admiral Horikor's assessment of the Macon crews proved astute, their ballista scoring several hits on the lead Torry vessels, fires igniting upon their decks.

The soldier in him urged him to act, but the sword held him back, becalming his spirit. 'Twas the strangest feeling Cronus ever felt in battle, as if detached from the mortal realm, observing the happenings below with serene calm. He had never seen battle at sea before, the movement of ships uniquely different from those of troops shifting on a battlefield. He felt Jentra's angst beside him, the older warrior warily watching the unfolding battle.

"Look!" Jentra shouted, his voice faint in the pressing air.

Cronus followed the direction of Jentra's outstretched hand, pointing to the lead ships of the Macon Fleet. Two were sinking rapidly, their bows dipping into the ocean. Then a third, its bow dropping suddenly, its crew clambering over its sides, jumping into the sea.

"Packaww!" Torry magantors sounded off his right, bearing fire munitions to attack the Macon Fleet. They too looked bewildered; their first targets sinking without reason. Their flock leaders pressed on, focusing on Macon ships further afield.

Cronus looked as a fourth Macon ship dipped to port, as if its entire hull was cut away. Within moments, it rolled over. A fifth ship went down at the bow, swallowed by the sea as a sixth broke in half amidship, its bow and stern pointing skyward, its center collapsing into the surf. The Torry warbirds held back, uncertain of what ailed the enemy fleet, wary of it extending to them. Cronus pressed on keeping beyond ballista range, passing high over the sinking ships, trying to discover the cause of this strange phenomena. By the time he reached the vanguard of the Macon Fleet, three more ships were struck, going under in rapid succession. Then another off his left, the ship listing forty degrees starboard before rolling over. It was almost a pattern, the ships going down one after another, each adjacent to the next. He scanned the sea around the next likeliest target, an intense light emitting from a small dark shadow passing near it, the beam of blue cutting the hull at the stern before passing on.

"Raven!" Cronus laughed like a madman, following the mini-sub's course beneath the surface, swerving amidst the Macon Fleet like a versk hunting its prey. Only the Earthers could make the impossible look so easy. Within moments, the entire Macon Fleet would be sunk. The Torry warbirds held back, frustrated by their lack of targets. They would have to dump their munitions and return to the *Plexus* until the admiral readjusted his plans. The larger question was why? Why were the Earthers doing this? Did they find out about Kato? Were they now in the war? If so, where would they appear next? He needed to follow the sub back to the *Stenox*, which could be anywhere beyond the horizon.

"Cronus!" Jentra's voice drew him from his thoughts just as the sword urged him to turn sharply north, spotting two dozen magantors take shape beyond the fleet's left flank, their dark forms obscured by the graying sky.

Wind Racer moved of his own volition, driving headlong toward the enemy host. Cronus could hear Jentra curse, trailing him, trying to keep pace. Admiral Horikor's instructions to hang back and let his riders engage the enemy were useless when his mount had a mind of its own and the sword with it. He couldn't fight either, let alone when they were both of one mind.

"So be it." Cronus surrendered his will to the sword and mount, drawing the blade, sweeping through the tepid sky.

* * *

Admiral Morita stood at the prow of his flagship, *Queen Galena*, the only trioar in the Torry 5th Fleet, his gaze narrowed severely, trying to make sense of the sinking Macon ships. He was wary to send his ships into the enemy midst, fearing his fleet suffering their fate. Whatever bedeviled the Macons could very well strike them in kind.

"Magantors!" the lookouts shouted, warning them of the approaching enemy warbirds.

Morita shifted his attention northward; the approaching magantors spread across the horizon, half bearing fire munitions, their deadly loads dangling expectantly below their necks. Torry ballista crews readied shafts as Torry magantors sped to blunt the attack. He braced himself for the Macon advent, realizing his good fortune with the Macon Fleet could just as quickly turn sour with their aerial assault. Once again, fortune smiled on the good admiral, when a great white-gray avian swept from the east, striking the enemy left, its rider wielding a glowing sword.

"Kenti!" Morita marveled, watching as Wind Racer swept under a Macon warbird, gutting it across the breast, the beast thrashing briefly before tumbling to the surface. The great avian continued on into the Macons' midst, dispatching another before the skies were crowded with other Torry magantors joining the fray. Within moments, another Macon warbird tumbled to the sea, its riders thrown clear. A Torry magantor followed, its left wing crippled by the talons of a Macon warbird. Arrows could be seen passing back and forth with the magantors maneuvering in the graying sky.

"Ready arrows!" a ballista commander shouted.

Several Macon magantors broke free, driving on the Torry Fleet.

Giant shafts spewed from the Torry ships. One struck a Macon warbird in the throat; the bird's beak dipped forward, dropping into the sea. Another veered off; a shaft embedded in its right wing. The remaining continued on, delivering their munitions, flames bursting across the decks of the *Cagan's Hammer* and the *Iron Torch*, before flying off. The skirmish north of the fleet quickly waned. The remaining Macon warbirds retreated, leaving half their crews dead or dying in the waters below. Eight Torry magantors shared their fate; the rest returned to the *Plexus*. Morita ordered two ships to recover enemy prisoners bobbing in the waters where their ships went down.

* * *

"Are you certain?" Jentra asked, standing upon the deck of the *Plexus*, with Admiral Horikor and Captain Tullen looking on.

"I know that ship as well as any Araxan, Jentra. It was Raven. I am sure of it," Cronus said, another magantor passing overhead, setting down on the deck behind them.

"How can you be certain?" the admiral asked.

"I saw it move under the water, firing its lasers on the Macon vessels. You must have seen it as well, Jentra." Cronus looked to his comrade.

"I saw…something." Jentra couldn't really describe what he saw, but it clearly unsettled him.

"What did you see? Just put it to words," the admiral asked.

"Looked more fish than vessel, swerving beneath the surface like a versk on the hunt." Jentra shook his head.

"These Earthers are your friends, King's Elite Kenti?" Captain Tullen asked.

"They risked their lives to rescue me from Fera, Captain. If that is not friendship, then what is?"

"I've seen firsthand what Kato and Thorton are capable of, so this wouldn't surprise me," Jentra snorted.

"If it is them, can you find them and ask what they plan to do next?" the admiral asked.

"I was going to follow them back to the *Stenox* but was drawn off by the enemy magantors. They could be anywhere out there." Cronus waved a hand over the starboard side of the deck at the endless ocean.

"If they took it upon themselves to sink one Macon Fleet, might they sink another?" Tullen asked, imagining the destruction of the enemy navy with little loss in exchange.

"Perhaps, *if* I can find them," Cronus said.

"I dare not spend long in the search. We must use this victory to its fullest, for time is fleeting," Horikor said.

"I will send out our scouts, Admiral," Captain Tullen said.

"Not far beyond the horizon, Captain. I wish to recall them quickly. Meanwhile, we must disembark Commander Corvis's troops on the first clear spot we find," the admiral said.

"And prepare to meet the other Macon Fleets certain to come our way," Jentra said, before he was struck by an idea.

"Jentra?" Cronus asked, noticing the odd look transfixing his face.

"If we can't find the Earthers, we can use the next best thing." Jentra looked each of them in the eye. "Unless we find them, the Earthers role in this must not be known."

* * *

The search for the *Stenox* proved futile. Wherever they were, Cronus could only guess. The Torry Armada continued east, finding a small coastal village where they could begin to disembark. The 5th Fleet positioned itself east of the landing site, awaiting the arrival of the Macon 1st and 2nd Fleets while the Torry 2nd Fleet unloaded the Torry garrison troops two ships at a time while magantor scouts from the *Plexus* scouted inland for enemy ground forces and the surrounding sea for their fleets. After unloading, the ships joined the 5th Fleet, guarding the approaches to the landing site. Among the survivors of the Macon 4th Fleet fished from the ocean was Admiral Gara, who was presented to Admiral Horikor upon the *Plexus*. The poor wretch was in a disordered state, a vacant, forlorn look in his weary eyes.

No sooner than the twelfth ship disembarked, Torry magantors spotted the Macon 1st Fleet to their east. Admiral Horikor quickly sent a magantor bearing a flag of truce, the scout circling the Macon Fleet, bearing the blue banner in full view before setting down upon the deck of the fleet's flagship, the trioar *Magyar's Dagger*, where stood Admiral Goren, a grizzled sailor with a lean, sharp face and penetrating green eyes. Admiral Goren was horrified to discover Admiral Gara climbing off the back of the Torry magantor, before the warbird took to the skies, returning to the Torry Fleet. Admiral Gara told the horrific tale of his entire fleet being sunk by the Torries' secret weapon—a sea creature controlled by their mystical powers. Only two Torry vessels were sunk and three heavily damaged, a devastating loss ratio to the twenty Macon ships sunk, taking most their crews with them. He also relayed of the disembarking of the Torry 1st Army, which were crowded on vessels stretched as far as he could see. Their twenty thousand men would be marching on Cesa, with nothing but the city garrison to stop them. Further compounding their problems, one of the Torry warriors was armed with a Sword of Light, which inflicted heavy damage to their magantor corps.

The ultimatum was clear. The Torry commanding admiral would grant them one day to withdraw their fleets to the east, and abandon Cesa. If not, the Torries would unleash their secret weapon upon their fleets and the city, slaying everyone who dwelt there. Admiral Goren was further surprised that the Torry admiral returned their prisoners taken from the wreckage, sending them one ship worth at a time, nearly three hundred in all, each repeating Admiral Gara's horrific tale of a Torry secret weapon, a mysterious *sea beast* that could waylay a fleet in moments. Unbeknownst to Admiral

Goren, the Torries released another one hundred prisoners ashore, where they would spread word of the Torries terrible power. Before he could send word to Cesa, the harbor was already in panic.

Holding to his course was now untenable, forcing Admiral Goren to withdraw, sending word to Admiral Vulet, commander of the Macon 2nd Fleet, to return to Null, securing the isle and raising conscripts. Goren would withdraw to the east, joining his strength to the 3rd Fleet, where Admiral Talmet was currently sailing west to meet him. He advised Commander Clyvo, the commander of the garrison of Cesa, to declare the port an open city and withdraw his troops to Fleace. When questioned by his subordinates of his capitulation, Goren reminded them of his duty to preserve the Macon Navy and would not risk it for so little gain. They would hold position east of Cesa, awaiting the king's orders. He sent missives to General Ciyon, commander of the Macon 3rd Army, advising him of their untenable position and that he should withdraw to reinforce the capital, consolidating with the Cesa and Fleacen garrisons while waiting for the 1st and 2nd Armies to come to their aid, using their combined strength to crush the Torry Army. It was the conservative play at this point. Surrendering Cesa without a fight was preferable to risking its five thousand defenders when they were needed at Fleace. His subordinates questioned why the Torries didn't simply sink all their fleets if they were able. He asked that question of Admiral Gara, who responded by handing him a sealed scroll from the ranking Torry, the Elite Prime of the Torry Realm.

Admiral Goren,

We have destroyed the Macon 4th Fleet by means I am not at liberty to reveal. Let the testimony of the survivors bear witness to the power we wield, a power we used to destroy the Benotrist Fleets in the Yatin Campaign. I am guided by the mercy of Prince Lorn, to spare your men further destruction. This mercy is not lightly given, a mercy that was not extended to our Benotrist

THE CHRONICLES OF ARAX

foe, and is offered to appeal to your king's good sense and reason. It is Prince Lorn's wish that no human realm should suffer needlessly or be embittered by needless suffering, sowing in the hearts of your people a hunger for revenge. Our true foe dwells to the north, the gargoyle peoples that have plagued the realms of men long before the reign of Kal. We desire only peace with the Macon Empire and will promptly depart from your lands once this crisis is resolved. It is our intention to seize Cesa and await your king's response to Prince Lorn's demands. We shall not advance our fleets beyond Cesa unless assailed by your ships.

Jentra Damasen,
Elite Prime of the Torry Realm

Admiral Goren read the missive one last time before tucking it away, giving the order to withdraw.

* * *

Three days hence
Cesa

Cronus stood upon the stone wharves of the Macon harbor, looking out across the serene waters of the tropic port. The Torry armada sailed into the harbor that morn, uncontested. They were greeted by empty streets and open piers. Large granaries towered behind him, holding the principal export of the Macon Realm, harvested from their rich farmlands and shipped to Nayboria, the Casian League, and points beyond. The most prominent features of the harbor were its massive circular docking facilities, connected to the wharves by sturdy-built bridges, home of the Macon 1st Fleet. The facilities were tall enough to cover the vessels docked beneath them, each housing five ships. The banners of the Torry 2nd and 5th Fleets now blew proudly above the circular structures, with the banners of the Torry 1st Army gracing the summit of the city forum, a blue hammer and ax upon a field of white. Cronus looked off to his right where the Torry sigil lifted in the breeze above the forum, the massive columned structure dominating Cesa's skyline.

"We shall see if our prince's deception works," Jentra snorted beside him, shaking his head.

"The Macon admiral believed it," Cronus said, regarding the Macons' believing their paltry garrison force was the Torry 1st Army.

"It would take an armada many times our size to move twenty thousand men. You would think their admirals would have seen that." Jentra couldn't believe their good fortune.

"Under normal circumstances, that would be true, but men lose their sense once confronted by events they cannot explain," Cronus said.

"Aye. If I witnessed our fleet suffering a similar fate your Earther friends visited upon them, I wouldn't be thinking clear either." Jentra shook his head.

"Don't sell yourself false, Jentra. You were clear thinking enough to use it to our advantage."

"There is an old soldier's proverb that says, 'Successful victories are always followed by immediate actions. Victories must be capitalized, or their gains are fleeting.'"

Cronus pondered this. Though they lacked the means of repeating the destruction of the Macon 4th Fleet, the enemy didn't know that. Jentra used this unknown factor against them, forcing their withdrawal without a fight. Their objective wasn't the destruction of the Macon Fleet but the seizure of Cesa and the positioning of a ground force in the enemy rear. The Earthers' intervention effectively achieved both and destroyed a Macon Fleet as well. Now they held Cesa with almost their entire force, both land and sea, intact.

"Corvis's troops keep pouring in," Cronus said, observing two more units parading along the adjoining avenue. The fleets brought one telnic into port with them, the rest taking the overland route from their drop-off point to the west.

"Aye, the rest should arrive by nightfall," Jentra said.

"Corvis will sleep better once they are accounted for and the walls sufficiently manned."

"Corvis wouldn't sleep well if he outnumbered the enemy ten-fold. The man is a miserable wretch," Jentra snorted.

"Then why does he command the Cagan Garrison?"

"He is distant kin to Regent Ornovis."

"And Prince Lorn trusts him to carry out this mission?" Cronus didn't like the sound of it.

"The man may be a miserable wretch, but he is a cautious wretch, and now that he holds a strong defensive position, that caution will be an asset rather than a liability. We were sent to strengthen his spine to attack the city or frighten them into a stalemate using your plan to mask our weakness in the surrounding hills," Jentra said with a hint of admiration.

"We didn't need to though," Cronus pointed out.

"Aye, but it gave Lorn the idea of masking the garrison as the 1st Army and that played a large role in the Macons' abandoning Cesa without a fight. Once again, Lorn's gamble paid off." Jentra felt like laughing if he weren't so weary.

"He believes his God guides his decisions."

"Maybe he does." Jentra couldn't believe he said that. Even a pragmatist such as himself had to admit there could only be so many coincidences before they were no longer coincidences.

"One could ascribe the prince's successes to sound planning and leadership," Cronus said.

"The Yatin Campaign should never have begun if you only knew the state of our southern armies a year before the war began." Jentra shook his head.

"I knew it wasn't good with the time I spent there. The local politics was dreadful," Cronus recalled the incident when he first met Raven and the retaliation he suffered for protecting the Earther.

"I recall certain commanders of rank demanding the head of an upstart unit commander named Kenti who *betrayed* upstanding Torry citizens in favor of a barbarous Earther." Jentra gave him a knowing look.

"How did you become aware of that?" Cronus asked curiously.

"Did you ever wonder why nothing came of it, other than your next promotion being apparently delayed?" Jentra asked.

"No," he said, knowing there were whispers that he was unworthy for a telnic command, but considering his young age for the position, thought nothing of it at the time.

"A certain Torry prince overruled any censure of a certain Cronus Kenti stating that he was most worthy of any promotion the crown thought him suited but insisted that he remain as commander of 5th Unit of the 9th Telnic of the 3rd Army. It is as if he knew what role you would play at Tuft's Mountain and the involvement of the Earthers, which was instigated by your capture."

"He told you of this?"

"Aye, before we sailed from Cagan. The prince has held an interest in Cronus Kenti for some time, it seems, an interest he would ascribe to visions from Yah."

"And you believe him?"

"I don't know, Cronus. I've spent more time with him than anyone, even his mighty sire. All I know is when he has these *visions* of his, they are always true. It was his God that told him to oversee the reform of the southern armies, preparing them for war long before Tuft's Mountain, protecting you and meeting Terin in the wilderness after his escape from Fera—these things don't just happen. Rushing off to Torry South to aid the Yatins while Torry North was threatened—no one of a right mind would have done that. Now this, sending us here just as your Earth friends suddenly appear, destroy an enemy fleet and disappear, leaving the Macons befuddled. I have to ask if he knew this would happen?"

"If his God is responsible for his clairvoyance, I wish nothing to do with him." Cronus shook his head.

"Why?"

"He sent Terin and Kato to their deaths. No righteous God would do that," Cronus sighed, looking out across the water.

"I was there when Terin fell. The boy was touched by a madness I can't explain. The things he did in battle defy reason," Jentra recalled.

"I know well what he did in battle. I know well what he meant for our cause, and if Yah is true, he sent him to his death. I can't help but worry of the difficult path before us without Terin."

"You will never sleep through the night if you look at all that lies before us. Don't worry of Tyro, the gargoyles, or Morac's spring campaign. Focus only on the task at hand. We win in Macon and worry about the rest later," Jentra advised.

"Victory here is now in Lorn's hands," Cronus sighed.

"And we have the more irritating task to attend."

"And that is?" Cronus asked.

"To sit here and wait."

CHAPTER 3

The Macon-Torry border
West of the Borin Gap

Dadeus Ciyon, general of the Macon 3rd Army, stood over the table in his pavilion, where a map of southwestern Arax was unfurled. Dadeus was the heir of House Ciyon and nephew of the late General Dorven Ciyon, who garnered fame putting down a revolt in the Caveus Region along the headwaters of the Clev. Unlike his contemporaries, Dadeus was a youthful twenty-three-year-old, with strikingly handsome features. His long black mane framed his boyishly attractive face and piercing hazel eyes. He was a favorite at court, his charm winning him his rapid promotion through his favor with the Queen Mother. His fellow generals despised him for his arrogance and pompous airs. He gained renown for his bold and flamboyant nature, attired in matching gold mail, greaves, and tunic, with a plume of red feathers running the middle of his golden helm.

Dadeus Ciyon looked over the many missives he received in the previous two days, troubling news from Cesa and the happenings at Sawyer and Yatin, trying to determine the meaning of it all. The siege at Sawyer dragged on, with General Vecious refusing to storm the city, granting the defenders a lifeline, though a tenuous one at that. With much of the 1st Army joining the 2nd at Sawyer, it left precious few troops to guard the capital. The commandant of Cesa abandoned the port without a fight, withdrawing his troops to the capital, giving the Torries a foothold on his southern flank. Reports of a Torry mystery weapon decimating the 4th Fleet were obviously overblown, but the effect on morale was not. The survivors spread tales of the hopelessness of their cause, panicking their people and soldiers alike. It appeared King Mortus's belief that the Torry prince was too occupied in Yatin to interfere with the Sawyer Campaign was now proven false. The Torry prince managed to salvage the remnants of the Yatin Empire, slaying Yonig and dealing Tyro a major defeat, decimating his legions and driving the survivors back to the Tenin-Telfer line. The Torry 4th Army would soon be returning south while the Torry 1st Army was supposedly now occupying Cesa. That last bit didn't sit with him. He was experienced enough to know that the Torries couldn't have moved so many troops by ship in so short of time. If the banners of the Torry 1st Army graced the walls of Cesa, it didn't mean the entirety of the army was there. Prince Lorn likely split his force, leaving a smaller force guarding the border. Or if they had managed to move the entire 1st Army by ship, then the border was presently unguarded or guarded by the dregs of Torry South.

General Ciyon considered these factors as his commanders of telnic gathered around, debating which actions they should take.

"We must remove ourselves to Fleace. The capital must be protected at all cost!" exclaimed Fen Zaden, commander of 3rd Telnic.

"And leave the border unguarded? Madness," Coln Vladek, commander of 8th Telnic, countered.

"Should the Torry 1st Army advance upon Fleace, our armies at Sawyer may not return in time," Jex Fortev, commander of 9th Telnic, reasoned.

"To leave the border unguarded would open the way to our richest lands. We would be undone," Kellis Havel, commander of 2nd Telnic, said.

"The answer is obvious, gentlemen, if you think several moves ahead, which any general of worth would demonstrate." Ciyon smiled knowingly, moving the marker representing the Torry 1st Army to Fleace, where the markers representing Commanders Clyvo and Novin guarded the capital.

"It is not obvious to me, General," Fen Zaden said.

"The Torry Navy controls the straits of Cesa and has landed a sizable force at Cesa, which is likely to move on our capital. I believe it is only half the Torry 1st Army that rests there. But if it is the entire army, the garrison troops of Clyvo and Novin would at most be outnumbered two to one, their ten telnics to the Torry twenty. If not, they would be close to even, which is more than sufficient to hold the city until reinforcements from Sawyer arrive." Ciyon smiled.

"If we return, we could make certain the capital's fate," Jex Fortev said.

"The capital will endure against whatever force the Torries have disembarked at Cesa. If we move to cover Fleace, they will bring the rest of their force through the Gap of Borin and then march on Fleace. Meanwhile, we would hold the city until Generals Noivi and Vecious come to our rescue, garnering the glory of victory while others at court whisper of our leaving the border unguarded. There is no profit in acting the anvil when posterity only remembers the hammer," Ciyon said, his words gaining purchase with his commanders.

"Then what do you suggest, General?" Fen Zaden asked.

Ciyon smiled, moving the marker of his 3rd Army across the Torry Border, stopping at Cagan, knocking over the harbor garrison. "We take their capital before they take ours," he declared. Most importantly, he would win the glory over his fellow generals, by being the hammer who didn't need an anvil.

* * *

Two days hence

Ciyon sat astride a spirited white *ocran*, looking across the gap of Borin, a narrow green vale cradled between forested hilltops towering above either side. The bodies of Torry soldiers lie strewn across the small vale, their blood staining the grass where they fell. He expected a stronger defense, but the enemy broke upon contact fleeing across the gap and reforming upon a small rise two leagues to his west. They were little better than conscripts, likely of peasant stock, testament of the Torries overextending themselves. His own men marched in good order, practical gray mail over bloodred tunics, sunlight reflecting off their spear tips as they continued through the gap in long columns.

"Packaww!" The sound of magantors careening through the sky above echoed through the air, the Macon warbirds scouting the lands ahead for any trickery the enemy might employ. The previous days' skirmishes cost both Torry and Macon magantor patrols dearly, each losing three warbirds in the exchange.

Ciyon's ocran shifted slightly as one of his outriders approached, the scout's lathered mount panting heavily as he drew up alongside the general.

"Report!" Ciyon ordered sternly, sunlight playing off his resplendent golden cuirass and helm, his matching cape billowing in the gentle breeze.

"The Torry infantry have re-formed on the distant rise. They have been reinforced and now number 4 telnics strong. We attempted to circle the rise, but they have a small cavalry contingent guarding their flanks, nearly fifty in strength, General Ciyon," the scout reported.

"Could you see what lies beyond the rise?"

"Nothing but empty ground between the rise and the Horns, General," he said.

The Horns of Borin, he mused, *the unique landmark denoted on every map of worth.* They were two high ridges of gray rock, aligned north-south. The more prominent north ridge jutted straight north; the lesser horn ran northwest to southeast, with a prominent gap between them. Beyond the horns were nine leagues of forest, bisected by a narrow road leading to the Torry heartland beyond. The forest was of greatest concern, where an inferior force could harry his advance, inflicting heavy casualties on his army. Of even greater concern was his long supply train that would follow, provisioning his army. A clever enemy would be certain to attack that vital weakness. But he was clever too and had plans to counter that. He would need to advance with measured care, mindful of tactics to counter his strength. Whatever force the Torries left guarding their frontier needed to be dealt with first. Already his troops discovered hundreds of straw soldiers throughout the gap, an obvious Torry attempt to mask their weakness. His first task was clear, however, the elimination of the force gathered upon the small rise ahead. If they expected him to fritter his troops assailing that position, they will be sorely disappointed, but deal with them he would.

"Sound advance!" he commanded.

* * *

The Torry soldiers awaited the Macon 3rd Army upon the low rise, aligned along its summit in ordered ranks, the sigil of the Torry 1st Army emblazoned upon their banners, a blue hammer and ax upon a field of white. Even from afar, Ciyon noted that only the forward ranks were outfitted with mail and greaves, the center and rear armed little better than peasants. Despite wearing the distinct Torry uniform of tan or white tunics and steel helms, Ciyon doubted all these men were regular levies, for they took great pains masking their weakness. They held the rise with four telnics against his ten, many armed with pikes, expecting him to charge the hill.

"A peasant weapon." Ciyon smirked, the evidence further proof of the poor quality of troops arrayed against him. He paraded forth before his men, his distinct golden armor and attire standing out among the sea of gray mail and red tunics of the Macon Army. He ordered his small cavalry contingent to the extreme flanks.

"The enemy waits upon us along that rise!" Ciyon shouted, addressing his men, pointing to the Torries to their west. "They mean for us to assail them! We are not fools, nor are we hasty. Never give an enemy what he wants, only what you want to give him. Follow your commanders, and the day will be ours!"

With that, the Macon Army marched forth, sunlight reflecting off their ten thousand helms, in blinding radiance. The Torries waited expectantly as they drew nigh, prepared to receive them until Ciyon spilt his army, sending four telnics left and four right, with two stopping at the base of the rise, four hundred Macon archers taking up position behind them. Macon magantors drew from the east, bearing fire munitions, the Torry ranks wavering with knowing dread. Macon archers commenced firing, shading the forward slope with arrows, just as the magantors dropped their first loads, fire splashing across the hillside.

Hundreds of Torries abandoned the rise, dropping their pikes and fleeing down the far slope before the Macons moving around their flanks could cut their retreat. Fires erupting along the forward slope fueled the panic; hundreds more broke ranks as men thrashed amidst the flames, others raising their shield against the barrage of arrows spewing from the Macon front. It was all too much—the entire Torry Army fleeing the battlefield, racing down the far slope toward the Horns of Borin and the safety of the forest beyond.

Ciyon wasn't expecting them to break so soon, his flanking troops unable to cut the retreat before the Torries slipped free, forsaking their shields and whatever armor they had to hasten their feet. The Macon cavalry, numbering a scant fifty healthy mounts, raced ahead, harrying the Torry flanks, cutting down men from behind, easy game for the skilled riders. Torry magantors soon appeared, driving his own avian from the sky, while others dropped fire munitions upon his pursuing troops. Ciyon ordered his two telnics at the base of the now emptying rise to advance and seize the high ground while he raced his mount around the left flank to join the pursuit.

The battle, now a rout, progressed painfully with the Macons chasing after their prey; the Torry soldiers forsaking all sense of order, fleeing toward the break between the Horns of Borin. Some were overcome, skewered from behind; with others dropping to their knees in surrender. The Macons struggled themselves in keeping order, their ranks coming uneven and broken in places but driven by the need to overcome the Torries before they escaped to the forest beyond.

General Ciyon rode apace, racing his mount alongside the left flank of his pursuing troops. He flinched as two magantors swept dangerously close, a Torry warbird being chased by a Macon magantor. A Macon avian faltered off his right, gliding to the surface, nursing a crippled wing. He cursed as the first Torry troops attained the Horns, passing between the jagged slabs of ominous gray stone.

Harroom!

Horns sounded in the distance, giving him pause, but couldn't place the source.

"Packaww!"

Torry magantors screeched overhead, dropping fire munitions amidst his troops. Ciyon cursed this nuisance, for all his scorpions remained with his archers, far to his rear. More Torries flooded through the gap in the Horns, continuing to the forest beyond. His men started to break ranks, hastening forth to chase the enemy before they escaped. Torry cavalry emerged along his flanks, skirmishing with his own cavalry, fighting to a draw by appearances. Most of the Torry cavalry were still in Yatin, by last reports, but it wouldn't require much for them to outnumber his paltry contingent. Cavalry was another asset he lacked in sufficient numbers, most being assigned to the Sawyer Campaign. He pushed on, following his men through the gap, the jagged rocky slopes of the Horns looming upon either side, the damnable retreating Torries closing on the forest, always just out of reach through their retreat. Ciyon was eager to push his men through the gap, the unique geological feature creating a narrow funnel, causing his ranks to crowd, squeezing through the dangerous choke point.

Harroom!

The sounds of horns echoed strongly through the din, long lines of infantry emerging from the trees ahead to either side of the retreating Torries, who began to pass into the forest, only to retrieve fresh armor and rejoin the ranks holding the front. General Ciyon looked on in dismay, his folly unfolding before his eyes in horrific splendor. The banners of the Torry 1st Army lifted above the ordered ranks aligned to his front, the blue hammer and ax on a field of white. It appeared as if the entire 1st Army was deployed to his front, which begged the question, What force did the Torries disembark at Cesa?

"Packaww!"

The terrible cries of Torry magantors sounded above, sweeping over the treetops from the west, a dozen warbirds bearing fire munitions. Within moments, the deadly loads carpeted the narrow gap where the trailing elements of the Macon Army were now passing through. Fires erupted through the deadly space, creating a deadly blaze along their primary avenue of retreat.

The moment of decision was upon him—to stand and fight or break and run. Ciyon hated the choices. With the Horns towering behind him, any move to circumvent them would string his army out while the Torries smashed them from the side. To withdraw through the fire-ravaged gap would cause a crowding disaster, with the Torries falling upon those trapped on this side, trying to squeeze through. He could lose half his army in such a panic, inflicting far less on the Torries. He noted a distinguished rider upon a black ocran, waiting in the center of the Torry line, where the fleeing soldiers now re-formed, surrounded by a score of riders wearing matching silver mail over the sea blue tunics of the Torry Elite. Beside the man rose the standard of the house of Lore, a gold crown upon a field of white.

Prince Lorn, Ciyon mused, his mind going in a thousand directions, before coalescing around the only viable option he would accept. He recalled what his uncle once taught him that even a foolish plan forcefully executed improves the odds of its success.

"Close ranks!" he ordered his drummers, who began to relay the command.

"Forward!" he directed to the enemy center. He would split the Torry Army and pass within the forest where they couldn't be overwhelmed by the Torry numbers. He might even slay Lorn in the process, breaking their morale. If not, their two armies would fight a thousand melees in the forested battlefield, bloodying them in mutual slaughter, which was the most optimistic outcome he could hope for. Despite his many vain faults, Ciyon would rather die with honor than submit to defeat.

The Macon 3rd Army lumbered forth, dressing their ranks as they advanced. Once they drew nearer, Ciyon gave the order to charge, to collapse the Torry center before their wings enveloped him. His men closed the distance, stopping short of the Torry line to close ranks and interlock shields as Torry archers unleashed a terrible volley. Dozens of men dropped to Ciyon's front, arrows feathering their ranks.

"Onward!" commanders shouted over the din, urging their men on the two armies clashing in a torrent of crashing steel and slamming shields. The Torry center held at the forest edge, positioned in front of prepared defenses, traps, and palisades of jutting stakes. Once pressed, the Torries withdrew behind these positions, forming a strong middle upon which the Macons threw themselves.

Ciyon cursed as Lorn withdrew into the forest, his men repositioning behind their foul entrenchments, while the Torry flanks marshaled forth to envelop him. Torry magantors made easy sport of his congested ranks, fire munitions exploding in their midst. Several fissures broke along the Torry front but closed before they could be exploited. The battle raged through endless hours, the Torries methodically encircling them, cutting them down layer by layer. Reinforcements of Torry cavalry overwhelmed the Macon riders, now controlling the periphery of the battlefield.

Ciyon was now afoot, fighting alongside his men, jabbing his short sword between the seams in his shield and the man to his right, finding purchase with Torry flesh, blood staining his blade. He jabbed again, just as a mace swung overtop his shield, striking his helm. Ciyon crumbled to the ground, with the world turning dark.

* * *

"He will live," a woman's soothing voice said as Ciyon stirred.

He opened his eyes, finding himself abed on a cot inside a great pavilion, with a lovely woman in a matron's dress sitting his bedside. He found his hands affixed to the cot and a blanket drawn halfway up his naked chest.

"My lady?" he asked through his hoarse throat. She was holding a strange device, which she appeared to be putting away.

"You were gravely injured, General. Be thankful my late husband's healing device repaired the damage," Ilesa said, putting a cup of water to his lips.

"Late husband?" He made a face, not understanding the reference.

"A great and beautiful man and another casualty in this awful war. My prince will have words with you, and I have others that require treatment." She stood, bobbing a curtsy to a man behind her and stepped without. By the torches spaced across the pavilion, he knew it was night, wondering how long he had been unconscious. There were others in the pavilion—Royal Elite and commanders of rank—but the man who stepped to his bedside was obviously the Torry prince. He was black of hair, with piercing blue eyes that looked through you, as if baring your soul. His mail and tunic were bloodstained, testament to his close involvement in the battle.

"Dadeus Ciyon, general of Macon 3rd Army, I am Lorn, son of Lore," Prince Lorn said, taking a seat at his bedside, his voice strangely comforting. Ciyon didn't know what to make of this.

"Your Highness, I would bow but seem to be detained," Ciyon answered in kind.

"The misfortunes of war, Dadeus. In another time, we might've been good friends," Lorn said sadly.

"You are generous to say so, Your Highness. Alas, I find myself your prisoner. I shall return your good manner with honesty, as is my nature. I am loyal to my king and will reveal nothing of his plans," Ciyon affirmed.

"Yes, your honor is well noted. But I caution you to discern the difference between honor and pride." Lorn smiled, as if privy to Dadeus's nature.

"Pride is no weakness, and humility no grace," Ciyon snorted.

"Pride blinds the eyes and spoils the soul, Dadeus. Was it not pride that led you across the border to win yourself the glory of taking Cagan rather than protecting your king?" Lorn's words cut like a sharpened knife.

"I made a calculated risk and fell for your deception," the general said bitterly.

"I simply allowed you to see what you wanted to see. As any wise general would attest, it is wise to know your adversary. Pride is your weakness, Dadeus. It is an affliction I know well," Lorn sighed. There was no triumph in his voice.

"Pride has been a better master to you than I, it seems." Ciyon shook his head.

"Pride has not ruled my path for many years, for I know my many faults."

"Spare this poor fool your pieties. You are a crown prince and future king, boasting great victories in Yatin and now here. What but pride could rule your path?"

"If pride ruled my path, Tyro would already hold dominion of our world. I know what pride dwells in your heart, Dadeus, for it once ruled mine, until I was gifted a vision of where that would lead. I sit humbled before you, a shadow of the wretched creature I once was."

"And what brought about this grand transformation? Did your father, the king, strap your backside, or a fair maiden spurn your advances?"

"Yah happened."

"Yah?" Ciyon laughed. "You are speaking with ancient deities now?"

"He is alive now as he was then, and he is the only one. There are no others," Lorn said.

"Very well. You spoke with your God, and he humbled your spirit. Why tell me this? You have won a great victory. The spoils and glory are yours. The Macon Empire is open to your invasion, so why waste words with me?"

"The battles in Macon are still secondary to the true threat looming in the north. I would have your service if you disavow your king. I can place you high in my counsel. If your king is brought to heel, I would have you lead a Macon Army at my side to fight the enemy that threatens us all."

"You are speaking of the gargoyles, I presume. As much as I detest the vile creatures, I am a sworn sword of my rightful liege. I took an oath to serve King Mortus and will not stain that honor."

"Commendable. I have put that question to your commanders of telnic, seven of which survived the battle. Three have accepted my generous offer and will forswear their oaths to King Mortus at the appointed time."

"Traitors! Which of my men would do this?"

"The 1st, 3rd, and 8th commanders of telnic have agreed to my terms. The others have chosen death," Lorn warned ominously.

"Gaiv Lucen, Fen Zaden, and Coln Vladek," he whispered harshly, rebuking them for their treason. All three were his strongest supporters, constantly speaking his praises.

"Those are the ones," Lorn said, gauging his reaction.

"And you will kill those who will not betray their oaths? And you dare speak of my pride? You have no honor, Prince Lorn!" He nearly spat.

"Indeed, it seems your honor might exceed your pride, General. We shall see if your courage survives the trials ahead," Lorn said cryptically, calling his guards to remove Ciyon from the tent.

"Your Highness," General Lewins, commander of the Torry 1st Army, addressed Lorn, entering the pavilion after Ciyon was escorted out.

"General, I know the hour is late, and time is fleeting. Make your report as brief as possible," Lorn said tiredly. They had both seen enough bloodshed this day, and the night would prove equally painful.

"Yes, my prince. We have secured the Gap of Borin, just to our east. The rear echelons of the Macon Army escaped, along with most of their archers. I count at least three full telnics slipping our pursuit but few commanders of rank, including one of Telnic. Of the other nine telnic commanders, two were slain, seven captured. Enemy dead number over two thousand, the rest captured or missing. Of our own casualties, eight hundred dead or missing, twelve hundred wounded. These numbers are all crude estimates, I am afraid."

"How soon before we can be on the march?"

"Two full days to attend our wounded and prepare our prisoners for transport, then we can continue with at least fifteen telnics battle ready."

"I want ten telnics on the march by midday tomorrow. Lady Ilesa will clear the wounded in quick order and can catch up with the army en route. The same with the trailing telnics. Send word to Cesa. I want Corvis to march north with three of his five telnics. The rest will remain and fortify the harbor. We must move on Fleace with utmost haste," Lorn said.

"Aye, my prince," the general agreed. "And might I say, Your Highness…splendidly done," the general said proudly, Lorn proving himself as a worthy future king of the Torry Realm.

* * *

"Bless you, my lady," the Macon soldier cried out, Ilesa healing his disembowelment, ending his torturous agony.

"You will live, soldier. Remember this mercy of Prince Lorn," Ilesa said, before moving on to the next wounded prisoner.

Lorn ordered all the mortally wounded to be treated first, whether Macon or Torry. Ilesa worked feverishly through the night, hoping the device's charge would last until dawn. She paused operations before dusk, giving the device a full charge. She lost count how many perished before she could render aid. She finished with the Torries first, before moving on to the Macon prisoners, but less severely injured Torries would have to wait until the critical Macons were treated first. Other matrons worked further down the line of wounded men, keeping men alive long enough to be treated and determining those who could endure from those who could not, prioritizing those requiring her immediate attention. She thought of how Kato's regenerator changed their priority of healing, or *triage* as he called it. They would operate under these guidelines while the device still worked.

Oh, Kato, I miss you so, she wanted to cry, her heart breaking at the memory of him. She recalled his gentle smile and easy nature and his beautiful eyes. She knew Prince Lorn meant well when he thought to keep her at the palace at Cagan until she gave birth but couldn't bear it. She needed to be here, using Kato's wondrous gift to help these desperate men. This was the legacy Kato would've wanted to be remembered for, and it kept her busy, too busy to dwell on what she had lost.

The next soldier lay upon the ground, whimpering piteously, an arrow embedded in his right eye, the tip protruding through the side of his head. Once again, it was Kato who prioritized these types of injuries, knowing the severe pain to induce *shock*, as he would call it. He said men could quickly expire from such injuries.

"Hold him still!" she ordered two of the soldiers guarding her, the others standing vigil for any threats. Lorn assigned these men to her for the campaign, each handpicked by their commanders for their fighting skill. Ilesa was a valued asset that Lorn safeguarded, not only for the device she carried but for the man who loved her.

The guards held the man steady, instructing him not to move. Whether he understood anything at this juncture, they could only guess. Ilesa quickly removed the arrow, the man screaming as it tore free. Within moments, she placed the regenerator on his head, initiating it. He quickly gasped, the pain washing away like snow in a summer rain. The man blinked slowly in disbelief, seeing her clearly, the surrounding torchlight playing off her face.

"My lady," he started crying before other guards removed him to the pen where the healthy prisoners were being kept.

* * *

Lorn and Galen watched Ilesa work from a distance, the unusually warm night air a blessing for the wounded men. Lorn's guards fanned out around him, keeping a constant watch as the camp bustled with activity. There was still some fighting to the east, Torries and Macons stumbling upon one another in the dark, but for the most part, the battlefield was secure. Lorn couldn't help but think of Kato as he watched Ilesa move along the line of wounded men. He trusted Yah to have his hand in all things and had to trust in him in this as well. Losing Kato and Terin was a blow that would doom any cause, but as long as Yah guided his path, he had to believe in their chances. Once again, Yah delivered his enemy into his hands, opening the way into Macon proper. He would not dwell on what they lost but on the next task before them.

"Walk with me, Minstrel," Lorn said, stepping away.

"Of course, Your Highness, where my prince leads, I shall dutifully follow." Galen smiled.

"There are few things as eerie as night after a battle," Lorn sighed as they walked, passing between two of the hundreds of cook-fires spread throughout the encampment.

"A grim affair, my prince. The battlements of Corell are similarly afflicted, especially in the still of night."

"A poet once spoke of the *Ghosts of Battle*, of disjointed spirits wandering the lands where they fell," Lorn said, recalling the tale.

"Savieus of Milito, he was a famed bard who spent his youth as a soldier in the Casian Army," Galen recounted.

"Yes, Savieus. I wonder what he would write of the battles that afflict us now?" Lorn reflected sadly.

"A great bard would sing of things great and small, grand or terrible, of love and loss. Such are the things of life, my prince. How can one know beauty without seeing the opposite? How can one love peace without suffering war? Cannot the written word substitute for experience? If one can learn of war, one can learn of its follies without suffering it," Galen pointed out.

"A truly wise man can learn by the experiences of others, but fools require self-education, and the world is never short of fools." Lorn shook his head.

"Then the Torry Realm is blessed for its wise future king," Galen smirked.

"A healthy fear of Yah is the source of true wisdom. If I remain faithful, men will ascribe to me foresight and intellect, though each would be unearned."

"Faithful to your God. Minister Antillius spoke to this as well. He is a fellow acolyte, I assume?"

"Yes, and a good man and a better friend." Lorn smiled.

"I concur with your assessment. I took delight in the minister's company. He is a most learned man. He took unique interest in the ruins of ancient Tarelia. He was most grieved by the loss of its famed library during its sacking, the endless tomes of antiquity lost to the ages. I always take delight in my fellow lovers of knowledge. Perhaps I shall pen a ballad of the famed Squid Antillius," Galen said amusedly.

"You would have no shortage of material when singing his praises, Galen."

"True. The same can be said of you, my prince. Your legend grows with every battle."

"Glorify Yah over me, and I shall be in your debt, Minstrel. To him, I owe every success."

"It was not Yah I witnessed leading our men or throwing himself into battle," Galen recalled Lorn moving amidst the lines, leading the decisive left pincer that finally broke the Macon ranks. "Despite your wisdom, I must question it when considering the times you risked your life this day."

"The safest place upon the field of battle is where Yah places me, Galen."

"And do all his followers hear his voice or only his elect?"

"I cannot speak for all his followers, only myself, and I can only hear when my heart is emptied of self and filled with him."

"And would the great Yah be offended if I attempt to pen a ballad in his name?"

"You would have to ask him yourself, Galen," Lorn said whimsically.

"I shall consider it, my prince. Do I require similar precaution when penning your fell deeds?"

"As I said, as long as you place Yah's glory before mine."

CHAPTER 4

Bansoch
Queen Letha's palace

She lay abed, her tortured mind awash in memories, memories of Raven repeating themselves over and over, always ending upon the shore of Lake Veneba.

"Raven," she called out, his image fading cruelly from sight, his dark eyes staring intently into her golden hues.

"Tosha," her mother's voice called out, drawing her from her restless slumber.

She opened her eyes, finding Queen Letha sitting the edge of her bed, her head tilted to the side, gently stroking Tosha's hair, her face painted with worry.

"Mother?" she asked, wondering why she was in her chamber at this time of night, moonlight shining dully through her open window.

"The guards overheard your fevered ramblings and informed me."

"You needn't trouble yourself. I am well," she said tiredly, sweat catching her hair to her face despite the cold night air.

"Well?" Letha raised a skeptical brow. "Your windows are drawn open, letting in the frigid air, and yet you lay sweating like a furnace. Matron Telesa says you are having twins by the size of your womb." Letha ran a hand softly over Tosha's belly. She looked terribly uncomfortable.

"Twins?" Tosha wasn't expecting that. That increased the odds of bearing a boy, which would please her father. What if it were two boys? Would he claim them both? Would her mother allow it? Or two girls?

"It is rare but more likely through a maternal line that bore twins in the past. I was a twin," she reminded her.

"Is that why this pregnancy has been such torture?" Bearing a child was supposed to be pleasurable, yet she was sick from the start.

"I don't know. I never asked your grandmother how she fared. I can only tell you of my own experience, and it was joyous." Letha smiled, rubbing Tosha's belly.

"You and father were still in love then?" Tosha asked. Her mother rarely spoke of those days.

"I was…and I thought he was also. More the fool, was I?"

"Father loved you. He speaks of you fondly, Mother. Does not your likeness adorn my chamber, carved by his own hand?" Tosha looked over to the side of her chamber, where a visage of Letha was cast in white marble with obsidian molded into flowing locks and agate set in her eye sockets, staring back at Tosha with powerful intensity. The statue stood nearly nine feet, towering over the room like a sentinel guarding a great treasure. Facing this statue upon the opposite wall stood a similar likeness of Tyro's mother, her image cast from his memory. Both stood vigil, guarding Tosha in spirit while her father lived so far away.

"Love? What could he know of love when his heart waxes cold? His love died with his first wife. If he held any true affection for me, he wouldn't have conspired to seize our isle."

"Father never speaks of that," Tosha said, her weak defense of his honor the best she could manage in the face of her mother's vitriol.

"What is there for him to say? He knows what he did. We need not have this discussion right now. You need to rest. I didn't mean to wake you, but I was fearful you might be ill." Letha lovingly stroked her forehead. She closely guarded her greatest fear that something would befall her precious daughter, her only child. She was advised repeatedly to take a second husband and sire more heirs in case something befell Tosha, but her heart couldn't bear it. To do so would also

71

risk Tosha's life, her second husband's kin profiting from her death. Political marriages were often a balance between risk and gain. What concerned her as much as an assassin's knife was the birthing bed. Despite ruling a matriarchal realm, it was a vulnerability her male contemporaries on the continent did not suffer.

"It was just a nightmare that I suffered, Mother."

"A nightmare or memory?" Letha asked suspiciously.

"What do you mean?"

"You called out his name again," she said.

"Whose name?"

"Your consort's. Why does he torture you so? Did he harm you?" she asked darkly.

How should she answer? The hurts that cut deepest were all mental, from real to imagined. She didn't dare mention the times he roughly handled her or spanked her like an errant child. Revealing such a thing would hardly endear the queen to Raven.

"He should be here by now. That is the hurt that pains my heart and spoils my sleep."

"And you fear he will not be here before the birth." Letha guessed what she was truly scared of, Tosha's silence confirming that summation.

"He…he will be here," she affirmed after a painfully long moment of silence.

"You don't sound so certain. Your captain Raven is highly unpredictable if his reputation is to be believed."

"He will be here," Tosha insisted, refusing to contemplate otherwise.

"I hope so. Nothing would unify the Traditionalists and the Reformers against us more than you unable to demonstrate control over your consort."

"I am sorry to put you in this position, Mother," Tosha apologized.

"You followed your heart, Tosha. I am not one to cast judgment in that regard, though it does place us in a difficult position. Your marrying Raven offended the Traditionalist bloc in the forum. Only

Darna kept them in line long enough for me to appease them by denying the Reformers' petition to amend the stratification laws."

"And if Raven doesn't present himself, it will infuriate the Reformers that you sacrificed their ambitions for mine, and if Raven doesn't show, it will be for naught." Tosha shook her head, weary of it all. She was heir to the realm. She should be allowed to choose her consort, politics be damned.

"It will cripple my regency, forcing me to appease the Traditionalists to keep one flank secure while I offend our true allies in the Reformist bloc," Letha sighed, wishing she didn't have to share this burden with Tosha, but as her heir, she needed to know the dangerous ground they were on.

"A queen shouldn't have to bend to her lessers, especially in matters of her own household," Tosha growled bitterly.

"A true queen is answerable to her people and their concerns, Tosha. We are not tyrants, and we rule by Federation."

"Our word is law, and that should be enough to still their wagging tongues."

"We must give them time to accept Raven, time to see that he is not a threat to the Sisterhood. But first, he must present himself. Rest, my beautiful daughter." She kissed her forehead before stepping without.

Tosha ran her hands over her bulging stomach, thinking of the two precious lives growing within. She took an extra pillow, stuffing it between her legs and another beneath her back, trying to find the correct combination to ease her discomfort. She couldn't help but think of all those nights she shared with Raven in the wilderness as he held her captive. When they weren't fighting, they would spend their nights lying beside each other, staring at the stars, her head resting in the crook of his arm, her cheek pressed against his thick chest. She recalled how he smelled, finding it strangely comforting and familiar. They were precious moments amid their arduous trek, but she savored them. Strangely, she didn't recall the hardships as much as those wonderful moments she spent with him. She regretted what she did to him at Axenville. It was petty retaliation for all his sins, just as childish as his antics were in his revenge for her betrayal at Fera. It

73

was an endless cycle of revenge, and it needed to end. There was so much she wanted to say to him when he arrived, but mostly she just wanted him to hold her.

Please come soon, you big oaf. She smiled before drifting to sleep.

* * *

The following morn found Queen Letha within her inner sanctum with Councilors Neta Vasune and Voila Arisone, each sitting upon settees. Letha sat regally, her midnight-black hair set high upon her head, her gray eyes regarding each of the women with cool indifference. It was her *queen's face*, as Tosha would oft describe it, the regal mask with which she began every interaction. The settees were placed in a circle, with a small table set in its center, with refreshments resting upon it. Letha wore silver robes over a long golden tunic that reached her ankles, holding a goblet in her left hand.

"Councilors, it is pleasant to treat with you as always," Letha greeted the women, extending her goblet for a male servant to refill it. He hurried forth from his post along the chamber's near wall with a pitcher of water in hand. He wore a white Calnesian tunic that stopped short of his knees, with long auburn tresses framing a youthful face. Two others stood near the councilors, similarly attired. Each was a son of a noble house, placed in service to the queen by their mothers, hoping to attract the eye of other great houses. Being a personal servant to the queen was a very prestigious and competitive post.

"Thank you, Joyan," Letha emphasized the boy's name so her visitors would learn it.

"It is a pleasure to serve you, my queen." The boy bowed deeply before stepping back to his position. Joyan was the second son of Dejara Guloz, matriarch of House Guloz. Dejara was a councilor aligned with the Merchant bloc within the ruling forum, a bloc whose votes swung between the Traditionalists and Reformers, often providing the deciding votes in most matters. The Merchant bloc were often referred to by their moniker Queen Makers, their tie-breaking votes usually determining the queen's agenda. The other serving boys

74

were the noble sons of leading Traditionalist and Reformist houses, chosen by Letha to appease each group.

"My queen, we are pleased to be received," Councilor Neta Vasune formally began. She was a sturdy-built woman with silver tainting her short cropped auburn hair, her light-olive skin fairer than most of her contemporaries. She wore burgundy robes over an ankle-length blue tunic, her expressive green eyes regarding the queen guardedly.

"We are grateful for the granting of this audience, my queen," Voila Arisone added. She was of an age with Neta, with discerning hazel eyes and black hair coiled in thick braids draping below her shoulders. Her formal attire matched Neta's in scope but with rich emerald robes over black tunic.

"I assume you wish to discuss the agenda for this afternoon's forum," Queen Letha guessed their purpose. The ruling forum of the Federation rested at the opposite end of the Via Melida, the central avenue that started from the queen's palace. The broad roadway bisected the heart of the city, with large stone edifices lining its length, including such wonders as the Great Library, the Hall of Statues, and the Grand Bazaar. The grandest of these architectural wonders was the queen's palace and the ruling forum, each distinct in design but majestic. The forum rested on the eastern hilltop of Carnela that overlooked the mouth of the harbor, its large pillars the first thing any sailor sees upon approaching Bansoch.

"We do, my queen," Neta Vasune said with hope visible in her expressive green eyes.

"Boys, leave us." Letha dismissed her attendants, who bowed and withdrew, leaving the three women alone to discuss these delicate matters.

"Proceed." Letha waved her free hand for them to continue.

"As you are aware, my queen, the measures put forth during our previous session failed to pass," Voila Arisone said. She left unsaid that the queen's silence on the matter doomed their passing.

"Most unfortunate, Councilor. Though I see the merits of the provisions, as queen it is often prudent to leave such bold propositions to the forum to gain consensus, lest my interference cause further division." It was a clever answer but false. Queen Letha had routinely interjected in the edicts proposed in the forum, the queen's voice able to move dozens of votes from one side to another. The provisions that failed were to allow free men permission to leave their homes without escort, to ride in public areas, and speak in the forum on behalf of their house. Although Letha supported these measures in private, she could not openly endorse them for two reasons. They were highly controversial and required consensus for them to be accepted by all factions. Second, her standing with the Traditionalists was strained by Tosha choosing a foreign consort, an Earther no less.

"My queen, our more traditional-minded sisters mistake our leniency with our menfolk for weakness. Nothing is further from the truth. We are simply asking that we treat our sons, husbands, and fathers with common decency," Neta Vasune said. Her forebears were longtime advocates for the rights of their menfolk since their house was reduced to only sons several generations before, their daughters killed by plague. They were forced to wed their sons to lower class houses, who were willing to give up their second or third daughter to take up the name of House Vasune. Such a thing is perilous, the survival of one's house depending on the ability of the new union to sire a daughter as heir. Should the elder matriarch die before such an heir is produced, the house would fall fully under authority to a lower-class wife, who by rights of marriage, owned their husbands and therefore their estates. Such unfortunates could always be set aside if the wife so chose. Neta's grandmother was fortunate to be the heir of such a union, forever changing their loyalty to the Reformist cause. Neta herself had three daughters and two sons and desired for her sons to be given the same advantages as her daughters.

Voila Arisone's concerns were for the survival of her house, not for the desires of her sons. The proposals put forth to the ruling forum were pushed by her desperation to overturn the inheritance laws of the Federation, after losing both her daughters. She was left with two sons and wanted their birthright preserved, not subject to the power of others, should she die.

"Today's proposals involve amending the inheritance laws, I am told," Letha said, proving she was aware of the proceedings, without revealing how deeply she was aware.

"Yes, my queen, and we doubt they will pass without your public support before we put them up for a vote," Voila said, failing to mask her desperation.

"Though I sympathize with your cause, Councilor, I am wary to choose one side in such an important domestic initiative. As queen, I am duty-bound to give official decree supporting unanimous decisions of the ruling forum. Should I intercede on your behalf, the measure would likely pass by the narrowest of margins and sow division in the realm. You must gain the support of your Traditionalist sisters. I am certain a compromise can be reached," Letha explained.

"If such a compromise was possible, we would not be here pleading our cause, my queen," Neta sighed.

"I have given my daughters in service to the realm, my queen. My eldest, Sorela, was first mate on the *Morning Star*, the pride of the 1st Fleet, and lost in a storm," Voila explained, barely containing the rage of her emotions. Letha knew well the fate of the ship, a bioar galley that was lost six moons ago, patrolling the northeastern coast.

"My second daughter, Velesa, was thrown from her ocran, breaking her neck during her training in the royal cavalry. Is my house to be punished for these misfortunes?" Voila asked. The death of her daughters made her a new convert to the Reformist cause, but it was out of necessity for the preservation of her house, not belief in their merits.

"I could pass a royal decree specific to your house, Councilor, ensuring that your eldest son retains his name, protecting your house from his wife's potential interference," Letha offered.

"A royal decree can be overturned by future queens, my queen. I dare not trust my house to the fickle whims of a future monarch. I need the law formally amended," Voila said.

"A royal decree is the law of the land, Councilor!" Letha declared, weary of this discussion. If Tosha hadn't wed a foreign consort, she would be able to support such controversial legislation, but her hands were tied. She only dared exercise her clout in military and foreign matters.

"Please understand, my queen, that most of the Reformists are small landowners and local craftswomen and guilds. Few of us are wealthy compared to the large estate owners of the Traditionalist bloc or the Merchant class. Few of us have the luxury of sheltering half our family members because they are male. Is it not enough that we must compete with the slave labor that undercuts our profits? Beyond this, my queen, it breaks my heart when I look into my sons' eyes and know they must suffer such indignities," Neta said.

"Have you thought of bargaining with others in the forum? My cousin Darna leads the Traditionalists but is ever opportunistic in advancing her position. She has three daughters with which to wed your sons and sons to wed your heir, Councilor Vasune. Perhaps she might compromise on the inheritance laws in exchange."

"Guardian Darna has already arranged a nuptial for her eldest and heir," Voila sighed in exasperation.

This was news to Letha.

"A slave, no less. One she plucked from the auction block." Neta shook her head.

A slave? Letha was taken aback. It was not unheard of but surprising for so powerful a house such as Estaran to decide. She would leave it at that with her guests. She would have more trusted sources look into her cousin's activities.

"If not Guardian Darna, there are other houses you might negotiate. As for the crown, I must hold to neutrality in these matters," Letha said, her words obviously not pleasing her guests.

"If that is your decision, we must accept, my queen," Neta sighed tiredly.

"I do not mean to sound callous or disinterested in your plight, Councilors. I am well aware that former queens have taken more proactive positions in domestic affairs, as have I early in my reign. As stands our current position in the greater world, however, I am singularly focused on matters of state and military readiness. I know both of those issues are foremost in your hearts as well."

"The safety of the Federation is ever our primary concern, my queen. You have our full backing in this regard," Voila reassured, though her conviction sounded lacking.

"And that safety hangs upon the outcome of this great conflagration sweeping over the continent. Our position of neutrality may be untenable. Should that day come, I will need every councilor in the forum to speak with one voice." Letha stared intently in each of their eyes.

"Might I speak honestly, my queen, without causing offense?" Voila asked.

"Proceed," Letha said.

"You risked much with your marriage to Tyro, a decision you regret by the events that followed. Now our crown princess has chosen a a a man as consort who brings little value to the throne, and if the rumors are to be believed, one who has inflicted great insult on the Benotrist emperor. Should we expect war with Tyro? And would not such a war threaten the independence our forebears have fought to maintain since our founding?"

"Queen Melida led a Tarelian expedition to topple the Soch Empire, to counter the gargoyle threat spreading over the land, establishing the Sisterhood was a means to that end, not the end itself, Councilor. Our first duty is to stand against the gargoyles, not to hide upon our isle until they overwhelm all of Arax. Should we wait until they unite all of Arax against us? Or should we contest their dominion while our strength still holds meaning?" Letha regarded her coolly.

"Of course, my queen, forgive my impertinence." Voila bowed.

With that, the councilors were excused, leaving Letha much to consider. She summoned her captain of the guard, Lucella Sarelis, a statuesque warrior with short, dark hair and studious green eyes. She wore golden cuirass and greaves over a knee-length black tunic, the uniform of the royal guards.

"My queen." Lucella bowed after entering the chamber.

"Lucella, rotate anyone whose loyalties you doubt within the palace garrison with new recruits from the Dalacia Region," Letha said. Since the incident with the pirate raid that saw Tosha and the other princesses taken captive from her very walls, Letha was ever cautious with her security. Since that event, she posted all magantor forces farther inland and away from the palace.

"As you command, my queen," Lucella bowed knowingly, for the Dalacian Region to the southwest was a royalist stronghold, the soldiers there hailing from rich bloodlines with proven loyalties.

"Once that is accomplished, I need information on the activities of Guardian Darna."

* * *

Terin shuffled around the table, carrying a pitcher of wine while refilling Darna's goblet. His thin garments afforded him little protection in the cool afternoon air while serving their table upon the veranda attached to Darna's private chamber. Darna and Deva enjoyed a private meal, with Terin the only servant attending them. He shuffled across the stone patio as deftly as his shackled feet would allow, the thick steel bands circling his ankles proving difficult to manage. He was careful not to spill or drop any item, the scars from his last whipping ever in his thoughts. Ever since that night, he became singularly focused on escaping, the vision of the Sword of Light ever present in his mind. The vision was a gift from Yah, calling out to him the blade's location; even now its intense power was pulsating from within Darna's chamber, just indoors, hidden behind secret panels that concealed it from prying eyes. Escape was all he had now, but it was joyless, the news of Corry's death robbing him of his greatest desire.

"Be still, boy," Deva scolded, running a hand along his leg as he poured.

Terin kept still, his eyes trained to the floor after filling her goblet, suffering her touch.

"Your mistress has spoken to you directly," Darna said icily.

"Yes, Mistress," he replied with that hateful appellation. Ever since Deva returned to the household, she was cold toward him, as if he had wronged her in some way. For the life of him, he couldn't figure what he could've done. What could it be? He was the one offended, suffering her slights and humiliations. Her entire household was no different, each treating him as the lowest of slaves like Darna and her daughters or something worse like Gaive, Darna's husband, who despised him to his core. Only Guilen treated him decently, but even that relationship was transactional, motivated by Guilen's desire to learn to read. Whenever Terin brought up a plan of escape, Guilen dismissed it out of hand as impossible. Further complicating his plans was the plight of his fellow captives, especially Criose, who would suffer terrible torment for his rebellion. They needed to escape together, and Guilen's help was essential. Terin could hardly plan the details under the restrictions he suffered. Once he broke his shackles, he needed to escape immediately, for doing so would alert Darna of his intentions. He therefore needed Guilen, but convincing him was another matter. A snap of Deva's fingers drew him from his thoughts. He knelt beside her chair, careful not to lose his balance with his cumbersome shackles.

"His deportment is much improved," Darna dryly observed, before taking a bite of her food.

"Itara has been most helpful in his training. She deserves a reward for her earnest efforts," Deva praised the house steward.

"His posture is excellent, and his grooming, impeccable," Darna noted his straight back, bowed head, and rich garment. He wore the scandalously brief tunic of a house slave, its short sleeves and hem baring his limbs to the cool outside air.

He winced under their scrutiny, wishing Yah give him leave to snap their necks and be done with this. He instead released a quiet breath, swallowing his rage, which did not go unnoticed as Darna gripped his chin, lifting his eyes to hers.

"He acts well-behaved, but he can't hide the defiance in his eyes." She turned his head side to side as he steadied the pitcher in his hands.

"Is this true, Tera?" Deva asked as Darna released his chin, calling him by the name they had given him.

"I live only to serve you, Mistress," he said as calmly as he could, his eyes trained to the floor.

"Such a poor liar you are, child." Darna shook her head.

81

"Kiss Mother's feet, Tera!" Deva commanded, testing his obedience as Darna extended a sandaled foot from the hem of her gown.

Patience, Terin, a voice cautioned in his mind, tempering his anger. He carefully set aside the wine pitcher, shuffling closer to Darna, pressing his lips to her foot.

"Now, mine," Deva said coldly.

Terin repeated the humiliating act, further losing his dignity with every passing day. Was this their plan, to strip away every part of his individuality? To leave him a shell of his former self? He wasn't a fool; he knew why they wanted him. It was his Kalinian blood, to sire daughters with Deva, which could be used as weapons against Tyro. Why else keep him here? The Benotrists would gladly pay many times what he cost Darna, to see their greatest enemy fall into their hands. Tyro didn't know of their relation as far as Terin knew, but if he did, he would probably offer even more. Darna was clearly wary of the Torry kingdoms knowing that she held him. It was also curious that they changed his name. Who were they keeping his identity secret from?

Deva called for her guards, ordering them to take Terin to his chambers, leaving her alone with her mother.

"You should be wary of how you treat him, Deva," Darna warned as Terin was led away.

"When has the treatment of slaves ever concerned you, Mother?" She sipped her wine.

"You went to great lengths to make him believe the Torry princess jumped to her death, so you could fill her place in his heart. After all that effort, why are you destroying any kind feelings he might have for you? Not that I care, for it is my opinion that a mistress should do as she wants."

Deva sat there for a time, looking off in the distance to the surrounding hillsides. She couldn't honestly answer the question. Perhaps she was angry with him for rejecting her, if not outright, then through those pitiful sad eyes of his. Another part hated how she wanted him. This made her vulnerable in a way she never felt before. There was another voice whispering in the back of her mind that there was nothing she could do to change his heart. It was that last voice that she knew was true, and it fueled her rage.

"I changed my mind," Deva said, refusing to look at her mother.

"Apparently," Darna said dryly.

"I'll not lower myself to such tactics to win the affection of a slave. I am his mistress. I am the 4th Guardian of the realm. I will do my duty, and he shall do his."

Darna nodded, quietly approving of Deva's sudden change. She was always concerned that Deva lacked the cold logic and sternness required to rule their house. Kindness and appeasement only invited attack. Her attempt to befriend Terin was a prime example of such folly, a folly Darna allowed her to pursue. Failure is the greatest educator, tenfold more instructive than success.

"Very well, on to more pertinent matters. It appears our queen has lost all support with the feckless Reformers," Darna said, eyeing Deva to see if she could ascertain the importance of what she said and plan to take advantage.

"'Tis hardly a surprise with Tosha's foolish choice for consort. Queen Letha has to demonstrate strength to the Federation and our adversaries abroad. She doesn't have time to entertain the Reformers' fancies." Deva took a sip of her wine, still not looking at her mother.

"You've stated the obvious. Now display your insight," Darna pushed.

"We take full advantage of the desperate," Deva said coldly, setting her goblet down on the table.

* * *

Terin sat on the edge of his bed, looking down at his hands, lost in thought. He was surprised to be back in his room, having spent every night since his whipping in a cold cell. Here he sat, his left ankle shackled to the wall by a long chain, and his ankles still joined by the heavy shackles. They were certainly taking no chances with him. He was actually surprised they left his hands free, but where would he go? He still burned with shame with his treatment and their changing his name.

83

"Stand when your mistress enters your room!" Deva's voice drew his eyes to the doorway behind him, as she strode into the chamber, wearing leather mail over thick wool shirt and trousers. She obviously spent time in the training yard after her meal before visiting him.

Terin stood, not saying a word as she circled his bed, stopping in front of him, her hazel eyes staring into his blue.

"I thought in this room I was to address you as Deva?" he asked, wondering if their informal talks were at an end.

"Sit."

He sat, weary of her pettiness. Only Yah prevented him from grabbing her by the throat and choking the life out of her. He wondered what she wanted as she stood over him, staring at him with cold hatred. There was certainly a change in her that for the life of him he couldn't understand.

"What troubles you, Deva?" he asked, daring to use her name.

Nothing.

"What do you want from me? I am chained and at your mercy. You've had me whipped, branded, and worked to death. You've stolen me from my homeland and degrade me constantly. You changed my name. Making me kiss your mother's feet is a new low, even for you," he said with as calm a voice as he could manage.

Still nothing. She just stood over him, her nostrils flaring with heated breath.

"If you hate me so, just kill me and be done with it," he challenged. He started to rise until being met with her hands on his shoulders, driving him back on the bed, before climbing atop him, her knees straddling his hips and her hands on either side of his head.

"Listen carefully, *Tera*. I don't care if you desire me or not. I don't care if you are happy or miserable in this house. All that matters is that you take your place at my side like a dutiful husband of the Federation. That will be your only focus once we are wed. Is that understood?" she whispered harshly.

"It is understood." He glared up at her. He couldn't imagine ever wedding such a woman. She was pretty and unattractive at the same time, which didn't make sense unless one actually saw her with their own eyes. She lacked the barest feminine qualities of empathy, nurturing, and warmth. Her beauty was like a statue, cold and indifferent. He instantly thought of her father, Gaive, the insufferable patriarch of House Estaran, who hated Terin so intensely. The miserable wretch spent a lifetime wed to Darna. Was he the way he was because of suffering her abuse for so many years, or was he always a miserable wretch?

Will I end up like him if I wed Deva? Terin thought miserably, considering a lifetime of loveless drudgery. That was rather optimistic if he thought about it. The thought of the Sisterhood actually enduring for twenty years with no one to stop Tyro's aggression was lunacy. The world needed him on the battlefield to stop this from happening. The Sisterhood needed him on the battlefield, and he said as much to Darna and Deva to no effect. "You can't reason with unreasonable people," his father often said. Perhaps that was why his grandmother fled before Tyro could find her, knowing he couldn't be reasoned with. Just like his grandfather, Terin knew Deva was equally unreasonable. He needed to escape and would do so, with or without Guilen's help. Meanwhile, he needed to play the broken spirited slave.

"In three days, we are having several guests for a dinner gala where you will be formally introduced as my betrothed. You will attend me throughout the evening as my companion and be seated with the family," she said, studying his face.

"Won't your guests be suspicious upon seeing my shackles?" He shook his left foot, the sound of clanging chains echoing in the chamber.

"Our guests have better manners than to ask."

"You have an answer for everything." He shook his head.

"I am the 4th Guardian of the Sisterhood. I should have answers to simple questions."

"Fair enough." He shrugged, wondering when she would let him up.

"You will be spending the next days learning from my father on the managing of this household. There is more to that than you would guess. I expect you to obey him and learn from him. Your days serving at the table are now over, but they can easily return if you fail to meet my expectations."

"I will do as you wish...*Mistress*," he said that last word with mock servility.

"See that you do."

Terin flipped her over, pinning her to the bed, catching her by surprise.

"I will do my duty once I take our marital vows, Deva, but know this...I will never be tamed."

"We shall see." She smiled evilly, looking forward to that challenge.

* * *

The following morn found Terin and Guilen sitting a stone bench in the garden, behind the palatial estate, two guards standing post beyond earshot, keeping watch on Terin's every move. Terin's brief garment was replaced with a long silver Calnesian tunic with red stitching along its hem and sleeves, symbolic of his change in status and long enough to cover his shackles.

It covers the shackles but doesn't silence them. Terin mentally shook his head, wondering how he was expected to conceal that fact from their guests when their nuptials were formally announced. He was surprised Guilen met with him this morn, as he was expected to suffer Gaive's instruction.

"I need you to read this parchment." Guilen deftly removed a scroll from the folds of his robe, carefully setting it between them so that no one else could see.

Terin thought to refuse him since Guilen refused to help him escape, but that would close off any chance to sway him in the future. A squid once told him in his brief apprenticeship, "People often change their minds."

"Where did you get this?" Terin asked, looking it over as well as he dare, without raising suspicion. Fortunately, Velecia and Rutesha were on guard duty, neither overly keen observers, though Velecia could transition quickly once bestirred. Terin kept his movements subtle, seeing no reason to be careless.

"From Mother's sanctum. She is gone until midday. I always take advantage of these times to look over documents she leaves lying about, especially ones with my name upon them." Guilen tapped a finger to the middle of the scroll where his name was affixed.

"It appears to be a marriage contract with a woman named Relina Vola. It includes an agreed dowry of one thousand gold and a seat in the forum. Do you know this woman?" Terin asked.

"Unfortunately. She is a commander of Telnic and daughter to General Vola of the 2nd Army. She is a most disagreeable woman," Guilen recalled a previous encounter with Relina. She was a sour-faced, belligerent woman, with cruel manners. A life with her would be tenfold worse than his first marriage.

"An unwanted marriage. You have my sympathy," Terin said dryly, a long silence passing between them.

"I'm not marrying her."

"You're not?"

"No. I'll not wed, and neither will you."

* * *

Three nights hence
Darna's estate

Criose stood statue-still beside his fellow Torry slaves, awaiting the next guest to arrive. A long golden carriage made its way along the road that ran from the valley below to the front of Darna's manse, the clopping of ocran hooves sounding off the stone surface. Criose kept his eyes trained to the ground, trying his best to avoid another lash for his insolence. He and the others labored painfully every day since they were brought to this foul place. He caught sight of Terin on occasion, his young friend suffering far less than him, but the strain was still evident in his broken stare. Of course, that was early on. Terin was livelier now, a light taking root in his eyes that gave hope to Criose in turn. The nature of that hope was confirmed when their young master informed him of their plan to escape. He kept that plan from his fellow captives, lest they let it foolishly slip from their lips. He waited until the day of their escape to tell them. Contacting their young master was difficult under the constraints placed upon them. One thing Guilen made clear was that they needed to be prepared to fight if necessary. Criose snorted at that. He would do whatever was necessary to escape this place. Once they made that first step to freedom, there was no turning back, for the consequences of failure were worse than death.

"Slave!" Veya Cluse, the vice steward, called Criose forth as the carriage came to a stop. Veya was a harsh-faced woman with a shaved head, who demonstrated cruel pettiness with the slaves in her charge. She stood forward of the others, clad in loose Calnesian trousers, and blouse in bright green, with a thick black cloak to fend off the chill late-afternoon air. Her attire was in stark contrast to the slaves' brief livery.

Criose felt her lecherous eyes upon him as he tended the team of ocran as the footmen stepped off the carriage, opening the door for their mistress.

"Councilor Gaina." Veya bowed her head, greeting the matriarch of House Gaina, a stick-thin woman with discerning brown eyes and silvered hair.

"Mistress Cluse," Fala Gaina greeted the vice steward, disappointment painting her smile, obviously expecting a member of House Estaran to receive her.

"Master Guilen is receiving each guest this evening, Councilor. He will be with us shortly." Veya anticipated the unspoken question on propriety.

"My daughter, Inese," Fala introduced her heir, a woman of nineteen years with braided dark hair, wearing thick emerald robes over matching tunic.

"Mistress Inese." Veya bowed as the woman stepped from the carriage.

"Guvo, Dalen! See to Councilor Gaina's carriage," Veya ordered two of the stable slaves forward. They bowed deeply before relieving Criose, who as primary attendant, returned to his place behind Veya.

"Follow the stable slaves and be on your best behavior," Councilor Gaina ordered her footmen and driver, who bowed before following Guvo and Dalen to the carriage grounds near the stables.

Criose posted, standing quietly as he felt the eyes of the councilor upon him. He overheard suggestive comments passing between her and Veya directed at him and the others. Despite her banter, Veya made it clear that he was exclusive to her. He found her repulsive but had little choice but to endure her advances until they escaped. He recalled an incident several days before when she caught a female indenture exchanging glances with him. Veya had the girl and him beaten for the *offense*. Veya constantly alluded to her standing with the mistress and Darna's agreeing to gift Criose to her when she started her own house. Darna was known to be generous with her most loyal attendants, allowing them their choice of her male servants that were not exclusive to another. Darna was rumored to favor a particular field slave and valued her vice steward's discretion in the matter. The most powerful matriarchs took such liberties once their childbearing years were passed, protecting the bloodlines of inheritance upon which their federation depended. Having sired five children, Darna was now free to indulge her carnal interests.

"Here is Master Guilen, now Councilor," Veya said cheerfully as Guilen and Dorath descended the wide steps that led to the front atrium of the manse, each dressed in shimmering silver tunics that swirled about their ankles.

"Councilor Gaina." Guilen bowed respectfully as he reached the last step; Dorath repeated his brother's reverent gesture.

"Your father oversaw these duties for Guardian Darna's previous gala. As this is your first attempt in doing so, I suggest you plan accordingly when multiple guests arrive and not leave one waiting with house subordinates," Councilor Gaina admonished, studying Guilen's response.

"My apologies, Councilor. Anticipating this, I went to retrieve my brother to help escort guests to the main atrium. If you would follow Dorath, he shall escort you and your lovely daughter. Mother eagerly awaits you." Guilen bowed again, masking his distaste for the vile woman. Usually, it was members of the Traditionalist bloc that were insufferable. Councilor Gaina was a staunch Reformist who pressed for laws to raise the status of male citizens.

"Very well." Gaina sniffed as Dorath executed a practiced bow before offering his arm, which she took.

Guilen ordered Veya to accompany them, as he awaited the next carriage, which made its way toward them.

Guilen took this moment to draw Criose aside.

"When the last carriage departs tonight," Guilen whispered in his ear.

* * *

Terin stood beside Deva in the receiving line as the guests entered the central atrium, each name heralded by the house steward, Itara Vosen. He was fourth in line, standing between Deva and Thesta, both girls dressed in matching gold trousers and blouses of flowing Calnesian fabric. They stood in contrast to his bright-silver tunic with gold stitching along its long sleeves, his shackles hidden within the garment's long hem. He struggled not making his chain rattle as he moved deftly about. He kept his hands clasped in front of him, raising his eyes only when greeting each guest as Deva introduced him.

Upon occasion, Terin would steal a glance around the spacious chamber, noting its rich detail and furnishings. The central roof rose some ten meters to the center, with slowly spinning lanterns suspended from the stone supports, casting images of stars and half-moons upon the upper walls as they spun, torchlight passing through the distinct shapes cut from the sides of the lanterns, producing the dazzling effect. The surrounding walls were solidly built with thick brown stones with speckles of white and gray. Large archways were centered on each wall, leading to each direction of the manse. Tables were set across the dark stone floor with house slaves moving among the seated guests, serving wine and bread.

Terin noticed Veiya, Deva's personal slave, giving him dirty looks whenever their eyes met. The pitiful wretch was jealous of her attentions since Terin arrived. The fact that the man was envious was beyond him. The entire situation was madness, beside the fact Veiya was a gelding, laboring forever in Darna's household.

I'll either escape or die, Terin reassured himself, not willing to spend another day in this place.

"Councilor Fala Gaina!" Itara Vosen, the house steward, announced as Dorath escorted the famed Reformist to Darna at the head of the receiving line. Dorath bowed deeply to his mother and stepped back.

"Such a lovely child," Gaina congratulated Darna, admiring the boy's comely face and graceful manners.

"Your words are most kind." Darna smiled, pride for her younger son evident in her blue-gold eyes. "And your daughter, I presume?" she asked, her gaze falling upon the young woman escorted by her vice steward.

"Yes, my daughter Inese," Fala said, drawing Inese beside her.

"Guardian Darna, my mother speaks well of your fortitude in the forum," Inese greeted her.

"I am flattered, Inese. Your mother is equally formidable, I assure you."

"Perhaps our aims need not be in conflict. I look forward to your thoughts on the matter, Guardian," Fala added.

"Yes, we have much to discuss," Darna said before introducing them to the rest of her family, making a special point on introducing Terin, though referring to him as Tera.

"So the rumors are true, you intend to wed your heir to a slave," Fala observed the collar gracing Terin's throat.

Terin held his tongue, feeling Fala's gaze upon him, keeping his own eyes to the floor. Yah tempered his anger, keeping him from responding to such invectives. If he managed to escape this place, he could look back to this time as a lesson in patience and understanding. He was becoming very good at observing his surroundings and truly listening to what others said. One thing was certain, and that was he would never look at slavery the same ever again.

"He's pretty enough," Inese commented, raising a bemused brow while gifting Deva a flirtatious wink.

"Indeed," Fala agreed, though she could barely conceal her disgust. She fought for the rights of free-born men in the Federation while Darna opposed such measures. It was little wonder Darna cared not, as she saw slaves as equal to true-born sons if she planned to wed one to her heir. Fala could count more than one hundred suitable matches for Deva from some of the wealthiest, loyal, and noble houses in the Federation. What was so special about this boy to pass so many others up?

Fala and Inese politely moved on as the steward heralded the next guest.

"Arch Councilor Lutesha Dorvena and her heir, Elesha!" Itara Vosen heralded Darna's closest ally and fellow Traditionalist.

"Welcome, Arch Councilor." Darna clasped arms with her friend.

"Guardian," Lutesha said, a knowing look passing between them. There was much to discuss once the formalities of the evening were concluded.

Terin cringed when Lutesha stopped in front of him, recalling the last time he had the displeasure of seeing her and her daughter, the night Elesha shared the awful tale of "Corry's death."

"Most elegant attire, Tera." Lutesha brushed his shoulder.

"You are most kind, Arch Councilor," he politely said.

"Not as revealing as the outfit you wore when we last met, but then again, this night is when you are formally recognized," she added before moving on, Elesha sharing a smile with Deva, before following her mother to their seats.

"Councilor Neta Vasune!" the steward heralded the Reformist councilor, escorted by Guilen. He quickly bowed to his mother before stepping away.

"Welcome, Councilor. I hope this evening finds you well," Darna greeted.

"It is not often I dine with my strongest adversary in the forum. This night is certain to be eventful. I have on good authority that the princess has begun her labor," Neta said, the last comment drawing Darna's curiosity.

"And her consort is still absent?" Darna asked.

"If he presented himself, I am not aware." Neta shook her head.

"Yes, he would be difficult to overlook."

Neta agreed before moving along. After the last guest arrived, House Estaran found their places at the high table, overlooking the others. Joining them there was Gaive's mother, Mearna Tolus. The evening proceeded with wine and food. Gaive, Guilen, and Dorath sang while playing harps, to the delight of Mearna. After this, Darna announced the betrothal of Deva and Terin to a chorus of cheers.

Terin stood beside Deva, receiving the unwanted attention with as much grace as he could manage. He tugged at the collar of his garment, feeling it constraining his neck even more so than his slave collar. The women seated across the chamber regarded him with a strange mixture of interest, lust, and hostility. Darna and Deva each spoke to the assemblage, but he didn't hear a word they said. As soon as he retook his seat, Darna asked Guilen to stand.

"I am pleased to announce that my daughter's betrothal does not stand alone. My eldest child, Guilen, is to wed commander of Telnic, Relina Vola, daughter of General Vola, who commands 2nd Army. General, would you and your daughter please stand!" Darna declared as General Vola and her daughter gained their feet.

"I welcome your son into our family, Guardian. May our union be blessed," the general said.

Terin regarded the woman warily. She stood of a height to him, with short cropped hair, silvered with age, and a heavy face. Her daughter was equally fierce, each dressed in leather trousers and blouse, with heavy cloaks that appeared as bland as their personalities. If Guilen was repulsed, he dared not show it. Terin gave the man credit for politely bowing as Relina stepped forth to take his hand, formally accepting their betrothal.

The night continued with more songs, wine, and desserts. Terin almost pitied the house slaves as they kept pace with the guests demands. His pity was tempered by their mutual hatred for him, each of them giving him heated glares throughout the night. He found their animosity misplaced since he had done nothing to them. Were they truly jealous of his new position? Deva was a conniving shrew, lacking any warmth. Despite her physical attractiveness, she lacked the feminine strength he found so inviting in Corry. Her touch held all the allure of a reptile.

It was then that Guilen spilled his wine on Terin while passing behind him, drawing Darna's ire.

"You foolish boy!" she admonished, coming swiftly to her feet.

"My apologies, Mother. Let me help find something for Tera to change into." Guilen quickly bowed while setting his goblet on the table, swaying briefly as if drunk. Drunkenness was frowned upon in males, and they were never offered much to drink. Guilen obviously couldn't hold what little wine he had partaken.

"How can I expect you to handle your duties as greeting host if you are in such a state?" she asked.

"I am capable of performing my duties, Mother," he affirmed, quickly standing erect.

"See that you are. You may take Tera and help him change."

* * *

"Was that wise? They will question if you can return to your duties," Terin said as Guilen guided him toward his chamber.

"I had to hasten our plan. Mother intends to gather the visiting councilors to discuss matters of state. Now is the time for you to do what you said you could do," Guilen said, looking over his shoulder to see if they were followed. Luckily, the guards lingered at the end of the corridor.

"I can. Just take me to your mother's chamber."

Guilen wondered what was in his mother's chamber that would set Terin free, but that was why they had chosen this night. Most of his mother's guards were occupied protecting their guests and the perimeter. The corridors were mostly empty. They quietly made it to her chambers, slipping quietly inside.

Though he had been here before, his eyes were trained to the floor, unable to take in the details of the room. Terin was immediately struck by the chamber's austere design and furnishings. It was the chamber of a person of simple rank, with a modest bed and chest, with a large window and doorway that opened to the veranda overlooking the surrounding hillsides. A series of stone blocks rested along the room's perimeter, each of varying height and shape, arranged in no particular order. He saw the image in his vision, recalling which to approach.

"What now?" Guilen asked, keeping a nervous eye upon the door.

"You truly do not know what is kept here?" Terin asked in wonder. The look on Guilen's face confirmed his ignorance.

"Let me show you," Terin said, stepping toward the third block along the near wall, a square stone nearly one-yard square. He knelt at its base, pressing his hand to the floor, feeling a flat stone shift with his pressure until he could grip its sides, lifting it free. Guilen stared in awe as the floor opened to a small crevice below. Terin reached his arm into the dark opening, sliding his hand beneath the base of the stone block.

Guilen's eyes drew wide as Terin withdrew a glowing yellow sword, its light illuminating the chamber in blinding radiance. Terin felt renewed; the power of the blade shot up his arm, coursing through every fiber of his flesh, his countenance alit with terrible power. In two quick swings, he struck the heavy shackles from his ankles.

"How?" Guiled gasped.

"This is a Sword of Light, forged by the smiths of ancient Tarelia," Terin said, replacing the floor stone to its proper position.

"The legends are true," he marveled.

"Yes, just as I told you."

"But how did you know to find it here?"

"It called to me. My Kalinian blood gave me a vision. Now let's proceed with your plan."

* * *

Deva sat beside her mother, their ranking guests gathered in the private sanctum, leaving the rest of the guests still celebrating in the central atrium. Darna and Arch Councilor Lutesha Dorvena, represented the Traditionalist bloc, with Neta Vasune, Voila Arisone, and Fala Gaina, representing their Reformist guests. Deva was surprised her mother included her in this delicate meeting, explaining to her that as her ascendance drew nigh, she needed to assume greater duties as the future head of House Estaran. She was miffed when Guilen returned to the festivities without Terin, claiming he became ill and was asleep in his bed, positioning guards outside the chamber.

Her brother seemed distracted sharing this information and hurried off to attend to his duties, seeing a few of the guests off. If she wasn't distracted with the meeting at hand, she might investigate his strange behavior.

"The princess is in labor this night with no sign of her consort," Councilor Gaina began.

"His absence might be excused if he was a monarch of equal standing or a son of one of our noble houses," Neta Vasune added.

"With one hand, our queen allows this offense to our realm, and with the other denies mercy for the rights of our true-born sons," Fala Gaina bitterly stated, all affinity for their queen gone.

"Is it our place to question our rightful queen?" Lutesha asked, measuring the Reformers' sincerity.

"Are you truly going to ask such a question at this juncture, Arch Councilor?" Fala Gaina asked darkly, their previous overtures putting the matter to rest.

"Perhaps I overstepped. Let us start again. What specific laws would win your loyalties for advancing Guardian Darna to the throne?" Lutesha asked.

"Amending the laws of inheritance to start with," Neta Vasune said.

"We will not equalize sons with daughters before the law. That is a dangerous slope we will not pursue," Lutesha countered.

"We are not asking for equality but to allow sons a place to inherit should we not have daughters to pass on our authority and wealth," Fala said.

"Perhaps a compromise could be reached. What else do you want?" Darna asked.

* * *

Terin crept through the darkness, the light of Darna's manse illuminating the hilltop behind him. He slipped away from the estate through Guilen's chamber window after changing into a pair of loose woolen trousers and shirt with thick woven sandals. He kept the sword hidden within the folds of a cloak, lest its light give him away. He made his way, carefully keeping watch for guards posted along the curtain wall surrounding the base of the hill and others conducting routine patrols. Thankfully, most of the soldiers were guarding the front of the estate, few looking in his direction as he made his way to the stables. He stopped at the edge of a field near the stables, watching men lingering near each carriage lined up along the pathway. They were obviously the drivers and footmen of each.

Terin kept low, crouching behind the ditch lining the edge of the field, seeing if he could make out Criose or the others in the darkness. His patience was rewarded upon finding Guilen make his way along the pathway, two guards escorting him to the stables. Once Guilen reached the stables, Terin recognized Criose stepping into the torchlight to greet him with a deep bow. Guilen immediately ordered all the carriages to be sent to the front of the manse to await their mistresses. His escort guards returned as well, leaving one last carriage. After a few moments, Guilen started walking toward the field, obviously looking for him.

"I am here," Terin whispered, standing up.

"Come quickly," Guilen said as they ran back to the stables where Criose and Guvo awaited them, with Dalen and Zaran sitting on the carriage beside a distraught-looking driver, a young girl of sixteen years, Dalen holding a dagger to her throat.

"Criose." Terin smiled, embracing his friend.

"Well-met, Terin." Criose lifted him off the ground.

"We must make haste," Guilen scolded them. "Terin, there is an ocran saddled and ready for you. The rest of us will be in the carriage. Stay close to us and react if need be."

* * *

"Where is he?" Darna snarled, storming through the corridor; Itara Vosen, her steward, trailing at her heels.

"The guards are scouring the estate, Guardian Darna. Master Guilen hasn't been seen since he went to the stables earlier this night."

"Who saw him last?"

"The guards who escorted him there."

"And why didn't they remain with him?"

"He ordered them to guard Master Dorath, who was at the front of the manse, seeing guests off."

"He wouldn't have just disappeared. He was either taken or…" Darna stopped midstride, an awful suspicion passing over her, only to be confirmed by Deva rushing toward her from the adjoining hall.

"Terin's missing!"

No sooner had Deva uttered those words than Veya Cluse, the vice steward, reported that the carriage of Voila Arisone was missing, and her footmen found tied and gagged in the stables.

* * *

Bansoch
Queen Letha's palace

Tosha lay abed, her feet spread, pain coursing her womb. She shouted in agony, hateful thoughts of Raven repeating in her brain, and curses from her lips.

"What ails her?" Queen Letha asked the chief matron, sitting at the end of the bed, awaiting the birth.

"A strange affliction, my queen," Matron Telesa said, perplexed by Tosha's birth pains.

Birthing was a euphoric experience for Araxan women, more powerful than erotic fulfillment, constant pleasure sweeping over their flesh. Tosha's labor was a tumultuous mix of unimaginable pleasure and unbearable agony, and Telesa did not know why.

Is the child cursed? Letha kept that thought to herself, holding tight to Tosha's hand, her daughter gripping her desperately.

"Curse you, Raven!" she screamed, squeezing as the first baby drew near, blaming him for the pain. He was the root of her agony. She didn't know how but knew it was true. Even more so, she cursed him for breaking his promise, his promise to be here for this most important event. Now she was shamed by his absence, and so was the throne.

"Don't think of him, Tosha. Just push." Letha squeezed her hand.

"Aaargh!" She pushed, pain and euphoria sweeping over her in equal measure; the cool night air blew through the open window, drying the sweat on her brow.

"I see the head," Matron Telesa said as the crown began to emerge. She reached out, receiving the baby after an arduous session of labor.

"A prince!" Telesa declared, her sister matron cutting the cord before handing the bawling babe to a third matron who brought the child to the wash basin arranged in the chamber. There, it was attended by several sister matrons who cleaned the child, wrapping him in swaddling clothes before presenting it to the queen.

Tosha caught her breath, her head pressed against the bed as if it were stone. Her weary golden eyes looked desperately to her mother holding the child.

"A handsome boy," Letha assured her, her gray eyes dancing with delight as she beheld her grandson.

"Is he…is he well?" she asked.

"His coloring is strange, but he is healthy," Letha assured her, guessing his light reddish-brown skin was from his father.

Raven, Tosha thought bitterly, before the pains began anew. Letha kissed the boy's wrinkled forehead, blessing the prince before passing him to a royal attendant.

"I see the next child," Chief Matron Telesa said, after another bout of labor, leaving Tosha a weeping mess, overcome with pain and pleasure.

"A princess!" Telesa declared triumphantly, holding the child aloft.

"An heir for the realm!" the other matrons shouted, heralding the birth of their new princess. The girl was quickly prepared and presented to the queen.

"A name, my queen?" Telesa asked.

As queen, Letha held final authority in the naming of a crown royal.

"Tosha?" Letha deferred to her daughter, who still lay abed, her anguished face barely able to appreciate the moment.

"Ceana," Tosha said, choosing the name she selected long ago, the namesake of her renowned ancestor, the Great Queen who ruled their isle three centuries before.

"A perfect choice," Letha affirmed, holding her granddaughter aloft, proclaiming her birthright.

"Aaargh!" Tosha winced, pain washing over her.

"What ails her?" Letha handed the princess over to a matron, returning to Tosha's side.

"A third child!" Telesa gasped.

Another bout of pain and pleasure contorted Tosha into a quivering wreck as Letha stroked her forehead, whispering words of comfort into her ear. Chief Matron Telesa grew eerily quiet, drawing the child from the womb, audible gasps escaping the lips of her sister matrons standing over her.

"Telesa?" Letha asked, hiding the concern from her voice, the disquiet of the matrons as they went about cleansing the child, doing little to calm her fears. One look from Telesa caused the queen to step near to see for herself.

"A boy," Telesa whispered, the simple words unable to convey what she couldn't describe.

"Hand him to me." Letha took the child, her eyes drawn wide, looking down at his face. She stifled a gasp, staring into his silver eyes that stared back at her curiously, as if she was the most interesting thing any creature had ever beheld. His skin was covered with inky black scales, their patterns crisscrossing his flesh. He was far larger than his siblings, with a wide flat nose, and a strange grin stretching his lips. For the life of her, she didn't know what to make of him.

"He is…different," Telesa said, stopping herself from calling him something worse, like an abomination or freak.

"Yes, and very strange," Letha observed, running a finger over his cheek, which drew a grin from the child that melted her heart.

"His skin is quite hard," Telesa said.

"Almost like stone," Letha added.

"Mother?" Tosha called out, obviously concerned by what they were saying.

"You have another son, Tosha, a healthy boy, though I warn you that he is different."

"I want to see him," she said determinedly.

Letha set the child in her arms as Tosha stifled a gasp, tears pouring down her cheeks as her son looked up at her.

"Raven, where are you?" she cried, holding the infant to her breast.

* * *

The following morn

They rode through the night moving apace south and east, using the roads and putting as many leagues between themselves and Darna's estate as possible. The clear, moonlit sky illuminated their path and the open fields that lined either side of the road. They came upon only a few passersby, and none stopped to challenge them. Terin trailed a short distance at times and rode ahead at others, keeping constant vigil. Luckily, they reached the outskirts of the port village of Caltera without incident before sunrise.

They stopped upon a hillside overlooking the small port below. Terin, Guilen, and Criose stood in front of the carriage, taking stock of their surroundings. A half dozen ships were in port, their masts peeking above the rooftops surrounding the inlet, upon which Caltera was built. The small port village was surrounded by a ring of hills, with the only road leading straight inland, where they stood.

"The village looks quiet," Criose said, tightening the hold on his sword. He didn't intend to loosen his grip until he was on a ship and far away.

"Looks can be deceiving," Terin said warily, looking for any sign of troops in the port. He could only see a few people stirring in the village, tending various tasks. He saw two young boys drawing water from a well at the base of the hill where they stood.

"You are certain there is a ship that will take us?" Criose asked of Guilen.

"There should be any number of foreign-flagged vessels moored here at any time if my mother's log tablets are accurate. We only need to bribe them with half the gold I acquired from my mother."

"Stole, you mean." Criose grinned.

"It is my proper inheritance, a small price for her to pay for a lifetime of insults." Guilen lifted his chin indignantly.

"What if you can't bribe a ship to take us on?" Terin asked.

"It is a possibility, but if gold does not motivate them, your sword should move them," Guilen encouraged smugly.

"Let's hope it doesn't come to that," Terin sighed.

"The difficult part might be getting to the ship without raising suspicion," Criose said.

"I suggest we ride full gallop. It's a small port, and we should be at the docks before anyone has time comprehend who we are or what we are attempting," Terin said, stepping away to mount up.

"You heard the man, Dalen, keep a tight hold on her!" Criose said. Dalen was still sitting beside the driver, his dagger concealed behind her.

"You do as we ask, and you shan't be harmed," Dalen whispered in her ear.

"I am already harmed. Councilor Arisone will extend my indenture for this failure," the driver lamented sullenly.

"Then come with us," Dalen offered. He could tell by her silence that she was mulling it over.

They were suddenly on their way racing down the hillside, coming swiftly upon the village outskirts. A young slave boy jumped out of their path as they passed, the lad giving Terin a strange look as he trailed the carriage. They passed between two level wooden structures, weathered by the salty sea air. The carriage wheels sounded audibly off the cobblestone road, drawing unwanted attention as they drew closer to the wharves.

"Halt!" a woman's voice called out as they passed once she saw Terin mounted, and trailing the carriage.

Terin didn't spare her a glance, shouting for Dalen to hasten his pace before others took notice.

"Halt!" the woman screamed again, chasing after them, others taking up her call. Sailors began pouring out of a building to their right, some brandishing weapons. By the time they noticed the source of the commotion, the carriage had already passed them by.

Several soldiers in gray mail over dark-brown tunics stepped into the street up ahead. Terin raced out in front riding straight through them, his sword cutting one their blades in half, causing the others to jump clear.

Terin spotted a Casian-flagged vessel among several Sisterhood and mercenary galleys, a black anchor upon a field of gray, the sigil of Port West, blowing freely upon its forward mast. He raced along the wharf, causing the crews of the ships they passed to stare in disbelief. He rode straight for the Casian vessel, giving the onlookers little time to register what they saw. The carriage followed, stopping at the gangplank of the Casian ship as he circled about, keeping an eye out for any pursuers.

Guilen quickly exited the carriage. Criose and the other Torries emptied out behind him, keeping close as they approached the Casian ship. They were soon met by several crewmen in mustard tunics and leather caps, who escorted them to their captain, who in turn flatly refused to take them.

"I have one thousand gold certras to pay our passage to Cagan," Guilen offered.

"And lose my head? Are you touched, boy?" the silver-haired captain growled.

"Only if they catch you, and they won't," Guilen reasoned, though the captain was having none of it.

"You will earn the favor of the Torry crown prince," Criose added.

"And why is that?" the captain snarled, about to draw steel. He took note of Criose's slave collar and wanted nothing to do with it. If he helped these fugitives, he could never return.

"Our friend is the Torry champion, Terin Caleph!" Criose declared.

"Caleph is dead, drowned at Carapis, if the rumors are true," the captain said, backing a step.

"He was washed ashore with the lot of us, taken by slavers and brought here. If you help us, Prince Lorn will richly reward you," Criose pleaded.

"Aye, if true. But why would I believe such a yarn?" With that, the captain's eyes drew wide, staring over their shoulders to what was unfolding upon the wharves.

Terin raced along the piers, driving off several mounted warriors, his blade snapping swords ere touching them, their steel shards flying off his blade. Before he knew it, Terin was on foot, fending off several sailors from a mercenary vessel, all men, clad in thick leather and furs, intent on subduing the escaped slave and win the Federation's favor.

Terin no sooner chased off the soldiers when the mercenaries were upon him. He fell into his deadly trance, charging into their midst.

Split!
Thrust!
Spin!
Thrust!

He cut down two in quick succession, his blade taking another across the throat, the man's head spinning into the air. He took a fourth man at the shoulder, the wretch's left arm dangling by the barest of threads. The man stumbled, his screams piercing the morning air like a dagger to the ear. It was too much, and the others broke ranks, returning to their vessel.

"Come aboard!" the Casian captain relented, his eyes transfixed, watching Terin standing amidst the carnage, his blade glowing with

THE CHRONICLES OF ARAX

a terrible golden hue. It was both beautiful and terrifying, beguiling to behold.

The others quickly scurried aboard, with Dalen pleading with their driver to join them.

"Come with us, Moira. Freedom now is worth more than any reward given after ten more years of bondage," he pleaded. She finally relented, taking his hand and following him up the gangplank.

The crew immediately sprang into action, untying the ship from the wharf and preparing to lift anchor. Guilen called out to Terin to climb aboard, but the Torry champion held off, regarding the danger the other vessels posed.

"What's he doing?" Guilen shook his head as Terin raced up the gangplank of a Federation vessel, splitting the upraised shield of the sailor guarding entry to the ship. She stumbled briefly before jumping over the side, avoiding losing her head.

"He's crippling her!" Criose said as Terin swung at the forward mast of the vessel, the sword cutting it clean through, its furled sail failing with the mast upon the starboard bow, its weight carrying it overboard. Terin did the same for the center mast before racing off the ship and boarding the next.

"We don't have time for this. Tell him to hurry back, or we leave without him!" the captain barked, eager to get underway.

* * *

Terin raced onto the next Federation vessel, a sleek-hulled merchant galley with a double mast and single deck of oars. The female crew fled upon his approach, wanting nothing to do with the maddened warrior wreaking havoc in the port. Some jumped overboard; others ran below deck, leaving him free to cleave their mast poles.

"Terin! Make haste!" Criose shouted from the wharf, having ran from the Casian vessel to fetch him.

Terin caught his breath, regarding his friend briefly, before staring out across the small port, his golden mane lifting in the breeze. He crippled three vessels, and the others' crews were in complete disarray. He need only to run back to their ship and sail away, putting this nightmare behind him.

"Go! I am right behind you!" he shouted, waving Criose on while stepping off the ship. A few of the port's residents gathered at the end of the street to his left, holding position, wary to advance anywhere near him. Others were securing their slaves, lest any thought to join this rebellion.

"Terin!" Criose called out again from his right, urging him to make haste.

Only instinct kept him from heeding his friend's plea. He noticed movement upon the rooftops of the structures lining the waterfront, sunlight reflecting of polished helms as archers took up position. The sound of ocran hooves slapping stone echoed through the nearby streets until a column of riders swept onto the wharf off his left from the adjoining avenue. They wore the familiar golden armor and silver tunics of Bansoch garrison, with the black cloven crown upon a field of white emblazoned upon their crests, the sigil of the harbor garrison. He spotted Darna riding at the front of this considerable host, with Deva upon her right, and Sela Yorin, her second, upon her left.

"Terin!" Criose pleaded, their ship preparing to push off.

Run, Terin! Yah whispered to his soul, urging his disciple to obey his will, but Terin stood transfixed, tempted by revenge. His mind was plagued by the countless tortures and humiliations inflicted upon him, each repeating in his mind over and over, each more terrible than the last. He felt the power of the sword coursing through him, melding with his Kalinian blood, restoring him to his full glory. He wasn't chained and helpless anymore. He was the blood of Kal, the champion of the Torry Realm, and the Sword of Yah. All of Darna's might shrank before the power he wielded.

"Terin, NO!" Criose shouted in vain as Terin ran in the opposite direction, straight into the gathering host, one man against hundreds, their hooves echoing like thunder.

Terin fixed his eyes upon the lead mount, recognizing Darna's cruel blue-gold eyes through the slits in her steel helm, a plume of red feathers running down its middle. Arrows bounced off the roadway around his feet, each missing him. He stopped suddenly, bracing for impact as Darna drew nigh, his blade steady in hand.

Sela Yorin, Darna's 2nd, swept in front of her commander, bearing down upon Terin, who shifted to his right, bringing his sword across her ocran's throat. Sela lowered her lance, trying to skewer him, but he moved with unnatural speed, his blade slicing her mount's head with one terrible strike. The beast tumbled to the ground, tossing her into the air. Time slowed as she stared at the ground below, hanging briefly before dropping to its unforgiving stone surface.

Terin spun, evading the dying beast before cutting down another rider pressing near, his blade taking the ocran at the knees. Darna cursed as she rode past him; Sela's dying ocran separated him from her. Deva came up alongside her, her eyes transfixed by Terin's fell handiwork as he moved behind them, cutting down ocran like straw training dummies. They eased their gallop, turning slowly about so as not to be trampled by those following on their heels. Upon her signal, her cavalry backed away, forming a perimeter around Terin, their lances leveled upon him. The riders that were thrown from their mounts struggled to their feet before fleeing his blade.

Terin paced around the beasts littering the street, his eyes sweeping Darna's soldiers, challenging them to come and take him. He spun his sword, sunlight playing off its magical blade, illuminating his countenance. He was beautiful and terrifying to behold. Several shifted nervously, their skittish mounts growing restless.

"Come, Darna! Fight me! No chains grace my ankles. My friends' lives are not yours to use against me. I'll slay every one of your people if I have to, to get to you!" he challenged.

Darna regarded him coldly, the beat of her heart deafening her thoughts.

"The rest of you will die by my blade if you do not flee!" he continued, the power coursing his veins emboldening his prideful heart. "I am the blood of Kal, the son of Jonas, and champion of the Torry Realm! No one will deny me my vengeance this day!" He leveled his sword toward Darna, a wicked grin twisting his lips, nothing but revenge filling his heart, crowding all else, leaving only a dark caricature of his former glory. He did not notice the darkening sky encroaching from the north, the wind sweeping before it, nor his comrades' ship pushing away from the wharf. He was blind to everything but hate.

"Mother?" Deva asked nervously, drawing her mount closer to Darna. Whatever overcame Terin had unnerved her.

"Be still!" Darna whispered harshly, her own heart losing its steel, her soldiers faring little better. She could see them losing faith, even their mounts shifting nervously beneath them. It felt as if Terin surrounded them rather than they him. Then as all seemed lost, the heavens answered.

Crack!

A bolt of lightning flashed brightly before her, paining her eyes, striking the Sword of Light in Terin's outstretched arm. She opened her eyes, finding Terin lying upon the ground, unmoving.

* * *

"The fool!" Criose cursed, watching the terrible scene unfold from the stern of the Casian vessel, Guilen standing beside him, crestfallen at their friend's madness and misfortune.

"Madness. Utter madness." Guilen shook his head sadly.

"Raise sails!" the captain ordered as the wind miraculously picked up as Darna's warriors flooded the wharf behind them, firing arrows as they drew away beyond their reach.

CHAPTER 5

Seven leagues southeast of Darna's estate

The cold took him, engulfing him in its frigid embrace. It was all consuming, burrowing into his soul. He stared into complete darkness, lonely and afraid, drowning in a hopeless abyss. He called out to Yah, but there was no answer.

Yah cannot dwell in a pride-filled heart. Lorn's words came painfully to mind.

Terin opened his eyes, staring at the stormy sky above, wondering where he was. He could only bemoan whatever fate awaited him, his eyes rolling back into his head, letting the darkness take him.

"What shall we do with him?" Deva asked, riding beside the wagon where Terin was chained. He lay upon the bed of the wagon, his hands bound behind him, and feet shackled, his body shaking uncontrollably at times. He mumbled incoherent nonsense; his mind lost in delirium.

Darna rode beside her, trying to answer that question herself. She thought he was dead with that lightning bolt. The fact he still breathed proved the boy's fortitude. But why did it strike him? Was the lightning drawn to the sword? It never did so with her. She looked down to her side, where the Sword of Light again rested in its proper place. Many of her soldiers regarded the blade with awe, never realizing their commander possessed it all along. It was a closely guarded secret of the Sisterhood, the two Swords of Light wielded by General Melida and her sister Telisa to overthrow the old Soch Empire. The swords were forged in ancient Tarelia and given them to aid their quest. Since that day, they were passed down to the descendants of those powerful women; their bloodlines joined every few generations to strengthen their bond. As a direct descendent of General Telisa, Darna was the keeper of this Sword of Light, just as Queen Letha was guardian of the other, a direct descendant of Queen Melida. The swords were kept secret as much as possible; only a select few knowing of their existence. Only in times of invasion were they fully revealed, and their existence again fading to legend once the crisis passed. Was it any wonder every invasion of the Sisterhood met with ruin? Two Swords of Light wielded by daughters of Tarelia proved too much for any invader.

How did Terin learn of the sword or its hiding place? This baffled Darna. Guilen did not know of it, only Deva, and she spoke not of it to him, which brought the question back to Terin. How could he have known? Mystery surrounded the boy; that much was certain. She wondered what other powers he possessed.

The blood of Kal. She finally concluded, for it was the only explanation.

"Mother?" Deva asked, waiting for an answer to her question.

"We have much to consider. Keeping him as I intended may not be possible."

"What do you mean?" Deva didn't like the implication.

"No chains will hold him if he ever attains the sword again. We may have to consider a more…permanent solution."

* * *

Ninety leagues southeast of Bansoch

"Zoom in," Brokov said, standing over Corry's shoulder.

She adjusted the controls, sitting at the console in the weapon's control room. She had grown accustom to handling the remote discs, shrinking and expanding the images sent back to the ship. The image projected on the viewscreen was of a spacious dwelling in the center of Bansoch, the residence of General Jani, supreme commander of the Sisterhood Armies. The disc hovered some two hundred feet above the structure, the large stone edifice dominating their vision. The foregrounds of the manse were easily visible, where a few slaves were busy working. The slaves' faces were identified one by one, none matching Terin.

Corry sighed in frustration. The *Stenox* was only a few hours from reaching Bansoch, and they needed to find Terin. They sent four discs on ahead, each monitoring estates of commanders of rank or powerful councilors in the forum. Operating the discs so far remotely, they could only effectively operate four. Since Corry was most familiar with the political structure of the Sisterhood, they let her choose where to begin the search. General Jani and Councilor Lutesha Dorvena were the first priorities, their respective discs arriving first, sending back the live feeds they were now seeing.

"We need to get inside the structure to complete our search of the estate," Brokov said.

"How do I do that?" Corry asked, looking back over her shoulder.

"Very carefully. Luckily, it appears we have a nice overcast building up. A little rain will help conceal the disc, at least until we get inside."

With that, Brokov reached over her shoulder, touching the console. The disc hovered directly over the structure before descending to the roof. From there, it glided to the edge of the building, sliding slowly down the front wall, its smooth surface taking on the color of the white stone of the structure. It continued its slow, careful path into the large manse, clinging to the ceiling but keeping within the shadows.

"This might take a while," Brokov grumbled.

* * *

The bridge of the Stenox

"Nervous?" Lorken asked his friend while sitting the helm.

Raven sat the captain's chair, his head resting on his right fist as he stared at the endless blue expanse, with ominous gray skies crowding the horizon.

"Why would I be nervous?" he mumbled.

"Oh, I don't know. Maybe seeing your wife? Waiting for her to give birth? Being a father?" Lorken rattled off the obvious reasons.

"I'm not nervous. It's like my dad used to say, 'If I wasn't here, I'd just be somewhere else.'"

"That doesn't make any sense." Lorken made a face.

"Makes more sense than what you're saying."

"I simply asked if you were nervous about what awaits you in Bansoch, trying to give encouragement to my friend," Lorken explained.

"Encouragement? You're just trying to get me to act all mushy. I don't work like that."

"Forget I asked. Sometimes I think Zem has more emotional range than you."

"Emotional range? Since when are you Mr. Sensitive? Marriage life must've cut off your balls. Whatever happened to the Lorken who shot first and asked questions later?"

"Things change, Rav. We all have to grow up eventually."

"That's a nice way of saying you're a whipped dog. Well, Tosha isn't putting a leash on me. I can tell you that!" he growled.

"A leash? You'd be lucky if she didn't plant an ax in your thick skull. I got to warn you. Araxan women are supposed to experience great pleasure giving birth, but that didn't work out for Jenna."

"You think Tosha will experience the same?"

"It's a real possibility."

"Wonderful, just another reason for her to be pissed at me. Hopefully, Brokov has a few things in his medical kit that will help with the pain. I better bring the healing machine along just in case there's complications."

"Healing machine? You mean the tissue regenerator?" Lorken corrected him.

"Healing machine is easier to say. Since when are you an aspiring intellectual, anyway?"

"Compared to you, I'm a Rhodes scholar."

"If I remember, my grades at the academy were higher than yours, and we had the same major."

"No, I was a double major while you took elective courses to pad your grades, like *the meaning of large breasts in natural history*," Lorken grinned.

"It was *female anatomy*, and you took it too, numbskull. And it wasn't an easy course either. There are no easy courses at the academy." Raven had a point. The acceptance rate for Space Fleet Academy was less than 2 percent of qualified applicants, with cadets requiring to meet high academic and physical standards.

"Well, Tosha chose you despite your limitations. Hope you make the most of it."

"Tosha will be fine. I'm more concerned with her mother. Who knows what that woman is like?"

"Corry speaks well of her."

"I'm sure she does," Raven grumbled.

"Maybe you'll win her over with the gift we got her," Lorken said, regarding the fist-sized pearl they extracted from their remote isle in the Eastern Sea, an uninhabited island a thousand leagues east of Torn. It was there that they first landed upon Arax and constructed a base of operations. The isle was home to enormous oyster-like creatures, producing pearls of incredible size. They selected a pure black one for Letha and a white one for Tosha. Ones of that size were nowhere to be found on the continent.

"Hopefully, she'll be more grateful than Tyro. All we got for returning his daughter was treachery. I swear, is it beyond these people to show a little gratitude or even say thank you?"

"You two certainly didn't hit it off very well. It kind of reminds me of Admiral Kruger and that major sent by the IG to oversee flight operations. I thought the old man was going to have him ejected through the space lock." Lorken smiled at the memory. Admiral Kruger was commander of the battle carrier *Stalingrad*, where Lorken, Raven, Zem, and Thorton were assigned before their reassignment to the mission that brought them to Arax.

"I would've helped him do it," Raven recalled the insufferable Major Prescott with his snooty airs. He kind of reminded him of Galen. "I still wonder why he just up and departed just when he started investigating our squadron party on Delta Station." Raven wondered, referencing his squadron's shore leave excursion on the Titan lunar base, where numerous Space Fleet codes were violated involving entertainment of questionable moral value.

"Probably had to do with someone altering his medical charts and issuing him daily injections of estrogen without him knowing it." Lorken grinned.

"You did that?"

"With a little help from Thorton and Colonel Chang's niece, Bao, who worked in ship operations. We were seeing each other at the time."

"How much estrogen did you give him?"

"Enough to sprout a generous pair of—"

"All right, I don't want to picture it." Raven shook his head.

"Oh, we had pictures all right. Bao kept extra copies." Lorken smiled at the memory.

"Why am I just hearing about this now?"

"You were the squadron commander. We didn't want you to get caught if they started looking into it. Commanders are the first ones they ask. Besides, the admiral told us not to tell you, so you could have *plausible deniability*."

"Admiral Kruson found out about it?"

"Yeah, he kind of figured it out pretty quick." Lorken scratched his head.

"And he didn't bust you for it?"

"No, he thought it was brilliant and covered our tracks."

"The admiral was a good man. I miss the cantankerous old bastard. He was going to take Thorton and me—"

"Thorton and *I*," Lorken corrected his awful grammar.

"He was going to take Thorton and *me* to his home in Bavaria. He wanted us to see a famous castle there and visit the Alps," Raven recalled.

"Neuschwanstein," Lorken said.

"What?"

"The name of the castle. It's quite famous. That is the one in Bavaria. Didn't you ever go there when we were in Brussels?" Lorken asked.

"No, I never heard of it."

"You're hopeless. All the years we spent in the academy and you never visited Neuschwanstein?" Lorken shook his head.

"I went to a castle one weekend," Raven countered.

"Which one?" Lorken didn't believe him.

"The one in England."

"There are a lot of castles in England, Rav. Which one are you referring?"

"The one near the white cliffs. It's along the coast."

"Dover."

"Dover is in Delaware," Raven refuted.

"Dover is the capital of Delaware but also the name of the castle that overlooks the *white cliffs of Dover!* I swear, you must've been hit on the head sometime in your life." Lorken rolled his eyes.

"Comments like that are why I'm not taking you with me to meet my mother-in-law."

"Who you taking with you?"

"I'm thinking Arg—"

"Argos stays here. You can't leave us alone with Orlom and Grigg. You need to take one of them with you."

"I can't take either of them with me. They'll do something stupid like set their fur on fire or look up the queen's skirt or something worse."

"They're bound to do something even worse if you leave them both here without enough supervision. You need to take one of them with you."

"All right. Might as well flip a coin. Probably should go with Orlom since I let Grigg man the helm last night."

"You what?" Lorken gave him a look over his shoulder.

"Don't give me that look. He did fine. We are on open ocean. What was he going to do, run aground or hit a rock?"

"With Grigg, anything bad is possible. We're lucky we didn't capsize."

"He kept a steady course. He's usually well-behaved for you and me. It's Brokov that they save their biggest screwups for."

"You and *I*," Lorken corrected him again.

"Nobody likes a grammar nag, Lorken. Marriage is turning you into a killjoy."

"Fair enough, but I married a sweet and kind girl. What are you going to be like after spending time as Mr. Princess Tosha?" Lorken laughed.

"She'll be taking my name."

"No one can pronounce your real name, and she definitely won't call herself Mrs. Raven."

"We'll probably just agree to disagree," Raven sighed, the fight draining out of him already.

"I'm sure everything will work out," Lorken lied.

"As long as she and the baby are safe. Childbirth is dangerous in primitive worlds like this one."

"You'll have the regenerator with you if you need it. Just call back to the ship, and we'll send it ashore."

"Thanks. Maybe we can use it on a few of the locals who are disabled. Might win us a few brownie points with the queen."

"Never a bad idea to spread a little kindness."

"Yep, but we've been doing that since we arrived on Arax, and we've made more enemies than friends," Raven snorted.

"But the friends we made were worth it," Lorken rightly pointed out.

"Yeah, I guess you're right. Let's hope the kid is alive like Corry thinks."

"I don't know. Her story sounds crazy if you ask me."

"Yeah, she's nuttier than a fruitcake, but if there's a chance she's right, we got to take it."

"Hopefully we can find him."

"If he's anywhere on that island, we'll find him."

"You really think they made a slave out of him?" Lorken asked.

THE CHRONICLES OF ARAX

"That seems the way they do things on this planet. Prisoners of war were often enslaved in our ancient times."

"True, but I never heard of women taking male captives back then."

"These women are a little different. Besides, the size differences here are not as significant as on Earth. Hell, half the time I can't tell the men from the women anyway."

"You got a point. Some of the men here are quite pretty."

"If that's what you think, maybe you should bunk in a different cabin."

"I didn't say I favored them, moron. I just stated the obvious. How else can you explain women able to take so many men captive, if the rumors of the Sisterhood are true?"

"Why do they have to go through all the trouble? There were a lot of fellas back in the academy who would've volunteered to be abused by a woman," Raven recalled.

"Whips and chains, lots of pain." Lorken laughed, recalling much the same.

"What they saw in it is beyond me." Raven shook his head.

"To each his own, I guess, but I don't think the Sisterhood is filled with dominatrices, Rav. That's just a sick fantasy of some degenerates. These women would dispel that notion in a hurry. If Corry is right, the place is anything but pleasant for any slave brought there."

"Then we better find Terin and get him the hell out of there."

* * *

Bansoch, Queen Letha's palace

"She's beautiful." Letha smiled as Tosha sat upon her settee, cradling her daughter in her arms.

"Beautiful but hungry," Tosha said tiredly, the princess suckling her breast. One child was enough but three? She was grateful her mother arranged an army of wet nurses and attendants, lest she lose her mind. Her daughter was the priority of the court, but Tosha insisted on partially nursing all her babies.

117

"Did you sleep last night?" Letha asked, running a finger along her granddaughter's cheek, stroking a lock of coal-black hair.

"As much as can be expected," Tosha sighed. Though her mother intended the wet nurses attend the babies at night, Tosha couldn't help but intercede throughout the evening. She couldn't sleep anyway, her mind awash with worry, exhaustion, and disappointment.

"You must rest. We need our wits now more than ever."

"He lied to me," Tosha said in a deathly whisper.

"It was always a possibility," Letha tried not to say *I told you so*.

"Raven keeps his promises, at least those that hold meaning to him," she recalled his promise to Leanna to rescue Cronus.

"There could have been any number of reasons for his delay, Tosha." Letha tried to assuage her pain.

"Excuses are the weapons of liars."

Letha took a deep breath. There was much to consider before she held court. Members of the ruling forum were already gathering in the throne room, waiting to treat with her. Word had already spread of the birth of their new princess, and nobles and dignitaries came to offer tribute and honor. Letha was no fool, for these guests would offer silent judgment for the scandal they found themselves in.

"Do not let those fools question our position, Mother. I have borne a princess of the realm. She is strong, fierce, and will be a worthy queen one day." Tosha fixed her steel gaze upon her mother, her golden eyes burning like embers.

"No one will question her legitimacy, Tosha. As queen, I will refute such slander as treason," she assured her.

Harroom!

The sound of horns echoed through the palace, causing their eyes to turn sharply to the window. Tosha and Letha approached the door, stepping onto the terrace overlooking the palace grounds and the city beyond. They stared below, where soldiers raced to the outer battlements. Beyond the palace walls, the streets of Bansoch were abuzz, people scattering and taking shelter as horns sounded the alarm, echoing from the shoreline to the city's outer walls and beyond.

Tosha froze, for there, upon the mouth of the harbor, gliding across the surface was the *Stenox*, its distinct bluish-silver hull making its way toward the city.

* * *

"Well, it looks kinda peaceful," Lorken said as they entered the Bay of Soch, the city of Bansoch dotting the distant shoreline. The water matched the graying sky, the building surf a sign of a coming storm.

"We'll see if it stays peaceful once we get closer. What's that thing up ahead?" Raven asked, his eyes drawn to a structure upon a rocky isle guarding the approaches of the city.

"Looks like some kind of watchtower by the looks of it," Lorken said, expanding the image on his viewscreen as he sat the helm.

A fire quickly ignited atop the tower as they drew near. They could see several figures standing upon the battlements, observing them as the flames flickered above them.

"That can't be good," Raven said.

"Looks like they sent a signal to the city, warning of our arrival," Lorken guessed.

The signal was soon relayed by another stone tower upon the shoreline, east of the city, two leagues off their starboard bow.

"Must be a relay system. I see another one further west near the edge of the city," Lorken pointed out.

"Guess they know we're here. Should give them time to arrange a welcome party when we pull up to dock," Raven said.

"Let's hope it's a *nice* welcoming party," Lorken quipped.

"Our luck's bound to change at some point. In reality, this is still just a family visit."

"It's the family we're talking about that concerns me," Lorken said, and as if to prove his point, several war galleys came boldly into view as they passed between the watchtowers.

"You had to open your mouth," Raven growled.

"Relax, Rav. What are they gonna do, lob rocks at us?"

"I did plan to go ashore, you know."

"Don't worry about it. Tosha doesn't want any harm to come to her husband, her sweet little Raven. I'm sure you'll receive a hero's welcome," Lorken smirked.

"If so, then why are they exposing their broadsides?" Raven said as the Federation warships turned hard to port, their crews aligning all their catapults toward the *Stenox*. The ships were all bioar galleys with triple masts. Each was lined with catapults and large arrow munitions along their decks. The ships looked well-built from native paccel wood, stained bloodred. The flag of the Sisterhood 1st Fleet graced the forward mast, a flaming sword upon a field of black. They could see the sailors positioned along the upper and lower decks, arrayed in copper-hued mail over red tunics.

"Do you want to sail around them, sink them, or have a chat?" Lorken laid out his options.

"Might as well talk." Raven shook his head before raising Argos on the comm.

"Aye," Argos responded, standing watch upon the 3rd deck, enjoying the view of Soch Harbor in the open air.

"Raise the blue flag, Arg. I'll be right up in a moment," Raven said as Lorken set direct course for the Federation ships.

* * *

"This breeze feels good," Raven said, stepping off the ladder as the wind rolled across the bow. He stood beside Arg, resting his forearms on the forward wall, overlooking the sea ahead.

"I agree." Arg's nostrils flared, the exposed fur on his head rippling in the salty air.

The Federation warships loomed directly ahead as Lorken reduced speed, easing the *Stenox* to a crawl. Raven noticed one of the officers on the center galley with three braided cords adorning her shoulders, wearing a steel helm with blue feathers running down its middle. Lorken must've noticed her as well, maneuvering the *Stenox* toward her vessel, her rank indicating a commander of squadron.

"She looks like a real beauty," Raven grumbled under his breath as the Federation commander stood amidship with her muscled arms crossed, staring daggers at them through the slits of her helm.

"She looks a sturdy lass. She could bear a human male many hearty children." Argos respected the woman's strength.

"Yeah, but don't go saying that too loud. I got a feeling she wouldn't take that as a compliment."

"I don't understand you humans. Siring strong heirs is the primary duty of males and females. It is a measure of worthiness and a matter of pride."

"I should've been an ape. Your people make a lot more sense."

"Yes," Argos agreed.

The *Stenox* eased to a halt, well within range of the galley's ballista, hoping they would honor the parlay. Raven gave Argos a look that said, "Here goes nothing."

"Hi!" Raven smiled and waved at the crew of the galley, who returned the gesture with the warmth of a glacier.

"Who bids entrance to Bansoch?" the commander asked, her cold brown eyes fixed on Raven. She obviously knew who they were but needed them to formally identify themselves.

"I'm Raven, captain of the *Stenox*. This is Argos, champion of the Ape Republic and my good buddy," Raven said in good humor that was lost on them.

"You are the consort of Princess Tosha?" the commander asked.

"I'm her husband," he confirmed, not liking the term *consort*.

"You will follow us to the appropriate docking facility set aside for you. Once there, you will be escorted to the palace, where you are expected."

"Well, lead the way." Raven gave her a casual salute, a broad smile on his lips, knowing the woman hated it.

* * *

They guided the *Stenox* to a spacious stone wharf along the royal docking area, an isolated area where the queen's private barge was moored. The queen's palace rested on the hillside above, just to the east. A small army met them at the wharf, arrayed in disciplined ranks, their black mail polished to a bright sheen, their spears resting in their right hands, and square black shields in their left. A commander of Telnic stood before the assemblage, dressed in uniform black mail over silver tunic of the harbor garrison. Beside her stood a silver-haired woman dressed in flowing burgundy blouse and trousers, with gold cape billowing behind her.

Zem and Brokov joined Lorken on the bridge, staring at the activity on the wharf through the viewport, all wanting to see Raven make a fool of himself. As soon as they dropped anchor, Raven stepped onto the wharf, causing the ranks of soldiers to immediately level their spears, which caused him to begin exchanging heated words with the silver-haired dignitary and Telnic commander.

"What's he doing?" Brokov asked.

"Making friends like he usually does." Lorken shook his head.

"His diplomacy requires refinement," Zem stated the obvious.

"It looks like he isn't winning them over," Brokov said as Raven kept a tight grip on his holstered pistol.

"This isn't good," Lorken said as the commander of Telnic started drawing her sword.

"Where's Arg?" Brokov asked.

"Still on the top deck. He is far too intelligent to enter a potentially hostile port without assurances," Zem pointed out.

"What was Raven's plan, just to jump off the ship and walk up to the palace and say hello?" Brokov asked.

"Moron," they all said at the same time.

* * *

"Like I said for the thousandth time, Tosha is expecting me!" Raven growled at the two women.

"Princess Tosha," Galana Vesin, the royal steward, again corrected him.

"Either get out of my way or I move you out of my way!" Raven threatened, causing the soldiers behind them to take a step forward.

"We shall gladly escort you to the palace, where you are expected, but you must leave your weapon behind and place yourself in our custody," Telnic commander Glora Delvar said through clenched teeth, glaring heatedly at him.

"Mistress Vesin, Commander Delvar," Kendra politely addressed the two women, stepping off the ship to join Raven.

"Your name and title?" the royal steward asked.

"Kendra Sarn. I am the former vice magistrate of Axenville and new crewmember of the *Stenox*. Another crewmember and myself will accompany our captain to the palace. We have been assured of safe passage to this realm by your crown princess. In regards to Captain Raven's weapons, he is entitled to self-defense as he will be surrounded by thousands of soldiers. Considering the reception he received at Fera, you can't possibly expect him to leave behind his only means of protection," Kendra explained.

Corry prepared her for this, even identifying each of the women standing before her. It would be easier for Corry to speak on Raven's behalf, but she needed to keep herself hidden until they find Terin.

"No one is allowed in the queen's presence armed, especially a man such as him." Commander Delvar held firm.

"Listen, girl. I could flatten this whole city if I wanted, and there isn't a damn thing you could do about it. Now we can do this the easy way or the hard way!" Raven growled, his bluster not having the effect he intended.

"We will skewer you where you stand, *boy!*" Commander Delvar responded in kind.

"Raven, please." Kendra stepped in front of him.

"Stay out of this, Kendra." He glared over her shoulder at the insufferable commander.

"Do you really want your visit with Tosha to begin with bloodshed?"

His silence was the closest she would get to a *no*.

"Allow me to help you."

Raven threw his hands up and backed away. He wished he had followed his original instinct and stunned the crowd before setting ashore. He'd already be at the palace by now. Of course, he would have the same problem once he got there, but he hadn't figured that out as yet.

"Mistress Vesin, might we start anew?" Kendra asked politely.

"Proceed," the royal steward conceded.

After much deliberation, Kendra managed to broker a compromise. Raven would retain one pistol and bring one bag of personal possessions, which he would bring from the ship. Kendra and Orlom would also retain a pistol but no other weapons. They would proceed to the palace with an official escort, where they would present themselves into their official custody.

Raven went back to the ship to grab his things. Fetching his bag from his crew cabin, he stopped on the bridge on his way out.

"Keep looking for the kid and let me know as soon as you find him," Raven said to Lorken, Brokov, and Zem, who all stood there looking at him curiously.

"Once again, you made another great first impression." Brokov grinned.

"It wasn't my fault. I was nothing but nice to those girls."

"You didn't actually call those distinguished ladies, girls, did you?" Lorken asked.

"I might've said it once or twice."

"Well…good luck." Lorken shook his head.

"I'll be fine. What are they gonna do, beat me up?"

"You're right. They could never do that," Zem said since they only outnumbered Raven several hundred thousand to one.

"What's in the bag beside the pearls for Tosha and her mother?" Brokov asked.

"Just a change of clothes and gifts for the baby."

"What gifts?" Lorken asked.

"A diamond necklace if it's a girl. Zem helped me cut one, and Lorken helped with the chain."

"The cut was perfectly symmetrical," Zem praised his fine work.

"What if it's a boy?" Lorken asked.

"I'm giving him one of our spare footballs." Raven smiled as if it was the best idea ever.

"A football?" Brokov made a face.

THE CHRONICLES OF ARAX

"What's wrong with football? Every boy should have one. We might not be on Earth, but there's no reason these people can't learn a real game. The boy should be a dominant defensive tackle next to the lightweights on this planet," Raven said proudly.

"You're hopeless." Brokov shook his head.

"A father can dream, Brokov. Now, you boys, be good while I'm away. We might be a while. I'm not sure how long we'll have to wait for the baby to pop out."

"Don't worry, Rav. We'll keep in contact several times a day. We can even switch out with Orlom and Kendra to give them a break if this stay drags on," Brokov said.

"Hopefully, I'll find out what to expect when I get to the palace. Wish me luck," Raven said, making his way to the door.

"You'll need it," Lorken said.

"Don't do anything stupid." Zem shook his head.

"Try not to be yourself, and it will all work out," Brokov added.

* * *

Queen Letha sat her throne, staring out at the gathered assemblage with discerning gray eyes. She wore the garb of a warrior queen, with golden cuirass and greaves over a bloodred tunic, her muscled limbs displayed for effect. A golden helm rested in her left arm, and a sword rode her left hip. A dozen royal guards were aligned to each side of the throne and another dozen at the base of the dais upon which the throne rested. Each guard wore black steel breastplates, vambraces, and greaves over silver tunics. Their black steel helms stretched below their cheeks, their eyes staring out through their narrow slits. Each held a spear in their strong hand and shield in their weak, each black as a moonless sky.

The throne room was a cavernous chamber with a high-domed ceiling, and twelve pillars aligned along either side, supporting the ceiling's weight. Each pillar was carved from white granite, contrasting the blue-stained ceiling above, which appeared as a false sky with torches bracketed high upon the walls, illuminating its surface. The floor was mirrored dark-blue stone, like the surface of a wine dark sea. Upon the walls were frescoes, richly detailing events from the Sisterhood's storied past. Upon the east wall, dominating its center, was the likeness of Queen Melida slaying Vagar, the Soch King upon the hill where the palace stands, in year 326.

Queen Melida's visage stood over the fallen Vagar, holding his severed head into the air as her soldiers cheered. Upon her right stood her sister Telisa, standing upon a pile of slain enemies, her countenance as fierce as Melida's. They each held bronze-hued swords emitting a golden light. Upon her right was Commander Zur Zellion, her lover and consort, his own sword stained with the blood of many Soch.

The battle of Bansoch dominated the fresco, the visage painted larger than the other scenes of their history, which bled one into the other. The sack of Tenin Harbor dominated the west wall, a glorious triumph of the Federation Navy in 577, their expedition led by Queen Melina III. The painting showed the great harbor in flames, the Sisterhood freeing thousands of female slaves held by the Yatin monarch. Queen Melina III was depicted standing triumphantly before the cheering throngs of freed women. Beside this visage was the wedding of Queen Melina III and King Zar V, king of the Middle Kingdom, the first union of the two Tarelian Realms.

Further along the west wall was the battle of Faust, where in 704, Queen Velima II led the Sisterhood Fleet into the Bay of Faust, destroying the Yatin Fleet and capturing the Yatin Crown Prince Yagnar. A kneeling Yagnar was prominently depicted bowing before Queen Velima upon the battered ruins of Faust, where she claimed him as her consort.

"My queen, this insult upon our realm cannot go unanswered," Arch Councilor Lutesha Dorvena declared, standing prominently in the fore ranks of the congregants. She was a known ally of Darna, the queen's cousin, and staunch Traditionalist. Like most of those gathered in the throne room, she came to officially honor the birth of Princess Ceana.

"And what course would you propose, Arch Councilor?" Letha asked, her neutral demeanor not betraying her suspicions of the women.

"The man is a known ruffian, his barbarity cloaked by their mysterious powers. He offends the throne by purposely arriving after the birth of the princess, disgracing the crown, our people, and the Federation," Lutesha argued.

"You didn't answer the question, Arch Councilor," Letha regarded her sternly, Lutesha withering under her gaze. Plotting with Darna in secret to depose the crown was one thing, but facing the queen herself in the throne room was quite another.

"He should be arrested and forced to surrender his weapons to the Sisterhood. His crew should be detained and made to swear loyalty to the throne. Then and only then can we be certain of their allegiance," Lutesha said all too quickly, her voice sounding uncertain.

Letha thought the suggestion daft but kept that to herself. If the rumors regarding the Earthers were true, she doubted anyone's ability to detain them.

"What of you, General?" Letha looked to her ranking commander, Elise Jani, supreme general of all Sisterhood Armies.

General Jani stepped forward, her bright, polished cuirass and greaves resplendent, matching her proud carriage and cold steel eyes. "Arch Councilor Dorvena is not wrong in her desire to see the Earther brought to heel, my queen. How to affect such a thing is another matter altogether. Since the Earthers' arrival to our world, I have sought knowledge of their capabilities, gleaning whatever tidbits of information I could. It is my opinion that they cannot be brought to negotiate without leverage. Their captain is on his way here as we speak. Perhaps we could detain him, using his life to keep the others in check. Such a thing is not without risk, however, and I would proceed only if a peaceful alternative cannot be reached," the general advised.

"Anyone else?" Letha's gaze swept over the assemblage.

"Why else would he come but to pay homage to his rightful queen?" Councilor Adela Luiven offered, her brown eyes looking to the others for affirmation.

"Pfftt"—Councilor Mearana waved off such a notion—"if that were true, he would have returned with our princess when she sailed from Tinsay. No, he stands apart. Such an insult cannot stand. His very presence is a threat to the Federation. He must be punished."

"And you would look to the army to administer justice, I assume," General Jani gave her a dark look.

"Who else could subdue him?" Councilor Mearana countered. "Should our queen call upon you to do so? Then it is your duty to see it through. This Earther cannot be allowed to disrupt the delicate balance that we fought to uphold since our founding. His mere presence would give our underclass ideas to rise above their station."

Letha noticed Darna standing quietly in the center of the chamber, impassively observing the discussion. She had seen little of her cousin recently. There were rumors that she was having difficulty with a slave she picked out for her daughter to wed. The fact that she would purchase a slave for Deva rather than join her with another ranking house was most curious. If Letha was not otherwise occupied, she might investigate this slave that troubled Darna so much.

"What is your opinion on this matter, Guardian Darna?" Letha decided to force her tongue.

"A demonstration of power would be my choice of action, oh Queen. But unlike Councilor Mearana, I would not do so out of fear that this Raven will incite our slaves to rebel. The slaves know their place and will not lift their eyes from the ground or their knees from the dirt. We are mightier than nervous worriers fearing every calamity, real or imagined. We have ruled this isle for over a thousand years," Darna declared.

"Then why would we need to demonstrate our power?" Letha asked.

"Because we can!" Darna crossed her arms, emphasizing the point.

Letha considered every opinion, but thought them rash.

"I will speak with Captain Raven before deciding what course of action to pursue. When he arrives, escort him hither!" she commanded the captain of the royal guard, Lucella Sarelis, who promptly bowed and marched out of the chamber, her cape billowing in her wake.

* * *

"I don't think they like us, Boss," Orlom said all too loudly as they followed their escort through the palace corridors. The looks the guards and courtesans gave them was a mix of loathing, fear, and disbelief. The one thing everyone had in common was dead silence.

"What gives you that idea?" Raven snorted.

"Their frowns," Orlom answered, Raven's sarcasm going over his head.

"Would you two be quiet?" Kendra growled over her shoulder. It was bad enough their presence was disturbing the status quo, the last thing they needed was to spark another argument with the royal guards before they reached the throne room. Thankfully, she was able to convince the royal steward to allow them to retain their weapons as long as Kendra took the lead, effectively representing the Earthers. A woman in such a position put the garrison more at ease.

"Tosha owes me a big one for all this," Raven grumbled.

"A big what?" Orlom again said too loudly, his voice calling more attention to them.

"A favor. A big, fat favor for making me go through all this bother. She could've met me on a secluded beach somewhere without all these people around giving me funny looks." The situation reminded Raven of a time in the academy when he called members of the Women's Leadership Forum a bunch of nags. *Or was it hags?* He tried to remember. The response they gave him was the same look these women were giving him now.

Kendra rolled her eyes, wondering what Tosha was thinking marrying Raven in the first place. Even Argos and Grigg knew this was going to be a disaster. For some stupid reason, Orlom was slow to pick up on that fact but would quickly come around. Of all the Earthers, Tosha just had to pick Raven. Kato or Brokov would have at least been civilized. Well, thankfully she didn't choose Brokov. Kendra smiled to herself. The hardest part of this mission for her was being separated from him for the next few days. With that thought, she found herself coming to a halt before a large open archway, opening to a cavernous chamber—the throne room.

* * *

Upon entering the throne room, Raven found the chamber quite impressive, nearly as large as Tyro's but more decorative and inviting. The same could not be said of its occupants. He guessed there were one to two hundred people gathered to either side of the chamber, each giving him strange looks. Most were downright hostile, usually he had to open his mouth before receiving such scorn. He wondered what exactly Tosha told them about him. The small procession finally stopped at the base of the raised dais where sat two thrones. One was empty, a lesser chair made of pure silver. The second was larger by half, made of gold, where a strikingly attractive woman sat with black hair that was tainted with silver, wearing armor over a red tunic, revealing a pair of attractive legs. Her stormy gray eyes were fixed upon him with terrible intensity. This had to be the queen; he correctly guessed. He could imagine if Lorken were here and read his thoughts, telling him, *Well, no shit.*

"My queen, I present Raven, consort of the crown princess," Galana Vesin, the royal steward, announced, standing in front of them where she knelt, followed by the rest of their escort, leaving Raven, Grigg, and Kendra standing.

"You are in the presence of Queen Letha, 1st guardian of the realm. Kneel or be knelt!" Darna declared, stepping from the crowd to stand before the dais.

"Make me!" Raven growled, forcing her back a step.

"You dare threaten me?" Darna glared at him, taken aback by his towering stature. The rumors greatly understated his presence. He was unlike anyone she had ever seen.

"If I did, what are you gonna do about it?"

"If you were my consort, I'd have you flogged!"

"You would need an army," Raven shrugged.

"If an army wouldn't suffice, I would rather jump from the highest cliff than bed a brute like you!" Darna sneered.

"If we were wed, I'd push you," Raven said, about to push her out of the way.

"Raven," Kendra warned, reminding him not to make things worse.

"Have at it, kid." He waved her on, tired of the whole spectacle already. He looked around the room for any sign of Tosha, wondering where she was.

"Queen Letha, I speak on behalf of the Earthers. I am Kendra Sarn, former vice magistrate of Axenville, former man-hunter, and now crewmember of the *Stenox*," Kendra declared.

"You are of Raven's crew?" Letha asked.

"I am, Your Highness. I was selected by my fellow crewmates to speak on their behalf as a woman's voice holds greater worth in the Federation," Kendra explained.

"A logical decision but unnecessary. I would speak with your captain," Letha said.

That was all Raven needed to step forward, standing at the base of the dais with the queen's guards standing directly before him.

"I'm Raven. I'm sure Tosha has told you about me. Is she here?" He looked around one last time to see if she was hiding in the crowd.

"She is in the palace" was all that Letha offered.

"Is she all right?" Raven's concern evident in his tone, which Letha found reassuring.

"She is well."

She's not real talkative, he thought to himself, wondering where to go from here.

"You have questions as do I." Letha sensed his unease.

"You're not kidding. Should you go first or me?" Raven's informal tone drew the ire of the entire assemblage, save the queen, who stared at him as if studying a strange oddity.

"You may ask the first question," Letha said.

"If Tosha is here and well, why isn't she here to greet me? I traveled a long way and came just as I promised I would."

As soon as Raven asked, Tosha stepped from the shadows behind the first pillar to the right of the throne. She was dressed as if ready for battle, silver polished cuirass and vambraces over leather shirt and trousers, her armored boots sounding audibly off the stone floor. Raven's eyes alit upon seeing her, black eyes meeting gold. Letha regarded her curiously, not realizing she was nearby all along. She looked nothing like she did a brief while ago. She looked like a warrior queen, not a new mother barely off the birthing bed. Her black hair was bound tightly into a bun upon her head, drawing the skin of her forehead taut.

"Tosha." Raven smiled as soon as he saw her.

She said not a word, taking her place upon the lesser throne at her mother's side, her silence evidence of her displeasure.

"You will not address the crown princess so informally!" Galana Vesin warned, taking her place upon the queen's left, the gasps circling the room evidence of his breaking protocol.

"It's a little late for formalities, Lady. Tosha and I are wed." Raven dismissed their objections.

Galana meant to reply when the queen interjected.

"Enough, Galana. Captain Raven is our guest. He is also an Earther, and their protocols are less formal than ours," Letha said before ordering her guards to back away, giving her a clear view. She knew there was nothing stopping him from killing her if he truly wanted to. The reverse was also true, for he couldn't stay every spear and arrow trained on him.

"Thanks. Every other royal court I've visited has been a little touchy about all that kneeling crap." Raven gave her his stupid grin, which took her aback.

"As you can see, Tosha is present and healthy," Letha said, not missing the strange look on his face as he looked Tosha over.

"Something troubles you?" Letha inquired. Before he could answer, Tosha ordered a servant boy stationed off to the side to attend to her, her eyes drifting suspiciously to Kendra. Tosha ordered the servant to rub her ankles, lovingly stroking his hair as he did so. Letha was taken aback by Tosha's behavior, wondering what caused her to act so?

"Raven!" Kendra said in alarm as he stormed up the steps of the dais, grabbing the servant by the collar of his tunic, tossing him to the floor behind him. The unexpected move took everyone by surprise, the queen's guards quickly surrounding him.

"Don't touch my wife!" Raven growled.

The servant stared up at him from the base of the dais, eyes wild with fright.

"He is a servant, Raven, not a suitor," Kendra said, helping the boy to his feet.

"Get this outta my face." Raven pushed a guard's spear away as Tosha stood from her throne, stepping toward him, her golden eyes burning into his.

"Tosha!" Letha warned, wondering what had come over her.

Tosha didn't respond as she continued to stare up into his dark eyes, her mind a maelstrom of emotions—jealousy, lust, anger, longing—each vying for dominion.

"I thought you were pregnant, or was that a lie too?" he asked angrily, looking briefly to her stomach.

Slap!

The sound of her hand upon his face echoed through the chamber. Every eye was riveted to the two of them, the entire scene becoming surreal.

"Tosha!" Letha's voice thundered in warning.

Tosha gave Raven one last look before storming out of the throne room; several guards following her.

"What was that all about?" Raven growled, watching her leave.

Letha was again taken aback by the entire scene, wondering if Raven and Tosha were touched by madness. She couldn't miss the sudden change in Tosha's demeanor once in Raven's presence. Nor could she understand Raven. By reputation, he was a dangerous mercenary who instilled fear in kings and emperors alike. That was not what she saw. He acted like an overgrown child. His jealous rant was strange. Was he truly envious of the servant touching Tosha? Could he not see that she arranged the scene on purpose? And why did Tosha do so? Was she equally jealous of Raven's female crewmate? The only thing that was apparent was that they were either madly in love or equally insane. She needed to speak with Raven without this spectacle.

"I would speak with Raven in private. Galana, please escort his companions to the guest apartments arranged for them," Letha commanded.

* * *

"You are not what I expected," Letha said, standing upon the terrace of her chamber, overlooking the harbor. She could see his vessel below, its bluish-silver hull contrasting the wooden galleys moored beside it. Tosha spoke of its awesome power. She could tell by its aura the power it held. She had to be very careful in dealing with the Earthers. The foolish council she received in the throne room suggested confronting them directly. Did they consider the ramifications if that went poorly? She would consider all options but needed to meet with Raven in private. She needed to learn who he truly was. They were alone, save for the two guards posted at the archway behind them, which opened to her private chambers.

"What were you expecting?" he asked, setting his large bag on the floor beside him, the cool wind pressing upon his face.

"By reputation, you are a terrifying mercenary and cunning warrior," she said, turning to look into his dark eyes.

"I'm really quite lovable," he said with that stupid grin he seemed to use all too much.

"I don't know about that, but from what I observed in the throne room, you are acting like a lovesick child. Tosha is acting the same, which is most unlike her. She was always a dutiful, serious girl, ever mindful of her place as my heir. Since meeting you, she has acted strange, unpredictable, and rash."

"You can say that again." He made a face.

"Say what again?" She didn't understand.

"Just an expression of my people. It means I agree with you. Tosha has acted strangely since the first day we met. I saved her life, you know, rescued her from Molten Isle, and she thanked me for that by biting my nose."

134

"What?" Letha hadn't heard this from Tosha.

"Yep. Then she argued with me every moment we were together until we reached Fera. Once we got there, she tricked me into marrying her and tried to knock me out with some sleeping concoction."

Letha closed her eyes, trying to picture everything he was saying. For some reason, she believed him.

"After escaping, she caught up with me far to the east, but I took her captive instead. She later escaped near Axenville, where she stuck a drunken mob on me. When we parted at Lake Veneba, she finally told me she was pregnant. I could've strangled her then and there for putting our unborn baby in danger with all her antics." He shook his head.

Letha learned by his comments that he cared for the health of their children. That was a point in his favor on the mental list she was making to measure his character.

"I told her to return here and take care of herself for the baby's sake and that I would join her before she gave birth. Now I show up just to find out she isn't even pregnant!" he growled.

Letha looked at him even more strangely, if that was possible.

"You believe she lied to you?" she asked incredulously.

"Does she look pregnant to you?" he asked before a sad look overcame him. "She didn't lose the baby, did she?"

"No. And she didn't lie to you. She gave birth to your children a few days ago."

"Children? Days ago? They came this early?"

"Yes, you have three children. Yes, it was a few days ago, but they were not early."

"Full term is two hundred and eighty days. We are not anywhere near that mark. I came early, with time to spare, just as I promised," Raven pointed out.

"What baby requires such a lengthy period of growth?" Letha asked.

"All babies do, at least on my wor—" He stopped midsentence, realizing his mistake. Why hadn't he thought to ask someone about the difference in gestation periods between Araxans and Earthers?

"I see." Letha closed her eyes, realizing the misunderstanding.

"No wonder Tosha's angry." He threw his hands up.

"I am certain she will becalm herself once the truth is revealed."

"Calm herself? Not likely. She's meaner than a gut shot grizzly," he said, the reference lost on the queen.

"She will understand, though it might take time," she tried to reassure him.

"I need to straighten this whole thing out. Where is she?"

"I will take you to see her after we finish speaking. There are matters we need to address."

"What matters?"

Letha stepped toward the table set behind them, where a pitcher of wine rested with two goblets. She filled both, offering him a drink.

Raven gave her a look, remembering the last time he was offered a cup of wine. Letha rolled her eyes, switching the goblets, offering her own, which he reluctantly took.

"If either of us intended the other harm, Raven, we would both be dead."

"What makes you say that?" he asked, taking a generous gulp.

"Because I am queen, and my army surrounds you. You, on the other hand, command great power, a *dangerous* power."

"You think I'm dangerous?" He smiled, liking the sound of that.

"Very much so, and you know this. Don't go seeking compliments. It is unbecoming." She rolled her eyes.

"A man can dream. Tosha never compliments me for anything. Are you sure you're her mother? You seem a lot nicer."

She nearly spit out her drink. Was this the Raven she heard so much about? He was so much a child. He almost seemed harmless, even if he towered over everyone.

"You think me kind?" She managed to ask.

"You seem so, and I have a pretty good sense about people, like when I first met Brokov. I knew he was a jerk, and time has proven me right." He smiled, far too pleased with his explanation.

"He is one of your crew," she said, recalling their names as Tosha explained them to her.

"He's the 1st officer, my 2nd in command. He's not so bad when he keeps quiet, which is never. Kendra likes him for some strange reason."

"She is fond of him? Are they betrothed?" Letha asked. If true, it would ease Tosha's jealousy of the woman.

"They like each other but haven't taken it that far yet, at least as far as I know. Then again, what do I know? I didn't realize I was married to Tosha until someone explained it to me after."

Letha smiled at his humor. He was so different from anyone she knew and understood Tosha's attraction to him.

"So what did Tosha have, boys or girls?" he asked.

"One girl and two boys. I am certain you are anxious to meet them."

"That's why I came besides seeing Tosha."

"Good answer." She smiled.

"I'm learning. I'm not used to all this marriage and relationship stuff."

"I am sure you will manage, though I doubt you'll ever conform to the expectations of court. My people are very particular on the proper decorum of a royal consort."

"Like the lady giving me a hard time about kneeling," Raven said.

"Guardian Darna," Letha said, taking a sip from her goblet.

"She's a real beauty." He rolled his eyes.

"She is my cousin." Letha smiled, seeing how he would react.

"It's like my dad used to say, 'You shake any family tree, and a few nuts will fall out.'"

Again, she nearly spit out her wine, understanding the meaning but not the words of his phrase.

"Yes, she can be…difficult."

"She reminds me of my 8th-grade English teacher, Mrs. Ives. She was a mean old witch who hated my guts. I got kicked out of her class so much I spent more time in the principal's office than her class. Wasn't so bad though. He was a good man and taught me how to play chess. We'd play almost every day that year. I didn't do so well in English, but I whipped everyone in school at chess," he rambled on as Letha listened with the patience of a saint.

"Darna should give you a wide berth from now on, but such is the sensitive balance we must strike in court. Our people are ever fearful of what you represent."

"Tosha should've thought of that before marrying me."

"She thought she could convince you or tame you if necessary." Letha shook her head at Tosha's foolishness.

"I've heard how the men are treated here, so I'll pass on being *tamed*."

"I am not foolish enough to disagree with you, but there are parameters we need to agree upon."

"I'm listening."

"For one, I can't have you exploring the city or the outer castle. It is best for you to remain in the inner palace during your stay. Even here, you will need a royal escort. Two—and this is very important— you should speak to no one outside our house, except for the servants attending you."

"Are you afraid I'll offend everyone I talk to?" He smiled.

"Your mere appearance will offend them, I fear."

"Come on, Mom, I'm not that ugly, am I?" He gave her his stupid smile again.

"You are certainly not ugly, young man, and what did you just refer to me by?"

"Mom. It's short for *mother*. My people often call their spouse's mothers by that title. Since you're the friendliest royal I've met on this planet, it sort of fits. In fact, you're the only royal I met who isn't a complete ass."

She just stared blankly for a moment, at a loss for words.

What have you done, Tosha? The question repeated in her brain.

"Oh, I almost forgot. This is for you," he said, fishing an object from his bag before handing her a fist-sized black pearl. It was unbelievably large and beautiful to behold.

* * *

138

Tosha stood upon her terrace overlooking the harbor, lost in an emotional storm. Why did he so easily upset her? She longed for him in his absence, but when he finally presented himself, she wanted to scream. Her eyes were fixed on the *Stenox* docked along the royal wharfs. How she hated that ship. He would soon climb aboard that vessel and sail away. She would ask him to stay, beg him to stay, but it wouldn't convince him to remain. Of all the men in the world, why was it him that claimed her heart? She closed her eyes, feeling the late-day breeze upon her face, the familiar smell of salty air caressing her nose.

"Guardian," a young wet nurse called out from behind her, carrying her daughter.

"Bring her here, Ivessa," she commanded, taking Ceana into her arms.

"I will see to the princes, Guardian." Ivessa bowed and withdrew.

Tosha held the infant lovingly in her arms, losing herself in the child's golden eyes that stared curiously into her own. She never thought to love anyone or anything as she loved her precious children. Tosha swayed gently, rocking the baby in her arms. She discarded her warrior garb for a loose shift, the folds of her skirt swirling around her ankles.

"Beautiful," Raven said.

She turned at the sound of his voice, finding him leaning against the door to her chamber, his presence filling the archway.

"How did you gain entrance here?" She wanted to say something else but felt the urge to challenge him.

"Your mom let me in." He smiled, coming off the archway.

"Weapons are not allowed in *my* daughter's chamber," she said, regarding his holstered pistol.

"That's a good rule. I wouldn't want a stranger bringing a weapon anywhere near Daddy's little girl." He ignored the challenge, setting his bag on the floor before stepping near.

"You will speak with reverence when referring to the Princess Ceana." She refused to back away, staring up into his dark eyes.

"I'm not letting you get me mad and start a fight, Tosha. I know why you're angry. I said I would arrive for the birth, and I missed it.

Earth women give birth much later than you. I thought I was early, but there you have it." He ran a finger along her cheek, caressing her face.

Tosha bit his finger as it neared her lips.

"Oww! Why'd you do that?" he yelped, backing a step while shaking his wounded digit, her teeth marks visible between the joints.

She just glared at him, her chest rising with labored breath.

"If you weren't holding our baby, I'd take you over my knee," he growled.

"You will not lay a hand upon me here, Raven! I am the crown princess of the Federation and 2nd guardian of the realm. No one here will tolerate your misdeeds!"

"You think your people can stop me?" he challenged.

"Still your lying tongue! I spent every moment since my return defending you, suffering the judgment of our nobles for your absence. Your thick skull may not understand the scandalous nature of an absent consort, but it challenges the legitimacy of royal heirs."

"If it was that important, you might've explained the differences in gestation periods before we parted!" he growled.

"And you might have spoken of the pain Earth women suffer birthing their children!"

"What's that supposed to mean?" He decided to play dumb, after Lorken explained the pain Jenna suffered.

"It means just what I said."

"Well, of course, women suffer birth pains. It comes with having a baby," he stated the obvious.

"Only your cursed race suffers so, and now me by extension." She glared at him.

"Women don't feel pain during childbirth?" He made a face, hoping Jenna was unique in her suffering.

"Of course not. We feel *pleasure*, except with you, it was both pleasure and unspeakable pain!"

"How's that my fault? You might've asked a few questions before marrying me."

She'd have slapped him if she wasn't holding their baby. She could only glare at him and turn her back. She fixed her gaze to the horizon, seeing nothing but her own rage. She didn't really want to be angry with him. She wanted to hold him, touch him, and kiss him, but was captive to her situation, trapped by her position. Her mother warned that she couldn't serve the realm and the leanings of her heart. She was the future queen, heir to two realms. Why couldn't she have what she wanted? She wanted Raven, and she wed him. If only he was willing to stay, she could have both her birthright and the man she loved, but she knew him too well. He would never stay, and she couldn't make him.

"Tosh," he said gently, turning her back around, staring intently into her eyes.

She couldn't bear to look at him but couldn't look away. Did he miss her as much as she missed him? Did her absence rend his heart, like his pained hers?

"I don't know what to tell you to make this better, Tosh. I don't want to fight with you. All I thought about these past months was you, Tosh. You!" He put his hands on her cheeks, and this time she didn't bite him.

"I needed you, and you were not here."

"Do you want me to go? If it's too late to fix this, I can…"

"Is that your answer, to run away?" she growled.

"Then what do you want?" he asked, still holding her face in his hands.

"You know what I want. I want you to stay with me."

"I can't stay here. This is no place for a man. Your people would be calling for my head after a few days. They're probably calling for it now, and all I did was say a few words in the throne room."

"You often spoke fondly of your family back on Earth. What would they think of you for leaving your children for some boyish adventures?"

"That's playing dirty."

"What would they think?" She pushed.

"They'd tell me to take you with me."

"Your mother would never have you raise our children on the sea."

"We can work something out. I'll be back often enough. I just can't stay here. I have responsibilities other than—"

"You have responsibilities to me, Raven. To *us*," she emphasized, lifting Ceana.

"What about your responsibilities to me?"

"What is that supposed to mean?" she asked.

"We don't have to stay here. You can come with me."

"I will be queen." She lifted her chin proudly.

"And I'm the captain of the *Stenox*, which puts me above any king in this world."

"You conceited—"

"It's true. Who is more powerful, me or any of the idiots wearing a crown on this world?"

"You are not royalty by blood, only by marriage through me," she pointed out.

"I'm talking about power, not royalty. Royalty is un-American, and I'd never accept it, and neither will our boys."

"What do you mean?" Her eyes narrowed severely.

"Our daughter might be queen here one day, but the boys won't be her subjects. They should have a good American upbringing. General Matuzak has granted us citizenship in the new Ape Republic. We can go there and avoid all this kneeling nonsense you people are so fond of."

"We are not living with the apes! Are you touched?"

"I'm not the crazy one who marries someone without telling them, *Wife!*"

"Don't pretend you hated it, *Husband!* You could not wait to share my bed. I saw the lust in your eyes that first moment we met."

"Yeah, but did you ever think to simply be nice and tell me you felt the same before going through with your deception?"

"That would have only delayed our wedding. All I did was hasten the process."

"Hasten the process? You skipped everything in between *hello* and *I do*. We nearly got killed escaping dear old Dad's castle of horrors, not to mention traipsing through the woods fighting your soldiers, the elements, and *graggloggs*. You could've died out there as well.

Maybe you should think things through before making rash decisions. That's why I should be in charge, to keep you out of trouble."

"Lower your voice, you fool!" she whispered harshly, his rising volume causing the guards to stir.

"I didn't come all this way to argue with you. We can talk about all this nonsense later," he said before taking hold of her shoulders, pressing his lips to hers. It was deep and passionate and surprisingly gentle. "I really did miss you," he said once their lips parted.

"And I you," she sighed.

"Of course, you did." He grinned.

"Must you ruin every good moment with your tasteless humor?" She rolled her eyes.

"You like my humor, and who can blame you with how boring your life was before me."

"You're hopeless." She tried not to smile, but he had that irritating ability to make her act out of character.

"Yeah, the same as you," he said, his smile having the desired effect on her.

"Would you like to hold your daughter?" she offered.

"Uh, sure." His confidence disappearing in an instant.

"There is nothing to be afraid of," she said, placing the baby in his arms.

"She's so tiny. I don't want to break her," he said, losing himself once she stared up, studying his face.

"You won't break her." She smiled, loving the effect Ceana had on him.

"She has your eyes," he said, gently rocking her in his massive arms.

"And your temper, especially when she is hungry," she added.

"I'm not the only one with a temper," he reminded her.

"Fair enough." She knew better than to deny it.

"She is so beautiful, the most beautiful girl I've ever seen."

"I'll try not to be jealous." She smiled, loving how he loved their child.

"You'll just have to accept being the second most beautiful woman in the world." He smiled, running his thick finger down her nose.

"Would you like to meet your sons?"

"Lead the way."

She gave Ceana to the wet nurse before leading Raven to the adjoining chamber, where the other babies were resting. The two chambers were joined by a wide, lit corridor that also connected to her private chamber. She paused before entering, taking his large hands into hers.

"I must warn you before you see them." She looked worriedly into his dark eyes.

"Warn me about what?" He didn't like the sound of that.

"The youngest is…different."

"Different?"

"He is…I don't think…" She couldn't put it to words.

"Show me."

She relented, leading him through the archway. The chamber was well furnished yet cozy, with a large tended hearth centered on the far wall, and large fur rugs covering the light stone floor. A young woman stood over the two cribs in the center of the chamber, holding one of the babes in her arms.

"Guardian." The woman bowed her head upon their entering.

"Hand him to me, Meara. You've earned a respite. There is a tray of food in Ceana's chamber. Eat of it as you will before returning." Tosha dismissed her.

"You are most kind, Guardian." Meara bowed, regarding Raven warily before stepping without.

"Your son, Tyros," Tosha said, stepping near him so he could see. The boy looked much like him, with a tuft of black hair upon his scalp, and dark penetrating eyes that were instantly drawn to Raven.

"Hey, little buddy." Raven couldn't stop smiling.

Tosha was overcome with joy seeing his reaction. It was a side of him she never expected. Perhaps fatherhood would change him.

"Tyros is no name for a future all-American linebacker. He looks like a Jake to me. That was my grandfather and uncle's name,"

Raven recalled his favorite relative, his mother's youngest brother, who taught him to hunt, fish, and most importantly, to play football. Of course, being half Tejano, his uncle was talented singing that style of music, which Raven couldn't carry a tune.

"My father would not approve," she reminded him.

"Jake will grow on him. With a name like Tyros, people will make fun of him behind his back, kind of like Brokov."

"No one would dare," she said indignantly.

"Tell that to Lorken and Brokov. I'd never live it down. Isn't that right, Jake?" he asked, touching the boy's nose.

"You're impossible." She should've known he would have issue with the naming.

"I'm just looking out for my son. He'll thank me later."

"I should have considered your corrupting influence." She could just imagine the things Raven would teach their children.

"That's not corrupting. That's fatherhood. There are a lot of things I'll teach my boys. Speaking of which, where's his brother?"

Tosha nodded toward the crib to his left, fearing this moment. Would he accept the child? Would he reject him? Would he blame her for his deformity? Before another question crossed her mind, he already had the baby in his arms, the boy emitting a gurgling sound.

"I wonder what caused this?" Raven asked curiously, examining the baby's inky black skin that crisscrossed his flesh in scaly contours.

"No one can tell me," she said, the anguish evident in her voice.

"He looks healthy though, heavy too," he said, noting the child's heft. Raven started laughing, noting the stupid grin on the boy's lips and his piercing silver eyes staring up at him.

"You like him?" she asked. He didn't seem repulsed by the child's appearance.

"I love him." He gave her the most wonderful smile she ever saw. His unfailing love for their child melted her heart, wiping away all her worries.

"You are not concerned by his...uniqueness?"

"He's different, but that's not necessarily a bad thing. He might not be pretty, but he looks happy and strong. All he needs is a name that fits. Let me see. He looks like a big rock, so...Ujurak," Raven recalled his father's Inuit village in Alaska, near Anaktuvuk Pass, and the native word for rock, which seemed fitting.

"Ujurah?" She made a face, unimpressed by his choice.

"*Ujurak,*" he corrected her. "It means rock."

"You are not naming our son after a rock." She narrowed her eyes severely as she put *Jake* over her shoulder, patting his back.

"It's kind of catchy, Ujurak. We can call him Uju for short."

"No!" she whispered harshly, not wishing to disturb the babies.

"Uju and Jake." He decided, liking the sound of that.

"We shall discuss this later," she said as Meara appeared. Tosha passed off her children and led Raven by the hand to her chamber.

* * *

"This place is nice," Orlom said excitedly, jumping on the bed in the guest chamber.

"Get down before you break it!" Kendra growled, losing her patience. If she knew she would be babysitting Orlom by herself on this mission, she'd have jumped overboard at sea. She couldn't wait to give Raven a piece of her mind when he joined them, whenever that would be. The chamber given them was quite impressive, with rich furnishings, large windows, and an archway to an outside terrace overlooking the courtyard, the city, and the sea beyond. Four life-sized statues stood along each wall, each a queen of old, if she were to guess. She hoped Orlom wouldn't break them, but that was probably too much to hope for.

"Beds are for jumping," Orlom continued, giving her a toothy grin.

"Perhaps in your homeland that is so but not here. Now get down before I have to send you back to the ship!"

"Boss would let me do it." Orlom sulked, jumping down to the floor.

"Raven would tell you the same. The last thing he needs is for you to cause trouble."

"I don't cause trouble. Me and Grigg help everyone. Who do you think helped Brokov make his flying thingy?"

Before Kendra could put that notion to rest, Queen Letha entered the chamber, escorted by a flax of royal guards, who posted at the door.

"Your Highness," Kendra greeted politely while Orlom stood beside her with a stupid grin on his face.

"I hope you are pleased with your accommodations," Letha said, her gaze sweeping the room.

"They are exceptional, Your Highness," Kendra said.

"The bed bounces good." Orlom grinned as if he paid her the greatest compliment.

"I am pleased it is to your liking." Letha ignored whatever Orlom meant, her tact putting the young gorilla in a good mood.

"We are curious of our captain's whereabouts. When can we see him?" Kendra asked.

"In the morning. He and the princess will spend the evening with their children." Letha left unsaid what else they would be doing.

"I see," Kendra sighed, not liking the situation. Raven could be dead for all they knew, even though that wouldn't make sense.

"Your captain is safe in my home, Kendra, as are his friends. You are both new to his crew, if my information is correct," Letha said, guessing their concerns.

"We are. I joined them at Axenville, and Orlom at Gregok. Our fellow crewmates will rotate with us throughout our stay, if that is agreeable with you, of course?" Kendra asked.

"I would very much like to meet every member of your crew. Since Captain Raven is now a member of my family, it is wise to know his friends."

"You will find some more agreeable than others." Kendra gave Orlom a disapproving look.

"Yes, Fatty is not very nice." Orlom nodded, as if Kendra was referring to Argos.

"Fatty?" Letha lifted a curious brow.

"His moniker for Argos. Argos is not fat, Orlom. He is General Matuzak's champion and a great warrior," Kendra corrected him.

"He is a dumb, dumb. The pretty queen will not want to see him," Orlom pointed out.

Kendra face-palmed, wondering which of her idiotic crewmates thought it a good idea to send Orlom along.

"I am certain Argos will represent the Ape Republic honorably. I am in his debt for his brave deeds at Molten Isle," Letha said, regarding Argos's participation in rescuing Tosha.

"I know I can speak on the others' behalf to say they are truly honored to have aided in that endeavor," Kendra said.

Letha understood why the Earthers sent Kendra with the first shore party. She could actually treat respectably with Royals and women of power. She guessed the others shared Raven's willful ignorance or Orlom's crude manners.

"And I would be honored if you each join me for dinner," Letha said, which brought an overexuberant reaction from Orlom.

* * *

They stood upon the terrace of Tosha's chamber, looking out over the ocean as the sun set behind them, the surface of the water disappearing into the eastern horizon, melding with the starlit sky. Tosha closed her eyes, feeling the ocean breeze in her hair.

"Tosha, I…" Raven began before she cut him off.

"Just hold me," she said, keeping her eyes closed as he embraced her from behind, his thick arms wrapping protectively around her. She was tired of the arguments, the pettiness, the constant struggle for dominion that defined their every interaction. She would set aside those battles for tomorrow. She needed a night of peace. She needed to set aside her worries.

Raven held her for a time, a strange sense of belonging overtaking him, as if he was finally made whole. Why did she have such power over him? She was right about one thing; he did want her the moment he first saw her. A woman has a way of knowing a man's heart, seeing through the steel veneer he places between them.

"Tosha?" he whispered.

She didn't respond, resting the back of her head against his chest. He scooped her into his arms, carrying her inside and gently setting her on the bed. She smiled as he stood over her, watching as he removed his thick jacket, tossing it on the floor, followed by his pistol belt. He let it drop where he stood, not caring if it was in arm's reach.

"You are very trusting." She smirked.

"What are you gonna do, beat—"

"Beat you up? I just might." She finished his stupid line.

"All right, you can hit me all you want but no biting." He grinned, stripping off his boots and shirt, his muscles bulging on his thick chest. Tosha hated the way just looking at him made her shudder.

"What about your trousers?" she asked as he started to climb into bed.

"They come off once you're fully naked," he said, tugging at her loose shift.

"You dare look upon the crown princess of the Federation unbidden? Such insolence," she teased.

"Yep." He smiled, crawling over top of her, staring intently into her golden eyes.

"Then you must be punished," she whispered, reaching up to kiss him, pressing her hands to his cheeks, brushing her lips to his.

He grabbed her hands, pinning her to the bed, crushing his lips to hers. He wanted her for so long, dreamed of her for so long that it drove him to the brink of madness. She returned his passion with a fire of her own, pressing her body to his, her inhibitions swept away like leaves in the wind.

"Tosha, I…" he began to say as their lips briefly parted.

"Don't ruin this by saying something stupid," she growled, maneuvering herself on top of him, devouring him, her passion kindled by their long separation. How she longed for this moment, sharing her bed and her home with this man who ignited such fire in her heart and her womb.

"*Bahhh!*" A child's cry echoed from the adjoining chamber, killing the moment. Tosha lifted her lips from his mouth, craning her head toward the archway to the corridor.

"Which one is that?"

"Tyros." She recognized the cry.

"You mean *Jake*," he corrected her, his comment drawing the expected reaction, the one confirming he said something stupid.

"The wet nurse will take care of him," she sighed, torn between her desire for Raven and her need to attend the child.

"Go get him." Raven smiled, easing her off him.

"It will only take a moment," she said.

She returned a moment later, carrying the baby in her arms. He made room for her, helping her into bed. She snuggled under his right shoulder, holding the baby to her breast. Raven cradled her under his arm, looking down as the baby suckled, his little mouth moving so delicately. It was the most beautiful thing he ever saw.

"What do you think?" She looked up at him, her golden eyes sparkling like he never saw before. Motherhood changed her. There was a tenderness he never noticed before.

"Beautiful."

"Are you referring to me or our son?" She smiled.

"Yes," he said, kissing her forehead.

She knew at that moment that he truly loved her. Within moments, the babe fell asleep, suckling her breast, and she followed, lost in peaceful slumber for the first time in many nights.

Maybe tomorrow. Raven smiled, holding her as he too fell asleep.

CHAPTER 6

Darna's estate

"Is he awake yet?" Darna snarled upon stepping from her carriage.

Deva greeted her in front of her palatial estate in the dark of night.

"He stirred briefly earlier this evening," Deva said, falling into step beside her as she ascended the steps to the entrance, passing between several household slaves bowing deeply as they passed.

"It's been three days. I will wait no longer. He'll begin to receive his punishment come morning, awake or not," Darna said bitterly. She came straight from the palace, her mood soured by the foul Earther.

"How fares our queen?" Deva dared ask.

"The princess bore three children—two pathetic males and an heir. I had the displeasure of meeting her poor choice for a consort." She couldn't hide her contempt.

"The Earther finally appeared?"

"Unfortunately, but three days late. Scandalous!"

"Does he match Terin's description?"

"Unfortunately. It matters not, for he will soon be dealt with. We shall hold the throne and the leverage over Tyro and not deign to lend our might to the Torry cause as my foolish cousin is wont to do."

"Letting them bleed each other is the wiser move," Deva agreed.

"We must hasten our plans with the contemptable Earther's arrival. We must be careful of his foul magic if the rumors are true."

"Should we interrogate Terin of their capabilities when he wakes?"

"Not yet. That might lead him to conclude his friends are here. He must never suspect."

"How do you plan to punish Terin?" Deva wondered if her betrothal still stood.

"You shall still have him, but he is too dangerous in his current state."

"What do you intend, Mother?" Deva asked as they passed within, stopping in the center of the outer atrium.

"He must be impaired."

* * *

The following morn

He stared sightless into the empty void, inky blackness enveloping him in its deathly embrace. His heart felt like ice, lifeless, and cold. Terin wept silent tears; his dreams were tormented by dreadful nothingness, dreams he could not wake from. He heard voices calling out to him at times but could do naught but lay still and shudder, captive to the torment consigned him.

"Wake up!" the most awful voice snarled in his ear, drawing him from one tormented abyss to another. Terin's eyes fluttered, painfully struggling against the dim torchlight that glared like a blinding sun.

"W..." his words strangled in his parched throat.

"Give him water," Darna ordered the slave attending him.

Terin partook of it gladly; water never tasted so sweet.

"You've been asleep for three days, avoiding the punishment due you for your crimes," Darna began, standing over him like a hellish apparition.

Terin found himself abed on a stone bench, his hands shackled to his side, and his ankles again joined by impossibly large chains that looked even more powerful than his previous bonds. His shirt

152

and trousers were replaced with a coarse brown tunic. His stomach ached of hunger, but none of his afflictions were as awful as the cold emptiness in his heart. He felt as if his spirit was sundered, rent from its anchor.

Yah? Terin cried out in his mind, his thoughts dying in an empty void. It then struck him...Yah wasn't there. He knew then and there that the power of his Kalinian blood was blocked. He never felt so powerless. The realization struck him like a blow to the head. His eyes fell again upon Darna, who glared evilly at him.

"Where did Guilen lead the others?" she asked.

"Whe-wherever the ship...would take them," he lied, each word coming painfully in his parched throat.

"Oh, you are such a poor liar, Terin." She shook her head.

"It is...the truth." He tried to convince her.

"He is going to Cagan, no doubt. He shall present himself to your prince and tell him of your whereabouts," she said, Terin's reaction proving it true.

"You will never catch him. If you let...me go, I will not speak a word of what you did." His plea sounded pitiful even to him.

"Your prince will be in no position to help you, and oh, how you will suffer. Bring him!" she commanded her guards.

* * *

Weapon's room of the Stenox

"What is that?" Lorken pointed over Brokov's shoulder as the transmitted image filled the screen to his left.

"What is what? It's just a grassy meadow," Brokov said as the disc passed over an open area upriver along the south bank of the Sova.

"Expand on that," Lorken pointed out a furry creature hopping through the grass.

"It's just an animal," an annoyed Brokov quipped.

"I know it's an animal, but I haven't seen one like that." Lorken reached over Brokov's shoulder, tapping the zoom control on the console.

"I've already cataloged it. The locals call it a *tersk*," he said, switching off the zoom, pushing the disc further upriver.

"It looks like a rabbit," Lorken said as the image faded. The creature was about as long as his forearm, with large ears, a flat nose, and enlarged hind legs.

"Yes, a very ugly rabbit," Brokov remarked, unimpressed with the comparison.

"Where's this disc headed?" Lorken asked.

"There are two smaller estates three kilometers up ahead, one belonging to a wealthy wine merchant, the other an ocran breeder. Neither looks promising, but we need to be thorough and check everywhere. Each owner is highly ranked in the Federation Army."

"What's the most promising disc?" Lorken asked, looking at the other two active screens. They were presently operating three discs. Using all of them at once was too much to process. Had they recorded Terin's image into the ship's archive when he was aboard, the ship's AI could do the search for them while operating all the discs.

"Disc 4," Brokov said, indicating the center screen, where the images fed back were of rolling hills and rich farmland. Lorken could see gangs of slaves working the fields, toiling in the morning sun.

"Where is that?"

"A rural estate belonging to the queen's cousin, a woman named Danla or Donna or something like that."

"That doesn't sound like an Araxan name," Lorken pointed out.

"I was half-asleep when Corry said it, so cut me some slack. I'm running on fumes about now." Brokov yawned. He and Corry were up all night scanning one estate after another, each owned by ranking members of the ruling forum. Each of those estates were nearer the harbor. Now they expanded their search outward, targeting the most promising holdfasts first.

"That estate is a lot farther out than these others that you passed up," Lorken said, noting the screen above where a digital map of the area was alit—the searched areas shaded green, and unsearched shaded red.

"Kendra said Raven had a run-in with this one in the throne room. Kendra didn't like the looks of her either, so she goes to the top of the list. Corry agreed. That's why we are passing over several other promising targets. If nothing shows up, we can always go back."

"Where's Corry now?"

"I sent her to bed just before you came down. She wants to be woken if we find anything, but unless we're staring at Terin's face, we're not waking her. Poor kid's been up through the night." Brokov yawned again.

"I still can't see how women can keep those men enslaved?" Lorken said, an image of slaves working the fields below the disc showing clearly in the viewscreen.

"Because the physical differences between Araxan men and women are less pronounced. If you look at those native to the isle, the females are larger and stronger than their male counterparts, likely a forced protein deficiency during their formative years. If you consider the history of the Sisterhood, you can understand their strict control of the population," Brokov dryly explained, regarding the brutality of the Soch Empire that preceded the Federation.

"Ever wonder what would happen if we left Raven here for a year or so?" Lorken chuckled.

"With no help or backup? It would be a grand comedy," Brokov agreed as he edged the disc closer to Darna's estate.

"We'd set up a remote feed so we could watch the crash up in real time." Lorken smiled evilly.

"It wouldn't take long for him to start running his mouth and causing a ruckus. He'd be dead or in the dungeon before we broke the horizon."

"No, Tosha would find a way to break him. He'd probably be washing and folding her panties and fetching things for her from the palace kitchen." Lorken laughed.

"Do Araxan women wear panties?" Brokov asked, looking over his shoulder at Lorken.

"Don't you know? I thought you and Kendra…you know." Lorken made a circle with left hand, drawing his right forefinger toward it.

"No. We haven't," Brokov refuted sternly.

"Relax." Lorken patted his shoulder. Knowing Brokov's high sense of honor, he and Kendra would wait to be properly wed. Lorken's expression quickly changed as the image on the center screen came again into focus.

Brokov followed Lorken's gaze back to the screen. There was some sort of activity in the area behind the large manse centered on the vast estate. A small army of soldiers appeared to be escorting a prisoner, the poor fellow's ankles bound by the thickest shackles they had ever seen, with his hands bound behind him.

"That's a lot of guards for one man," Lorken observed, counting over twenty warriors. Their current view was on the back of their heads, but something about the prisoner's golden hair gave him pause.

Brokov noticed the same thing, maneuvering the disc in front of the party, lingering some distance in the sky above, bringing the prisoner's face into view. Brokov locked on the man's head, expanding the view until his face filled the screen.

"Fetch Corry," Brokov said, but Lorken already cleared the doorway.

* * *

She burst into the room, her hair disheveled, with Lorken's thick jacket engulfing her shoulders, covering the top of her loose shift. Upon word of their discovery, she sprang from her bed, rushing into the corridor wearing only her night shift until Lorken draped his jacket over her. Lucas followed right behind her, he and Lorken struggling to keep pace.

Corry froze, standing over Brokov's shoulder, her eyes fixed on the screen. Her breath caught in her throat, looking into Terin's sea-blue eyes. He looked gaunt, tired, and soulless. Gone was the happy boy who won her heart, replaced by this morose creature. He looked breathtakingly beautiful, but it was a false and haunting beauty that bespoke a broken spirit.

"Terin," she whispered, her heart singing and breaking at the same time. He looked so sad that it broke her heart. She wanted to reach through the screen and wrap her arms around him. She wanted to hold him forever and never let go.

"He's alive," Lorken reassured her, touching a hand to her shoulder.

"Yes," she said, wiping a tear from her eye. He was alive. Beyond all hope, he was alive. *Alive.* Just as Jonas foresaw.

"Where are they taking him?" Lucas asked the question they hadn't thought to ponder.

Corry winced as Brokov expanded the image, bringing everyone around Terin into focus. She felt her heart jump in her throat as the guards roughly handled him, freeing his hands, only to bind them atop a pole, stretching them taut over his head.

"Are they about to…" Lorken began to ask when they all saw a stern-faced woman with hard brown eyes standing behind him, brandishing a whip. The guards stripped him to his waist, stepping away before the first lash fell.

"No!" Corry screamed as if the cruel leather struck her own flesh.

They stared in disgust as each lash fell, blow after blow leaving cruel, bloody welts across his back. Terin relented after the fourth lash, his screams tearing Corry's heart.

The image suddenly spun upside down, before spanning the surrounding landscape with dizzying speed, Brokov struggling to correct the disc.

"What happened?" Lorken asked.

"I'm trying to figure that out," Brokov growled, feverishly working the console. The image started to flutter, fading in and out as it passed quickly away from Darna's estate.

"Is that a beak?" Lucas pointed at the edge of the screen.

"You've got to be kidding." Brokov shook his head.

"What ails your device?" Corry asked, desperate to know Terin's fate.

"A bird snatched it. It's probably taking it to its nest. Of all the things that could go wrong, what are the odds of that?" Brokov growled, trying to break the disc free and failing miserably. These discs were his first successful attempt and were hopelessly fragile. The next generation of discs would be sturdier and armed.

"Then send another disc to that location," Lorken said.

"No shit, Lorken, wish I thought of that." Brokov gave him a look over his shoulder after already rerouting disc 5.

"We need to rescue him immediately," Lucas said, relaying Corry's thoughts on the matter.

"We're not doing anything until we scan every part of that estate and the surrounding area," Brokov pointed out, sending disc 1 to scout the lands south of the estate and disc 2 east along the coast for a possible extraction point.

"Terin is in danger. We don't have time to wait!" Lucas pleaded.

"He appears to be suffering punishment, not execution, Lucas. I trust Brokov to plan his rescue with both haste and care." Corry steeled her heart. She would not let anguish cloud reason.

"I won't waste any precious moments, Corry. I promise you that," Brokov said, appreciating her fortitude and logic.

"I'll raise the shore party and let them know," Lorken said.

"I will prepare. Lucas and I will be going with the rescue party," Corry declared firmly.

"I figured you would," Brokov said.

* * *

Queen Letha's palace

"How was your night?" Letha asked as the servant placed her breakfast upon the table. She sat on her terrace, enjoying the balmy sea air as Tosha joined her.

"It went well." Tosha took a sip from her goblet after another servant topped it with water.

"Just well?" Letha raised a skeptical brow. Tosha hadn't seen her husband in months, and their first night together merely went well?

"We were interrupted," Tosha said quietly, looking out toward the sea, imagining him leaving her again at some point, disappearing over the horizon.

"Interrupted?" Letha asked, dismissing the servants with a wave of her hand.

"Tyros. He required attention."

"You have wet nurses for that."

"I know, but—"

"You felt the need." Letha knew well that feeling, the maternal need to tend your child.

"Yes."

"Was Raven disappointed?"

"He encouraged me to fetch him," Tosha said defensively.

"He did?"

"Does that surprise you?" she asked, her gaze shifting sharply to her mother.

"Everything about your husband surprises me."

"How so?"

"I was expecting a brutish ruffian, which he supposedly is by reputation or a cold-hearted mercenary. Instead, I find a lovesick child in an enormous body. He is *nothing* like you described," she said with good humor.

"He is exactly as I described. Do not be fooled by his simple nature. It is a poor act. He is deviously clever."

"He loves you," Letha said, choosing her words like a sharp blade.

"He—" Tosha closed her mouth, unable to refute the obvious.

"Don't you dare deny it or your love for him. It is as clear as a cloudless day, and not at all what I expected. Sadly, it will not end well either."

Tosha narrowed her eyes severely, as if to challenge that remark.

"Oh, don't give me that look, child. You know as well as I that he cannot stay here unless he is willing to submit to our authority, something we both know he would never do. He will have to leave at some point, and that too will be scandalous in the eyes of our people, weakening our position."

159

"I am aware of this," Tosha bitterly confessed.

"And what do you propose to do about it? The only choice is him submitting and staying or—"

"Or what?" Tosha asked.

"You could go with him."

"Go with him? What about the throne? What about you?"

"You could abdicate your place in ascension, giving your crown to Ceana. She would stay, of course, and rule in your place once I am gone."

"Leave my daughter?" Tosha shook her head. She couldn't do that.

"Those are our options, Tosha. To think otherwise is ignoring what is for what you wish it to be. As queen, I have no such luxury, and neither do you. If Raven stays, he must kneel and pledge his loyalty to the throne, something I cannot and will not enforce. It has to be his choice. And deep in your heart, I don't think you want him to submit. He challenges you, as you challenge him. What you share is rare, and in a way, I am equally happy for you and jealous."

"I am heir to two realms. Should I not have who I want as my consort and on my terms?"

"You are my heir, and no other. Do not fancy yourself inheriting your father's doomed empire. It is a house built on sand. Even now the storms of war are turning against him. When they reach him, his foundation will crumble. I'll not have you or my grandson caught up in his destruction, and we both know you are not his true heir." She left unsaid who that true heir was.

"Terin will never claim it," she said.

"No, and neither will Tyros." As far as Terin was concerned, Letha received ill tidings, rumors of his fall in battle. She kept that from Tosha for now, knowing she was fond of him. Raven should be told though. Perhaps it would be useful in turning Raven and his friends to her true purpose.

"I made a promise to Father, a sacred vow. How can I deny him?" Tosha said with little conviction.

"A vow you do not wish fulfilled. You know well of what I speak. As far as betraying your father, you can set aside your guilt, for I will absolve you of such a sin. By royal decree, I forbid you from handing my grandson over to Taleron," she declared, using Tyro's true name.

"Father will be livid."

"And the blame will fall on me. He will not have the boy. Perhaps he would be safer with his father."

"I will not be parted from my son!" Tosha snapped.

"Then you will go with him!" Letha pushed.

"I will not leave my daughter."

"Your sons are not safe here, Tosha. You will have to make a choice."

"Raven will stay. He will not leave me. He will stay and protect his children," she said defiantly.

"Are you certain? Do you know that he has made other commitments?"

"What do you mean? Does it involve that woman on his crew?" she asked darkly.

"Kendra is courting another." Letha smiled at Tosha's jealousy.

"Who?"

"The one called Brokov. You can put your mind at ease. Raven's heart is safely yours. You have turned him into a lovesick fool, and he has returned the favor by the look of you. It is a pitiful sight to behold. Both of you are ruining your reputations. If matters of state were not in play, I would stand aside and enjoy the spectacle. You are both quite amusing." She smiled.

"That is not very helpful." Tosha rolled her eyes.

"I should have some pleasure from this mess you created. I must confess, after meeting two members of his crew, I look forward to meeting the others."

"And what do you think of his new crewmates?" Tosha took another generous sip.

"You do not favor Kendra. Jealousy is unbecoming of you." Letha shook her head.

"She betrayed me at Axenville," Tosha said icily.

"Betrayed you? Your father planned to betray her and every citizen of that freehold. Did you think a vice magistrate would not be aware of his antics? She wisely sought a new alliance. She is an impressive woman, one I wish served the Federation."

"You offered her a place here?"

"I did."

"And?"

"She politely refused but might reconsider in the future. Much depends on her romantic aspirations with Brokov, if I were to guess."

"She would base such a decision on a male?" Tosha shook her head.

"And you are one to judge?"

"And the more the fool I am," Tosha sighed.

"Do not regret your choice, Tosha. Raven seems a fine man. I see why you chose him." She smiled kindly.

"You…you agree?" Tosha found that surprising.

"He is acceptable." She left it at that. Her endorsement would only go so far with their nobles however.

"You spoke of other commitments?" Tosha recalled where their conversation shifted.

"Oh, yes. It seems your consort has pledged fealty to the Ape Republic."

"HE WHAT?" Tosha hissed.

"He has joined cause with his ape friends and his crewmates as well."

"Why? Raven has been adamant that he kneels to no one!" Tosha said bitterly since he wouldn't kneel for her.

"Apes don't kneel or acknowledge any as king. They select their leaders just like the Earthers. In fact, they have based their new republic on an Earth doctrine of governance. The Earthers have advised them on this transition and accepted their invitation to join their republic."

"Their ape friend told you this?"

"Orlom? No. He has the mental acuity of a gnat. Kendra spoke of it. Orlom is reckless, prone to accidents, and a constant source of mischief, if Kendra's assessment is accurate, which I believe it is."

"Then why is he on their crew?"

"Because your soft-hearted husband doesn't have the heart to send him home or his fellow dimwit, Grigg."

"Grigg?"

"Another ape prone to mischief."

"I thought you found his crew interesting and looked forward to meeting the rest?"

"I do. Orlom may be clumsy and careless, but he is most entertaining. He is far different from Raven and Kendra, each unique in their own right. I understand the others are equally diverse."

"They are." Tosha rolled her eyes, taking another sip of water, wishing it were wine.

"Is there something you wish to add?"

"They are unique."

"I established that already."

"Lorken acts much like Raven but is dark in color. Brokov is very intelligent, his color very fair. Kato is smaller in size. But of all the Earthers, you will find him the most agreeable."

"Kato is not with them. The rumors of him fighting at Corell and Mosar are apparently true," Letha interjected.

"Father will receive that news poorly."

"Which seems fair considering your father has an Earther of his own."

"Kato is no match for Thorton. I fear for him should they meet."

"You are fond of him."

"Yes. Everyone who meets Kato is fond of him. He is very polite and kind. He is nothing like the others."

"And yet you choose one of the others." Letha smiled.

"Raven is crude, but—"

"You find him to your liking."

"Unfortunately. Like my mother, I am hopelessly drawn to an unreasonable man."

"You could have chosen a handsome boy from one of our noble houses. Perhaps your cousin, Guilen? Darna would have been pleased to renew our blood ties."

"The men of our isle are too tame," Tosha said, politely omitting a more detailed summation of their shortcomings. She wanted a challenge in a mate, not an obedient pet.

"They only appear so. Our people give them little chance to prove otherwise."

"You could always change that, Mother," Tosha pointed out.

"I planned to, but then my daughter surprises me by wedding an Earther."

"And I undercut your ability to help the Reformers," she said guiltily.

"Yes, your marrying the son of the leading Traditionalist would have given me leave to appease the Reformers."

"Should I apologize?" Tosha asked, though Letha knew she would never mean it.

"Greater stability for our realm or my daughter's happiness?" Letha lifted her hands, as if balancing the two.

"My choice is not without benefit," Tosha said icily.

"Your husband's power aligned with us is a considerable boon, but his loyalty appears elsewhere."

"The apes are Raven's friends, but I am his wife. Should anyone dare challenge our position, he will be standing beside me—that I promise!"

"Like Melida and her consort Zur Zellion?" Letha said, regarding the first queen of the Sisterhood and her lover and warrior who fought beside her.

"Our people forget that our first queens had strong consorts standing beside them, men of ancient Tarelia, able swordsmen all," Tosha said.

"Yes, they have forgotten much of our early history. Perhaps Raven will remind them that queens should have strong men beside them. If not, his mere presence will give them reason to pause."

"It should, unless they are fools. Raven is the most powerful man in Arax," Tosha said proudly. *Did I just say that?* The thought suddenly struck her. She never defended him so fiercely. She recalled all the barbs and insults they traded between them. She realized that though she was free to attack him, no one else could, not in her eyes anyway.

"My queen!" Galana Vesin, the royal steward, interrupted, waiting at the archway.

"Galana, what brings you to my private chambers?" Letha asked, such an infringement being most unusual.

"Pardon my intrusion, Your Majesty, but an issue has arisen with our...guests," Galana said diplomatically, regarding Tosha briefly as she spoke.

"Now what?" Tosha moaned.

* * *

The last thing Tosha expected to find on the palace green was her husband tossing a strange-shaped object to one of her mother's servants, with several palace guards trying to grab him. Once the object left his hand, they ignored him and raced back across the palace green, where another guard tackled the servant to the ground. Further confounding the situation was Orlom, who hooted excitedly, seeming to congratulate the guard who pinned the servant to the ground. Raven led several other palace servants up to where the boy was thrown to the ground, gathering them into a circle, speaking in hushed tones while the guards looked on.

"What is the meaning of this?" Letha asked harshly to Kendra, who stood off to the side, watching over Raven and Orlom's pistol belts and jackets, as well as a half dozen swords belonging to the palace guards.

"A stupid game, Your Highness." Kendra shook her head.

"A game?" Letha raised an unimpressed brow.

"Yes, an Earth game he first introduced to the apes, and now looks to start up here."

"It is unseemly!" Councilor Mearana tsked, standing by the queen's side. Tosha noticed the councilor's son, Luten, standing shame-faced beside her, his blond head downcast. He too was a palace servant, placed in the queen's service at the behest of his mother. She noticed his rich emerald tunic soiled and torn at the sleeve, indicating his participation in Raven's game before being discovered by his mother, who promptly removed him from the field.

Of all the things Tosha never expected to one day see, seeing Raven involving guards and servants in this strange activity topped the list.

"Blue fourteen! Blue fourteen!" Raven called out after the servants formed a line in front of him, facing the guards and Orlom, who were strung out in a line opposite them.

"Set! Hike!" Raven shouted, an obvious signal to the boy squatting in front of him to hand him the strange object. Raven quickly backed away as the two lines came together, with two of the guards breaking through, chasing after him. He swatted one away with his left hand, tossing her in the grass, while the second lowered her shoulder, driving into his back. She barely moved him as he flipped the object to one of his team members, a young noble named Jarvel Torun, of House Torun, a diminutive boy of fifteen years with thick dark hair framing his comely face.

Jarvel caught the object, turning up field and running before being struck in the chest, the blow knocking him to the ground and the object bouncing from his grasp. The guard who delivered the blow dove toward the object, which seemed to hold some significance, but it bounced beyond her grasp. Another guard ran past her, scooping it up, and ran in the opposite direction, with Raven futilely chasing after her. Raven had many powerful attributes, but speed wasn't one of them. The guard stopped at the other end of the field, throwing the object down, celebrating her victory with an odd dance. Tosha watched dumbstruck as Raven walked back to lift Jarvel off the ground where he still lay.

"You'll live. Just shake it off." She heard Raven tell the boy as he pulled him from the ground, nearly throwing him in the air.

"I…I can-n-not breathe," Jarvel gasped, hunched over with his hands on his knees, his tunic half torn from his shoulder, and his bare knees bleeding.

"Just got the wind knocked out of you. It shouldn't hurt that much. She's only a girl," Raven said, his comments drawing disapproving looks from the palace guards nearby and a stupid grin from Orlom who was celebrating with his teammates.

"Girls and me are beating you, Boss," Orlom hooted excitedly.

"That's because that old bag took my best player." Raven jerked a thumb toward Councilor Mearana, who stood red-faced, staring back at him.

By now all the guards and servants were aware of the queen's presence and knelt, with the commander of the guard detail stepping closer to address the queen, before she, too, knelt. Orlom retrieved their football, tossing it to Raven as they walked over to greet Tosha and the queen, stopping short of the kneeling commander of the guards. Tosha shook her head as Raven shrugged after she gave him that look that asked, "What were you thinking?" He and Orlom just stood there without a care in the world, pretending to look around as the queen addressed the commander.

"Rise and report, Vena!" Letha ordered, her severe tone indicating she wanted to know what this activity was and who approved it.

"Your Majesty," Commander Vena began, explaining how she was tasked with guarding their guests and catering to their needs. When Raven presented the football as a gift to his sons, Vena inquired what it was, making certain it was safe. Raven failed in explaining what it was before dragging her outside to demonstrate. At this point in her story, Raven interrupted.

"We decided to gather up a few of your people to play the game, so Vena here could understand what I was talking about," Raven interjected, receiving strange looks from the growing entourage surrounding the queen.

"We decided boys against the girls, and I played on the girls' team, and we won!" Orlom emphasized with a stupid grin, his remark earning him a strong shove from Raven that sent Orlom flying.

"A poor loser." Kendra shook her head.

"We would've won, but she took away our best player." Raven raised an accusatory finger to Councilor Mearana.

"This barbaric game is inappropriate for young noblemen of the Federation. Just look at him!" Mearana hissed, drawing attention to her son's disheveled state.

"What's wrong with a young boy playing football? How do you expect him to grow to be a man without toughening him up a little?" Raven argued. He wanted to say they shouldn't put the boy in a dress but thought better of it. He would never get used to their strange attire.

"A young man should concern himself with his domestic duties, not violent activities that might disfigure him. You need to learn your place, Consort!" Mearana glared daggers at him.

"Yeah, and who's going to make me, you old bag?" he growled back.

That remark drew everyone's attention, most putting their hands to their face. Kendra rolled her eyes. Tosha closed her eyes and shook her head. Mearana looked to have an apoplexy. Orlom chuckled. No one noticed young Luten's smile, standing beside his mother. He actually liked Raven and relished the break from court protocols and serving in the palace.

"Enough!" Queen Letha commanded, reproaching both of them. "Councilor Mearana, Captain Raven is my son by marriage and a royal guest. He is deserving of your full respect!"

Mearana straightened her robes and lifted her chin indignantly, regaining her composure. "My apologies, Consort…Captain Raven. My outburst was inappropriate," she managed to say without too much sputtering.

"All right." Raven didn't know what else to say, which only drew more disapproving looks from everyone except Orlom, whose attention was drawn toward a strange-looking bird circling overhead.

"And, Raven, you are my son by marriage and a prince by the same right. I expect you to treat members of our ruling forum with their due respect," Letha admonished with as gentle a voice as she could use yet still get his attention.

"All right." He again shrugged innocently.

"That means apologize, Rav," Kendra added, explaining what the queen politely left out.

The queen thought an apology was obvious but overestimated Raven's ability to understand that.

"Sorry," Raven said as if that simply covered his insult. The looks he was given were enough to convince him to add a few more polite words.

"Your son is pretty fast. He is welcome to come with me to the Ape Republic. General Matuzak started a new league, and he could use a receiver with his hands and speed." Raven nodded toward Luten as if the compliment would win Mearana over to his cause. Adding further to the awkwardness, Raven gave Luten a thumbs-up, a gesture no one understood, though Luten smiled, giving one back.

"A most generous offer, though young Luten will have to politely refuse because of obligations to the court," Letha answered, intervening before Mearana responded with expected ire. A look from Letha was enough to move Tosha to intercede.

"Raven, come. We are expected elsewhere," Tosha said, taking him by the hand.

"What about our game? The boys want a rematch. Ain't that right, fellas?" He looked over his shoulder to the palace servants kneeling behind him. One seemed amenable to the idea, and the rest, terrified.

"You lost, Boss. Me and the lady humans need to celebrate our victory." Orlom grinned, his comments going over like excrement thrown upwind.

"The ladies have duties to attend, Orlom. We should return to our apartments," Kendra advised, handing Raven his jacket and pistol belt.

"Commander Vena shall escort Orlom. I am sure the kitchen servants have prepared a hearty breakfast that is waiting for him," Queen Letha said as Tosha led Raven away.

Her food comment lit a fire under Orlom's feet. Kendra remained briefly behind, sharing a few words of conciliation with Councilor Mearana, apologizing for Raven's temperament, and assuring her of his harmlessness. Whether the rigid woman was moved by her words, she could only guess, but the queen appreciated the attempt.

"At least one of them is civilized," Mearana commented as Kendra stepped away.

"Her reputation precedes her," Letha said, explaining Kendra's deeds as a manhunter and magistrate in the Troan Region. Even in Bansoch, Letha heard tales of her long before she joined the *Stenox* crew. The Sisterhood had a storied history recruiting women of great renown from the continent, bringing them within their fold.

"She serves the wrong master. She belongs with us, my queen," Mearana said.

"She serves no one, Mearana. The *Stenox* crew consider no one their master or king, each sharing equally in their bounty."

"Barbarians," Mearana sneered dismissively.

"Perhaps, but I wish no hostility between them and us. Am I understood, Councilor?"

"As you command, my queen." Mearana bowed.

* * *

Tosha led Raven back to her chambers, a flax of royal guards escorting them through the wide lit corridors. She noticed his glance out of the corner of his eyes every few steps, admiring the close-fitting gown she wore. She inwardly smiled at the desired effect it had on her less-than-subtle husband. She internally scolded herself, wondering when she became so wanton.

Curse him! She bitterly thought how Raven caused her to act so out of character. She should be thinking of ways to punish him for his insolence, for his lateness, for him being his natural self. Why did she choose a man she was completely unable to control? Perhaps her inner self-realized chains and whips wouldn't work and resorted to feminine charm.

So be it. She smiled to herself, deciding to use whatever means she had to tame the beast.

"What's with that evil smile trying to form on your lips?" he asked, his remark causing the nearest guard to stiffen. The woman's helm shifted quickly in his direction. They were certainly wary of him, not knowing how to react to him speaking so informally with their crown princess.

"You're incorrigible." Tosha sent him a flirtatious glance.

"I know that look, Tosh. You're trying to be mad at me, but deep inside, you're happy that I don't follow your silly rules around here."

"Don't flatter yourself, you insufferable pirate." She rolled her eyes.

"You missed me, didn't you? All these months apart you were lying in bed, dreaming of your brave rescuer, wondering when I would sail back into your boring life."

"Do you ever wonder when to shut up before ruining a moment?"

"No, not really. I usually just say whatever comes to mind."

"So I've noticed, as has everyone else in the palace."

"What are they gonna do, beat me up?" He grinned.

"No, that's my job," she said, passing through the doors of her chamber. She ordered the guards outside, closing the doors before turning into his arms, crushing her lips to his.

"Strip!" she hissed, pushing him toward the bed.

"Thought you'd never ask." He smiled, stripping off his jacket, shirt, and pistol belt, leaving them where they dropped before she closed on him like a hungry tiger, pushing him on the bed. She struggled working his left boot free, tossing it over her shoulder before attacking the other. He helped her loosen his trousers as she stripped them off and his undergarment with them.

"It's exhausting just getting you ready for bed," she panted, loosening her dress, letting it fall from her shoulders.

"Come here, girl." He smiled, lying on her bed, enjoying the view.

"Don't use that insolent tone with me, *boy*. I am the crown princess, and you are my consort. You are to kneel in my presence and address me with extreme deference," she admonished, climbing overtop of him, looking down into his dark eyes.

"What are you gonna do..."

"Oh, I am going to beat you up," she growled, crushing her mouth to his, savoring the taste of his lips. Oh, how she longed to do this, devouring him upon her bed, making love night after night until the end of their days. She tingled, feeling his fingers run along her spine, caressing her back, before moving to her shoulders. She felt the power of his large hands pressing on her arms, knowing he could snap them at will. His physical power was intoxicating, invoking a thrilling vulnerability that drove her mad.

No! She couldn't let him have such power over her. She needed to exert power over him, drive him to the brink of madness and desire, and submit him to her will. If the power of her throne couldn't break him, her feminine power would.

"I like this side of you." He managed once again to say something stupid.

She slapped his face.

"Just shut up and do as I tell you for once," she snarled.

Raven just shrugged, allowing her to have her way. Was this what he was fighting the whole time? Maybe he was an idiot. She took her pleasure of him, time and again, before he flipped her on her back, pinning her to the bed.

"My turn." He smiled, running a finger along her cheek and over her mouth, gently tracing her lips. She smirked, playfully biting his finger.

"You are the most beautiful woman I've ever seen and the biggest pain in the ass," he said, an infectious grin playing across his lips.

"And don't you forget it," she growled, grabbing hold of his face to emphasis her point.

"And don't you forget this," he countered, his mouth moving below her lips.

* * *

"You know, I still haven't had breakfast," he said, lying upon her bed with her head upon his chest, staring at the ceiling. Raven finally noticed the frescoes painted in intricate detail, running from the walls to the domed apex above, the midday light fully illuminating them.

"You are thinking of food after what we just shared?" she asked sleepily, her eyes closed as he ran his hand through her hair.

"Nothing wrong about thinking of that. I'm just hoping your food is as good as our ship's."

"Only you would question the quality of food from the royal kitchens. It's far better than anything you have on the *Stenox*. I assure you," she said dreamily.

"I'll have to take your word for it."

"As well you should."

Raven cocked his head sideways, trying to align his eyes with the fresco above. It was a visage of a woman dressed in bright mail and silver tunic, with windswept black hair, standing upon a battle-scarred shore, wielding a glowing, bronze sword, emitting a brilliant golden light. Beside her, stood a man similarly attired, with intense dark eyes, wielding a longsword and a shield, with a white tower emblazoned upon its crest.

"Who's the lady?" he asked, pointing with his free hand, his question drawing her left eye slightly open.

"General Melida, the conqueror and first queen of the Sisterhood," she said proudly, loving the feel of his thick chest beneath her cheek.

"She was a good-looking woman," he said, admiring her feminine face and shapely legs peeking below the hem of her tunic.

"She was a beautiful woman but a fiercer warrior."

"Who's the man beside her?"

"Commander Zur Zellion, a Tarelian warlord who fought by her side in every battle. They were rumored to be lovers. They wed when she became queen. Whenever she held court, he stood beside the throne, her warrior and champion." She couldn't help but think of herself upon the throne with Raven beside her.

"Do you have an outfit like that?" he asked, imagining her similarly attired.

"Of course," she said, turning her head to look him in the eye.

"You should wear it."

"Why?" Her eyes narrowed suspiciously.

"You have nice legs, and you should show them."

"Commander Zellion wore the same uniform. I should have one made for you, fair enough?" She smiled wickedly, knowing exactly what he would say.

"I ain't wearing a skirt, Tosh."

"It's a tunic. The men from your world only wear trousers?" she asked.

"Yep. Skirts are for women except for some countries. There is an island called Fiji, where the men have to wear loose skirts with no undergarments because of the intense heat and humidity, or else stuff starts growing on their balls."

"You could have spared me that knowledge." She made a face.

"If you ever go to Enoructa, it is similar to Fiji."

"Enoructa? The lizard men? You've been there?"

"Yeah, one of our new crewmembers is from there. Do you want to go there some time? I can take you."

"My place is here, my love, and so is yours," she sighed, running her fingers over his chin, resting her head back on his chest.

"I can't stay here, Tosha. We both know how that would end. But you could come with me. Think about it. We could sail around the world, visiting every port. We can raise our children without worrying about anything but ourselves."

"Raven, I can't simply leave. I will be queen one day. I have a responsibility to uphold. I must sit the throne, and as my consort, you should stand beside me."

"Well, I'm captain of the *Stenox*, and I have a responsibility too. And as my wife, you should stand beside me."

"Brokov is more than capable of being captain of your little ship."

"Brokov has been a staff officer since the academy. The *Stenox* needs a real leader in charge. And don't insult my ship by calling it little," he growled.

"I shall call it whatever I please. It is beyond me how you obsess over it. You have a family now, Raven. You will stand aside for Brokov, who is more than capable of sitting in the captain's chair and doing nothing, which is what you do." She was sitting up at this point, their sweet romantic moment long passed.

"I don't do anything? Being in command means making sure everyone else is doing their job, kind of like what you do. When you sit that throne someday, I can say the same for you."

"You cannot compare overseeing an entire realm to a single ship, which only proves my point that you should be the one to submit."

"*Submit?* Don't confuse me with the wimps on this island, girl. It will be a cold day in hell when I submit to you. You should submit to me. You could be my cabin girl and give it a good cleaning."

"What did you just say?" she hissed, leaning closer, her nose nearly touching his.

That's all it took for them to smash their lips together, rolling over on her bed, lost in another fit of passion.

* * *

It was late afternoon when Raven came strolling into the guest chamber in good spirits, carrying his jacket over his shoulder before tossing it on the settee in the middle of the room. Kendra stood impatiently at the archway of the terrace, with her arms crossed, tapping her foot. Orlom sat on his bed along the far wall, chewing on a tosi fruit with his boots off and wiggling his furry toes, without a care in the world.

"What's wrong with you?" Raven couldn't miss her annoyed look. It was the same face most women gave him with disturbing regularity.

"Besides the fact we've been waiting for you for half the day, nothing."

"I was busy."

"With your wife, I assume," she said.

"Trying to convince her to come with us when we leave."

"And you expect her to walk away from her home, surrender her throne, just to be with you?" Kendra shook her head.

"Hey, life with me is pretty good, and a woman would be a fool to turn me down."

"Unbelievable." She rolled her eyes.

"She's lucky to have you, Boss," Orlom added, before pushing the rest of the tosi in his mouth.

"See, he gets it." Raven jerked a thumb toward Orlom.

"You could say we should all jump into a furnace, and he'd explain why it's a great idea," she couldn't believe what suck-ups Orlom and Grigg were when it came to Raven.

"If Boss thinks we should, there must be a reason," Orlom said, proving her point before reaching for another tosi from the bowl resting at his bedside.

Raven just shrugged as Kendra gave him a look to say "I told you so." At that, Kendra motioned for him to follow her outside on to the terrace.

"All right, spit it out," he said, knowing she was itching to say something beyond prying ears as they moved to the edge of the terrace.

"They found him," she whispered.

"Found him? Where?" he asked too loudly, causing her to put her hand over his mouth.

"Shh! They found him at a rural estate fifteen leagues inland." She removed her hand.

"Is he all right?" he whispered.

"He is alive."

"What's that supposed to mean?"

"He was being whipped when they saw him."

"Whipped?"

"Yes. Brokov said it was quite vicious, but he should be alive."

"Should be? Don't they still have eyes on him?"

"The observing disc was damaged during the whipping." She went on to explain what happened with the bird.

"When do they want to send in the extraction team?"

"Tomorrow, by the sound of it. They are scouting avenues of approach and departure as well as equipment preparation."

"I'll tell Tosha I need to return to the ship for a day."

"Why?"

"If the kid is here, I'm going to go get him."

"Brokov said you'd say that, but thinks you should stay here."

"Why would I do that?"

"To not raise suspicion, you big oaf. We don't know if the queen or your princess are aware of Terin's captivity, though I doubt they are."

"They'll have to move out of port to conduct the raid, and once they do, it will raise the queen's hackles," Raven pointed out.

"Just tell our hosts that our crewmates are going fishing to fill our stocks."

"They might buy that, but who is going to lead the rescue op?"

"The Torry princess insists that she will," Kendra said.

"That's a terrible idea. Tell her to stay put on the ship and leave this to us."

"You've already had this conversation with her a thousand times. She is going, and that is that."

"Wonderful," he growled.

"She'll be fine, and she'll have plenty of help. You couldn't go anyway because your new mother has a gala planned for you tomorrow night."

"What?" He didn't like the sound of that.

"A gala, to celebrate the birth of the new royal heir, and to formally welcome you into her house. You and Tosha must renew your marital ties in the custom of the Federation," she said all too happily.

"What's that supposed to mean?"

"Probably a formal ceremony, the sort of which you will hate. I'm looking forward to it."

"I'm sure you are, but I'm not going to do anything stupid I don't want to."

Did he just say that? She shook her head. Since their first meeting, Raven did one stupid thing after another.

"Don't even say it." Raven knew that look.

* * *

Queen Letha's throne room

Minister Veda approached the dais, his burgundy robes swirling about his ankles, his discerning pale eyes trained upon the foot of the throne. His apprentice, Merith, trailed him, keeping a respectful distance as the Torry trade minister presented himself to the queen. They stopped short of the dais, kneeling upon both knees, their heads bowed with deep reverence.

"Rise, Minister Veda!" Queen Letha declared. She sat her throne, receiving dignitaries coming to honor the birth of her grand-daughter on behalf of their respective realms. Minister Veda was the second ambassador she received this day. He arrived at Bansoch five days before, meeting first with her minister of trade and her palace steward. Today was his first official visit with her.

"I am honored to be received, Queen Letha." Veda bowed again after gaining his feet. "On behalf of the Torry Realm, I offer our congratulations on the birth of your new princess."

"We warmly welcome you, Minister Veda. We have not had an official ambassador from the Torry Realm since the unfortunate incident at Molten Isle. I hope your journey was not unpleasant," she said.

"The seas were fair, oh Queen, but I humbly apologize for our unseemly delay. We were forced to wait upon our navy to make safe our passage. Our victory at Carapis cleared our path."

"War interrupts the affairs of state, Minister Veda. I am pleased the Torry Realm wisely chose a minister of trade as their acting ambassador. We will certainly utilize your knowledge to further align our interests in that regard."

"Of course, oh Queen. That was foremost in Princess Corry's decision to send me." Veda left unsaid his more urgent mission, to sway the queen to the Torry cause. Minister Antillius was the preferred choice for this task but was required at Sawyer to deal with the situation there.

"Your princess is wise indeed, Minister Veda. We have received word of her valiant defense of Corell."

"She is honored you think so well of her, oh Queen. She oversaw the defense of Corell with the brilliance of the great kings of old."

Letha smiled proudly upon hearing this, overjoyed with the courage of her beloved niece. She looked forward to treating with Veda in private, learning the more intimate rumors from the Torry court. She had already begun maneuvering her realm to a war footing, preparing to intercede on the Torries behalf. Such a thing was not easily done, however, considering the isolationist bent that dominated both the Traditionalist and Reformist ranks.

"Hopefully your people now see the fruit of sound female leadership, Minister Veda. Let Princess Corry be an example for others to follow."

"Our princess has been a light in the darkness, oh Queen. Every fighting man at Corell knows her worth, and those elsewhere shall be convinced once the full telling of the siege is shared."

"Should any need convincing, you may send them here. My people shall enlighten them."

"Should any scoffers or malcontents persist, we shall graciously accept your offer, oh Queen," Veda said.

"I look forward to treating with you in more private settings in the coming days, Minister Veda," Letha said as the Torry minister and his apprentice bowed and withdrew.

Letha received dignitaries from Yatin, the Casian League, the Macon Empire and Tro, before the Benotrist emissary, who waited impatiently in the adjacent hall, was introduced.

"Jetar Slars, regent of Tinsan Province and emissary of Emperor Tyro!" the palace steward announced as the slender man with silver braided hair walked boldly across the throne room, adorned in flowing Calnesian robes of emerald and gold. His small army of attendants and guards were ordered to remain without, as the palace guards escorted him to the queen.

"Regent Slars, I welcome you to my court." Letha regarded the man evenly as he knelt, keeping him in place for a painfully long moment before giving him leave to rise.

"I am honored, oh Queen. I have come to offer my emperor's deepest respect and congratulations," he said reverentially, leaving unsaid his true opinion of her poor treatment of the Benotrist delegation. He had been at Bansoch for a full fortnight, asking for an audience with the queen, only to be refused until now.

"Your emperor is most gracious," Letha lied, her cool gaze sending a chill down Jetar's spine.

"Emperor Tyro has sent gifts for the princess—chests of gold and two hundred yards of Calnesian cloth, spun to utmost perfection. For his grandson and heir, he has sent a pair of swords, personally crafted by his master of arms. Accompanying me is a master swordsman of the Imperial Elite, Guise Valeyan, who shall instruct the young prince in warfare, and Colbo Tailen, master sage, who shall instruct the prince on matters of state until the emperor calls for him to reside at Fera."

"The prince shall remain at Bansoch until I grant him leave, not before."

"It is our understanding that if Princess Tosha birthed a male child, he would be raised at Fera, after he was weaned, oh Queen," Jetar said, wary of Queen Letha's silent gaze.

"Then your understanding is wrong, Regent Slars. My grandson will remain under my care and protection indefinitely."

"The emperor will protest—"

"If my former husband wishes to make official complaint, inform him to do so in person, here in Bansoch, where you now stand!" Letha watched as Jetar Slars paled, before bowing and slithering away like the serpent he was. She would be damned before giving her grandson over to Tyro. She was reluctant to do so when Tosha first mentioned it years ago, but after Lore's death, she would never agree to it.

Letha held court until late in the day, treating with foreign emissaries and petitioners from the Federation, appealing to the crown to settle disputes between houses. There was an unconsummated marriage and demand for a return of the groom's dowry. There was another dispute between landed gentry, each claiming land transformed by the shift in a river's flow, which moved their boundaries. Letha would prefer to pass on these duties to her steward but refused to shirk her duties to the realm. The great advantage to her marrying outside the realm was her impartiality in domestic disputes, a factor overlooked by those urging the throne to strengthen ties to its vassals through marriage.

* * *

Darna's estate

The early evening found Darna in her private sanctum, downing a goblet of vintage Bedoan wine, thoughts of the contemptable Earther torturing her mind. For the first time, she wondered if her plans were for naught.

"Our guests are here, Mother," Deva said upon entering the chamber, finding her mother's disordered state unnerving.

"Send them in," she said, her glazed eyes fixed to the statue of her ancestor, Gelenda Estaran, her grandmother six times removed.

"In here? Are you certain?" Deva asked, knowing this chamber was never used to host guests.

"These walls have no ears."

"If something troubles you, Mother, I should know of it."

"The Earther might be a larger problem than foreseen."

"Was Terin's description accurate?"

"Nothing the boy said could prepare us for the threat the Earther poses."

"What is he like?" Deva asked, recalling the awe with which Terin spoke of his friend. She wrongly thought it was boyish adulation, but the look on her mother's face chilled her heart.

"He is as human as any other male, and he will be dead before tomorrow night ends. Send in our guests."

* * *

Neta Vasune was first to enter, regarding Darna guardedly, girding herself for the task at hand. She was followed by Lutesha Dorvena, who brought the full weight of the Traditionalist bloc. Jetar Slars came next, followed by another Benotrist emissary dressed in dark, crisscrossed leathers, wearing a longsword upon his left hip, a short upon his right, and a belt of daggers across his chest. An armed male was a rare sight on the isle, and mostly forbidden, especially on Darna's estate. The fact the man wore them so brazenly proved his importance. Deva suspected he was more than an emissary. His stern countenance quickly eased into a diplomatic smile.

"Guardian Darna, I am humbled by your eminence," the warrior greeted her with a natural charm that felt out of place with his profession.

"You are an emissary of Emperor Tyro?" she asked.

"I am Nels Draken of the Imperial Elite. I will oversee the mercenaries in your coup."

The Imperial Elite? Deva was taken aback, wondering how highly placed Nels Draken was in the emperor's court.

"Emperor's Elite Draken traveled directly from Fera after treating with the emperor, who has granted me full authority to oversee the empire's interests," Jetar Slars explained.

"Emperor Tyro sends his regards, Guardian," Nels began. "Minister Slars has informed me on the details of your plan, which I shall participate, leading the free swords in their designated task. Before we discuss this further, I need to hear from your lips the reassurances the emperor demands."

"As I agreed with Minister Slars, no harm shall come to the royal family, save for the Earther, whose head I demand."

"The emperor would prefer Raven taken alive but understands the impossibility of that aim. The lives of the remaining royals are nonnegotiable. The queen and the princess will be given over to us. The Princess Ceana shall be given to you and wed to your youngest son. You shall be acting regent until she assumes the throne," Nels said.

"And in return, we will ensure Federation neutrality," Neta said. She left unsaid the concessions she extracted from Darna to bring the Reformists into this alliance.

"Yes, Federation neutrality is of extreme importance to our interests," Jetar agreed. Only the threat of Letha drawing the Federation into the conflict on the Torry's side, convinced Tyro to agree to

Darna's overtures. This coup would return Letha and Tosha to Tyro, as well as his promised heirs. Even this was not enough for Tyro to usurp Tosha's birthright. He needed to preserve his granddaughter's inheritance, thus binding him to Darna through marriage. Darna, in turn, would reign as guardian regent until Ceana came of age and place her future granddaughter upon the throne after her, one sired by her beloved Dorath. Darna would also provide a female born of her house to Tyro to wed his heir, further binding their new union.

"To the death of the Earther and peace between our realms," Deva declared, her salutation receiving little more than pleasant nods.

"Reserve the celebration for after our victory. There is still more to discuss in bringing it to fruition," Darna tempered Deva's zeal.

"Quite correct. Your queen holds a formidable position, and the Earthers are dangerous to an extreme. I have fought beside them and against them and can attest to their strength," Nels added.

"Then enlighten us," Darna ordered, needing to glean every detail pertaining to the Earthers.

* * *

His pounding lungs muffled the terrible snarling sounds trailing him. He ran naked through waves of grass, with no sense of direction, the guttural sounds of snarling lincors drawing closer, pursuing him through the endless grassy sea. Terin stumbled, falling headfirst into the ground, struggling back to his feet, limbs failing under the strain. A powerful weight struck him, pinning him to the ground, fangs digging painfully in his back, tearing his flesh like barbed daggers.

"Agghh!" He awoke, pain drawing him from his terrible dream, returning him to his waking nightmare.

"Be still!" a weak male voice commanded. He recognized it as Veiya, Deva's personal slave who hated him profusely.

Terin winced as Veiya ran a wet cloth over his back, taking no care avoiding the deep tears in his flesh. The pain was excruciating, the merest brush of the cloth reverberating through his body. He felt the bloodied welts running from his neck to his hips, leaving his back a bloody ruin. He found himself face down upon a stone bed, his hands stretched in front of him, shackles binding his wrists to the wall. His ankles were similarly affixed to the end of the bed, thick shackles holding them in place. He was nearly naked, save for a brief kilt of brown wool.

"Where…" the question died in his parched throat.

"Be silent, or the mistress will have you beaten again," Veiya happily reminded him.

"Where am I?" he ventured again, his anguish too much to bear.

"The dungeon." Veiya decided to answer, anticipating the response he hoped to get from him.

Terin crooked his right eye open, scanning his surroundings. He was surrounded by four gray walls, with a torch bracketed beside the doorway opposite him. He could only guess how long he had been here, his brutal beating still fresh in his mind. He shuddered recalling the awful pain of the lash falling time and again. Perhaps he was fortunate not being able to see the ruin of his flesh. He couldn't remember a pain worse than this, not even his brandings.

"Agghh!" Terin winced as Veiya roughly cleaned his wounds, running the wet cloth over another deep gash.

"Be thankful the mistress ordered me to tend you. I have other duties to attend, ones far more important than this," Veiya hissed.

"Then attend them. My health doesn't matter." He gritted through his teeth as Veiya scrubbed another wound without a care of tenderness. Terin's back was aflame, but a frigid chill coursed every other part of him, especially his heart. His body was wracked with chills and fever, twisting him miserably as he fought his bonds to no avail. Even worse was the emptiness engulfing his mind, a caliginous void of hopeless despair. One thing was perfectly clear. Yah had forsaken him, for he felt nothing, knowing his Kalinian blood was stripped of its power.

Yah cannot dwell in a prideful heart. Lorn's words repeated in his mind. His pride brought this upon him. Yah warned him to run to the ship, to forsake vengeance for the deliverance he provided. Terin closed his eyes, trying to dam the tears squeezing through his lids. He truly had nothing now—no pride, no power, no hope…no Corry.

Even if he escaped, he now brought nothing to the Torry cause. His power, which was always a part of him, was gone.

"Leave us!" Darna's voice drew his eyes open.

Veiya bowed and hurried from the room. Terin wondered if she had been nearby all along, hiding in the shadows. She loomed over him; Deva was standing beside her with her arms crossed.

"Did…you…did you come to finish me?" He managed to ask.

"Finish you? Oh, my dear child, I have only begun to extract the debt you owe. You will beg for death, willing to crawl on your belly and kiss my feet, pleading that I give such mercy, which I shall not." Darna squatted beside him, running her fingers through his hair.

"Where did my brother go?" Deva asked, caring little for her mother's games.

"He won't answer you, Deva. He is too proud. I wonder though if he will beg when his true torture begins." Darna smiled wickedly, sending a chill down his spine. She was the evilest person he had ever known. He then understood what Cronus must have suffered in the dungeons of Fera.

"Your brother will…seek out Prince Lorn, and he will hold you to account. So do your worst and be done with me." He coughed.

"Oh, you stupid boy. Do you think I haven't anticipated that?" Darna painfully stretched her wicked smile, running a finger along his cheek.

Now what? he thought miserably, trying to decipher her meaning.

"By the time your prince learns you are here, there will be a new ruler of the Federation, one not as friendly to your Torry Realm. Even now there are forces moving against Queen Letha, an alliance of Reformists, Traditionalists, and Benotrists led by me. You should know that our queen is hosting an old friend of yours," Darna offered a glimmer of false hope.

"A friend?" he asked suspiciously.

"Yes, a most unpleasant man. If all goes as planned, I will let you see him tomorrow evening, or…the morning after," she said cryptically, savoring the look on his face as he struggled to work out whom she was referring.

"Why tell him now?" Deva asked, thinking it foolish to warn him.

"Because the agony of anticipation will be as torturous for him as the beating we gave him," Darna said, running her finger around his right eye to emphasize her next revelation. "The Earther Raven is at the palace. I will kill him tomorrow night and bring his head for you to see. You will look upon that wondrous sight, burning it into your memory, for it shall be the last thing you shall ever *see*."

Terin made a face, wondering if this meant she would kill him. Could he be so lucky?

"Oh no, child. Death would be an escape, which I am not at liberty to give. I still have plans for you, plans you will fulfill. I am simply removing the hope that you will ever be free or threaten me ever again."

Terin paled, realizing what she intended. He looked to Deva, who simply stared back at him, her face a mask of cruel indifference.

"Of course, we must be careful. Blinding slaves is a delicate procedure if you do not want them disfigured. One must hold the burning embers near enough to complete the task, but not close enough to mar their features," Darna said, her words striking their mark.

Panic took him, realizing his awful fate should she prevail— Raven dead and him trapped forever, blind and helpless, a slave to this wicked house.

"Rest well, slave." Darna smiled, stepping without. Deva gave him one last look before following her mother out.

* * *

Bansoch, Letha's palace

The evening found Raven, Kendra, and Orlom as guests at the queen's table, joining Councilor Mearana and her heir, Galena. Letha was seated at one end of the table, and Tosha, the other. The dining chamber was smaller than the greater halls used for larger galas but more intimate for smaller parties. Modest torchlight provided an air of ambiance, with two golden chandeliers hanging overhead at each end of the stone table. The ladies were dressed comfortably in loose Calnesian gowns of varying hues; Queen Letha gifted Kendra an emerald dress, which she thanked her for. The queen was not surprised, however, when Raven and Orlom refused the garments she provided them. Both came as they were, clad in their black trousers, shirts, and jackets, with their pistols holstered at their sides. Tosha was miffed by their refusal but not surprised, knowing she might never instill culture in her husband. He was a hopeless barbarian.

"I welcome each of you to my table this evening. Let us partake." Letha snapped her fingers, signaling the servants to commence. Four young male servants moved about the table, filling goblets and serving platters of food, each impeccably attired in long golden tunics and scented with fragrance befitting servers at the queen's table. Each was a son of a high noble house, including Mearana's son, Luten, who constantly withered under his mother's scrutiny. Raven was oblivious of the interaction, recognizing his teammate from earlier.

"Hey, Lute, good game today, buddy," Raven said all too loudly, using the abbreviated name he gave him when they played.

Luten blushed, feeling everyone's eyes upon him while filling Tosha's goblet.

"It is breaking protocol to familiarly address those serving unless the queen directs otherwise," Luten's sister, Galena, said, sitting across the table from Raven.

"Relax, miss, I was just telling your little brother he did a heck of a job today. He has good hands and quick feet and picked up the game fairly quick."

"And what makes you believe such an unseemly display should be celebrated? Young noblemen should not be engaged in such activities. Their attention should be focused on the betterment of their houses and improving their marital prospects. As a royal consort, you are expected to learn this," Councilor Mearana said, staring down Raven from across the table.

"Captain Raven was kind to acknowledge your son, Councilor. We should be mindful of his intentions," Letha interjected as Raven was about to say something obnoxious as he was inclined to do. When Letha asked both Raven and Mearana to join her, Tosha questioned the wisdom of it, knowing they hated each other. Letha looked at it from another perspective, trying for them to bridge their differences. She knew the only peaceful way to salvage the situation was for her people to accept Raven and for Raven to not interfere with their social order. And as Mearana was her closest ally and a fierce loyalist, she was the first Raven needed to win over.

"You are wise, my queen," Mearana relented.

"And you are a trusted confidante and friend, Mearana," Letha added before looking to Raven. "Councilor Mearana simply meant to advise you of etiquette, Raven. No offense is intended. We are of different worlds, you and I. We can emphasize our differences, disparaging what we don't understand, or we can respect each other. We can accomplish this by learning each other's culture and history. I am certain Mearana is as curious as I about your home world. Would you care to elaborate?" Letha deftly shifted the conversation, maneuvering two hostile factions to a place of her choosing. This was a skill Tosha needed to develop to be an effective queen.

Kendra sighed tiredly as Raven happily told them of his time on Earth, focusing on his football heroics and piloting skills, speaking at length of trivial matters that did little to explain anything of his home world.

"It was 14–10 in the 4th quarter. We were leading the Melbourne Academy with one minute left in the game. All our points, by the way, were scored by our defense. Lorken couldn't complete a pass if his life depended on it, so it was up to our defense to bail us out." He paused, jerking his thumb toward his chest, implying himself. "They had the ball 1st and goal on the two-yard line. I timed the snap perfectly, cutting through the left side A gap, hitting the QB during the handoff, forcing a fumble, which our free safety scooped up and went ninety-eight yards in the other direction. I wish you all could've been there," Raven explained happily, receiving blank stares as they hadn't a clue what he was talking about, save Orlom. The young gorilla listened attentively, hanging on his every word.

"Great story, Boss. Tell us another," Orlom said eagerly.

"I think one football story is enough, Orlom," Kendra interjected as Raven was about to continue. "It would be easier if our host could see Earth, in order for them to better understand. Brokov anticipated such a need and wisely sent along a tool to aid us." Kendra fished an object from her satchel that she brought with her.

"Why didn't he tell me he sent that along?" Raven snorted as she placed a circle-shaped object upon the table.

"Because you would have broken it somehow, as you often do," she scolded him before pressing a lever on the side of the object.

Letha stared in wonder while the others gasped as a three-dimensional image hovered above the projecting device. They looked on as a hologram of Earth rotated above the table, highlighting its oceans, continents, and nations. They stared as the image of a man appeared beside the Earth, dressed similarly to Raven, but of slighter build and very light of skin.

"Hello, I am Brokov," the man introduced himself. "I am the 1st officer of the *Stenox* and prepared this demonstration for each of you to understand where we came from."

"What sorcery is this?" Mearana gasped, taken aback.

"It is science, not sorcery," Brokov's image replied, able to respond to her statement.

"Your world is round. The wisest among us have speculated on the nature of our own world, believing this to be true," Letha said curiously.

"Shall I continue?" Brokov's image asked.

They silently listened as Brokov explained the theoretical formation and history of Earth, highlighting the great technological leaps that propelled mankind to the stars. At different points, the Earth shrunk, revealing Solar System Prime, and then further shrinking, revealing the greater universe.

"From Solar System Prime, we began to explore the galaxy, scouting the nearest star systems and later terraforming barren worlds to expand our civilization to a multitude of worlds," Brokov explained, using the visuals to reenact the process. He then described their encounter with another space-faring civilization, the Aurelians, and the war that followed.

Tosha couldn't keep her eyes from the visage of the space battle, where Raven and Thorton engaged dozens of Aurelian fighters. Her heart went to her throat as Raven maneuvered his fighter, dodging heavy blasts from the Aurelian command ship, before disappearing into the open bay of the warship. A large explosion followed, the ship imploding before breaking apart as Raven's fighter emerged from the ship's opposite end.

She looked at Raven, who sat to her right, seeing him in a new light. She then began to realize who he actually was before coming to Arax. She was equally proud of his deeds and abhorred by his recklessness.

"What?" Raven asked, shrinking under her withering stare as she shook her head.

"Why do you court death? Listen to me, *Husband*. There will be no more such foolishness!" she growled before leaning closer, her voice dropping to a whisper. "Or I will beat you up," she said before he asked that stupid question. For the first time since she met him, he was speechless, staring back at her like a berated child.

Mearana looked upon Tosha with renewed respect. Many of her contemporaries feared Tosha was acting like a lovesick girl, marrying the untamed Earther, spellbound by his influence. Those fears were only compounded by those who actually saw the intimidating Earther. She hated to admit that he was the most frightening human she had ever encountered. Tosha, however, exerted incredible power over him. It wasn't a physical dominance that the women of the Sisterhood used to great effect but a mental one. It took a powerful personality to influence a man like Raven. The Earther might never conform to their expectations, but he wasn't a catalyst for their destruction either. In fact, with him at Tosha's side, she would be a powerful queen, Raven complimenting her power in a way that Tyro never could for Letha.

Brokov continued the presentation, revealing the events that followed that historic battle, ending with their fateful mission that brought them to Arax. At the conclusion, the images disappeared, leaving them speechless for a time until Letha broke the silence.

"How many people live on your world, Raven?" the queen asked, struck by the majesty of Earth and its great cities and wonders.

"Three billion."

"Three billion?" Galena asked in disbelief.

"Give or take. It was much higher several hundred years ago, but our birthrates dropped since then. Some of our cities have more people than your Federation," he said.

Letha felt like a small insect discovering the true size of the larger world. All the concerns her people had about Tosha wedding a stranger and fearing his insolence paled next to the greater threat. Even the gargoyles were insignificant compared to the power of the Earthers' realm. Their people journeyed the stars, harnessing a power her people couldn't hope to develop for thousands of years. What would stop them from taking over Arax?

"What can we expect should your people ever find our world?" Letha asked, taking a sip from her goblet.

"I don't know if that will happen. They have no way of tracking us. We passed through a wrinkle in space. I'm not certain we are even in the same galaxy anymore, so who knows." Raven might as well have been speaking his native English, for they could barely understand what he was talking about.

"You didn't answer the queen's question, Rav," Kendra reminded him.

"In all honesty, I couldn't tell you. If our fleet discovers Arax, an Earth-type planet inhabited by humans…" Raven shook his head.

"What would they do?" It was Tosha now asking the question, her face a mask of worry.

"For one thing, your existence would be the greatest discovery in our history. If the government could keep it secret, they would tread carefully, sending emissaries to each kingdom and scientific teams. Eventually, news of their discovery would get out and draw public interest from everyone on Earth. The problem wouldn't be an invasion from our governments or bureaucracies, for they would be pleased to make contact with another human civilization. They would make overtures for an alliance and mutual cooperation. The problem would be the public," Raven sighed.

"The public?" Mearana asked, her original concern over Raven changing to outright fear of what might follow.

"Once everyone on Earth learns of humans such as yourselves, native to an Earth-like planet, they will start coming here to see for themselves, and then *Katie bar the door.*"

"Katie?" Kendra asked.

"It's an expression. It means 'everything will go crazy,'" Raven poorly explained.

"What would they do?" Letha grew more concerned.

"Most would just come to have a look, curious to explore your planet and meet your people. They wouldn't mean to cause harm but couldn't help disrupt your society. Add to that, that any one of them will introduce technology that could drastically transform your world and sometimes not for the better."

"You are saying we would be an oddity to them, a form of entertainment?" Mearana was horrified by the thought.

"To some, yes. You have to understand that most Earth people aren't as sophisticated as me," Raven said in all seriousness.

Kendra put her hand to her face, shaking her head, the others equally horrified as Mearana.

"Come on, it's not all bad, ladies. If my people do come, they will improve you lives a great deal in everything from household conveniences to health care, not to mention my family," Raven explained.

"Your family, yes, tell us of them," Letha said, looking for the good news in all these revelations.

Raven went on to describe his parents, his Inupiat father, Texan mother, and his brothers and sisters. Tosha was surprised to learn that his late sister was wed to Thorton, their child being his nephew. She didn't ask what brought their friendship to an end but guessed it had to do with her death.

"If they do find us, I will take you to Earth to meet my family. There is much I want to show you," he said to both Tosha and Letha. "You, too, Mearana, you would like it if you gave it a chance." He smiled, including her in his invitation.

"Well, I don't think…" she stammered.

"Oh, lighten up, Mer. There's a whole galaxy out there to see. We have endless choices of holo chronicles, literature, music, and recreational activities. You can explore large canyons on Earth or the many planets we've terraformed. You can sail distant oceans or fly between the stars. There are countless romantic places you can enjoy with your husband…"

"Councilor Mearana is widowed," Letha said.

"Well, there are plenty of bachelors from Earth that would love to meet a beautiful warlord of the Sisterhood. My old skipper, Admiral Kruson, doesn't have a wife. He's a good man for a cantankerous old German." He smiled at the thought of Mearana wearing a dirndl during Oktoberfest.

"Raven," Tosha said softly, placing her hand in his to get him to stop talking.

"It is kind of you to think of me, Consort, but I fear my days of courtship are over," Mearana politely replied, the two of them striking a peaceful coexistence.

"Your gift was quite beautiful, Raven." Letha shifted the conversation, drawing attention to his generous tribute, the sort of thing to win Mearana's approval.

"What gift?" Tosha asked, looking to both of them.

"A black pearl of extraordinary size," Letha said, summoning another servant hither, presenting the gift for all to see.

"Where did you find a specimen of such size and hue?" Mearana asked.

"Near a small isle off the eastern coast. I brought a second pure white one for Tosha and this for our daughter." Raven fished the diamond necklace from his jacket pocket, giving it to Tosha.

"Raven, it…" She was taken aback, touched by his thoughtfulness. It was truly a gift worthy of a queen.

"Zem helped me cut it, and Lorken helped with the design." What he meant to say was that Zem did all the cutting, and Lorken did all the design.

"A fitting gift." Letha smiled, signaling the servants to continue with the meal. It didn't go unnoticed when Orlom and Raven helped themselves when a server brought a tray of meat, forking large pieces on their plates before the servant could do so.

"Don't go far away with that," Raven said, the boy giving him a strange look before serving the others.

Mearana shook her head. Raven's manners only confirming his unsuitability for life at court. She took a deep breath, checking her anger before considering his attributes. She resigned herself to the fact that he was who he was, and there was no changing that. She caught Letha staring at her before gifting her a knowing smile, probably reading her thoughts. As Letha's most loyal vassal and trusted confidante, Mearana would stand by her regardless. Perhaps they could limit Raven's interactions with their people.

The rest of the meal went without incident. Letha dismissed Tosha, who took Raven in tow, returning to her chambers. Kendra, Orlom, and Galena were excused as well as Letha invited Mearana to her private sanctum, leaving the servants to their duties. Letha retrieved a pitcher of wine from her side table, pouring two goblets.

"Your thoughts?" Letha asked, offering her a goblet, leading her out onto the terrace.

"I stand with you as always, my queen," Mearana answered carefully, taking in the night air, the lights of the city spread out below.

"Don't give me that *my-queen* foolishness when we are alone, old friend. Tell me what you think of him."

"I honestly cannot say. We have been friends since we were children, Letha. We've drilled side by side in the training yard. I've stood as your second when you wed Tyro, though I warned against it."

"Do you think Tosha has made the same mistake?"

"The Earther is no Tyro, but he is not an appropriate consort either. He is wild and unpredictable. He is like taking a lincor for a house pet, hoping it doesn't eat your guests," Mearana said, taking a generous sip.

"That is an apt description." Letha laughed, picturing it in her head.

"You will have to limit his interactions with our more traditional-minded sisters, else he'll cause them an apoplexy," Mearana snorted.

"They are a prickly lot," Letha said.

"You are too kind. They are a collection of small-minded brutes. They take wicked pleasure in suppressing men even their own kin. I am no soft-hearted Reformer, but I would never treat Luten or his brother the way they torture their sons," Mearana wanted only the best for her sons, hoping to find them good matches who would honor them.

"It was never Queen Melida's vision for our Federation. She would be aghast at what we have done," Letha sighed.

"You can hardly fix it now after Tosha's troublesome choice," Mearana said.

"True, but with the events sweeping the continent, we have graver concerns than appeasing the Reformers. If Tyro conquers the Torry Realm, we could eventually face a unified continent," she stated a long-held fear of the Sisterhood.

"A unified continent aligned with the gargoyles. I often wonder why so many of our sisters ignore the primary reason Queen Melida destroyed the old Soch Empire," Mearana said.

"A convenient oversight. If the Soch were not inadvertently aiding the gargoyles, the Tarelian order might not have sent her. Freeing the women enslaved here was simply a means to that end," Letha admitted.

"Our Federation was formed as a bulwark against the gargoyles. You might have wed Tyro to turn him from his folly, but you are still a Torry princess by blood and our queen by right. I know you wish to intercede on the Torries' behalf, but doing so now may not be possible," Mearana said.

"Will there be a better time? Tyro has been defeated at Mosar. General Yonig is dead. The Benotrist Fleet was smashed at Carapis. We could strike at Tinsay with our full might, and either take the city or render it useless. What's left of Tyro's forces in Yatin would have to withdraw or starve," Letha reasoned.

"Your spies are more informed than mine, so you know the blow suffered by the Torries at Carapis. Their mighty champion is dead, and without him, so is their cause."

Letha sighed, knowing of Terin's fall but not yet telling Tosha of it or Raven. The boy was Raven's friend, so Tosha explained. The news would certainly upset the Earther, and he was loyal to his friends as his reaction to Cronus's capture proved. Knowing who the boy truly was gave her a pang of sympathy for Taleron as well.

"I have heard, though it is strange, that the Torry minister hasn't spoken of it," Letha said.

"Why would they confirm that awful truth? They are here to seek aid and won't do so from a position of weakness. Informing us of their champion's fall would make them appear a poor investment. Equally troubling is the war the Torry prince is pressing in Macon."

Letha heard as well the troubling troop movements in Torry South and the Torry withdrawal from Yatin. She could hardly convince the Federation Forum to approve a war upon Tyro if the Torries were moving south. Such a thing would have to wait until the Torries' prospects improved.

"All you say is true, Mearana, but we cannot stand aside and do nothing."

"I've met your nephew and know his worth. If the Torry prince can bring the Macons to heel, then he can return north in strength. With Yatins and Torries behind us, only then should we strike Tyro a blow."

"So we do nothing?" Letha shook her head.

"No. You prepare the way. It takes planning and patience to maneuver the forum to your position. You are a wise queen, Letha, perhaps the wisest since Melida, able to see the larger picture most are blind to."

"A wise queen would not have wed a tyrant."

"Wisdom is born from folly. Do not disparage choices that make you stronger. Consider if you hadn't? Tyro might have committed all his resources to our destruction if his daughter was not your heir. Instead, your brief union has stayed his hand, purchasing us precious time to expand our navy. We are strong now because of that, and the enemy will feel the full weight of our power at the allotted time."

"You are a good friend, Mearana, a loyal friend. Only a loyal friend tells you what you need to hear in place of what you want to hear. We shall proceed with caution but proceed all the same. Unfortunately, I must present Raven to the realm at the royal gala tomorrow evening. He will either impress upon them Tosha's strength for controlling such a man, or—"

"Cause a panic," Mearana snorted.

"Yes," she sighed, taking another generous sip of wine.

"There is one advantage the Earther brings. He proves Tosha is no coward, and that will earn her respect, just like her mother and grandmother, who chose kings as their consorts over perfumed pets. Tosha's choice may displease some, but her daughter has the blood of kings flowing in her veins."

"But Raven is no king," Letha pointed out.

Mearana gave her a look. "Who would you rather face in battle, an Araxan king or Raven?" Mearana might not like Raven but respected his power.

"Fair enough." Letha smiled.

"No use fretting over decisions already made. You simply make the best of it. Present your new son to the people and hope he doesn't do anything foolish. Should any of your vassals have doubts, I shall be standing beside you."

* * *

"You never fail to surprise me," Tosha said, staring up into his dark eyes, standing beside her bed.

"You mean seeing my piloting skills?" He thought after she watched the holo video detailing his exploits.

"No. You were foolhardy and reckless. I meant my mother. She actually likes you," she said before bending over to unlace her sandals.

"Of course, she likes me. I'm lovable. She's not so bad herself."

"You're impossible." She laughed, touching a hand to his cheek. For the first time in her life, Tosha felt true contentment. Their argument earlier felt ages ago, replaced by the undeniable attraction that drew them together. It felt as if steel cables wound around them, binding them closer. It was simultaneously suffocating and intoxicating. He was the most frustrating person she ever knew, entering her ordered life like a tempest, tossing everything into chaos. The more she came to know him, the more the chaos felt like the natural order of things. It was exhilarating; their every interaction sparked conflict or passion or both. She was certain he was going to say or do something stupid tomorrow night at the gala. She still hadn't told him about it, knowing full well he would want nothing to do with it.

"Why are you smiling?" he asked, suspicious of the grin growing on her lips.

"You'll find out." She laughed, pushing him toward the bed before crawling atop of him.

CHAPTER 7

Bansoch
The queen's palace

The sword came suddenly toward Tosha's eyes; the morning sun reflecting off its blunted steel. Tosha brought her own sword to block the hurried strike, thrusting her second blade at Kendra's midsection. Kendra thrusted her hips backward from the sword's path, deflecting it with her own second blade. They quickly disengaged, circling each other in the sand of the sparring yard, before engaging again, their blades clashing in a dizzying storm.

Letha stood off to the side, observing the bout among her royal guards and guests, all gathered in the training grounds to spar or watch.

"The mercenary is quite skilled," Mearana said, tightening the straps on her vambraces, preparing for her own bout.

"Especially for one who favors the bow. Her sword handling is impressive, but her footwork needs refinement," Letha sagely opined just before Tosha planted her foot behind Kendra's, knocking her to the sand, her blades trained to Kendra's throat.

"Splendidly done, Mistress Sarn!" Lucella Sarelis, the captain of the royal guards, praised Kendra's performance, stepping forth to help her to her feet.

"I lost," Kendra grunted, taking Lucella's hand.

"I never lose, and you lasted longer than most." Tosha raised her training swords across her face, saluting Kendra's effort.

"Neither do I, until now it seems," Kendra said, returning the honor by crossing her swords across her face.

"Yes, but the sword is not your weapon of choice," Tosha said, handing her training swords to a young squire, the girl bowing before stepping away.

"In my previous position, I had to master all weapons—swords, axes, knives, and the bow," Kendra said, removing her iron helm, her light-auburn hair falling freely as another squire retrieved her swords.

"I can show you a few techniques to improve your sword-handling," Tosha said, her original distrust of Kendra replaced with polite acceptance. She would never admit that her opinion changed upon discovering Kendra and Brokov's amorous affections.

"My father said to learn from your betters, to never allow pride to deny improvement," Kendra said as they stepped from the training circle, their armored sandals kicking loose sand.

"Surprisingly, my father said something similar," Tosha recalled his many lessons. She learned as much about sword-handling from Tyro as her trainers and in far less time. Of course, he taught her the dirty tricks used by those who experienced years of combat, certain techniques her mother would find detestable. As a famed manhunter, she was certain Kendra knew many of these as well.

"Your father was a great warrior before he was emperor. I would very much like to learn what he taught you, Princess."

"As long as my mother's watchful eyes are elsewhere," Tosha said, her remark drawing a smile from Kendra.

"Perhaps you could teach Raven a technique or two, if his pride will allow it," Kendra said, staring ahead at the man in question, who stood beside the queen.

"Males are not allowed to train. It is only by my mother's permission that he is allowed to carry his weapons."

"Not even noble sons?" Kendra found that odd.

"Long ago, sons of forum members and princes of the realm trained in warfare but that ended after several led a revolt, trying to usurp the matriarchy."

"What happened to them?"

"They were brutally put down. The survivors were blinded including Prince Daru. Since then, males have been stripped of many of their freedoms."

"Thus, Raven cannot train in this yard?"

"Yes, but he doesn't know that, and I am not going to tell him," Tosha said.

"Just as well, for he wouldn't want to unless you told him he couldn't."

"Yes, that is exactly what he would do." Tosha laughed, just as her eyes met the man in question, standing between her mother and Orlom.

"Not bad, girl. You're pretty good with that toothpick," Raven said as they drew close. No sooner had they cleared the training circle, then a dozen royal guards hurried forth, pairing up for their morning bouts and drills.

"You don't refer to the princess of the Federation as girl, Rav. You undermine her authority when you do. As her husband, you should treat her honorably," Kendra scolded him, noticing the severe scowl torturing Mearana's face and the queen's annoyance. Her intervention was well received by both women, allowing them to stand aside as Kendra confronted him.

"You can always stay here if you want, Kendra," he growled.

"Perhaps you should stay and learn some manners. We are guests and should show a degree of respect for our host," she countered.

"I like her." Mearana couldn't help saying, a smile spreading across her lips, crossing her arms over her chest.

"Respect? I'm here, aren't I? I promised I'd come, and I did. Kissing anyone's ass was never part of the deal!"

"Kissing ass? Why would anyone apply such affection to another's posterior?" Mearana asked.

"It's just another of Raven's expressions," Kendra said.

"Do people of Earth actually kiss assess?" Mearana asked, still not understanding.

"It's figurative. It means 'ingratiating yourself to your betters,'" Tosha answered, having learned many of his ridiculous phrases during their time together.

"If Tosha wanted someone like that, she could've married the minstrel," Raven growled.

"Minstrel?" Letha asked.

"A traveling bard that happened across our path at Axenville. He journeyed with us to Tro before joining Cronus and the others to Corell," Kendra explained.

"A miserable scum who looks like a drowned rat. He's a real suck-up though, kept telling Zem how wonderful he is," Raven said.

"Rat?" Mearana asked.

"A rodent from Earth. Don't worry yourself, Councilor. Raven always uses phrases and references to his world knowing we have no idea what he is talking about," Kendra explained.

"I can always teach you things you would understand, Kendra. Give me a training sword and we'll have a go," Raven challenged.

"You don't use swords, Rav," Kendra reminded him.

"I did all right at Fera, fighting her father's champions." He jerked a thumb toward Tosha, recalling his trial in the pit.

Tosha winced, recalling the brutal display. One could hardly call it a sword fight considering Raven's unusual tactics. It was more of a brawl, with him bashing her father's champions over the head with a shield or picking them up and driving their heads into the ground. She needed to squash this idea of his before he learned that he wasn't permitted on the training grounds.

"Raven, we have other matters to attend," she said, taking his hand to draw him away, but her efforts were too late with Mearana's next utterance.

"You might as well go, Consort. Males are not allowed on the training grounds."

"We're not, huh?" he challenged, pulling his hand from Tosha's grasp.

She quickly stepped in front of him, cupping his face with her hands, drawing his attention away from Mearana.

"Listen, you big oaf, we have other duties to attend. We can discuss this later," Tosha said, their eyes locked before pressing her lips to his.

Her efforts were rewarded after they parted, taking his hand in tow, leading him successfully from the training grounds, the others looking on, impressed by her control.

"An impressive display," Mearana remarked, admiring Tosha's power over the beastly man.

"You can't tell Raven what to do, but you can sweet-talk him if you are kind or properly equipped." Kendra smiled, referring to Tosha's physical attributes.

"Boss likes her," Orlom stated the obvious.

"Yes, I believe he does, Orlom." Letha gifted the young Ape a knowing smile.

"Would our emissary from General Matuzak care to spar?" Mearana asked, inviting Orlom to join her in a bout.

"I thought males weren't allowed?" Kendra asked.

"Only human males. We have entertained Jenaii warriors on many occasions and would be honored to offer the same privilege to a brave ape warrior," Letha explained, her compliment inflating Orlom's healthy ego. Orlom handed his pistol belt to Kendra, following Mearana to a circle in the middle of the training grounds, leaving Kendra alone with the queen.

"Your friends are quite a handful, but you manage them well," Letha said, watching Orlom take up an unfamiliar fighting stance.

"If you think Orlom and Raven are difficult, wait until you meet the others, Your Highness." Kendra imagined the queen's reaction upon meeting Lorken, Grigg, Ular, Brokov, or the fates forbid... Zem.

"You provide a calming influence on them. My offer stands should you ever decide to take a place here."

"I am honored, oh Queen, though for now my place remains on the *Stenox*."

"And your heart." Letha smiled wryly, Kendra's silence confirming her affection for Brokov.

"The desire of our heart is impossible to deny. No woman can withstand its beguiling power," Letha added.

"No man can either from what I've seen," Kendra said.

"It is the frailty of humankind, the overwhelming desire that lends the wise to madness and the strong to weakness. Yet it is the essence of life, the elixir of unbound bliss, filling us with purpose. It is not just love, but the mere chance of it that drives us to greatness or ruin. Without it, life would be a dull affair. You are fond of this Earther, the one called Brokov?"

"I suppose." Kendra might as well shout a resounding yes.

"I wish you well. If he is anything like Raven, I suspect he is a better man than he likes to portray," Letha said.

"They are very different in most things, but in that regard, you are correct. The Earthers are brash, loud-spoken, and rude, but show their true measure where it counts. They are the best friends I have ever known, even though they had no reason to show me kindness."

"So Tosha chose well." Letha smiled.

"Yes, but don't tell Raven that, or he will be even more impossible to live with."

"Of course." Letha laughed.

Kendra quickly winced, watching Mearana receive a vicious strike to her shield arm. To the woman's credit, she countered with a skillful thrust to Orlom's belly, a clear win.

"That's two matches to one, if I am keeping an accurate count," Letha said as they again took up a start position.

"A classic struggle of power and experience. I've seen both win out, depending on the level of experience weighed against the level of power," Kendra opined.

"He is giving her as much as she can handle, by the look of it," Letha said, as Mearana found herself on her back with Orlom's sword at her throat, evening the match at two apiece.

"Orlom acts simple and childish, but is one of Matuzak's finest warriors. It speaks well of Mearana to hold her own."

"Mearana is an excellent soldier, one of our finest, so it speaks well of Orlom also."

Kendra politely nodded, but felt Orlom was holding back. The apes were stronger than Araxan humans, and she shuddered to think what an army of them could do in combat.

"I meant to ask you, Kendra, where your ship sailed off to?"

"My ship?"

"The *Stenox*. It pushed away from its anchorage first thing this morning. My people watched it sail out of the harbor, disappearing into the morning sun."

"Oh, Raven sent them to gather provisions for our next journey. Our food stores were running low, and the fishing grounds are rich east of here."

"Fishing?" Letha didn't believe it but wouldn't press the matter.

* * *

Guards saluted while courtesans and servants bowed as Tosha led Raven through the wide lit corridors of the upper palace. He drifted behind her, admiring the view afforded by the brief skirt of her leather tunic. Did this woman just give birth a few days ago? She turned quickly, catching him looking.

"What?" he asked innocently as she smirked, shaking her head.

"Come." She extended her hand, drawing him to walk beside her.

"I thought I was supposed to walk several paces behind you like a dutiful consort?"

"You are, but somehow you manage to turn it to your advantage." She rolled her eyes. Men of the Sisterhood never acted so brazen.

"Just admiring the view. You should wear that getup more often."

"I could say the same for you." She gave him a flirtatious smile, imagining him in a training tunic.

"That's not gonna happen, but if you're a good girl, you can see me naked once we get to your chambers."

"Patience, boy. We have other duties to attend…for now."

* * *

Darna's estate

Terin lay spent, gasping for breath. He tried in vain to free his hands, pulling futilely on his chains. It was useless, but he had to try. Whenever he thought to give up, Raven's face and his own grim fate came to mind, driving him to pull with all his might. He still lay abed on the flat stone, facing down with his ankles shackled to the wall behind him and his arms stretched out to the opposite wall. He was famished and weak with the loss of blood. He pulled again, the steel of his shackles digging painfully into his wrists.

Nothing. He couldn't budge the unforgiving steel. He winced, the slightest movement enflaming his ruined back. That pain was nothing compared to the emptiness of his heart. It wasn't the loss of Corry, though her death grieved him so. It was the absence of Yah. His God had forsaken him, leaving a cold emptiness with a festering darkness filling its cavernous void.

"Why have you forsaken me? If this is how you treat your faithful servants, it's little wonder the men of old rejected you!" he growled, his earlier humbled spirit giving way to self-pity and anger.

"Is this what you want, Yah? To slay the woman I love? To cast me in bondage? To see my friend die before Darna takes my eyes? Why give me the blood of Kal and prevent me from using it before taking it away altogether? Just let me die and be done with it!" he shouted, dropping his head to the cold stone bed and weeping.

He had no track of time, his cell hidden in the bowels of Darna's manse. The only light was the dim torch bracketed on the far wall beside the locked door. He began to shiver, his body wracked with fever. It felt the longest day of his life, every moment an eternal torment, both physical from his wounds and mental for what was to come. He drowned in a delirium of fear and fever, both torturing him with cruel delusions. He tried thinking of pleasant things, recalling his mother's face and father's love. If only he could go back again to the day he left home, retracing his steps to a different outcome. He would have told Raven to never set foot on this island, tell King Lore not to march to Kregmarin, to join Cronus on his mission at Tuft's Mountain, to prevent his capture, and to stop himself from pressing on at Carapis. Had he stopped before assailing the last ship or set ashore to ride out the storm, he would've never been captured and Corry would still live.

Corry, he wept, his last memory of her coming to him bright and vibrant, her golden hair lifting in the winter breeze where he left her upon Corell's battlements.

"No, take it away!" he pleaded, not able to bear seeing what he lost.

The vision only faded as the door creaked open, light flooding the chamber from the outer corridor. Still lying face down, Terin turned his head as Itara Vosen, the cruel steward of House Estaran, stepped within, followed by Sword Mistress Selenda, the commander of the household guard.

"He is secure," Itara reassured Selenda, a look of relief evident in her face.

"Good. While the guards are sweeping the grounds, I want him watched," Selenda ordered.

"I will remain with him," Itara said, not happy with being ordered about, her own authority subject to Selenda's in matters of security.

Terin froze as Selenda looked down at him, recalling the pain of her lashing. She took wicked pleasure in his beating. For some strange reason, the woman looked concerned. Or was it mere annoyance?

"Lower your eyes, slave, for the little time you have use of them!" Selenda hissed, her silhouette filling the doorway.

"Shall you perform the deed, or shall Guardian Darna?" Itara asked, standing over him, giddily anticipating his punishment.

"Guardian Darna has delegated that privilege to me." Selenda lifted her chin, steeling herself to the cruel task. Darna would do it herself, but Selenda was well experienced in blinding slaves. It had to be carefully done, else the slave might die or be severely disfigured.

"Perhaps then we can free his ankles of the noisome shackles he has been dragging across the floors. They are most irritating," Itara added.

"You think you won?" Terin coughed. "You think you can sit out of this war and Tyro will let you be? You are doomed."

"Tyro will not remove his granddaughter from her rightful throne. We are secure here, and in time, you shall give Guardian Deva daughters with Kalinian blood." Itara smiled. Within several generations, there would be hundreds of Terin's descendants on the isle, each with the blood of Kal, enough to stop any gargoyle invasion at the shore. As Darna's two most trusted servants, Selenda and Itara were the only ones beside Deva to know of Terin's unique Kalinian blood. Each were promised matches from Deva's children to wed their own future heirs. Itara had grandchildren who were yet infants, and Selenda had yet to wed. Darna even considered binding Terin to all three of her daughters, increasing the number of grandchildren of Kalinian Blood born of her house. It was the most rapid way of expanding the power of House Estaran.

Fools, Terin thought. They didn't have generations to wait before Tyro came against them. Besides, his blood was probably useless now since he couldn't feel Yah within him. He was lost, despair filtering to every part of him.

"Keep watch over him. I will return…" the words died in Selenda's throat. A flash of brilliant blue light illuminated the corridor behind her.

"Agghh!" she screamed, falling to the floor. Itara drew back against the wall, her eyes transfixed as Selenda lay writhing on the floor, a hole blasted through her spine, vapors rising from her burnt flesh.

Terin knew this was an illusion, a trick of the mind, paying him false hope. Selenda's deafening screams could not convince him otherwise. Three figures entered the cell, their images blurred by his fevered eyes.

"No, you don't!" A familiar feminine voice spoke harshly, before striking Selenda's right arm as the Sword Mistress reached for her dagger, the sword nearly removing her wrist.

"I got her, go check on Terin." He thought he heard Lucas's voice, but that was not possible; his illusion was growing stranger by the moment.

Itara scrambled to her knees, cringing as Lucas loomed over her while keeping a foot on Selenda's neck. If she as much as twitched, he'd take her head.

Corry's heart pounded in her ears as she knelt beside Terin, touching a hand to his cheek. He stared back, his sea-blue eyes looking back in disbelief.

It is a trick, he bitterly thought. He wouldn't close his eyes, fearing the beautiful illusion would disappear.

"Terin." She smiled. He was the most beautiful thing she had ever seen. She found him despite all odds. He was *alive.*

"Am...I dead? Is this heaven or a dream?" He couldn't take his eyes from hers, tears running down his cheeks. Did Yah finally grant him mercy so he could spend the afterlife with his beloved?"

"You are not dead, and I am no dream, my love." She started crying now, gently stroking his hair.

"This cannot be." His heart was beating heavy now, trying not to believe in something that would be taken away once he woke.

"Why can't it be?" she asked, her soothing voice caressing his spirit.

"They said you were dead." He wept, struggling to lift his head.

"Lorken, help me with these chains!" she shouted, drawing the big Earther from the doorway where he stood watch.

"Lorken?" Terin couldn't believe it, not even when his friend stood over him, giving him that mischievous grin before fishing a metallic device from his jacket pocket. He pressed the strange object to Terin's wrist.

Beep!

A metallic clicking sound followed, breaking the manacle. He repeated the process on his feet and opposite hand, freeing his limbs. Terin's arms eased, the constricting pain in his muscles fading.

"Who said I was dead?" Corry asked him, running her fingers through his hair.

"My mistress," he said, that foul appellation coming so naturally from his lips that he didn't think not to say it.

"Your mistress?" Corry asked darkly.

"Guardian Deva," he said, wincing severely as he tried rising, his back aflame.

"Lie still," she ordered, standing over him to examine his injuries. Her hand went to her face as she gasped. She felt suddenly weak, overcome by the sight of it. Raised bloody welts crisscrossed his back, with strips of flesh outright missing. This wasn't discipline but butchery. She started to cry even more, imagining the suffering he endured.

"That looks pretty bad, Terin. You must've really pissed these ladies off," Lorken said, calmly taking the tissue regenerator from his other pocket, sweeping it over his ruined back. If Lorken was bothered by the sight, he didn't show it.

Terin closed his eyes, a soothing sensation coursing the flesh of his back as the wounds healed, torchlight playing off his glistening skin. He thought of all the wounded soldiers Kato healed at Mosar, the wondrous device restoring them and removing their pain.

"Did Deva order you beaten?" Corry asked, her tears swallowed by a festering rage.

"Her mother," Terin sighed, struggling to a sitting position.

"Darna ordered this?" Corry growled.

Terin nodded, his body still weak from his ordeal. The Earthers' healing device couldn't restore his depleted nourishment. He felt Corry's hand touching the rough edge of his slave collar.

"Lorken, remove this abomination!" she hissed.

"Is that what I think it is?" the Earther asked, putting the metallic device to Terin's neck.

"Yes," Corry said with seething anger.

Beep!

"Not anymore." Lorken smiled, putting both devices back in his jacket, the collar snapping free.

"Where is the woman who beat you?" Corry asked, throwing the collar to the floor. The woman's face was carved in her memory, fueling her resolve. She must have looked at the frozen image on the ship's monitors for half the night before embarking on this mission.

Terin pointed at the writhing form of Selenda. Corry pushed Lucas's foot away, grabbing the crippled Sword Mistress by the hair, twisting her head around.

"I will never forget your face, or what you did to him," Corry said in a deathly whisper, before drawing her dagger, running it across Selenda's throat.

"What have you done?" Itara screamed, her eyes wild with fright, kneeling against the far wall, Lucas's sword keeping her in place.

"She tortured the Torry champion. The punishment is *death*! And who are you to question me?" Corry stepped around Selenda's twitching body, blood pooling beneath her feet.

"I…I am the steward of House Estaran." She lifted her chin, as if the title were a shield.

"Do you know who I am, Steward?"

Itara couldn't answer, terrified by Corry's dark countenance.

"I am Corry, princess of the Torry Realm and granddaughter of Queen Theresa, 1st guardian of the Sisterhood!"

'The Torry princess?' Itara cringed before gaining her nerve. "This is an act of war. Do you think the Federation will not avenge me?"

"You were party to the enslavement of our champion. *That* is an act of war. Finish her!" she commanded. Lucas drove his sword through her breast, skewering the vicious steward, twisting his blade before kicking her off its bloodied steel.

"We better get moving. Ular can't keep them busy forever," Lorken reminded her as she turned back to Terin, sheathing her sword and dagger, kneeling before him.

"Can you walk?" she asked, her countenance softening, looking into his sea-blue eyes.

"I thought you were dead," he repeated, his tears coming faster.

She couldn't hold back, wrapping her arms around his neck, squeezing with all her strength, refusing to let go. He returned her embrace, fiercely holding her as if she might disappear. They held each other for an eternal moment, their garments damp with tears.

"I thought you were dead. I thought I lost you forever." He couldn't stop crying.

"I thought the same when they said you drowned at Carapis." She couldn't stop crying either, her heart mending with each passing moment in his arms.

"They said you jumped from the battlements upon hearing of my death. It was all a lie," he said, pulling briefly away to look at her, his face a breath from her own.

"I thought so too, but your father spoke to me, changing my mind and giving me hope."

"My father?"

"He knew you were alive. He told us you were here." She was smiling now, joyful tears continuing to stream along her cheeks.

"How could he have known?"

"His God told him. It sounds like madness, I know, but it was the only hope I could cling to, and he was true to his word."

There was so much he wanted to say, so much he needed to say but not now. He pressed his forehead to hers, overcome with emotion.

"I hate to break up you lovebirds, but we need to move. It's going to take a few trips on the air ski to ferry everyone back to the ship," Lorken said.

"Not before I kill Darna." Corry stood, pulling Terin to his feet.

"We're going to have to kill half the people on this estate to do that," Lorken pointed out.

"I want her dead!" Corry's eyes were aflame.

"Darna's not here," Terin suddenly remembered. How could he have forgotten? His mind was a whirlwind.

"Where is she?" Lorken asked.

"What troubles you, Terin?" Corry asked, taken aback by the frightened look in his tired eyes.

"Raven," Terin said.

"Raven?" Corry made a face.

"She's going to kill him!"

* * *

Terin struggled keeping pace as they ran through the winding corridors of the manse's vast subterranean levels. So many awful memories of this foul place flashed through his mind. Corry stayed at his side, holding his hand, following Lucas and Lorken, who dispatched anyone they came upon.

"Two subjects around the next corner. Both male and unarmed," Brokov's voice broke through Lorken's comm. Terin wondered what was going on and how Brokov could see them if he was back on the ship.

"We don't have time to see if they're friendly or not," Lorken said into the comm in his left hand, his pistol in his right.

"I don't care what you do with them, just hurry back to the ship," Brokov said.

"Did you raise Raven yet?" Lorken asked.

"Still working on it. Just worry about getting back here," Brokov shot back.

Lorken closed his comm before clearing the corner, nearly running into the two men coming from the opposite direction. One was an older man, dressed in a long Calnesian tunic, a man of position in the house. The second was a house slave, by his diminutive stature and brief attire and the silver collar fastened round his neck. Both men froze in place as Lorken stood menacingly before them. Lucas quickly joined him, leveling his sword.

"What is the meaning of this?" Gaive shrieked, his eyes wild with fright, belying his haughty airs.

"Master, should I fetch the guards?" Veiya whispered in his ear, looking for any excuse to step away.

"Most of your guards are dead, boy, so I suggest you stay put until Terin can vouch for you," Lorken warned.

Terin? Veiya thought horribly. When he overheard the commotion in the bowels of the manse, he went to inform Master Gaive. He certainly didn't think the patriarch of the house would drag him along to investigate. Were these men friends of Terin? That thought was confirmed when Terin stepped around the corner, accompanied by a fierce and beautiful woman.

"Where are you taking him?" Gaive asked haughtily, unable to mask his disdain for Terin.

"Who's this idiot?" Lorken asked.

"I am Gaive Estaran, husband to Guardian Darna! Again, I ask, Where are you taking him? He is the property of House—"

Corry burst past Lorken, her left hand grabbing the pompous Gaive by the throat, her right holding a dagger in front of his left eye, pushing him against the wall.

"You dare speak of him with such disrespect? If I had the time, I'd take your tongue for such insolence, knave!" Corry hissed, thought of these wretched people treating Terin so poorly kindling her rage.

"I…my apologies…" he stammered, his bladder releasing as she tightened her grip on his slender neck.

"Did this fool have you beaten, Terin?" she asked, keeping her eyes on the quivering Gaive.

"He…" Terin wasn't sure if he should truly say.

"Tell it true, Terin!" Corry growled.

"Yes" was all he needed to utter for Corry to run her dagger over Gaive's throat.

"And what about this one?" She turned on Veiya, who was now on his knees, begging mercy as Gaive slumped to the floor.

"He's just a slave, guilty of pettiness, but nothing else," Terin's words stilling her wrath.

"Scram, kid, before she changes her mind," Lorken said as Corry pushed Veiya away. He scrambled to his feet, hurrying whence he came.

"Remind me never to get on your bad side, Corry." Lorken chuckled, taking the lead as they continued on.

* * *

They reached the outskirts of Darna's manse, meeting little resistance; Brokov magically guiding them wherever Darna's guards weren't. Lucas told Terin of the Earthers' flying disc, which allowed those on the *Stenox* to see all around them. It was just after dusk, the stars taking shape in the crisp air. They were moving north and west over the open fields surrounding Darna's vast estate, after slipping through a break in the outer wall circling the base of the hill, obviously Lorken's handiwork. How they ever approached unseen, Terin could only guess. They stopped atop a gentle rise, providing a clear view of the manse and its surroundings, where they caught their breath while Lorken used his pistol scope to scan afield. There in the distance, just south of their position, he spotted Ular running apace, several of Darna's guards giving chase.

"Do you see him?" Lucas asked, standing at his shoulder, gazing blindly in that direction.

"Yep, might have to give away our position," he said, taking aim at Ular's pursuers. Ular was armed with a laser pistol as well, so he wondered why he didn't use it. Maybe he couldn't see the guards trailing him in the dark.

"Is he in trouble?" Lucas asked.

"Not anymore." Lorken shook his head as the slippery Enoructan turned on his pursuers. Keeping low to the ground, he swept the legs out from under one of them, dropping the others with dagger throws before flipping back to his feet.

"Is he all right?" Lucas asked.

"I don't know who's more dangerous tonight, Ular or your princess. Let's keep moving," Lorken said, watching Ular retrieve his daggers.

"What about Ular?"

"He'll probably beat us there by the way he's moving. Besides, it won't take long for the guards to pick up our sign over these open fields," Lorken said, before noticing Terin shivering behind him, wearing naught but a skirted garment of some sort. He removed his jacket, wrapping it around his shaking shoulders.

"Thank you, Lorken." Terin tried to smile, but it was surreal, as if he were in a dream.

"Just don't lose it. I have the regenerator and other important tools in its pockets."

"I'll guard it with my life," he reassured him.

"That won't be necessary. Ular seems to have drawn off any of our pursuers. We best get a move on. Out transport is just over the next rise."

* * *

Over the next rise rested a grove of swaying frolog trees, where the tilled fields of Darna's estate bordered untended lands beyond. Terin struggled keeping pace, his weakened body suffering malnutrition. Once within the grove, his eyes were instantly drawn to a strange sight. Resting beside the trunk of a thick frolog was an elongated silver object that was longer than Lorken's considerable height.

"What is that?" Terin asked.

"That's our ticket out of here," Lorken said. The word *ticket* lost on his Araxan friends.

"It's another of their magical toys," Lucas added.

"They call it an air ski. It can hold three of us and fly at incredible speeds," Corry explained.

They waited only a brief time until Ular arrived, his bulbous dark eyes and scaly green skin standing prominently out as he emerged through the trees. Terin had never seen an Enoructan before, but his father had, and he spoke well of their people.

"Glad to see you in one piece, Ular. Good job with that diversion. We snuck in the manse unseen until we were well inside." Lorken slapped him on the back, the reptilian warrior growing accustom to the Earthers' familiar greeting.

"The pistol accomplished the task most efficiently. The brilliant flashes of light disrupted their response. I kept fatalities to a minimum, though several were unavoidable," Ular's voice rippled like running water.

"Well, hang tight until I come back. Unfortunately, our footprints left a pretty clear trail straight here over the tilled fields. Hopefully, they don't have the stomach for another fight until I come back to fetch you and Lucas. Come on, Corry, let's mount up," Lorken ordered, straddling his legs over the forward part of the seat of the air ski.

"I will stay. Let Lucas go first," Terin coughed.

"Hop on Junior before your girlfriend drags you by the ear," Lorken said, pressing the ignition switch on the console.

Corry didn't wait for Terin to comply, pushing him forward. Within moments, they were seated behind Lorken and on their way.

* * *

Terin held tight to Lorken while Corry held tight to him as they sped westward, the ski hovering just above the ground. The wind whipped his face, his hair fluttering in his wake, slapping Corry in the face. She didn't seem to mind, tucking her head tight to his back. He looked down as grassy fields passed swiftly below, their golden stalks visible in the moonlight.

"Hang on tight!" Lorken shouted over the wind, the ski lifting higher in the air, clearing the treetops of the forest ahead. The sudden shift caught Terin by surprise, the ground shrinking suddenly away. The tingling sensation one felt standing upon a precipice creeped over his flesh as they skimmed the treetops, before turning south toward the sea. It felt unreal, the fevered dreams of imagination, yet it was real. Beyond all hope, his friends found him.

Yah, Terin thought humbly, recalling his aspersions flung at his God for forsaking him. But he hadn't forsaken him. He delivered him from the hands of his tormentors to the hands of those he loved.

Forgive me, Terin cried, his heart mending with every league he drew farther away from Darna's manse. Yah delivered him and returned Corry from the grave Deva planted her in his mind. He felt shame for his lack of faith. Would his God ever forgive him?

"Oops," Lorken said, the ski dropping faster than intended at the other side of the forest, the sudden shift lifting them briefly from the seat.

Terin felt his stomach lift to his throat with that rapid descent. Flying a magantor was one thing, but the great avian never flew at this incredible speed, grassy fields and streams passing rapidly below.

"Here we go!" Lorken warned as the ocean came into view, dominating the horizon in inky darkness.

217

Whoosh!

The ski swept over the cliff overlooking the shore, dropping just above the surface before speeding out to sea, the smell of fresh salty air tickling Terin's nose with sweet liberation.

He was free. He knew right there that he loved his friends dearly and that they loved him. He said thank you, though the words were lost in the wind. He heard the waves lapping below them, moonlight illuminating the surface in its milky light. A fish leaped out of the water off their left, the sound of its gentle splash drowned by the wind in his face. The sea passed swiftly below their feet for several leagues before their speed rapidly eased, a dark familiar shape looming just ahead...the *Stenox*.

They circled the ship before setting down astern the 1st deck, where a large ape met them with his arms crossed over his powerful chest.

"Argos." Terin smiled at the familiar face as the ski settled upon the deck.

"Welcome aboard, Terin. It is good to see you alive and well, lad!" the gorilla's deep voice boomed as a furry hand lifted him off the ski with pitiful ease.

Corry climbed off before the large ape took such liberties with her.

"Take care of him, Arg. He's had a rough go of it. I'll be back as soon as I can," Lorken said, easing the ski back into the air before speeding off.

Guess he didn't need his jacket, Terin thought as his friend disappeared into the night.

"Come, let's get you inside." Corry took him by the hand, pulling him toward the door.

He paused briefly, taking one last look northward, in the direction of the shore that lay somewhere beyond the horizon. He was free. His nightmare had finally come to an end. He was overwhelmed with happiness, unable to comprehend it. It was almost anticlimactic. He was suffering, and then he was not. He was alone, and then his true love returned from the dead, bringing his friends with her to rescue him. He turned to her as she held his hand, a fresh tear running down his cheek.

"Corry, I..." He couldn't put words to what he was feeling, overcome with emotion.

"I know." He gifted him the warmest smile that sent his heart racing.

* * *

Bansoch, the queen's palace

The evening found Raven seated at the royal table in the great hall, overlooking the open floor below. The vast chamber was more like an auditorium than feasting hall, with long, wide tables running the length of each wall, set upon raised tiers, with the forward tables resting lower than those behind it, affording every guest a clear view of the open center floor, where performers entertained the gathered assemblage while they ate.

The queen's table was the only table upon the north wall while the other walls held three rows of tables, with the more prominent guests seated higher than those seated lower. Tosha sat his left, and Orlom his right. She explained to him that the Traditionalists were placed primarily upon the east wall, Guardian Darna seated in the direct center upon its highest tier, her daughter Deva sitting to her right. He noted the small army of personal guards standing behind Darna. Tosha explained that each member of the ruling forum was permitted five personal guards within the palace. As a guardian of the realm and blood relation to the queen, Darna was permitted double that number. There were scores of others gathered along the back of the east wall, the personal guards of other Traditionalist forum members. Most were similarly attired in polished steel mail over dark tunics or trousers. It didn't fail to amuse Raven that Araxan women were more likely to wear trousers than the men, especially on this island.

"They have all the charm of a starving Gragglogg," Raven said too loudly, remarking on the Traditionalists' sour disposition.

"Ssh!" Tosha scolded, before pointing out the other guests in the great hall. Seated opposite the Traditionalists were the Reformers, positioned along the west wall. Their most prominent members were Neta Vasune and Voila Arisone, each seated upon the upper tier, with their personal guards posted behind them. Raven didn't think they looked any friendlier.

"It's like sitting between death and the grim reaper." His comment lost on Tosha, though she understood his meaning.

"Do you require a muzzle?" She shook her head, wondering how they would get through the night without causing an incident.

"I might. Now who's that other happy bunch along the south wall?" he asked, regarding the mixed collection of forum members and foreign dignitaries.

"The upper tier is reserved for several members of the Mercantilist bloc and other Independent voices in the forum. The second tier is the ambassadors' row. The distinguished gentleman sitting in the center is the Torry minister, Veda. The man to his left is Guine Lovis of the Casian League. Tosha went through the list of dignitaries, pointing out the ministers representing Macon, Yatin, and Tro. She concluded with Jetar Slars, the regent of Tinsan Province, who Raven remembered when they delivered Tosha to Tinsay before journeying on to Fera. None of the foreign dignitaries were permitted weapons or guards within the palace.

"Is there a reason that, that Jetar character keeps eyeballing me?" Raven pointed out her father's ambassador, who was less than subtle in observing Raven from across the chamber.

"Need you ask why any of my father's ministers would look upon you suspiciously?" She rolled her eyes.

"Fair enough." He shrugged. He noticed four balconies to each corner above, with royal archers standing post upon them, overlooking the chamber. *Guess they have the high ground covered,* he thought to himself.

The chamber itself stood in stark contrast to the regal formality of the throne room. Whereas the throne room was made of marble and stone and adorned with gems, the great hall's walls were made of dark wood and decorated with drapes of varying hues. Though massive stone pillars supported the roof of the structure, even they were stained in hues of forest green and sea blue. The center floor was covered in treated timber rather than the mirrored stone of most royal halls. To Raven, it felt more hunting lodge than fabled hall, which was a point in Letha's favor as far as he was concerned.

"My esteemed guests!" Queen Letha began, standing from her seat to address the assemblage. "I have invited you to celebrate the birth of a royal heir, the Princess Ceana!" she declared, raising her goblet into the air.

"Princess Ceana!" the guests cheered.

"As most know, my daughter and heir has taken a consort, swearing her vows in her father's palace. Though hastily done, without my formal approval, it is within her right as 2nd guardian of the realm. The male she chose is a stranger to our world and unaware of our customs and protocols. I ask understanding and lenience from each of you if he should occasionally fail our expectations. He comes from an advanced civilization, where humans have created incredible wonders. The Earthers have not come here by purpose or ill intent. They are stranded on our world, without means of returning to their own, like a mariner washed ashore on a distant land. They have made our world their new home. We should look to Princess Tosha's mate as an emissary of his people rather than a mere consort. While here, he has sworn to follow our laws and respect the sovereignty of the Federation. I expect many of you have questions regarding his place in our royal house, or are curious to learn more of his native Earth. Let us put these inquiries aside this night and allow ourselves to be acquainted," Letha declared. With a clap of her hands, the celebration began.

A small army of servants began serving their meal, each a high-born son of a noble house, attractively attired, their mothers hoping they might catch the eye of available suitors. Raven recognized several of his teammates from earlier, more than one of them moving gingerly from their bruises. Sitting at the queen's table meant there were no other tables below them, giving them a clearer view of the open floor below. Unfortunately, it also put them in full view of the other guests seated in ordered rows along the other walls.

"So what's the point of the open area below? Is there more entertainment planned?" Raven asked just as the musicians moved to the edge of the chamber.

"It serves several functions, including the first dance, which you and I shall partake." She gave him a mischievous smile.

"Dance? Me?" He made a face.

"Are you lacking of that skill?" She didn't believe him.

"It depends on what kind of dancing you're talking about. If it's slow and easy, I'll be all right but don't expect me to do any of that funky monkey stuff."

"Funky monkey?" She gave him that look, wondering what in the world he was talking about. After spending much of the afternoon schooling him on proper etiquette and the order of events for the evening, she regretted not testing his dancing ability.

"As long as you keep it simple and slow, I'll manage," his words failing to reassure her.

"It will be respectful and measured. It is best if you feel inclined to do something, do the opposite." She smiled.

"I'll remember you said that," he said, taking a large gulp from his goblet, the sounds of his slurping echoing far too loudly, drawing disapproving glares from all corners.

Raven's slurping was soon topped by Orlom's, who followed with a healthy belch.

Why couldn't we have brought Argos instead? Kendra rolled her eyes, sitting at Orlom's right.

It was Luten who was designated to serve at the royal table, offering the queen the first serving from a platter of meat carried by another servant. The queen waved him on to serve her guests first. The queen was always served first but often ordered to be last. It was a practice her father and mother instilled in her at a young age, to always place your people before yourself. Even Letha's harshest detractors admired her sense of duty.

Not one to pass on a perfectly good meal, Raven gladly accepted a generous helping of whatever meat was on the platter. Tosha sighed, shaking her head as he took the prongs from Luten, helping himself to extra portions. That break in etiquette did not go unnoticed with the entire court looking on.

"Thanks, Lut, this looks really good, whatever it is." Raven slapped the slightly built boy on the back, nearly knocking him from his feet.

"You are most welcome, Consort." Luten bowed respectfully.

"Hey, none of that bowing and consort nonsense. It's just plain ole Raven, like we discussed during the game," he reminded the blushing youth, who was uncertain how to respond.

"Just do as he asks, Luten. It is fine," Tosha said, absolving the boy for breaking protocol when dealing with Raven.

"Yes, Your Highness, Raven." He nodded politely to both before serving Orlom, who repeated Raven's actions, to Kendra's chagrin.

"Let them serve you, Orlom," she admonished.

"But, Boss did it," he protested.

"He is the one person you should never imitate."

The festivities continued with the conclusion of the meal while appetizers and generous servings of wine continued to be offered. The musicians started up again with music that was more tranquil than upbeat. It reminded Raven of something from medieval Europe, dull and torturous. He noticed that all the musicians and singers were male, each with long hair that he mistook for women. He thought all Araxans were a little on the feminine side, but the lines were really blurred on this isle. He didn't care what Tosha said, he wasn't going to let his sons be raised here.

"First dance!" General Jani hailed, standing from her seat, raising her goblet into the air.

"First dance!" others chorused, joining in her call.

Queen Letha regarded Tosha briefly, ordering her forth with a wave of her hand, her eyes studiously scanning the crowd.

"Come." Tosha took Raven by the hand, leading him down the stairs of the dais onto the floor as a singer began a romantic ballad, the musicians following his key. Tosha led him to the center of the floor, where she held her open right hand before him. "Press your palm to mine and hold your left in the air behind you and follow my steps," she said, the bright torchlight above reflecting off her golden eyes and the sheen of her midnight hair. She wore a bright-golden cuirass over a black tunic, with her toned muscular thighs peeking below the hem of her garment. She wore matching greaves and vambraces, girding her limbs, the attire of a royal guard. For most festivities, he'd expect her to wear a gown of some sort, but this was a celebration of state, and she was clad as a guardian of the realm. She held her hand out, patiently waiting for him to begin.

"Let's do this my way," he said, taking her in his arms, catching her by surprise.

"What are you doing?" She scowled as he held her obscenely close, moving across the floor. The guests were equally appalled.

"This is how we dance on Earth, at least how most men know how to dance on Earth." He smiled, looking down into her golden eyes.

"It is not how *we* dance," she admonished him, though she didn't try to pull away.

"I'd look like a dork dancing your way," he said, holding her right hand in his left, with his other hand resting on her lower back and her free hand upon his shoulder.

"A dork?" She could only guess what that meant.

"A dork is an idiot or dolt, kind of like Brokov." He smiled, laughing at his own joke.

"Everyone is staring at us," she said.

"We're the only ones dancing. Who else would they look at?"

"It's *how* they're staring that concerns me."

"They're probably jealous of you for having such a handsome husband." He couldn't help himself.

"I believe the word you bring to mind is *terrifying*," she corrected.

"Terrifying? Little old me?" He gave her that hurt look.

"Yes, little old you."

"And what about you? Are you terrified of me too?" he asked, spinning her across the floor.

"I am not terrified of what is mine."

"Neither am I." He smiled, crushing his lips to hers, causing audible gasps from across the chamber.

They briefly parted as the song ended, concluding the first dance. It needn't be said that no other man there would be so bold with their spouse. Before the other couples could step onto the floor for the second dance, Councilor Vestana, a wealthy wine merchant seated upon the upper tier of the south wall, stood to address the assemblage.

"A song, Guardian Tosha!"

"A song!" others chorused.

Raven didn't like the way Tosha was suddenly looking at him with that smile she used whenever she was up to no good.

"Song?" he asked.

"It is a Federation marital tradition. Every groom is expected to sing for his bride. Usually, it is performed at their wedding dinner for all their guests to hear. Since this is your formal presentation to the realm, my people are calling upon you to sing for me now." She smiled wickedly, wondering if he would do it.

"You want *me* to sing?"

"Unless you are afraid," she challenged, enjoying seeing him squirm.

He looked around the chamber, seeing the hundreds of eyes looking back. Some were mocking; others were guarded; but most silently observed to see if he would go through with it. It was a test to see if he would bend to their expectations.

"I can't sing a lick, but I'll do it." He was damned if anyone called him a coward. Besides, he had just the song in mind—"It's Hard to be Humble," an ancient song by a man called Mac Davis.

And so he began, reciting the ancient ballad in good humor, his deep voice carrying easily in the still air. Some of the words were lost to the crowd, but the meaning was all too clear.

Unbelievable! Kendra shook her head, wondering if they would kill Raven after this performance. In all fairness, Tosha knew what he was like before she wed him, so the fault rested with her.

Queen Letha maintained a mask of indifference, guarding her true thoughts.

Darna glared at the spectacle below, disgusted by the Earther's brazen display. She saw Raven for what he was, a threat to their entire social order.

"When shall we…" Deva whispered in her ear, Darna's scowl warning her to silence.

Darna looked across the assemblage, observing her allies, both stalwart and those less so. So few would have courage to lead in what must be done but would follow a strong leader in achieving what they were too weak to do on their own. None of her Traditionalist sisters had the foresight or cunning to fulfill their aims.

"It is time we move closer," Darna said, gaining her feet.

* * *

Minister Veda sat among his fellow ambassadors, each quietly observing the spectacle below with mixed reactions. The Earther was so out of place in this environment that it was absurd. The fellow was terrifying to look upon, and he wondered how Terin ever made friends with him. Thoughts of the fallen Torry champion dampened his spirits. Despite his first impression of the boy, he proved himself an invaluable asset to the Torry cause. His death was disastrous, just as Kato's was. Unlike Terin's death, the death of Kato was not widely known, not yet, anyway. He intended to share that devastating news with the queen after he secured her alliance with the Torry cause, but Raven's sudden appearance changed that. He decided to try a bolder approach and inform the Earther of his friend's demise. One could easily guess his reaction. The Earther had many faults, but disloyalty to his friends was not among them. He was enthralled with the possibilities of what Raven would do to the Benotrist Empire to avenge his friend. If he couldn't draw Queen Letha to their cause, he would settle for someone far more dangerous. Merith sat his immediate left. It was only the boy's first formal event. Scribes and apprentices usually served in a less public capacity. Only when they neared completion of their apprenticeship were they introduced in a public setting. Normally a minister's apprentice would require many years of tutelage, but the war accelerated young Merith's training. Minister

Veda planned recommending his ascension to the king's ministers upon their return home.

"Are you enjoying your first formal gathering on this assignment, young Merith?" Veda asked as a servant refilled his goblet.

"I am honored to join you, Minister Veda." He gave the expected reply before catching the eye of a young woman sitting upon the west wall's middle tier. She lifted her goblet toward him and winked, the gesture catching him off guard.

"Careful, Young Merith. She is the daughter of a powerful councilor," Veda warned.

"I will be respectful, Minister." He looked away from the woman, certain not to offend her house.

"You misread the situation, Young Merith. The women of the Federation are direct in their aspirations. If not careful, you shall be seized and wedded before I can raise a formal protest. As the son of a noble Torry House, you are a favorable match to any lady of the Sisterhood."

"My family wouldn't allow it." Merith swallowed nervously.

"If a noble woman from Bansoch wed you, there is naught your family could do. Be wary, Merith, for any dalliance here can be easily taken as courtship." He laughed, enjoying his apprentice's discomfort. Showing such gaiety was out of character for the ever-serious Veda. Perhaps he had too much wine but didn't remember having that much. For some reason, his vision was out of focus, and why were the Earther's companions at the high table visibly upset? It was the last thing he saw before the world went dark.

* * *

"Kendra! Kendra, pick up!" Brokov's voice rang from her comm as she finished listening to Raven's awful singing.

"Brokov," she answered, lifting the comm to her lips.

"Take evasive actions. They are going to attack you and the queen. Hold on until we can send help!"

"Who is planning to attack?" she asked, looking around the great hall, struggling to hear his voice over the noise. She and Orlom gained their feet, causing a reaction from the guards behind them.

Harroom!

The sound of horns rang out from the outer palace, silencing the assemblage as every eye went to the queen. Before Letha could order her guards to investigate, Brokov's voice rang out clearly for all to hear from the comm in Kendra's hand.

"GUARDIAN DARNA WILL ATTACK RAVEN AND THE QUEEN!"

CHAPTER 8

"GUARDIAN DARNA WILL ATTACK RAVEN AND THE QUEEN!"

With that dire utterance, every eye went to Darna just as she and Deva stepped onto the floor.

"Is this true, Darna?" Queen Letha asked, standing from her seat, her guards closing ranks behind her.

"Now!" Darna screamed, drawing her sword, torchlight alighting its bronze-hued blade a fiery gold.

Raven drew Tosha behind him as Darna cut a woman standing between them in half. The crowd upon the floor scattered, clearing Darna's path as arrows flew from the balconies above. Raven drew his pistol, firing several blasts that Darna deflected, following the will of her sword, her eyes alit with this revelation, the Earther's weapon useless against her.

Zip! Zip! Boom!

Laser passed by Darna's shoulders, dropping two of her companions, followed by a third heavier blast tearing a hole in the floor between them, exposing the level below, large fissures webbing out from the blast point. Darna's feet stopped at the edge of the precipice; the screams of those dying below echoing through the massive hole.

Zip! Zip!

Darna brought her sword across her face deflecting Raven's blasts before backing a step; the fissures spreading beneath her feet.

"Raven!" Tosha shouted as a dozen warriors closed upon them from the opposite wall, each a guard from Reformists houses. Luckily, Tosha was armed, drawing her sword as the first came upon her. She parried a hasty strike, gaining her bearing as laser blasts spewed into the line of warriors from the direction of the royal table.

* * *

Letha received a shield from her nearest guard, holding it below her eyes as she oversaw the carnage erupting across the chamber. An armed cohort of guards loyal to the Traditionalists poured onto the center floor, led by Darna, her sword flashing brilliantly in the chaos. Reformist guards, similarly armed, advanced from the opposite wall, led by Voila Arisone and Neta Vasune. Dread washed over Letha as the Reformists traded blows with her palace guards, joining in Darna's treason. Raven and Tosha fought their way to the side entrance along the west wall; laser fire spewing from Raven's pistol as they withdrew.

Archers positioned upon the southeast and southwest corners of the chamber took aim at the royal guards below. From this distance, Letha could not tell if they were traitors or simply attired as royal archers. A pall of dust obscured her vision, spewed from the breaking floor. She marveled at the destructive power of the object Raven tossed between Darna and himself that tore a hole in the floor, spewing powdered stone through the air. She noticed many of those seated along the southern wall falling unconscious, either drugged or poisoned. Whatever it was, it did not pass her food tasters. It was obviously meant to neutralize anyone not involved with this treasonous plot.

Letha lifted her shield, an arrow bouncing off its thick steel. Her own archers returned fire from the northeast and northwest balconies, one shaft finding purchase in an archer's neck, the woman slipping beneath the parapet of the southeast balcony. The cries behind her proved the effect of their opponents' aim. She saw a royal guard lying upon the floor behind her, an arrow protruding from her eye. Others struggled to stand, with barbed shafts embedding their limbs.

Thump!

Another arrow punctured the table off her left, rattling the goblet where it struck. Blue light flashed off her right, where Kendra and Orlom spewed their deadly fire into the attackers moving across the floor. Darna withstood their barrage, laser blasts reflecting off her sword but finding purchase upon her allies. Raven and Tosha retreated under the cover of Kendra and Orlom's fire, holding at the archway of the entrance along the west wall, where the Reformists were positioned. They left a trail of slain guards in their wake, most falling to Raven's terrible weapon. Raven held position, the archway shielding them from the Reformist traitors above, his fire dropping everyone near the entrance, one of his blasts taking Neta Vasune in the knee. The Reformist leader dropped to the floor; her screams drowned in the din.

Tosha guarded his back, her own blade stained with the blood of her foes, including Fala Gaina. She gutted the Reformist councilor from hip to hip, her innards spilling to the floor as Tosha spun around her.

"My queen, the outer wall has been breached!" Lucella Sarelis shouted in her ear, the captain of the royal guard hurrying to her side under a hail of arrows.

"How? By whom?" Letha asked in alarm.

"Men. They appear to be mercenaries."

"Men! How many?"

"Hundreds, if not thousands. They passed through an open gate before the alarm was raised. We are holding at the inner palace for now, but we don't have the numbers to hold for long."

Letha winced, shielding her eyes as laser fire flashed behind Lucella's shoulder, Kendra and Orlom shifting their aim to the archers positioned upon the southern balconies.

"Hu! Hu!" Orlom shouted excitedly, spraying laser blasts to the southeast balcony, several hitting the mark by sheer volume.

Kendra took time to aim, fixing a steel-eyed archer in her sights, her laser grazing the woman's throat, sending the archer's arrow awry. Kendra cursed, her target crouching below the balcony's low wall and out of her line of sight.

Zip! Zip!

Lowering her aim, she sent two hurried blasts through the wall, one striking true by the scream that followed. She quickly shifted to the other archers upon that platform, dropping two while the others withdrew through an archway into an upper corridor.

* * *

Zip!

Raven dropped another attacker, a sturdy-built woman, clad in bright-red armor over a gray tunic, his laser passing through her breastplate as she lunged at him with a spear. He backed away from the thrust before firing, retreating into the main outer corridor.

"Raven, your left!" Tosha shouted a warning. She stood behind him, parrying another blade, her follow swing cutting her opponent's sword arm below the elbow.

Raven turned to the sight of several warriors rushing toward them, brandishing short swords or crossbows. The corridor was wide set, with a series of white stone archways along its length like the ribcage of a giant beast. Closely spaced torches illuminated the passageway, reflecting off its sheer black walls.

Zip!

Raven struck the first crossbow wielder in the shoulder, the weapon slipping from her failing grasp.

Whoosh!

The barb of the second crossbow grazed his left shoulder before his return fire pierced that warrior's legs, dropping her face first on the unforgiving stone.

Zip! Zip! Zip!

His following blasts struck the swords women in the thighs, each dropping short of his feet, their screams sounding off the walls.

Tosha strode past him, slashing at the back of their necks as they flailed about, finishing them.

"Why aren't you killing them?" she growled, finishing the last of them, before storming past him in the opposite direction.

"It's not my nature to kill women. Where you going?" he asked as she hurried off with a purpose.

"To see that our children are safe!" she shouted over her shoulder.

Raven ran after her, trying to raise Kendra on the comm to let them know.

* * *

With Kendra and Orlom's attention on the archers, Darna renewed her assault upon the queen's table, dozens of Traditionalists joining her charge, navigating the expanding fissures spreading across the floor. The festering hole ran north-south, separating Darna from her Reformist allies, many of whom followed Raven and the princess into the outer corridor.

Zip! Zip!

Darna deflected Kendra's laser fire, thankful for her sword's otherworldly ability. It wouldn't protect her fellow conspirators, however, forcing her to close the distance on Raven's contemptable allies, before she found herself alone. She cursed her misfortune, her carefully laid plans ruined by the Earthers and their foul magic. How they learned of her plans, she could only guess, but it forced her to commence her attack before the queen's guards were drawn off to engage the Benotrist-led mercenaries attacking from without. It was her plan to kill Raven and his friends in the sudden confusion, striking them from all sides. Adding to her disadvantage, the queen rotated out many of the guards whose loyalties she purchased, with those from the Dalacia Region. She planned to remove them all in one fell strike and blame the coup upon her Reformist allies, thus unifying the Federation around her, as the defender of Letha and the crown. She would have sent Letha, Tosha, and the princes to Tyro, telling her people they were slain by traitorous Reformers. She would then rule in Princess Ceana's name, using the child as a shield against Tyro and blaming Raven's death on the Reformers, thus appeasing the Earthers. Now it was all in ruin. She had to act quickly before the Earthers brought their full might to bear. She needed to take one or more of their crewmates hostage to gain her leverage to bargain. Such plans were quickly falling apart as the battle progressed. It was now a matter of surviving to the next moment. She bounded up the wide stair running along the side of the dais, where the royal table sat, meeting a thrusting spear with her shield, her follow strike cutting the weapon in half as she drove on.

Zip!

Kendra fired again, crouching behind the table, hoping to strike Darna while she was engaged with the royal guard. Darna deflected the laser; the blade twisting her arm in an unnatural angle.

"Withdraw!" She heard the queen command; the royal guards followed her through the large archway behind the royal tables, retreating into the upper corridor of the inner palace. She ordered Kendra and Orlom behind her as they passed through the archway. Kendra was taken aback as Letha drew her sword, a luminous golden light emitting along its ancient blade, matching Darna's mysterious sword.

Darna pushed on, step by step up the stair that ran along the side of the queen's table, royal guards failing to keep her at bay with their thrusting spears.

Split! Split!

She cut the tips of their spears, pushing the useless sticks away with her shield, moving forward; her opponents stumbling as they backed away. She hurried a step, hacking off the foot of a guard falling backward. The other guard scrambled to her feet, retreating through the archway as Darna finished her comrade.

Deva followed on her mother's heels, raising her shield while moving up the dais; the royal archers raining arrows from the balconies above.

Thump! Thump!

The sound of arrows bouncing off her shield rang in her ears. She spied Neta Vasune's heir, Leta, leading a cohort of Reformers up the opposite side of the dais. She saw Fala Gaina fall in battle and Voila Arisone lying below with arrows in both legs and Neta Vasune lying near the west entrance, nursing an injured knee. Her mother's allies fared little better, with several prominent councilors among the fallen, most victims of the Earthers' foul weapons.

* * *

Darna passed through the archway; royal guards stumbling to escape her fell blade. The thrill of her enemies fleeing before her elated her spirit. The power of the Tarelian blade was intoxicating. She wanted to do nothing more than cleave the world in half. She paused at the archway, waiting for her guards to keep pace and shield her advance, lest she step into a trap in the passageway beyond.

"Keep behind me, Deva," she ordered her daughter, before stepping through. The light of the passageway illuminating the wide corridor, with gray stone curving toward the ceiling above, the apex reaching the height of three women. There, before her, was her cousin and queen, the 1st guardian of the realm, blocking her path, wielding the sister blade to her own. They were two of the Swords of the Stars, forged by the smiths of ancient Tarelia and gifted to General Melida and her sister Telisa to topple the Soch Empire. They were passed down through the generations to the heirs of Melida and Telisa, both sisters' bloodlines joined and renewed through the ages to strengthen the unity of those wielding the mystical weapons. The two swords explained the endurance of the Sisterhood through the centuries, defeating their foes at the water's edge with the power the blades bestowed upon their wielders. In all that time, never had they been drawn upon each other...until now.

The two guardians spoke not a word as their comrades crowded behind them, transfixed by the power pulsating from their blades. Darna and Letha tossed their shields aside, the objects useless against the swords, as they gripped the hilts with both hands. They were upon each other in an instant, bursts of light igniting whenever the blades touched, bathing the passageway in ethereal brilliance.

* * *

"You are foreign," Tosha said without emotion before slitting the traitor's throat. The treacherous soldier was knelt by two guards loyal to the throne, holding her in place as Tosha interrogated her in the middle of the corridor. She gathered nearly a dozen loyal guards as she navigated the corridors of the palace. The traitor's brief interrogation revealed enough of the growing plot to instill in her the gravity of their situation. The attack within the palace was only to commence after her mother's soldiers were drawn off by the attack on the outer walls. Brokov's warning caused them to attack immediately, spoiling their plans.

"Remind me stay on your good side," Raven said as they moved along, looking back at the traitor's twitching corpse, blood pooling across the gray stone.

"You've never been on my good side," Tosha snorted as they drew closer to the nursery; her guards surrounding them as they moved apace.

"I haven't?" he asked stupidly.

"No, especially after that song you sang back there." She shook her head.

"I thought it was pretty good," he quipped as they came upon a small group of warriors clad in greenish mail over gray tunics, with the sigil of House Dorvena upon their crests, a known ally and coconspirator of Darna. Tosha and her guards were already upon them before Raven could get a clear shot.

"*Raven!*" Kendra's voice broke through his comm as he lowered his pistol, Tosha and her guards cutting down the hapless Dorvena guards.

"Raven here. I tried to reach you awhile ago. What's your status?" he asked.

"We are both with the queen. Where are you?" Kendra asked, irritated with his disappearance.

"I'm following a crazy woman," he said, wincing as Tosha gutted her adversary hip to hip before driving her blade into the dying woman's throat.

"*What?*" Kendra asked.

"I'm with Tosha, on our way to secure the children. Stay with the queen. We need to hold out until the cavalry arrives," he advised.

"Cavalry cannot attain the palace," she pointed out.

"Just an expression. Just find a defensive position until help arrives."

* * *

236

"Idiot." Kendra closed the comm, using the term Brokov oft used to describe their insufferable captain.

"Can I shoot now?" Orlom asked excitedly, standing behind the queen, with royal guards packed around them, the flash of clashing swords causing them to look away.

"Hold your fire. It's too dangerous in here should she deflect a blast," Kendra said, noting the width of the corridor, imagining their own blasts coming back at them.

"I can hold here. Your help is needed upon the battlements!" Letha commanded, overhearing her conversation with Raven and Orlom as she parried another thrust, countering with one of her own.

Kendra reluctantly withdrew; she and Orlom following several guards to the palace roof. The flashes from the queen's sword illuminated the corridor as she looked over her shoulder, the flashes visible even after she turned the corner.

* * *

It wasn't supposed to be this easy. That thought was foremost in Nels Draken's mind with his men pouring through the outer gate. Darna's agents were to open the gates only after his attack drew the queen's guards to the battlements, using the diversion to kill Raven during the initial chaos. Instead, there was little initial response to their assault, allowing his vanguard to hold the outer gate for his reinforcements, who were flooding into the palace proper. Not even the soldiers they slew at the wharves and the streets leading to the palace raised a response.

Nels raced through the open portcullis before leading two hundred men up the nearest stair, attaining the battlements of the outer wall while the remaining seven hundred advanced upon the inner palace. Nels allowed several of his men to precede him up the circling stairwell, the clash of steel above proving the wisdom of the selfish act. He pressed his back against the gray stone wall, dodging a body tumbling down the stair, taking out the feet of the man below him. The corpse's dark leather mail indicated it was one of his. By the time he continued on, several others moved ahead of him, clearing his path. He passed two bodies of palace guards upon the stairs lying beside three of his own.

The top of the stairwell came quickly upon him; the glow of the moon illuminating the opening with its dull light. Stepping onto the causeway that ran behind the battlements of the outer wall, he was greeted with the clash of swords and sights of battle. His men rushed past him, giving battle to the few guards posted upon the walls to meet them.

Did we catch them unawares, or did they truly guard their walls with so few? he mused, taking stock of the situation. His men were securing the section of the outer curtain wall where the main gate rested. He could make out palace guards moving along the outer wall from each direction, moon and torchlight reflecting off their helms and spears. He ordered his men to secure the turrets to either side of the gate, fortifying their position. A few well-armed men could hold back much larger numbers congested on the causeways. He felt secure in his position, watching the rest of his small army passing through the gate below, streaming north toward the gate of the inner palace. The curtain wall of the outer palace stood the height of seven men, running along the base of the hill upon which the palace sat. The inner palace was protected by a second curtain wall, the height of ten men, set much higher upon the hill, far above the outer wall. Beyond this rose the queen's upper palace, with towering minarets spiraling into the night sky.

A torrent of arrows greeted the invaders below the wall of the inner palace, archers firing blindly into the mass of infantry gathered before the closed portcullis of the inner gate. The alarm was sounded, alerting the entire palace to the assault, which Nels found odd in its lateness. Darna's agents prevented the first alert, slaying the signal sentries before they could sound their horns. Despite this, there was supposed to be greater resistance breeching the outer wall. No matter, for the entire garrison was now alerted; soldiers taking up position upon the inner battlements.

"Raise shields!" a mercenary commander ordered. His men interlocked their shields overhead, arrows bouncing off their thick steel. A team of ocran passed through the outer gate, pulling a ram, with an iron pike jutting from its end.

Fire ballistae spewed from the turrets overlooking the inner gate, splashing upon the interlocked shields, flames licking between their seams.

"We can't take much more of this," a mercenary commander barked in Nels Draken's ear, standing beside him, observing the battle from the safety of the outer wall.

"We press the attack until our allies can strike at them from behind. They need time to eliminate Raven before doing so," Draken said, his eyes following a flaming ballistae arc over the inner wall. Much of his view was hindered by the structures resting between the inner and outer walls, including a massive barracks off his left. The lack of activity in the structure convinced him its use was only maximized during war.

"Thank the spirits," the commander sighed as their own ballista were moved into position below the inner walls, as well as the ram, men wheeling it up to the inner gate. Royal archers concentrated their fire upon the men crewing the ram, their shafts feathering several, their bodies slipping to the ground. The cries of the wounded rent the air as men were struck by arrows or fire. Nels spotted several of his men running from the battle waving their arms while covered in flames.

No sooner than their first ballista returned fire, it was struck by a munition, igniting its oil barrel. Nels winced. A sheet of flame exploded below the inner wall, engulfing scores of his soldiers. His vision cleared, revealing the ghastly sight of men caked in flames, flopping upon the ground like fish thrown up upon the shore.

"If we don't breach the gate soon, I will order a retreat," the mercenary commander growled in Nels' ear.

"We have no choice but to press the attack. There is no alternative to victory, Varg," Nels answered far too calmly considering their plight.

"You can't convince men to withstand that!" Varg growled.

"They knew the risks when you recruited them for this mission. They also know their fate should we fail," Nels reminded him. He recalled that it took mere moments for Minster Slars to recruit Varg Galenca for this mission. The mercenary general already assembled this small army before Nels reached Tinsay upon his return from the Yatin Campaign.

"The men were promised all the riches and slave girls they could plunder, but such things have no worth to dead men," Varg answered back.

"Death is a mercy if we turn back now, Commander. Our allies will open the gates to us soon enough."

A mercy? Varg thought miserably of their fate should they be captured. The Sisterhood earned a reputation for cruelty dealing with invaders.

And so, they waited as each painstaking moment passed all too slowly; their casualties piled up before the gate of the inner palace like cordwood. The ram pounded away to little effect; its crew weathering flames and arrows to deliver each strike. They managed to dent the portcullis but not the heavy iron gate behind it. After a time, the sounds of battle rang out behind the gate as Darna's soldiers struck at the garrison troops from behind. Nels and Varg looked on as the gates finally swung open, and the portcullis raised.

"Remember that the royal family is not to be harmed," Nels reminded Varg before the general hurried off to join the assault.

The sound of their men cheering rang out as they poured through the gate, storming the inner palace.

Zip! Zip! Zip!

Nels winced as laser flashed from the battlements of a tower of the queen's upper palace, striking behind the open gates where Darna's soldiers likely were. More blasts followed, splashing all around and through the open gate.

"Curse that foolish woman!" Nels growled, knowing Darna failed to kill Raven. Their plan depended on neutralizing him, Kendra, and Orlom at the outset to prevent this very thing from happening. Nels was no fool and had no intention of lingering. He quietly slipped away, disappearing back through the outer gate.

* * *

Kendra and Orlom stood behind the parapet that circled the upper portion of the tower of Melida, its black and silver minaret spiraling above them. From here, they held a commanding view of the battle. A flax of royal guards protected the stairwell behind them, freeing them to concentrate their attention on the gate and courtyard below.

"It's almost too easy," Kendra whispered, using the night vision of the scope to great effect.

Zip!

She fired, striking a mercenary wielding a battle ax just as he passed through the gate, caving his skull.

Zip!

She struck another in the thigh before the first target hit the ground, his ax clanging off the stone of the courtyard.

"Woo-hoo!" Orlom grinned excitedly, spraying laser fire all around the gate. Many blasts missed their mark but caused chaos and fear all the same.

"Slow down, Orlom! Make your shots count!" she warned, uncertain of how long the laser batteries would last. She'd never seen one run out but didn't want to test that theory.

"We got to drive them away, or they'll swarm the palace!" he said with a stupid grin on his face, firing away like a madman.

She couldn't argue her point as an untold number already passed below their line of sight, storming into the palace. Royal guards were fighting among themselves across the inner battlements surrounding the courtyard. She couldn't shoot either group, unable to discern traitors from loyalists. It was all madness. She kept her sights trained on the male mercenaries, knowing which side they were on.

* * *

Tosha dodged a hurried thrust, bringing her sword down upon her attacker's blade before driving her shoulder into the woman's chest. The strike caught the warrior by surprise, knocking her back. Tosha spun around her stunned foe, chopping the back of her knee. A quick thrust finished her opponent as she stumbled to the floor.

241

Zip! Zip!

Raven shot another; his laser hit the warrior's breast and neck, dropping her several paces beyond Tosha farther along the corridor. Before he could ascertain further threats, Tosha hurried off, racing through the wide lit corridor.

"Hold up, Tosh!" he shouted, trying to keep pace.

"You're too slow," she shouted back before disappearing around the next corner.

"Even my wife's faster than me," he grumbled, trying to keep pace. The Araxans' great speed made up for their lack of size. He wondered how many traitors were in the palace, after coming upon three separate groups of them since leaving the great hall. He could barely get a shot in before Tosha tore into them, cutting them to pieces with all the rage of a mother bear protecting her cubs. Tosha sent the royal guards they came upon to help her mother, deciding that she and Raven could handle whatever lay ahead.

Just as well, he thought miserably, knowing the guards would also outpace him, leaving him in the back of the crowd, limiting his line of fire.

"Crap!" he growled, hearing the sound of clashing steel around the corner.

Tosha came upon the entrance to the royal apartments where a dozen queen's guards held the archway separating the royal residential wing from the palace proper. Facing the queen's guards were nearly twenty warriors and citizens of various loyalties attempting to breach the entryway, obviously intent on seizing or harming their children. Tosha came upon the attackers' rear, cutting one down from behind before several turned on her, the others committed to the threat to their front. Unfortunately for Tosha, the corridor widened significantly before the archway, allowing her foes to surround her. She was drilled relentlessly to counter such a tactic, closing swiftly upon the woman to her right, keeping the warrior between herself and the others. No sooner had she done so, then Raven arrived, his first shot braining her furthest attacker. He moved quickly to her side, angling his shots so the royal guards weren't behind his targets.

Zip! Zip! Zip!

Laser fire swept the corridor, dropping one after the other. Several charged futilely; others tried to scramble past him. Seven others dropped their weapons, kneeling and raising their hands in surrender. Only one remained standing, defiant with chin raised and sword leveled at Tosha.

"Wait!" Tosha commanded before Raven could shoot her or her guards could skewer her from behind. She recognized the warrior as Sela Yorin, Darna's second in command.

"Kill me, for I will never submit!" Sela sneered, tightening her grip on her sword.

"Oh, you are certain to die, Sela, but it will be inglorious and painful. Cripple her, Raven!" Tosha said.

Zip!

Sela dropped, a laser blast taking out her left knee. The guards were on her instantly, pinning her head to the floor, twisting her sword free. She would answer to this treason. Tosha would extract it by any means necessary once the immediate battle ended.

"Guardian Tosha," the commander of the guard dipped her head briefly, slapping her sword over her black shield, her gray eyes staring intently through the slits of her helm.

"Report, Commander," Tosha said. A cursory scan revealed nearly a dozen bodies littering the corridor before the archway. A few were royal guards, but the rest were their attackers. Each of these warriors were handpicked by the queen herself for their martial skill and loyalty, each a native of Dalacia. They accounted well of themselves, a tribute to her mother's wisdom in appointing them this task.

"This group of assailants attempted a breach of the royal apartments. They did not advance beyond this point. The royal heir and the princes remain in their quarters with Lady Ivessa," the commander stated matter-of-factly. If the woman was affected by the whole ordeal, she didn't show it.

"Very good. Tend our wounded and secure Commander Yorin," Tosha ordered, stepping past to check on the children, Raven following a step behind.

The two guards posted outside the nursery saluted as she entered; her mind singularly focused on the welfare of her children.

Stepping within, she found Ivessa standing before the cribs, holding Ceana in her arms, quieting the infant, the din of battle raging in the courtyard beyond the outside terrace.

"Your Highness." Ivessa bobbed a curtesy upon Tosha entering the chamber.

"The children?" Tosha asked as Raven circled the room, looking for hidden threats before stepping through the opposite archway to search the terrace.

"All present and well. What is happening?" Ivessa asked, her eyes evident with fright.

"An attempted coup that we are still suppressing," Tosha said, examining Ceana before looking after the boys, who were asleep in their cribs. Were they truly able to sleep through this ruckus yet awaken whenever she tiptoed out of the room?

Raven lingered on the terrace, looking out over the courtyard below and the inner and outer walls beyond. Laser flashed from a high point off his right, striking targets below to great effect. Taking a look through his pistol's scope, he found Kendra and Orlom atop the battlements of a tower, the name of which escaped him.

"What are they shooting at?" he wondered, scanning the activity at the gate below. "Crap," he growled upon seeing the mass of male infantry swarming the courtyard, half fleeing and half advancing into the palace. *That Darna is pulling out all the stops on this one,* he thought, sweeping his scope across the battlements along the outer and inner walls, trying to make sense of it all.

"The children are safe here. We need to help my mother," Tosha half shouted, stepping onto the terrace.

"I think we'll be more help here," he said, taking his first shot, his blast killing the next man he found, a disagreeable-looking soldier wielding twin blades.

"What are you shooting at?" she asked, alarmed by his direction of fire.

"Just the hundreds of men storming the palace." He fired again, piercing the skull of a warrior heading toward the palace, dropping him before he passed below his view.

244

"What?" she snarled, taking his pistol from his grip, looking through the scope.

"Hey, careful with that," he said, shaking his pinched trigger finger, wondering how she didn't manage to kill either of them with that impulsive stunt.

Horrified by what she was seeing, Tosha started firing, her hurried shots striking over a wide area.

"Easy there, Wyatt Earp," he said, trying to take his pistol back, but she was having none of it.

"What's wrong with this stupid thing?" she snapped, sounding more like Raven with that utterance.

"Use the sights and squeeze the trigger. Don't jerk it, and it will hit what you're shooting at."

His advice had some effect; her next shot managing to hit one fellow in the foot, the poor wretch face planting on the unforgiving courtyard.

"You know, it would be better if I use that," he suggested, standing there, feeling useless.

"Shut up." She smiled, her next blast piercing an unfortunate man in the groin. *I could get used to this,* she thought wickedly, gaining confidence with each pull of the trigger.

"Since you're doing that…" He busied himself raising Brokov on the comm, seeing if he could shed some light on what was going on.

"Brokov," he said, watching curiously as Orlom, Kendra, and Tosha lit up the night air. He waited no more than a second before calling out again.

"Brokov."

Nothing.

One second later, he shouted, "Brokov! Hey, you there?" He lost his patience at the end after three seconds.

"We're a little busy, Rav," Brokov answered.

"Why don't you send one of your disc thingies to the palace so we know what we're up against?" he suggested.

"What part of busy do you not understand?" came the obvious reply.

"Not as busy as we are with this bunch of party crashers pouring into the castle." Raven made a face. A fire munition struck the battlements along the inner wall. He could make out people leaping from the wall, caked in flames. *That's gotta hurt* was the first thought that came to mind. He couldn't make sense if those burning were the good guys or bad guys, or good girls and bad guys to be more accurate. Or was it good girls and bad girls? Or good guys and bad girls?

"You should be used to these kinds of receptions by now." Brokov rolled his eyes.

"If you have time to make wise cracks, then you can't be too busy to lend a hand."

"Are you inside or outside?" Brokov asked, ignoring his remark.

"Standing on the terrace of the upper palace, watching my wife greet her guests," he said as Tosha dropped another warrior climbing the steps to the inner battlements below, his body tumbling down the stone stair, tripping two others in his path.

"If you're outside, tell Kendra and Orlom to hold their fire."

"Stop shooting, Tosh," Raven said, before hailing the others to do the same.

"Why?" Tosha said, ignoring the request.

"Give me that," he growled, snatching his pistol just as brilliant flashes of laser burst across the harbor, igniting a galley into a ball of flame. By the look of things, the *Stenox* was already back at its designated wharf. Within seconds of the first ship going up, a second and third were struck; the *Stenox*'s heavy lasers making quick work of them.

"Who are they targeting?" Tosha asked, surrendering the pistol back to Raven.

"Probably the ships belonging to your guests storming the castle," Raven said, scanning the harbor with his scope as two more ships went up in flames. "This is getting pretty ugly." He winced as a sixth ship lit up the night sky, a sheet of flame illuminating the surface of the harbor. Brokov was really taking it to them by the look of things. Raven noticed smaller laser fire just beyond the outer walls. His quick scan found the familiar visage of his towering metallic friend marching methodically through the streets of Bansoch, blasting anything in his path.

"Here comes the cavalry," Raven said, watching Zem leading Argos, Grigg, and Corry toward the main outer gate, through which the mercenaries were retreating.

Whoosh!

A large object swept overhead, spewing laser fire, while circling the courtyard.

"What is that?" Tosha asked, drawing close to his shoulder.

"Brokov's new toy," Raven said as the air ski zoomed back and forth, spraying fire at the base of the palace before circling back to their position.

Tosha stared in wonder as the air ski hovered at the edge of the terrace, where a green-scaled Enoructan and a Torry warrior jumped off, landing at their feet.

"Wasn't sure we'd make it on time. Glad you're still alive," Lorken said, sitting the driver seat as Ular and Lucas disembarked.

"Lorken?" Tosha asked, wondering what to make of his sudden appearance.

"Beautiful as always, Tosha. Thought you could use some help, so we came straight here from Darna's estate," Lorken commented briefly before speeding off.

"Darna's estate?" Tosha made a face.

"I'll explain later. Tosha, meet Ular and Lucas," Raven introduced his new comrades.

"Your Highness." Lucas bowed briefly.

"Princess," Ular greeted, his distinct watery voice taking her aback.

There was no time to converse further as they still had a battle to win, which Raven reminded her. They left the children in the care of the royal guards, hurrying off to aid the queen.

* * *

Zem greeted the men fleeing through outer gate with laser fire concentrated on that choke point. Argos and Grigg stood to either side adding their fire to his own. Corry stood behind him, sword in hand, guarding their back. The heavy traffic fleeing through the gate quickly reduced to a trickle and then nothing. Scores of men lay dead or dying before the gate, piled in heaps where they dropped. Corry spared a glance at the macabre scene; the smell of burnt flesh torturing her senses. She saw men crawling away; their blood trailing behind them. Many just flopped about on the ground in agony. The bodies were piled hip high all around the gate, hindering their path. The scene was reminiscent of Corell, a sight forever haunting her memory.

"Hold fire!" Zem commanded with his deep metallic voice. Slinging his rifle over his shoulder, he strode forth, his heavy feet sounding off the stone surface.

"Stay back!" Argos growled, putting a heavy hand on Grigg's shoulder.

"We should help him!" Grigg futilely tried to break free of Argos's grasp.

"Stay put and cover the battlements until we clear the gate!" Argos commanded, following Zem, blasting any body in his path that twitched.

Zem went to work, tossing bodies out of the way. Grigg's eyes grew as wide as saucers, watching the giant Earther grab hold of a body by the neck, tossing it thirty paces to his left. The sound of the body striking the ground echoed sickeningly. More followed. Zem tossed bodies to either side of the gate like straw dummies. A wounded man crawled out of the pile, brandishing a sword, trying to strike Zem's leg. Zem snatched the sword in the middle of the blade, snapping it in half before kicking the poor wretch in the chest, driving him backward. Corry winced as Zem grabbed hold of the man's arm, pressing his boot to his ribcage, tearing the appendage off at the shoulder, before beating him with it.

Argos joined him, tossing enough bodies away to clear their path; the others following them through the gate. Once there, they discovered even more horrors, with bodies strewn over the palace grounds, the clash of steel ringing upon the battlements above.

"Who do we kill?" Grigg asked, confounded by the clashing steel in the dim evening light, with female warriors similarly clad battling each other all around them.

"Kill the men, wait on the others," Corry advised, knowing the loyalties of the male combatants.

Before Zem could unsling his rifle, a mercenary rushed him with an ax, swinging the weapon with all his might. The ax bounced off Zem's head, to no effect. A look of dread transfixed the poor wretch's face. Zem snatched the fellow's throat, lifting him in the air; the ax falling from his grip. The man drew a dagger, jabbing futilely at Zem's arm. Zem crushed his throat with his right hand, grabbed his head with his left, twisted it off, tossing it over his shoulder.

Not to be outdone, Argos grabbed a man's sword arm, bending it back at the elbow.

"Agghh!" his victim screamed, his arm bent at an unnatural angle. Argos twisted him to the ground before ripping his shield from his other hand, smashing his head in with it.

Another charged him with a leveled spear, which Argos deflected with the shield, holding it by the edge with both hands, bashing his attacker in the face. The fellow went down like a sack of grain, either dead or unconscious. Grigg put a laser blast in the man's head for good measure after Argos moved on.

Whoosh!

The air ski swept down from above, hovering between Corry and Grigg at knee level.

"Climb on!" Lorken said to the two of them.

"What of Zem and Argos?" Corry asked. Their two comrades were drawing further ahead, cutting a path of corpses across the palace grounds.

"Let them have their fun," Lorken said, shaking his head as Zem tossed another screaming wretch through the air. The body smashed against the upper wall of a stone structure before dropping dead to the ground.

Grigg didn't hesitate climbing aboard, rightly figuring Argos wouldn't let him join in the fun anyway.

"Where are we going?" Corry asked, seating herself behind Grigg.

"Kendra and Orlom could use some help," Lorken said, the air ski lifting suddenly into the air.

* * *

Raven and Tosha fought their way back to the great hall, gathering reinforcements along the way, with Lucas and Ular close beside them, the sounds of battle guiding them. Tosha interceded more than once on their behalf, preventing bloodshed between the men and her mother's loyal guards, the sight of armed strangers during battle causing obvious reactions. Upon entering the south entrance of the great hall, they were greeted by the bodies of drugged guests sleeping wherever they fell and the sound of clashing steel across the chamber. Tosha's concern was drawn to the hostile warriors holding position at the queen's table along the north wall, with her mother nowhere in sight. The battle raged along the middle of the chamber, on either side of the broken floor, where Councilor Mearana led a host of loyal vassals against the treacherous alliance of Traditionalists and Reformist councilors.

"Raven." Tosha pointed out Mearana falling to her back in the middle of the floor, her opponent's spear closing upon her prone form.

Zip!

Raven's blast took the warrior between the breasts, burning a hole clean through, but she fell forward atop Mearana. The loyal councilor managed to push the dying woman off her, blood soaking her front.

"This will be easy," Raven said, taking up position behind one of the long tables, with Mearana's loyalists occupying the floor below with the rebels holding the north side of the hall. They could simply stay put, allowing him to cut down Darna's soldiers with ease. Of course, that would've been a good plan if his wife, Lucas, and Ular didn't take it upon themselves to join the fray.

Ular moved with unnatural speed, darting ahead of the others and through the loyalists' ranks. Before they could ascertain his loyalty, he already slipped into the rebel ranks, running his blade across the back of a guard's knee wearing the livery of House Gaina.

Why doesn't he just use his pistol? Raven wondered, observing the Enoructan warrior move through the ranks like water, cutting one down after another. He was reminded of a lesson back in his academy days; the history instructor told them that soldiers reverted to weapons they were most familiar with during combat. The warriors of Arax were no different. Raven went back to shooting, remaining where he could do the most good, firing over the loyalists' heads, a heavy stream of laser fire gutting the rebels' ranks farther afield.

Mearana gained her feet; the blood of her foe dripping from her garment. Her soldiers stepped forward, shielding her. The royal guard to her right went to her knees, a spear driven into her thigh. Mearana split the spear before its wielder could drive it deeper, smashing her shield into the woman's face. The royal guard was pulled back to safety by those behind them, another taking her place. Mearana was taken aback as the one taking the guard's place was a male, clad in a silver cuirass over the sea-blue tunic of the Torry Elite. Beside him stood Princess Tosha, blocking a spear thrust intended for Mearana. There was no time to identify the man as the battle raged around them. She caught sight of Ular cutting a path through their enemy, opening a fissure which they quickly exploited. Laser fire passed overhead, further decimating their foe.

"The queen is somewhere beyond the north entrance. We must press on!" Mearana informed Tosha as the rebels started to give way, their lines crumbling.

"What of Darna?" Tosha asked, driving her sword into the ribs of a warrior engaged with another, delivering four quick thrusts before backing a step, waiting for the blows to take effect.

"She followed the queen through the north entrance with her damnable sword."

The sound of cheers rang out behind them as Lucella Sarelis, the palace's mistress of arms and captain of the royal guards, led a unit of palace guards through the east entrance. Their arrival was too much for the remaining rebels to bear, their fore ranks overwhelmed, and back ranks decimated by Raven's fire. A few escaped through the north entrance behind the queen's table, but most were slaughtered where they stood.

* * *

Kendra was pleased when Lorken brought Corry to their position upon the upper battlements of Melida's tower but horrified that Grigg joined her. Wasn't it enough for her to be paired with Orlom? The two young gorillas hooted excitedly upon seeing each other, firing a few blasts into the air, jumping about on the stone platform. She wondered how they managed to do so without falling over the parapet. She and Corry exchanged sympathetic smiles.

"We should help the queen. The others have things well in hand below," Corry said.

Indeed, they did, by the look of things. The mercenary attack was all but squashed between Kendra and Orlom's laser fire and Argos and Zem tearing through their ranks. Not to mention Lorken circling the palace, shooting everything in sight.

Harroom!

The sound of horns beyond the outer gates heralded the arrival of more reinforcements, a royal telnic led by Glora Delvar, the gritty commander dispatching two units of infantry to hunt down any mercenaries that escaped into the city, leading the bulk of her telnic into the palace. Where could the fleeing men escape to anyway with most of their ships sunk by the *Stenox*?

"We must be wary of Darna's sword," Kendra explained, passing through the archway of the tower. The guards protected their backs following them down the stairwell.

"Her sword?" Corry didn't like the sound of that. Terin did mention that Darna harbored one of the lesser Swords of Light in her rural estate. Unfortunately, by the time he thought to tell her of it, they were already aboard the *Stenox*. Did Darna bring it with her? If she was planning a coup of this magnitude, she certainly would.

252

"A Sword of Light, if what you said of Terin is any indication, the queen has one as well."

"Lead the way."

* * *

"I should be out there fighting," Terin coughed, sitting at the console of the weapon's room, beside Brokov.

"You can barely stand. Besides, your girlfriend wouldn't let you," Brokov snickered, expanding another image on their viewscreen.

"It is my duty to fight for her, not her for me." Terin cringed, thinking of her fighting while he sat useless on the *Stenox*. He ignored the reference to his *girlfriend*, though the Earther's crude moniker aptly described their bond. She came for him, forsaking her duties to the realm to enlist the Earthers to rescue him. To know he held such prominence in her heart filled him with joy. Despite this revelation, doubt lingered in the deeper recesses of his brain. Did she only love the man he was? He wasn't the same as before. Darna and Deva stripped away so much of his former self, reducing him to this pitiful wretch. He failed her, falling captive and having his power stripped away by failing his God. He could feel the difference since he was struck by the lightning, the severing of the bond that linked him so closely with Yah. He felt weak…so very weak, a shell of his former glory. If he felt it, then Corry could see it. Would she feel the same for him now? Or would her love turn to pity and then loathing, quietly blaming him for what he lost?

"Terin?" Brokov drew him from his melancholy.

"Yes…yes?" he stammered.

"You should go lie down. You don't look so good," Brokov said, further expanding the image on his viewscreen, where a merchant galley rested along the wharves, observing its crew for any sign of mischief. After dropping off the others, he withdrew the *Stenox* farther from the wharves, giving him a clear view of the ships along the piers. The mercenary ships were obvious at the outset, their nervous crews preparing to sail off if their mission failed. Now the docks seemed quiet despite the burning wrecks littering the harbor.

"I am well," Terin said.

"You're half naked and shivering with a blanket wrapped around you," Brokov pointed out before spotting the merchant galley's deck crew hiding below its forecastle for some odd reason. He couldn't tell if the galley was part of the plot or not, so he held his fire. It wasn't going anywhere at the moment, so he would leave it to the harbor officials to sort out. He moved the viewer to another ship, a sleek hulled vessel built for speed. There was activity along its deck, the crew readying to lift anchor. Several men clad in dark armor, brandishing swords, emerged from the adjoining street, rushing up the gangplank, indicating the vessel's loyalties.

Zip!

Brokov sent a heavy laser across the ship's bow, cutting a severe gash below the waterline.

"How about a little music?" Brokov said, whistling along as a rendition of the Beach Boys' "Sloop John B" began blasting through the ship's amplifier.

"Drinking all night / Got into a fight…This is the worst trip I've ever been on," Brokov hummed, switching to the lighter lasers, targeting individuals clambering onto the wharf. Their vessel's bow was dipping severely.

Zip! Zip!

He struck two soldiers in heavy mail; their bodies dropping on the pier.

"You make it look so easy." Terin shook his head. His friend's merry tune was a stark contrast to the horrific scene unfolding before them.

"Technology makes many things look easy," Brokov agreed, before continuing to hum along the strangely merry tune.

It was surreal. The Earthers existed in a world so different from his own. Even in the direst of times, they acted as if nothing was a bother. Was there anything they couldn't do? How many times did he try to escape and fail? Yet they arrive and free him in a day, as if it were a simple thing.

"This ballad reminds me of Kato." Terin smiled at the memory of Kato singing similar tunes at Mosar, as men gathered around a cookfire after a hard day of battle.

The Earthers were each unique in their own ways, but in one thing, they were alike…they made the world a brighter place to dwell.

"This is one of his favorites." Brokov smiled. His next blast took another mercenary between the shoulder blades after raising an ax to strike at garrison soldiers now pouring onto the wharves.

"Were you able to see him before coming here?" Terin wondered how his friend was faring, or if he was still in Yatin with Prince Lorn.

"Kato?"

"Yes."

"No. We came straight here once your girlfriend showed up at Gregok with a crazy story about you being captured. Your father had a dream about where you were held."

"And you believed her?" Terin couldn't believe they dropped everything to travel to the other side of the world for a mere chance of finding him.

"We were coming here anyway, Terin. It's a good thing too because Raven would've been later than he already was."

"You still came, and for that"—he paused, his throat tightening with emotion—"for that…I thank you."

"We don't leave a friend behind, Terin. We've shed blood together, you and us. You helped rescue Cronus. We don't forget things like that. Besides, we all think of you as our kid brother."

"I never had a brother or sister until I met Cronus, Arsenc, and then you," he sighed, wondering if this was all a dream, for it was too wonderful to be true.

"Every soldier has a brother, if not by blood, then by shared experience."

"That sounds like something Kato would say." Terin smiled.

"Who do you think I heard it from? Certainly not my other crewmates, I'll tell you that." Brokov chuckled. Raven and Lorken weren't very deep thinkers when it came to emotions, and Zem was lacking altogether in that department.

"I wonder how Kato is faring?" Terin sighed.

"Fighting somewhere in Yatin with your prince, from the last reports we got or in Macon. We came upon a sea battle between Torry and Macon Fleets on our way here."

"Another war?"

The Torry Realm could ill afford another enemy.

"Don't worry. We lent a hand." Brokov went on to explain their brief action and the sinking of the Macon Fleet.

"So if Kato was there, he should be safe," Terin said.

"That was why we did it, for him and Cronus, but who knows if he was there or not."

"The last time I saw him was at Mosar when he wed the Lady Ilesa," he recalled the small ceremony on the bank of the Muva.

"Lucas mentioned that," Brokov said. "He said she is a matron healer accompanying the army."

"Yes. She is beautiful and very kind." Terin smiled at the memory.

"A perfect wife for him. It reminds me of something my father once told me—that a man gets the wife he deserves," Brokov said.

"Do you believe that?"

"Yes, look at Raven." He chuckled, recalling all the abuse Tosha heaped on him.

* * *

Letha blocked another strike, backing a step through the archway into the grand corridor that ran the length of the upper palace. Darna pressed her attack, striking again from her right; the queen matched her blow for blow, neither sword yielding to the other. Their blades alit with each strike, bathing their countenance in otherworldly light. Those loyal to the queen aligned behind her, backing away as the two drew near and advancing if they pulled away. Dozens loyal to Darna did likewise, guarding her back, following the duel into the grand corridor.

Deva remained closest to her mother, never more than a few paces away, her eyes fixed to her counterparts guarding the queen, a line of royal sentries clad in black armor over silver tunics. Her mother purchased the loyalty of many royal guards, but the queen inadvertently reassigned them to barracks outside the city. It was coin poorly spent, further proof of her mother's endless follies, including arranging a detestable marital match for Guilen, leading to his escape. That meant the Torry prince would learn they held Terin, forcing her to proceed with this plot far earlier than she originally planned. Deva ordered their guards to fan out across the corridor's expanse. The grand corridor was akin to a great hall with a high-arched ceiling and broad staircases jutting prominently along its course. The nearest stair was behind the queen's guards, where several royal archers were perched, holding their fire lest an errant shaft strike their queen.

Deva shook her head, disgusted by the turn of events. Their plan was ruined once the Earthers named her mother a traitor, costing them the element of surprise needed to kill the Earthers at the outset, preventing their crewmates from learning who truly killed them. Now the Earthers were loose in the palace, slaying their soldiers at will and their other crewmates fully aware of House Estaran's subterfuge. Horns sounded without, heralding the arrival of more royal forces. There was no sign of their mercenary allies, another of her mother's plans going awry. She recalled her mother's instruction should their plans sour, one last contingency for her to execute if failure was imminent.

Letha felt a surge of strength driving her to go on the offensive. A strike followed a back strike. Darna blocked them with laboring breath, the power of the sword exacting a heavy toll. The swords were forged to fight gargoyles, gifting their wielders unnatural stamina and awareness. The benefit was dulled when facing another Sword of light. It was now a matter of their own conditioning and skill, with Letha more than her match in that regard. Letha meant to challenge her treacherous cousin, to ask the purpose of her betrayal, but fatigue didn't allow her to waste breath on useless chatter. She looked beyond Darna's shoulder to her crowd of treacherous conspirators holding position like her own guards behind her, both groups waiting for a victor to emerge. Once more reinforcements arrived for either side, the temporary pause would end, the winning side attacking Darna or herself from behind.

The sounds of battle echoed whence they came, growing louder with every passing moment. Other shouts were heard from the adjoining corridors. She needed to finish this fight should the new arrivals prove hostile. Letha thrust her sword; Darna parried the strike while backing a step. A second thrust followed. Darna backed again, only stopping with a strange look upon her face, as if she was plunged in cold water.

"Agghh!" Darna cried out. A sword emerged from below her chest; blood dripped from its tip.

Letha immediately struck Darna's sword arm at the wrist; her hand and sword fell freely to the floor as she sank to her knees, falling face forward, slipping off the blade piercing her back.

"My queen!" Deva said, lowering the bloody sword while taking a knee.

* * *

The last thing Corry expected to see upon reaching the landing of the central stair was Deva driving her sword into her mother's back in the corridor below.

"What is happening?" Kendra asked, standing at her side with Grigg and Orlom close on their heels, anxious to shoot something.

Orlom aimed his pistol at Darna's soldiers facing Deva and the queen.

"Orlom, wait," Corry said as the traitors started dropping their swords before kneeling in surrender.

CHAPTER 9

Bansoch
Throne room of the queen's palace

Queen Letha sat her throne, surveying the diverse assemblage with a myriad of emotions—relief, joy, exhaustion, surprise, but mostly anger. Tosha sat the lesser throne beside her, her golden eyes staring heatedly upon the traitors kneeling in chains in the center of the chamber. Most of the treacherous councilors were slain in the battle, with most of their soldiers. She recognized the Reformists Neta Vasune and Voila Arisone among the prisoners, each lying upon the floor with severe injuries to their legs. How many of their fellow Reformers were caught up in their treason would be determined. Among the captives were three men of rank, each mercenaries whose true loyalties she would extract under pain of torture. Arch Councilor Lutesha Dorvena was the highest-ranking Traditionalist among the prisoners. She looked much abused with her left arm missing below the elbow and a severe gash across her right cheek. The likely chief conspirator lay dead at the foot of the throne, victim to her own daughter's blade. Said daughter stood apart from the others, unarmed and unchained. Deva's action would be weighed against her role in this treason.

Nearly a hundred royal guards were positioned about the chamber. Their once resplendent black armor and silver tunics were stained with blood, their battle-weary eyes alert to any threat. General Jani stood prominently among her loyalists gathered along the east wall.

The general led the defense of the inner wall and helped root out the palace guards aligned with Darna. Councilor Mearana stood beside her, her bravery and zeal unmatched among all of Letha's vassals.

The foreign ministers in attendance during the gala were alive, yet still asleep from their drugged wine. Nearly two thirds of the councilors attending the gala suffered the same fate. They were removed and brought to their homes to recover. Letha placed Bansoch under martial law, ordering everyone to remain in their homes while her soldiers searched for any who escaped the battle.

Standing along the west wall were most of the *Stenox* crew. Kendra and Orlom she knew, but Grigg, Argos, Ular, and Zem were introduced to her briefly after the battle. The one called Lorken was tending their wounded with a healing device of wondrous power. She would meet them in private after the matters at hand were settled. Most surprisingly to her was who stood with the Earthers, her niece, Princess Corry, and Lucas of the Torry Elite. To discover that she came here in the company of Raven without presenting herself before now raised many questions, which Letha would have answered before this audience was dismissed. And of course, there was Raven. He belonged next to Tosha as her consort but stood with his crew, as he had much to account for, specifically how his crew came to learn of Darna's treachery.

"The night grows late, and we are weary to see its end, so I shall dispense with pleasantries and introductions, neither of which are appropriate at this time. General Jeni, please step forth and address the assemblage!" Letha commanded.

"My queen." Elise Jani bowed reverently upon reaching the dais. "The palace is secure. Hundreds of the conspirators are slain, along with an equal number of mercenaries. I oversaw the battle at the gates of the inner palace until we were beset by warriors of House Dorvena, from behind. At that juncture, the gate was breeched by the male mercenaries. The enemy was stopped shortly after by the Earthers positioned upon the tower of Melida, allowing our troops time to deal with the traitors at our back, before repelling the invaders. We were soon aided by other Earthers assailing the mercenaries from without and reinforcements from the harbor garrison. Most of the mercenary army were slain. We've counted seven hundred and twenty-three dead, and one hundred thirteen captured thus far."

"Seven hundred is a very high number, General," Letha said, considering most casualties in any battle are less than 20 percent, except for gargoyle engagements.

"The Earthers' weapons were quite…effective," the general stated dryly.

"Not just their weapons," Telnic Commander Delvar said, receiving disapproving glares from her fellow commanders for her interruption.

"Speak to what you said, Commander," Letha ordered, her gaze drifting to the Earthers standing off to the side.

"The metal giant tore men apart with his bare hands. We saw him toss others through the air like straw dolls. The large gorilla did much the same. It was quite fascinating to observe, oh Queen," Glora Delvar said with clear admiration, her opinion of the Earthers much changed since first greeting them upon their arrival.

"Zem and Argos like to show off," Raven explained, giving an innocent shrug.

"The use of a laser with possible friendly assets positioned behind your target represented unnecessary risk. Argos and I wisely chose to use other means of subduing the threat," Zem's metallic voice boomed across the chamber.

"I briefly inspected their handiwork, oh Queen. It was gruesome but effective," Lucella Sarelis, captain of the royal guard, stated, standing behind the throne with her arms crossed over her chest, surveying the assemblage for any threat.

"Do you have anything else to add, General?" Letha asked.

"I have not included among the dead the crews of the merchant vessels sunk by the *Stenox*. The last count is fifteen vessels burning or sunk, my queen," Jani stated.

Letha looked again in Raven's direction, her face masking the thousand questions running through her mind.

"It was pretty easy for Brokov to identify which ships those idiots came from," Raven added.

"Have we discovered the origin of the mercenaries?" Letha asked, though she had her own suspicions regarding that.

"All are free swords, oh Queen," Jani added.

"What of you, Deva? Any mercy depends on your complete honesty," Letha asked.

"The mercenaries were recruited by a Benotrist agent named Draken, who met with my mother at her estate, planning their treason with Councilors Vasune, Arisone, Gaina, and Dorvena!" Deva confessed.

"LIAR!" Lutesha Dorvena shouted. Neta Vasune and Voila Arisone chorused the charge.

"You wish to refute her claim, Lutesha?" Letha asked.

"She omits her role in this treason!" Lutesha growled.

"You admit to your treason then?" Letha asked, Lutesha withering under her own confession.

"Yes," Lutesha snarled.

"And you confess to attending this meeting?" Letha pushed.

"I did, but she was a part of it!" Lutesha said, her confession drawing gasps from the assemblage.

"Deva, fully explain your involvement!" Letha commanded.

Deva went on to explain her mother's recruitment of ranking Reformist and Traditionalist councilors, along with Benotrist agents, to usurp the queen. She further explained that the mercenaries were to attack the palace from without, and when the queen's soldiers went to quell the assault, the treasonous councilors would attack from within, killing the Earthers first before they could inform their fellow crewmembers on the *Stenox*.

"Did your mother not consider the Earthers aboard the *Stenox* would seek revenge?" Letha asked.

"She planned to place the blame on her Reformist allies, who were to be slain at the battle's end. They would be blamed for the entire coup, and my mother would present herself as defender of the throne," Deva said, drawing heated glares from the Reformists Neta Vasune and Voila Arisone, knowing they were played for fools.

Deva then detailed what Darna planned to do with the royal family. Tosha, Letha, and the two princes would've been given to the

Benotrists, whisked away, while Ceana would be a ward of House Estaran, with Darna ruling in her name.

"My father would never consent to that!" Tosha snarled, tempted to gut Deva where she stood.

"Oh, yes he would," Letha said dryly.

"Where's Draken now?" Raven asked.

"It is not your place to interrupt, Consort," Lucella Sarelis warned.

"You shall have a chance to speak freely, Raven," Letha graciously stated, stopping him before he said something offensive.

Raven threw up his hands, letting them have their say.

"My son by marriage has a point. Was Nels Draken among the dead or captured?" Letha asked.

"I will set my soldiers to the task, oh Queen, but we do not know what he looks like," General Jani offered.

"I know what he looks like, as does my consort's crew," Tosha said, wanting to know the level of her father's involvement in this coup.

"Very well. We will have one of you review the dead and the prisoners for any sign of him. As for you, Deva, why did you betray your mother?" Letha asked, curious of her motive. She didn't miss the look of pure loathing on Corry's face, the Torry princess glaring hatefully at the heir of House Estaran.

"I spoke with Mother, trying to convince her to forsake this folly, oh Queen. I warned her that it would destabilize our Federation, opening us to attack, but she rebuked me, threatening to disinherit me for my younger sister if I did not support her treason. Yes, I betrayed my mother, but to obey her would be treason to the crown. When I saw her occupied with your duel, I took the first opportunity I had to end her madness," Deva stated with enough passion to convince much of the assemblage.

"Are there any other crimes of House Estaran still unspoken? Answer now or be held to account?" Letha warned.

"I have stated truthfully, oh Queen. Any further crimes committed by Guardian Darna against the crown are unknown to me," Deva answered carefully.

"Very well," Letha said, regarding Deva. Her judgment required a delicate balance.

Deva slew her mother, choosing loyalty to the crown over her house, but did she do so because their cause was lost? Did Darna instruct Deva to do so beforehand if their plans went sour? Letha couldn't miss Corry's heated glare—her niece's gaze fixed solely on Deva—wondering what that was about.

"Any other words from those accused before I pass sentence?" Letha asked, observing the sorry state of so many councilors, who once held her esteem.

Silence.

"Very well," Letha concluded.

The lesser houses and mercenaries could be dealt with later, after her inquisitors extracted more information from them. The greater houses, however, required immediate judgment, quashing any chance of their treason spreading or their vassals rallying to free them.

"House Estaran's sins have not been fully vetted, oh Queen!" Corry stepped forward, drawing every eye to her and hers to Deva.

"Present yourself, Princess Corry, and speak to this charge!" Letha called her forth, curious of her sudden appearance during the battle and her connection to the Earthers.

Corry approached the dais, kneeling before the throne before given leave to stand.

"I have many questions for you, Princess Corry, the first of which is why are you here? How did you arrive? And why have you not presented yourself earlier? Each of these you shall answer after you explain your charge against House Estaran," Letha ordered.

"House Estaran is guilty of grievous crimes not only against the Federation but the Torry Realm!" Corry turned, pointing an accusatory finger at Deva, whose face was a mask of indifference, save for her eyes, which stared daggers at the Torry princess.

Deva recalled Corry's last visit to their isle, before she was taken captive by pirates. She felt nothing toward her then, but now she looked upon her with jealous hatred. This was the woman that claimed Terin's heart and loyalty, driving his rejection of her. Deva was curious what crime she would accuse her of. Even if they learned of Terin, it would take more than the single day that they spent at Bansoch to discover his whereabouts. She had time to move him to an even more secluded location, beyond prying eyes. Now that her mother was dead, she might spare his eyes. She would return him to her estate once the Earthers departed. All these plans crumbled to ruin with Corry's next utterance.

"House Estaran, including Guardian Deva, have taken Torry slaves, purchased through intermediaries smuggling their captives to the black markets of Bansoch. Most notable of their purchases was Terin Caleph, champion of the Torry Realm!" Corry declared, drawing a myriad of reactions throughout the chamber.

"How do know this, Corry?" Letha asked, leaning forward on her throne, waiting expectantly upon her every word.

"Because, oh Queen, we rescued him this very night from Darna's estate. It was Terin that told us of the plot against the throne and the plan to kill Raven," Corry explained, her eyes sweeping the assemblage, gauging their reaction to this revelation.

"And where is Terin now?" Tosha asked, coming to her feet.

Corry was taken aback by her sudden interest. Did Tosha know of her relation to him?

"He is aboard the *Stenox*, recovering," Corry said, giving Deva a dark look.

"Recovering from what?" Tosha asked, giving Deva an equally cold stare.

Corry couldn't quickly answer, her throat tightening with emotion. At this, Zem stepped forth to summarize Terin's injuries.

"Upon finding Terin in a holding cell in the subterranean levels of Guardian Darna's estate, our extraction team discovered injuries inflicted upon him, likely as punishment. The subject suffered 3rd-degree lacerations across his back, severe burns upon his chest and thigh. Lorken administered immediate aid to Terin's back, restoring him to a state where he could walk of his own volition. Upon returning to the *Stenox*, we conducted a brief but thorough examination, finding enlarged kidneys and bruising to his lung tissue. He was severely malnourished, with an impaired mental state. All conditions will improve with our tissue regenerator and proper rest and nour-ishment," Zem explained. Most of the assemblage, distracted by his metallic voice, missed half of what he said.

Corry closed her eyes, recalling his pitiful state when they res-cued him.

Tosha stormed down the steps of the dais, striking Deva across the face, her countenance frightening to behold, unsettling many of the onlookers. Nearly everyone in the assemblage wondered the cause of her strong reaction.

"Tosha, back away!" Letha commanded. Her daughter reluc-tantly obeyed; with Deva staring on in confusion.

"Speak to this charge, Deva!" Letha said sternly.

"My mother purchased Terin from the slaver Captain Veneva, who found him upon a beach at Carapis, where he was washed ashore after the battle. Veneva brought Terin and numerous other captives to Bansoch, selling the Yatins and Benotrists at auction and the Tories to my mother," Deva said.

"Torry slaves are forbidden by royal decree. Are you not aware of this?" Letha asked.

"I am aware, oh Queen. I was unaware of my mother's purchase until Terin was brought to our manse and presented to me as a mate. I later learned that he was Torry. Since he was to be my consort, his status as a slave would have been altered thus allowed by royal decree, or so my mother explained," Deva said, hoping she could talk her way out of this mess.

"Your mother was wrong as she was in many things. Were you aware that Terin is the Torry champion?" Letha asked.

"He spoke of it after coming into my possession."

Letha shook her head as did much of the assemblage.

"What else did you learn of him?" Tosha challenged.

"Speak truthfully, Deva!" Letha warned.

"He made extraordinary claims, oh Queen. Should I believe them, you would think me mad."

"Speak them!" Letha ordered.

"He claims…he claims he is of the blood of Kal," Deva said, half expecting Tosha to strike her again or Corry, by the murderous look in her eyes.

Several in the chamber laughed at the mention of the legendary king, but Letha's deadly serious face quelled their amusement.

"And do you believe him, Deva?" Letha asked.

Deva didn't know what she believed, wondering how to answer.

"There…there is something strange about him, some power that…I don't know, oh Queen." She shrugged.

"What power did you see in him?" Corry asked.

"I learned after the fact that my mother tested him."

"Tested? How?" Tosha asked.

"With gargoyle captives, pitting them against Terin."

The crowd stirred at this, more evidence of Darna's subterfuge. Gargoyles were forbidden on the isle, even captive ones.

"A test he obviously passed," Letha said icily.

"Yes, oh Queen. The creatures are terrified of him."

"Why was he punished?" Corry asked.

"Which punishment, Cousin?" Deva lifted her chin, declaring their kinship before the entire assemblage. The statement drew curious looks from those unaware of Letha and Lore's shared parentage.

"I saw him scourged! Whipped senseless by that foul woman, Selenda!" Corry hissed; her hand wrapped tightly around the hilt of her sheathed sword.

"How could you see it?" Deva made a face.

"The Earthers have many fanciful tools. One of them allowed me to see what you did. The woman who administered the punishment is dead by my hand before I slew your father!" Corry said.

"No!" Deva screamed, lunging at Corry before Tosha stepped between them, her sword at Deva's throat.

"Stand back, Deva!" Letha ordered. Deva's breaths grew labored, her eyes frantic, looking to Corry then Tosha and back to Corry.

This was a battle Deva could not win, causing her to back away, reason suppressing passion.

"Why would you kill my father?" Deva asked, angry tears staining her cheeks.

"He confessed to ordering Terin beaten. The champion of the Torry Realm beaten like an animal. The punishment is death, and you will do well to remember it!" Corry declared, confessing her own guilt for passing judgment on the patriarch of House Estaran.

"Corry, stand aside!" Letha commanded. "You have stepped beyond your authority. Only the crown can pass judgment on its subjects."

Corry looked stricken but relented, stepping back.

"As for you, Deva, I am troubled by your claims, but your mother's guilt overwhelms everything. Despite this, you knowingly kept a son of Torry North slave in your house, the Torry champion no less." Letha stood, looking out over the crowd, wishing the entire realm could hear what she was to say.

"Our Federation was not established to gain retribution upon men for the crimes of the Soch kings of old. General Melida and her sister, Telisa, did not journey from ancient Tarelia for the sole purpose of freeing female slaves and bringing the men of Soch low. Like all generals of the Tarelian order, they were sent to contest the gargoyles, whom the Soch were inadvertently aligned, by waging war upon the gargoyles' enemies. Melida and Telisa were unique in that they were given *two* Swords of Light to achieve this end—the very swords of my house and House Estaran." Letha looked down at the base of the dais, where Darna's sword rested, before descending the steps, lifting up the sister sword to her own, holding it aloft, the light of the chamber illuminating its blade.

"These swords were given us to contest our true foe," she continued, her gaze running the length of the blade before sweeping the crowd. "With these swords, we established our Sisterhood, to further that purpose. We freed all the women kept in bondage by the Soch kings of old, to further that purpose. Neither our Federation or the liberation of our sisters take precedence over our true *purpose!*" Letha roared. Her eyes swept the assemblage with terrible intensity, stopping on those of the traitors, who would've aligned with Tyro. "Know this, and know it well, if I could defeat the gargoyles by enslaving every man on Arax, I would do so. If I could destroy the gargoyles by freeing every male slave on this isle, I would do so. If I could destroy the gargoyles by sacrificing our Federation, and dooming each of us to death or slavery, I would do so. *Nothing* is greater than our original commission. As queen, I have allowed the forum to oversee the scale of our involvement upon the continent. No more. From this day forth, I declare queen's law until the crisis upon the continent is resolved!" Letha proclaimed, granting the crown complete military and diplomatic authority.

A chorus of whispers swept the chamber, some taken aback, others aghast, but most relenting to the need of it.

Letha set the sword back down upon the floor, retaking her seat upon the throne. There was still the matter of passing judgment upon the traitors and what to do with Deva.

"I shall defer judgment upon you, Deva, daughter of Darna, now 4th guardian of the realm," Letha said, drawing severe scowls from both her niece and daughter.

"She is guilty, Mother," Tosha protested.

"What of her crimes against the Torry Realm?" Corry added, standing at Tosha's side.

"I defer judgment to the one most aggrieved. I summon Terin to stand as her judge!"

* * *

Terin was surprised when Corry returned to the ship with Tosha, finding him upon the bridge with Brokov. No sooner had they stepped onto the bridge, Corry rushed into his arms, only letting go as Tosha stepped near, staring intently into his sea-blue eyes, as if searching for something.

"Princess Tosha, I..." he barely uttered before she took him into her arms, holding him possessively as Corry looked on with happy tears. Brokov stood back, wondering if they all hit their heads on something. Tosha eventually pulled briefly away, cupping his face in her hands.

"If I only knew you were here—" She shook her head, her golden eyes red with tears.

"I…I thought you might be angry with how we parted," Terin said, recalling his escape from Fera.

"I was only angry with Raven for risking everyone's life. If something happened to you, Father would be inconsolable," Tosha said.

"Your father?" A look of horror passed his face.

"He knows, Terin. Jonas is his son, making you my brother-son…my blood." Tosha held his face, not letting go.

Terin looked pleadingly to Corry, wondering if she could forgive him for that dark kinship.

"I already knew, Terin. Your father told Torg and I everything." Corry smiled, placing her right hand over Tosha's, pressing it harder against his cheek.

"You know, and you still…" he stumbled over the words.

"And I still love you, you foolish boy." She smiled.

"She traveled across the world to rescue you, Nephew. My cousin is deserving of your love and devotion!" Tosha said sternly.

"I am hers." He surrendered, looking back and forth between the two forceful women. Terin was informed of Corry's relation to Tosha after his rescue, recalling Torg mentioning King Lore's sister but not revealing who that was.

"Very good. Now let me have a look at you," Tosha said, stepping back after removing the blanket he had wrapped around his shoulders. She stifled a gasp at his burned chest, where they covered his warrior's brand with a crude marking. He was naked above the waist, his ragged kilt barely covering his essentials. Her blood boiled finding the brand upon his upper left thigh, a common slave marking. She shared a hateful look with Corry, both shaking their heads in disgust.

"This will not do. We shall find something in the palace for you to wear before presenting you to the queen," Tosha said.

"Presenting?" Terin drew away, a look of horror torturing his face.

"The queen summons you to court. You will state everything that happened since Carapis. Do not omit a single detail. Then you shall stand in judgment of Deva. My mother insists her fate rests in your hands," Tosha explained.

"I…" Terin turned away, his heart pounding in his ears. "I can't go back." He lowered his head, his back to them.

"Terin, it is safe now. Queen Letha is just and true. You saved her life with your warning. No harm shall befall you," Corry said.

"Darna is dead, Terin. She will never harm you again," Tosha added.

"Dead? How?" He turned, facing them again.

"By Deva's hand," Tosha said.

"Deva killed her mother?" He couldn't believe it.

"Yes, and makes bold claims of opposing her mother's treason. Only you can speak to this falsehood," Tosha said.

"Why cannot the queen pass judgment? I just want to leave." He felt so tired.

"She has, by naming you the final arbiter. If you refuse, Deva will be set free," Tosha warned.

"I…I can't go back. I don't ever want to see her again." He looked at them with the saddest eyes.

"Listen to me, Nephew. You are of the blood of kings and legends. You are further shielded by my protection. You are safe now. You must come and pass judgment on your tormentor," Tosha said.

"Go on, Terin. We got you covered," Brokov added.

Terin sighed, overcome by the memories of Darna's abuse, tormenting his every thought. Part of him still believed this was all a dream, and stepping foot on the island would bring it to an end, and he would again wake in Darna's chains.

"All right, what's the holdup?" Raven said, entering the bridge.

"Raven?" Terin tried to smile but was overcome with emotion, recalling the last time he saw his friend on the roof of Fera.

"It's me, Champ," Raven said, stepping between the ladies, ruffling Terin's head.

"Champ?" Tosha gave her husband a disapproving glare.

"It's short for *champion* since the kid got himself promoted since we last saw each other," Raven pointed out.

"Your cute little nicknames are disrespectful," Tosha said, stepping protectively to Terin's side.

"I am no longer champion of the realm." Terin lowered his head.

"You are free, Terin. The title is still yours and belongs to no other," Corry reassured him.

"You don't understand. The power has left me. Yah has forsaken me," he said, sighing sadly.

"How do you know?" Corry asked.

"I…I disobeyed him, and he…he left me. I can no longer feel his presence. I can't even lift a weapon," he confessed.

"That don't make much sense, Champ. Why don't you explain it a little better?" Raven said.

"I…I escaped, myself and several others, including Darna's son, Guilen," Terin began, detailing the events that followed, including the lightning strike, and Yah's words of warning. They were taken aback by his revelation. None truly understood his mystical connection to the ancient deity but comprehended what he lost.

"That's why you were beaten?" Raven asked, giving him a good look over.

"Yes, for that, I was scourged, but it paled to what Darna truly planned to…" Terin's voice trailed, not wishing to think of it.

"What did she plan to do, Terin?" Tosha asked, barely concealing her rage.

"She…" He couldn't answer.

"The bitch can't hurt you anymore, Terin, so just spit it out," Raven said.

"To prevent me from ever escaping again, she was going to… blind me." He lowered his head.

"WHAT?" Corry and Tosha growled in unison.

"When was she planning to do that?" Brokov asked.

"She boasted that it would happen after she presented me with Raven's head, wanting it to be the last thing I ever saw," he said, sharing a look with Raven.

"She was ambitious. I'll give her that." Raven shrugged, not appearing too worried about what might have happened.

"She might've succeeded if you didn't warn us," Brokov said.

"Yeah, I owe you one for that, Champ." Raven ruffled his hair again, drawing looks of disapproval from Tosha and Corry and a shy smile from Terin.

"Deva must pay for what she did. Her claims of opposing her mother's ambitions are clearly false," Tosha scowled.

"She will escape justice unless Terin answers the queen's summons," Corry said, touching a hand to Terin's shoulder.

"Then what are we waiting for?" Raven asked.

"I...I don't know..." Terin shook his head.

"Listen, kid, we got your back. All your enemies are dead or chained. No one's going to mess with you with me around. Not to mention Arg, Lorken, Zem, Ular, this idiot." Raven jerked a thumb toward Brokov.

"You are my blood, Terin. You are protected by my sword and my oath," Tosha affirmed.

"You are mine, Terin Caleph. I am a granddaughter of Queen Theresa and claim you before any other. You must treat with my aunt, the queen, and serve justice to Deva," Corry said, moving her hand to his cheek.

"Don't make me carry you," Raven warned.

"Very well," Terin sighed, knowing when he was beaten.

* * *

Upon reaching the palace, they were immediately ushered into the throne room. Tosha's plan to dress him in decent attire was dismissed; the queen demanding to see him in his current state.

"Courage, Terin." Tosha lifted his chin as they stood outside the throne room, before taking his hand, leading him into the grand chamber.

Corry was at their side while Raven slapped him on the back before stepping off to the side, joining his crewmates.

Terin took a deep breath, feeling every eye upon him, especially the queen sitting the throne, observing him with strangely inviting eyes as they drew near. As he stopped at the base of the dais, his eyes found Deva standing off to his right, watching him with guarded apprehension. He didn't miss Darna's corpse lying before the dais, beside her sword, or the curious stares from most of the assemblage

273

or the concerned looks on the faces of the conspirators, kneeling in chains. Upon seeing the queen, he started to kneel.

"Stand, Terin," Letha kindly ordered. "If what I have learned is true, you have done enough kneeling as of late. Tosha, I believe a formal introduction is warranted for our esteemed guest."

"My queen, I present Terin Caleph, champion of the Torry Realm!" Tosha declared.

"Let me have a better look at you." Letha motioned him to step closer. She sensed his unease, standing in their presence, half naked with only a ragged kilt barely covering him.

Terin faltered stepping beside the Sword of Light, the mystical power of the blade punishing him for drawing near, driving him to his knees. Corry and Tosha hurried forth, helping him to his feet.

"What ails you, Terin?" Queen Letha asked with genuine concern.

"My apologies, Your Majesty, I am…I am afflicted," he sighed, warily regarding the sword off his left, feeling Yah's presence emanating from its ancient blade.

"Afflicted? Is this more of Darna's treachery?" Letha looked sternly to Deva, who withered under her stare.

"Nay, Your Majesty, it is of my own doing, my own failure," Terin confessed. There were enough sins to lay at Deva's feet; he needn't ascribe her his own sins, for Yah would only punish him further for lying.

"Your own doing?" Letha raised a curious brow.

"Yes, Your Majesty," he said, feeling the eyes of the assemblage on his back.

"I want to hear everything that transpired since Carapis, Terin, in full view of this court," Letha briefly regarded the small sea of faces hanging on their every word.

"Can you do that, Terin?" Tosha asked kindly, touching a hand to his shoulder.

Terin just wanted to crawl into a hole somewhere and disappear, to forget his miserable existence, but looking back over his shoulder at Tosha and then Corry, he stiffened his resolve. *Yah, grant me the strength and words to do this,* he called out in his mind. "I awoke after the battle in the hold of a slaver ship…" he began, detailing his ordeal to the best of his garbled memory. As much as it pained him to recall the painful humiliations, it was equally unbearable for Tosha and Corry. Corry cringed thinking of him suffering so, scrubbing floors, slaving in the scullery, and bowing lowly to people unworthy to clean his feet. Tosha and Letha shared looks of disgust, thinking of him suffering such indignity so close to the palace, by their closest kin, no less. Deva listened with a mask of indifference. Terin's testimony damned her with his every utterance, her fellow conspirators staring daggers at her, realizing the extent of Darna's machinations. Terin's revelation of his Kalinian blood and Darna's plan to exploit it drew the gravest reactions from those looking on. Lutesha Dorvena shook her head in disgust for not knowing Terin's true identity. Councilor Mearana and General Jani felt ashamed by his treatment, neither considering the plight of slaves brought to the island before.

Terin finished his tale with his rescue, after going into his escape and recapture, as well as Darna's plans to blind him, which drew audible gasps from the chamber. It wasn't an unusual punishment for runaway slaves, but to do such a thing to the Torry champion was a grievous act. Once he was finished, all eyes fell on Deva, who stood before the dais, statue still.

"Do you contest what Terin said, Deva?" Letha asked.

"I opposed my mother's treatment of him, my queen, but I was fully aware of who he was," she confessed.

"So be it. For your crimes against the throne, I shall spare your life, but for the crimes against the Torry champion, your fate rests upon his judgment!" Letha declared.

Deva paled, looking to Terin, wondering what he would do.

"Give the word, Terin, and I shall order her stricken!" Letha said.

He stared at the floor, his thoughts a maelstrom of emotions. He recalled the thousand slights and humiliations and the endless drudgery slaving in her presence. How he longed for this moment, to exact righteous judgment on his tormentor. The endless days suffering at her family's hands repeated in his mind time and again; his anger building with each recollection. He felt the natural calling of

Darna's sword, urging him to pick it up and skewer Deva where she stood. The hunger for vengeance grew unabated, coursing his flesh, consuming him like a raging fire.

Mercy, the unseen voice whispered in his mind, tempering his vengeance. Was it Yah warning him or his own delusion? He pushed the thought from his brain, his anger building again, overwhelming his senses.

"AGGHH!" He was screaming, falling to his knees, the glow of Darna's sword exploding in blinding light, forcing the assemblage to shield their eyes.

Letha crossed her arms over her face; Tosha and Corry collapsed, trying to reach Terin. Deva was on her face, trembling in terror. The traitors were prostrate; the light of the sword piercing their flesh. Councilor Mearana turned away, squeezing her eyes shut; the light unbearable to behold. Raven and the others looked away, awed by its brilliant power.

"Mercy," Terin whispered, not begging for mercy but granting it. His pain washed away; the darkness gripping his heart melting like snow in a summer rain. The glow of the sword abated, dimming as Terin gained his feet. The crowd opened their eyes, staring dumb-struck as the Torry champion stood over the Sword of Light, reaching down to grasp it. Terin couldn't work his fingers around the hilt, as if the ancient metal was fused to the floor. The sword no longer hurt him but still denied him, as if it weighed a mountain. Terin released a sigh, overcome by a presence he did not feel a moment before. It was but a sliver of what he once felt, but the tiny part occupying his heart coursed his being with otherworldly power. He knew it was Yah, the deity returning, albeit in the smallest of measures.

It was then he realized everyone was staring at him, fully aware of the power he invoked in the sword. He found Deva on her knees but three paces away, looking up at him with pallid lips, overcome by what she just witnessed, believing her young life was at its end.

Mercy, he thought, repeating what Yah so clearly whispered in his mind. Could he grant such to Deva? Could he forgive her the pain she caused? Where had vengeance led him the last time? Following his own desires and wicked heart led to chains and suffering. Only

Yah's intervention spared him further torment; the deity sending the Earthers to save him. Terin stepped forth, standing over Deva; his face betraying the conflict that raged within but moments before until it eased into serene calm. He placed his right palm on her head.

"I would condemn you for your crimes, Deva, but Yah advises *mercy*. Yah has declared his will for all of you to hear, just as his glory shone for all of you to see. You shall not die at my hand, Deva, nor suffer as you have made me suffer. I give you back to your queen. She is wise and fair and has seen Yah's power, just as you have. Let his will guide you from this day onward or suffer for your disobedience as I have," Terin declared, for all the assemblage to hear, before collapsing.

Tosha and Corry hurried to his side before Zem strode forth, scooping him into his arms, following the two princesses out of the chamber.

Queen Letha stood from her throne, overlooking the sea of faces waiting upon her words with rapt attention.

"Lutesha Dorvena, you are charged with treason. Do you deny it?" Letha asked.

The arch councilor refused to acknowledge her.

"Bring her forth!" Letha ordered her guards, who dragged her to the base of the dais, forcing her head to the floor. Letha descended the wide steps, drawing her sword, bright golden light emitting from its mysterious blade. With one fell strike she struck Lutesha's neck, her head rolling across the floor.

"Neta Vasune! You stand accused of treason. State your innocence or suffer judgment!" Letha ordered her brought forth.

"I'll not bow to your tyranny, Letha. You are a false Sister, tainted by foreign blood, just as your daughter and granddaughter. Curse your—" Neta shouted.

The guards having enough forced her head to the floor before Letha removed it.

"I shall not suffer the bitter ramblings of traitors this night! Speak facts to your innocence or die in silence. Voila Arisone, you stand accused..." Letha continued executing every treacherous councilor in the chamber, ordering the captured males removed for interrogation, leaving only Deva to be judged.

"Deva Estaran! You stand accused of treason and crimes against the Torry Realm. I do not know your intent for killing your mother. It was either an act of loyalty to the throne or was ordered by your mother in the event your cause appeared lost. I delegated your punishment to the one most aggrieved by your actions, but his God intervened, as every soul gathered here bore witness. I ask of you again, Deva, what motive drove you to slay your mother? Swear it before Yah. May you suffer his wrath for speaking false!" Letha ordered.

Deva spoke truthfully against her will, an otherworldly power controlling her tongue. "*My* mother ordered me to strike her dead should our cause prove lost. I am guilty of treason, my queen." She sunk to her knees, feeling every eye upon her.

"As queen, I condemn you to death, but Yah demands mercy, for reasons I dare not question. Terin spared your life, and your crimes against him are many times those against me. Our world stands upon the precipice, beset by Tyro's legions, and should we falter, we condemn our people to thousands of years of darkness. This is something your mother either ignored or was willfully ignorant. I ask you, Deva, do you seek redemption, true redemption? Speak truthfully before Yah, he who granted you mercy."

"I...I ask your forgiveness, oh Queen. I...I seek redemption and will endure whatever punishment you declare, with humble acceptance." Deva bowed her head to the floor, overcome with a power she could not comprehend. *Was this Yah choosing my words?* she thought to herself.

"Very well. You shall state the full crimes of House Estaran before the ruling forum. You shall denounce the Traditionalist bloc and align your house with Councilor Mearana. House Estaran will be stripped of their guardianship until a time the throne deems it worthy. The sword of your ancestors will be returned to this royal house. Upon the redemption of House Estaran, it shall be returned through bonds of marital union to the throne. Every mine and galley owned by House Estaran is forfeit to the crown. Every slave held by House Estaran shall be inspected, manumission granted to any holding Torry blood. Every marriage of House Estaran shall require royal oversight. And lastly, House Estaran is stripped of all military and garrison authority," Letha declared.

CHAPTER 10

Terin awoke to the smell of fresh baked bread, finding himself abed in a spacious, richly decorated chamber with dark timbers crisscrossing the ceiling and carved statues to each corner. It was the most peaceful sleep he ever had, and if he dreamed, he didn't remember it.

"You're awake," a strong feminine voice greeted him.

He turned his head, finding Queen Letha sitting his bedside, with Tosha standing beside her. "Your Majesty," he said, trying to sit up but stopped by her firm hand.

"Rest easy, Terin. You are safe here," Tosha said.

"Where..." he began to ask.

"This was your grandfather's chamber, for the brief time we were wed, and private quarters of the queen's consort going back many years," Letha said.

"My grandfather." He shook his head, wishing no one knew of that.

"He wasn't always what you now see, Terin. He was a good man once, long ago," Letha sighed.

"Mother," Tosha disagreed, always defensive of her sire's reputation.

"And now he knows about me but how?" Terin wondered.

"The necklace that Morac tore from your throat. My father recognized it right away," Tosha said.

"Oh." Terin cringed, fearing it might be so.

"It wasn't difficult to surmise, especially when news of your unique abilities reached his ears. Only the blood of Kal invokes such

280

power and only a son of Joriah could explain your existence," Tosha said.

"Joriah?" Terin made a face.

"Your father's true name. Jonas is a crude attempt to conceal his given name," Letha said.

"What did he say when he learned who I was?" Terin asked.

"He is most keen on retrieving you," Tosha said.

"He can have me if he makes peace. I am loyal to the Torry throne."

"He doesn't care, Terin. He is possessive of what is his and what he believes is his, something my daughter has yet to understand." Letha gave Tosha a knowing look, to which Tosha rolled her eyes.

"He must know that I would never serve him," Terin said.

"He searched for your father and grandmother for many years before giving them up for dead and marrying me. He spoke of his first wife with great longing, grieving for her and what might have been. I thought I could change him, turn him from his dalliance with the gargoyles, but I was wrong. Now that he knows you and your father live, he will stop at nothing to claim you, as well as the sons that Tosha has born. He will have none of you—that I assure you," Letha affirmed.

"Minister Antillius spoke often of the bond shared between our realms. I see that now, though felt differently when I was in Darna's keeping," he said.

"If only I had known." Letha shook her head sadly. "As you now know, King Lore was my brother, a brother that I loved dearly. That affection extends to his children. My nephew spoke well of you, so Lucas tells me, and my niece could not have held Corell without you. You are very important to their cause and, thus, very important to me, Terin Caleph. More the fool was Darna for not seeing that," Letha said.

"I am not much use to them now." He lowered his eyes.

"How so?" Letha asked.

"As I explained in the throne room, Yah has taken my power. I no longer invoke great fear in the gargoyles or any of my enemies as

I once did. I cannot even lift your Sword of Light from the ground, a task any one can do, but Yah denies me."

"We all witnessed his power invoked by you through Darna's sword, so you are still yoked to the swords in some way," Letha said.

"It is difficult to explain," Terin said, struggling to put it in words.

"Do your best, Terin. We are patient," Tosha encouraged.

"When I disobeyed him during my escape, he struck me with lightning. I awoke to his complete absence, unable to sense him in any way. It was frightening to behold. When you live with something your entire life, a calming presence that you are not even aware of, then it is removed…" he trailed.

The queen and princess gave him sympathetic looks.

"But you feel his presence now, at least you did in the throne room," Tosha said.

"I feel his presence in the smallest of measures, just enough to know he has not forsaken me, but it is an inkling of what it was. But compared to the nothingness before then, it is pure rapture. Even a tiny spark of Yah's presence is like a candle in a caliginous void, its small light seeming as bright as a thousand suns."

"Can you restore your power?" Letha asked.

"Only Yah can do that. All I can do is follow his will, if he is generous enough to reveal it. It might be gone for good, or he might return it this very day. My knowledge of him is woefully ignorant. Perhaps Prince Lorn could advise me," he sighed.

"Have faith, Terin. Your God delivered you from Darna and, in so doing, saved my life and many others. Did it not occur to you that all you suffered served a greater purpose? Your warning saved this realm from falling to Darna," Letha explained.

"He could have just as easily warned you through other means," he said.

"Are you so clever to question the means he chooses? You are a fine boy, Terin Caleph, and I am very fond of you in the short time I have known you, but you are still a wee mortal before Yah's majesty. Where is this faith you speak of? If your God decides to use you for his purpose, who are you to judge the manner in which he uses?

You have suffered terribly at Darna's hands, but such is war, child. How many others have suffered worse? We are engaged in the greatest war in our history. Should the Torry champion endure its entirety unscathed?" Letha asked.

"I…am remiss. Perhaps I have not learned anything after all," he sighed.

"You have learned more than you know if you can see that you have learned so little. Fret not, for life is the greatest educator," Letha sagely advised.

"You must be famished, Terin. The servants brought you food," Tosha said, moving a tray to his lap from the table beside the bed.

"I…" He blushed, embarrassed by all the fuss for his well-being.

"Something humors you, Nephew?" Tosha raised a critical brow.

"It is just strange, is all. I went from serving at my mistress's table to being served by the crown princess in a day." He smiled, taking a bite of bread.

"If my father is possessive of his blood, so is his daughter." She touched a finger to his nose and winked.

"A fact her consort is slow in learning." Letha smiled.

"Eat well. You need to nourish your body and restore your strength, or you will upset my niece," Letha added.

"Displeasing a princess is always unwise," Tosha chided.

"Another fact my daughter's consort is slow in learning," Letha said.

Terin felt he was in a dream, sitting in the most comfortable bed, being fawned over by the queen and crown princess of the realm where he was a slave the day before. He sensed a genuine warmth in Tosha that was subdued when last they met. She seemed…happy. It was a strange paradox that she and Raven would find happiness with each other, knowing they were the two most different people he had ever known. It reminded him of something Kato once said, that there was one person you belonged to, and when you found them, you would know, as if they were the opposite piece of jagged puzzle, matching you perfectly. He recalled all the arguments Raven and Tosha shared, a constant battle of wills culminating in the events at Fera. Was it more of them fighting what their hearts were forcing?

Most people surrendered peacefully to their natural partners, like Cronus and Leanna, and Kato and Ilesa. That was why he fought Deva so desperately, his heart rejecting what she and Darna tried to force upon him, taking Corry's place in his heart. If it was Corry who bought him at market and demanded his complete devotion, he would have surrendered gladly, knowing she was meant for him. The thought was equally troubling and comforting, which brought an obvious question to mind.

"Where is Corry?"

"She is visiting the Torry minister, who is yet unconscious from his poisoning, as well as his apprentice," Letha said.

"She will be back shortly. She spent most of the night at your bedside," Tosha said.

"She claims she repeatedly finds herself sitting at your bedside after suffering the sword's power. You should be admonished for causing a princess such a bother." Letha gave him a fake scowl.

"I stand guilty, oh Queen." He raised his hands in mock surrender.

"Very wise, child. My niece gladly accepts your surrender. Now finish up and dress yourself. Everyone is waiting for you," Letha said, gaining her feet and pointing out the rich garments provided him.

"Everyone?"

"Yes, they have been waiting most of the morning for you to wake. Your friend Lorken plans to heal those brand marks on your chest and thigh once he finishes tending our wounded in the infirmary. Meanwhile, we all have much to discuss, and time is fleeting," Letha said.

"Thank you for your kindness, Your Majesty." He smiled.

"Should the heir of Kal expect any less from daughters of Tarelia?" Letha returned his smile.

* * *

The palace infirmary

"Just hold it steady and give it a moment to analyze," Lorken advised Matron Telesa as she held the tubular device over the darkened flesh of the palace guard who lay on the floor. Within moments, an image of the afflicted area hovered above the device in luminous red, with the healthy tissue represented by a green hue.

"How do we repair the injury without cutting her open?" Telesa asked, her comment drawing a nervous look from the patient writhing in pain, with her lower abdomen inflamed.

"The incision will be too small to see. The red area represents the source of the internal bleeding. The blue outline is the recommended procedure. All you have to do is press the initiate switch right…there," Lorken said, leaning over her shoulder.

Telesa followed his command, watching in awe as the source of the bleeding sutured, and the excess blood drained through the small incision, pooling outside the skin, the inflammation quickly subsiding.

"Not bad for your first attempt." Lorken patted her on the back.

The queen's chief matron found his casual manner strange compared to the reserved nature of the men of the isle.

"It is a wondrous tool," she said, moving on to the next soldier, her sister matrons helping the healed patient to her feet.

"It comes in handy, especially this newer iteration. The one Kato has is far more difficult to use than this baby, but don't go telling Brokov that, or he'll get a big head." Lorken chuckled, his terms lost on poor Telesa.

"You are most kind to help us, Master Lorken," she said, holding the regenerator over the next soldier's disjointed knee. The woman was moaning in agony since the previous night, waiting her turn.

"Just Lorken," he reminded her for what seemed like the thousandth time. They worked side by side throughout the night treating the wounded. Nearly all the serious injuries were treated, allowing them to work their way through the nonlife-threatening wounds.

"Lorken," she corrected herself, finding his presence equally invigorating and unsettling, unaccustomed to men in positions of power or authority. Like Raven, she found him otherworldly and overpowering, understanding why Tosha was so taken with them.

"That's better," he said, standing up as she continued with the next patient, stretching his back.

Telesa regarded him briefly before moving on, regarding his unusual attire and pistol hanging off his right hip. She wondered what Guardian Darna was thinking waging war on these men?

"You are a strange people, Lorken," she said, inspecting the next patient's nearly severed ankle.

"Oh, we're strange all right, but you need to narrow that down a little."

"The way you dress, look, and speak, to name a few," she playfully chided, initiating the device to repair the woman's ruined ankle.

"That's all right. We hear that a lot. That's what my wife says, anyway."

"A fortunate woman, despite your…peculiar attributes," she complimented.

"Thanks, I guess," he said, wondering if that was an attribute or mark against him.

"We favor attractiveness, attentiveness, and an ability to sire healthy offspring when choosing our mates in the Federation. Overwhelming strength and martial skill are not prioritized. Even so, there are many a warrior among my people who would choose a man such as you," she said. Her forward nature took him by surprise, which was natural for the women of the Sisterhood.

"I am flattered, Telesa. If I wasn't already wed, I might have taken you up on that."

"Such the pity," she teased, enjoying his company. Of course, no respecting woman of the Federation would consider taking the property of another woman, even from a foreign lady such as Jenna Talana. Of course, the idea that anyone could take an Earther against their will was absurd, though Princess Tosha managed as well as could be expected with Raven.

"Now if you keep flirting like that, my wife won't let me come the next time we visit." He smiled.

"She is always welcome to take up residence here. Any woman capable of claiming your loyalty would be a worthy sister of the Federation."

"Don't give her any ideas because she might be tempted just to keep me in one place."

"Very well, but you will need to return soon so we can have use of this wonderful tool. There are many crippled and deformed people on our isle that could benefit from its use."

"That won't be a problem, Telesa. That regenerator is our gift to you. We have built five of them now, one of which Kato took with him."

"A gift? Truly?" she gasped, looking up at him as she knelt over her next patient. His words caught the attention of the guards within earshot, who Queen Letha sent to watch over them.

"Yes, compliments of our crew. Just don't break it, and for heaven's sake, don't let Raven touch it." He grinned.

"Raven?"

"Yes, he's a klutz who breaks everything we give him, except his pistol." He shook his head.

She laughed, finding his humor refreshing. She believed her people would come to appreciate these strange men in time, and their actions the previous night went far proving themselves to the Federation and proving Princess Tosha correct in her choice of consort. Lorken patted her on the shoulder and stepped away, leaving her to continue treating the wounded while he went to meet the others.

* * *

It was all surreal walking through the corridors of the palace, escorted by Tosha with guards bowing as they passed. She held his hand, leading him to their private hall where the others awaited. The clothing given him was beautifully made, too finely made for his simple taste, but he wouldn't voice a complaint in the face of their kindness. They provided him a knee-length silver tunic with gold stitching along its hem and collar, with a black cape and finely woven sandals. He'd grown weary of wearing such things, wishing to dress like the Earthers, concealing himself from the appraising stares so many of the women of the Federation routinely practiced. He constantly caught himself starting to kneel upon entering any woman's presence, the humiliating act ingrained in him after so many beatings. But now, he was free, and part of him feared this was but a dream, a simple respite from his hellish reality.

"You are far too tense, Nephew. Relax, you are among friends now." Tosha tightened her grip on his hand, leading him through the archway to the private royal hall.

"Terin!" Lucas greeted him from the small crowd of mostly familiar faces, stepping forth to greet him, wearing the distinct blue tunic and silver armor of the Torry Elite, though slightly blood-stained and battle-worn.

"Lucas." Terin smiled, embracing his friend.

The others followed, like a breaking dam, each slapping him on the back or hugging him fiercely. Raven, Lorken, and Argos nearly knocked him over with forceful slaps on his back. Zem ruffled his hair like he was a kid brother, and Grigg introduced Orlom, both of them dragging him further into the chamber. Ular nodded respectably, honoring him as champion of the Torry Realm. Kendra was absent, helping Brokov aboard the *Stenox*. Queen Letha preceded him to the chamber, greeting him again as he entered her esteemed presence. Also in attendance were a number of Federation councilors and General Jani, each receiving him cordially, which took him aback. This was not a side of the Sisterhood he was accustomed. Corry was last to greet him, taking his hand in hers, before embracing him with the warmest hug he ever felt. He held tight, never wanting to let go. The others looked on, some observing respectably, others cheering. After the longest time, they parted, sharing in the festive atmosphere. Palace servants moved throughout the chamber offering food and drink. Only when Corry explained the servants were high-born boys serving honorably at court and not slaves could Terin receive their service without guilt. Gray stone walls and dark timber ceiling gave the chamber a rustic feel, more inviting than the formal hall he was expecting. Nearly everyone else was clad in warrior garb, armed, and battle weary. Few slept more than a few hours since the battle last night. Terin felt overdressed compared to everyone else, even Corry still wore her armor and sword.

"My aunt speaks well of you." Corry smiled, drawing him away to the side of the chamber.

"She was not what I expected." He shrugged.

"In a good way, I assume," she teased.

"In a very good way, but what else should one expect from the blood of King Lore?" he said. His comment drew an appreciative response. Corry loved her father dearly and loved Terin for feeling much the same.

"You seem hesitant though. Does it feel strange being here?" She sensed his unease.

"I...I catch myself starting to kneel in everyone's presence or feeling I should serve them food or drink," he said, ashamed of what he was forced to do for so long.

She touched a hand to his face, her heart breaking for what he suffered. Though the woman most responsible was dead, the scars in his mind would be slow to mend. "I feared for you, more than you can imagine." She smiled, her eyes moistening.

"I am so sorry for failing you, for making you think I was dead," he said.

"No need, my love. You simply followed the will of the sword, and it took you one step too far. Without doing so, Corell would have been overwhelmed, and the Yatin Campaign might have ended disastrously. The power you invoked in the Sword of the Moon is the reason for our victories, and I was remiss in judging you harshly at Corell. Forgive me for doing so?"

"There is nothing to forgive. You had every right. You are my princess, and you were burdened with so much."

"Your princess? You are the blood of Kal, my rightful king," she said with the deepest reverence.

"I claim no throne. Kal's kingdom is no more. I told Prince Lorn the same and swore myself to his service. He is the rightful king and the only king I will ever serve, and I swore an oath acknowledging it."

"You forsook your birthright?" She was taken aback.

"My birthright is the power of my blood, not a worldly kingdom. That is the purpose for which I was born, and even that is now impaired, if not gone altogether."

"You shall have it back. I can see that by the hope alit in your eyes last night in the throne room. You couldn't even stand near the sword when you first entered its presence. After it exploded in light, you were able to touch it," she said.

"Touch but not lift. I am still powerless to stop a gargoyle, let alone invoke fear in a thousand of them."

"What must you do to fix it?"

"Your brother says Yah cannot dwell in a prideful heart, so I must start there. I didn't think I had any pride left after being a slave. How wrong I was." he sighed.

"You think it was pride that brought you low with your failed escape? From what you said, it was more like justice. Darna deserved to die for what she did," Corry said adamantly.

"I didn't say she didn't deserve it, but Yah told me to run away and not to fight her, but I didn't listen. My pride demanded vengeance. I didn't care about justice. I wanted to cut her into pieces and watch her writhe in pain. That is why he struck me down and why my power is now blocked."

"I would have done the same. I wanted nothing more than to gut her myself and everyone who served her," Corry said.

"You are the strangest woman I have ever known." He smiled.

"Do you care to explain that comment, Terin Caleph?" She gave him a dangerous look.

"You can be as gentle and loving as Leanna and as fierce and deadly as Tosha, and I am hopelessly outmatched in every interaction we share," he confessed.

"Good. I am pleased you are wise enough to realize that. It will save me years of properly training you." She smiled wickedly.

"Training me?"

"Of course. Every wife must train her husband. It took my poor mother many years to get my father to dance to her tune before she was taken from us unexpectedly. My aunt never fully trained

Tyro, which explains his wild nature and the sorry state of our world. Tosha may not fare any better by the look of her impossibly incorrigible husband," Corry said, looking across the chamber where Tosha slapped Raven's arm for some apparent inappropriate comment.

"I don't think Tosha will train him as much as he will train her." Terin smiled.

"You might be right. He is the most stubborn man I have ever known." She rolled her eyes.

"Stubborn can be a good thing though."

"Oh, don't take offense for your friend's sake. He has many faults, but disloyalty isn't one of them. He will never admit it, but he does love you, in his brash earthlike manner. And without him, I could never have gotten here on time or even found you if I did."

"I owe both of you for that. Thank you," he said, touching a hand to her cheek.

"I am just glad to have you back."

"I am yours, though I don't have my power."

"I don't care. I would rather have you without it than ten others with it. It is selfish, I know, but what use is victory in the end without the one you wish to share it with?"

He started laughing, which drew another reproachful scowl from his beloved.

"Are you laughing at me, Terin Caleph?"

"Those were the same thoughts I had when I was first captured and every day since. I feared I would only escape after many years, only after you belonged to another. I pleaded with Yah, asking what was the point of anything without the one that you loved?"

"Silly boy, as if I would ever choose another. Our hearts are joined by bonds only your God himself could sunder. You will do well to remember that."

"Maybe I do need your training." He shrugged.

"Yes, admitting such proves you are trainable," she teased, moving a stray hair from his eyes, hooking it behind his ear. "Your hair is much longer now."

"Deva desired it longer, but I will cut it now that I am free." He hated how she controlled every part of his being.

291

"Don't. I prefer it longer." She smiled, though he didn't agree by the look he was giving her.

"Is that part of this training you are talking about?"

"I am just teasing you, Terin. You may cut it if it bothers you so."

"Thank you."

"Perhaps I shall do the same. We could be a matched pair," she said.

"I don't think it would suit you." He made a face.

"Are you questioning your princess, Terin?" She raised a critical brow.

"I give up." He raised his hands in surrender, seeing little hope in winning an argument with her.

"I accept your surrender. It is a pity Raven doesn't learn from you." She smiled, watching the large Earther receive another swat to his arm from Tosha.

"I think she likes him that way," he said.

"You may be right," she agreed after observing them for a moment, which caught Raven's attention, causing him and Tosha to start making their way toward them, Grigg and Orlom following on their heels.

"You look a whole lot better than last night, Champ," Raven said, causing Tosha to roll her eyes as they stepped near. "How is your ambassador doing?" Raven inquired on Corry's visit with the ailing Minister Veda.

"He is still asleep, his apprentice also. He should be fine as several of the councilors and foreign dignitaries have already awoken. If he still sleeps by tomorrow, Lorken says he will use the regenerator to revive him," Corry explained.

"Your pretty lady says you killed thousands. Tell us how you did it?" Orlom asked Terin excitedly, with Grigg nodding in agreement.

"There will be time for that on our voyage home, Orlom," Corry said, her comment reminding Tosha of their soon departure.

"You could remind my husband that he is needed here rather than the *Stenox*," Tosha said.

"You should come with us, Pretty Princess." Grigg came to Raven's defense.

"General Matuzak would throw you a great celebration, and everyone would come from every tribe to see Lady Raven," Orlom added, thinking it was a grand idea.

"Lady Raven?" Tosha gave them a look. That comment caused Lorken to overhear, where he stood off to the side conversing with Councilor Mearana and her daughter, Galena.

"Why don't you tell her your real name, Rav?" Lorken said, all too loudly, drawing many curious stares.

"After you tell them yours, LORENCE!" he shouted back.

"Lorence?" Terin asked.

"Lorence Kendrick Umaru." Raven smiled, revealing Lorken's true name.

"Lorence...Lor...Kendrick...Ken..." Corry surmised where the moniker of Lorken was derived.

"And what is your name, HUSBAND?" Tosha gave him a look, wondering how he hadn't told her this yet.

"Tell her, Rav, before I do!" Lorken said, drawing near with Mearana and Galena.

"I am waiting." Tosha leaned back with her arms crossed, an unimpressed look on her face.

"I doubt you can pronounce it." He shrugged.

"We don't all suffer your inability to call people by their correct names, Raven," Corry reminded him.

"Say it!" Tosha growled.

"Nanouk Mekiana. My full name is Nanouk Ethan Mekiana," he said, causing Lorken to grin, stepping into their growing circle.

"Nanut?" Grigg asked.

"*Nanouk*," Raven said defensively.

"It means polar bear in his father's native tongue. He was a very large and white baby unlike his older brothers." Lorken chuckled. Raven's father was native Alaskan, and his mother, Texan, her own lineage mixed heavily with Anglo and Tejano subgroups.

"Polar bear?" Tosha made a face.

"A large ferocious carnivore, lives in the cold at the end of the world." Lorken chuckled.

"That's very informative, Lorence," Raven punched him in the arm, which drew a larger grin from his friend.

"No matter your real name, thank you for coming for me, Raven," Terin said.

"Don't mention it, Champ. And that's *Uncle* Raven to you." He ruffled his hair. This caused Corry to roll her eyes.

"That goes for you too, Corry, once you two lovebirds hitch your wagons together," Raven added.

"Hitch our wagons?" Corry made a face.

"Get married," Lorken explained.

"You want the princess of the Torry Realm to address you as Uncle Raven?" Tosha gave him a look.

"Absolutely, don't want you children to get too lackadaisical when speaking to your elders," Raven said, his manners taking Councilor Mearana aback.

"You will get used to him after a while, Councilor." Lorken chuckled.

"Mer is coming around. We have an understanding," Raven said, using the nickname he had given the ever-serious councilor.

"Your language lacks refinement, and your manners are worse, but you have rendered a great service to the realm, and for that, I am grateful, Captain Raven," Mearana stated.

"No problem, Mer, glad we could help." Raven all but ignored the negative aspects of her summation.

"As for you, Terin Caleph, it appears we owe you a great debt. Your warning of Darna's nefarious scheme saved the realm. I am grieved by the poor treatment you suffered during your…time on our isle. Please accept my apologies for that unforgivable offense." Mearana regarded Terin with utmost reverence, his legendary adventures and Kalinian blood impressing her deeply.

"Thank you, Councilor Mearana." He bowed his head reverently.

"Perhaps Terin could instruct you on proper manners when addressing members of a royal court, Raven, or dare I say Nanouk?" Tosha said.

"Maybe you should worry about your mom, instead of giving me a hard time, Wife." He nodded his head in the queen's direction on the opposite side of the chamber, where she was listening to Zem ramble on for a long period of time with the patience of a tortoise, bless her soul.

"Does something ail the queen?" Galena, Mearana's heir and daughter, asked.

"Yeah, she's in danger of dying of boredom," Raven said.

"Boredom?" Mearana asked, finding it difficult to understand when the Earthers were serious or joking.

"Zem could bore a tree," Lorken added.

"What's he saying to her anyway?" Raven asked.

"He's talking about penguins again." Lorken shook his head.

"Not the penguin story," Raven said.

"Dare I ask?" Corry sighed.

"Penguins?" Tosha made a face.

"They are short, black-and-white birds that live on the ice on Earth's southern pole. Before we came to Arax, Zem submitted a formal proposal to the International Department of Animal Affairs on the wisdom of establishing a penguin colony in Greenland, an island near our northern pole," Lorken explained.

"Go save your mom." Raven slapped Tosha on the butt as she stepped away, giving him a dirty look over her shoulder, which he responded with an innocent shrug.

"I consulted Dr. Zhao of the Shanghai institute, the foremost authority in avian habitats and migration, a very intelligent human in my esteemed opinion. He agreed with my summation and included his name in my formal recommendation to the IDAA. The committee was still reviewing my proposal when I was unfortunately marooned on your world. By now I am certain that they have adopted my deeply thought-out analysis as official policy," Zem proudly explained, leaving Queen Letha at a loss for words. She found herself abandoned by the others, each finding a flimsy excuse to step away as Zem rambled on.

"Zem, General Jani wishes if you could recount the actions you and Argos took last night upon approaching the palace," Tosha said, stepping to her mother's rescue.

"I would be happy to give her a thorough report. It was a rather simple affair, really. Of course, it was my command decision to utilize our hand-to-hand skills to avoid friendly casualties, another advantage my superior skeletal structure affords me over you simple organics," Zem said, his gaze finding the Federation general standing in a corner of the chamber speaking with Lucas. Tosha sighed in relief as he stepped away.

"That was…interesting," Letha opined.

"He makes Raven seem humble by comparison." Tosha rolled her eyes.

"Which is no small feat," Letha smirked. "I wasn't being disingenuous. Zem is interesting, as are all of your husband's friends."

"You approve then?"

"They helped save our throne, of course, I approve," Letha said.

"And that should put to rest any misgivings the surviving factions have with my choice in consort." Tosha lifted her chin defiantly.

"Yes, since most of our staunchest opponents are now dead, in chains, or publicly disgraced, we are stronger than ever. Not to mention we hold the favor of the deadliest warriors on Arax." Letha regarded the *Stenox* crewmembers scattered throughout the chamber.

"They are still sworn to the Ape Republic," Tosha reminded her, irritated by that fact.

"And bound to you by the children you share. Besides, I don't see the conflict in our two peoples. In fact, I believe the time is right for us to reach out to General Matuzak, offering our formal acknowledgment of his new government."

"How so?" Tosha asked.

"I've spoken with Argos on my intention of sending an official envoy to Gregok, establishing formal diplomatic ties with the Ape Republic. He agrees, of course, and offers to transport our ambassador aboard the *Stenox*."

"Interesting. Who are you thinking of sending?"

"I would prefer Mearana, but I have need of her here with this failed coup and the reorganization of the forum that will occupy us in the near term. Instead, I will send Dejara Guloz. Her loyalties are as sound as any with her son serving me faithfully in the palace. As a merchant, she is familiar with the delicate trade negotiations currently underway between Matuzak, Tro, and the Casian League."

"A wise choice, Mother."

"I believe so, which brings us to another difficult decision," Letha said. The look she gave Tosha indicated her daughter would not like what she was about to reveal.

"And that is?"

"I spoke with Lucella before Zem. It appears several of our mercenary captives have already broken, each telling the same tale. It appears your father has several contingencies in place to retrieve his grandsons."

"His conspiracies died with the failed coup, Mother," Tosha said, not liking the tone her mother was using, the tone that portended she was about to say something Tosha didn't want to hear.

"Did they? Nels Draken is unaccounted for, as well as a number of others that the prisoners claim organized their attack. Darna was able to bribe many to her cause, including members of my royal guard. Many of them must now choose to come forward, beseeching my mercy, or hide, hoping to avoid any connection to this folly, or… they might decide upon a bolder move."

"Then what are you suggesting?"

"I intend to send your sons with their father, along with a wet nurse."

"Absolutely *not*!" Tosha protested. "I will not be separated from my children."

"This is not up for argument. The boys will go with Raven. Ceana will stay here. You can decide where you wish to go, though I warn you, if you choose Raven, I shall move Ceana above you in succession."

"How can you make me choose? You would condemn me in the eyes of one child or the others."

297

"There are times when a queen must make hard choices, Tosha. Now is that time. We are on the precipice of war. Families are divided all over the continent by this war your father started. If you are looking to cast blame, it lies at his throne!" Letha said.

"Mother, I…" The words caught in her throat.

"You have tonight to decide. I intend for the *Stenox* to set sail on the morrow."

"So soon? Why?"

"The plotters will be most desperate in the coming days. I intend to make the decision an easy one for the more ambitious. With their prize removed, they will quickly slip away, escaping our island to never return."

"I hoped to have more time," Tosha whispered, her heart shattering in pieces.

"And I wish I could to give it you, my beautiful daughter, but the hard choices are never easy. Think on it, my dearest," Letha said, before stepping away to speak with the others.

Raven couldn't miss the distraught look on Tosha's face once Letha stepped away. He quietly left the small group he was speaking with, coming to her side.

"You all right?" he asked, putting his hands on her shoulders.

"No," she barely whispered, looking up at him with red-stained eyes, before stepping into his arms.

* * *

The following morn

The queen and Tosha met them aboard the *Stenox* before seeing them off. Brokov finally greeted Queen Letha, giving her a tour of the ship, while Kendra settled the wet nurse Ivessa and Councilor Dejara Guloz into their cabin that they would be sharing with herself and Corry, along with the two infants. A number of Federation officials gathered along the pier to see them off, most watching out of curiosity at the strange vessel. Tosha lingered in the 2nd crew cabin, where Ivessa sat with the children. Raven stood in the doorway watching as

THE CHRONICLES OF ARAX

Tosha held Jake to her breast, hugging him fiercely before handing him to Ivessa and taking up Ujarak, pressing kisses to his black scaly forehead, causing the boy to giggle excitedly.

"I'll keep them safe," Raven tried to reassure her, but she was having none of it.

"You don't understand." Tosha shook her head, her heart breaking.

"Give it a little while for things to settle down here, and we'll be back, and this time, I'll stay longer," he offered, trying to stop her from crying.

"You'll stay?" She perked up.

"For a while, but I won't be doing any of the nonsense the other men of this isle do," he said adamantly.

"How long is a while?"

"A couple cycles of your moon, maybe longer. Much of it depends on your nutty dad. If he comes to his senses and sues for peace, I can stay longer."

"Then maybe I could come with you for a time as well," she conceded.

"Split the year, half here and half at Torn?" he offered.

"Yes." She smiled, stepping into his arms, holding Ujarak between them. She was tired of their squabbling, willing to meet him halfway. Their situation would never be ideal, but together, they could make it work somehow.

* * *

After a hundred goodbyes and farewells, the queen and Tosha prepared to step off. The crew were gathered along the stern of the 1st and 2nd decks. Zem managed to relay another of his tedious stories to the queen during Brokov's tour. Ular and Letha exchanged pleasantries, each offering to send official dignitaries to the other's realm. Argos told her that they would bring Matuzak's ambassador to the Federation on their next visit. Letha again offered Kendra a post in her palace if she ever decided to leave the *Stenox*. She also thanked

Lorken and Brokov profusely for the gift of the regenerator, which they would put to good use.

"Safe journeys, Nephew, and you, Cousin." Tosha pressed a kiss to Terin's forehead and Corry's cheek.

They responded with a warm embrace.

"Do not judge my people by Darna's crimes, Terin. We are grateful for your help in uncovering her plot and your valiant service in defending the Torry Realm," Letha added, pressing a kiss to his forehead and embracing Corry.

"It was my honor, oh Queen." Terin bowed. He and Corry stepped back as Raven helped Tosha and her mother onto the wharf.

"I am proud to call you my son." Letha gifted him a smile.

Raven responded by scooping her into his arms, giving her a hug. Every guard on the pier nearly drew swords at the afront. They eased, realizing Raven's familiar nature.

"Thanks, Mom. Maybe someday I can introduce you to my side of the family," he said, setting her down.

"I would scold you if I thought it would do any good." Tosha shook her head before he did the same with her, sweeping her into his arms.

"Scold away, Wife, just don't bite me." He grinned before she was on him, crushing her lips to his, causing everyone else gathered on the pier and on the ship to turn away, save Grigg and Orlom who hooted excitedly.

"Keep our sons safe," she said breathlessly once their lips parted.

"I got it covered, Tosh. If I can fly across the universe, sail from one side of Arax to the other and survive your father, I can handle our boys. How hard can it be?" He waved off her concerns. With that, he climbed aboard. The crew waved farewell before lifting anchor.

Tosha watched sadly as the *Stenox* sailed out of port, disappearing into the horizon, cursing her father for forcing this decision on her. She barely noticed when a messenger hurried onto the pier, beseeching the queen.

"My queen!" the young woman heralded, kneeling in Letha's esteemed presence.

"Rise and report!" Letha ordered.

"The Torry minister has awoken and asks for you and the Earthers."

* * *

"Minister Veda?" Letha said. She and Tosha entered his chamber, where he lay abed, a matron tending him.

"Queen Letha." He tried sitting up before she told him to lie still.

"What news have you that required us to hasten here, Minister?" Tosha asked.

"There is a delicate matter that I could not reveal when you received me in your court, a matter most sensitive in nature," Veda said.

"And how does it involve the Earthers?" Tosha asked, concern painting her expression.

"Few know this outside Prince Lorn and those in his company and those in the 4th Army, but soon the news will spread far and wide for too many know it, especially the enemy," Veda continued.

"Speak of what you are referring, Minister." Letha ordered, weary of his babbling.

"The Earther Kato was slain by Ben Thorton."

Tosha felt a pain in her heart, recalling him fondly, and knew Raven would receive this news terribly. Letha received it little better, knowing the Torry cause stood upon the precipice, with no Earther now to match Thorton and Terin's power impaired.

"Gather yourself, Minister, for we have much to discuss," Letha said.

* * *

Terin stood upon the 3rd deck, staring west over the portside of the ship. The Federation coastline was shrinking in the distance, and the *Stenox* broke north after clearing the bay of Soch. Corry stood at his side, neither speaking for the longest time, lost in thought. He wondered if this was all a dream, a merciful vision to escape his

301

endless torment, but feeling Corry's hand in his proved it was real. He should rejoice, shouting joyfully over the waves of his sweet liberation, but instead, he simply stared numbly in the distance, indifferent to everything but the warmth of her hand.

"Terin?" she asked, freeing her hand, moving it to his cheek.

"Yes?" He looked at her, gaining his senses.

"You look so sad." She smiled wanly, her heart breaking with his morose spirit.

"I am but also happy. It...it is difficult to put in words..." his voice trailed.

"You are free. Darna can no longer hurt you."

"Yes, but the damage is already done," he sighed, feeling weak and helpless.

"You are alive, and free and—"

"And I have you." He smiled, finishing her sentence.

"Yes." She smiled in kind.

"You came for me, believing the ramblings of my father over good sense and reason." He shook his head, amazed.

"I didn't like what good sense and reason offered." She shrugged.

"Good sense and reason are no match with a willful princess." He laughed, his mirth warming her heart.

"No, they are not, and neither are you, Terin Caleph." She gave him a false scowl.

"And I am wise enough to know it." He smiled.

"That is good, for I value wisdom in a husband, else I might bear stupid children."

"Husband?" He couldn't stop smiling.

"Of course, I didn't come halfway across the continent for just a silly boy I knew." She couldn't stop smiling either.

"You didn't?" He raked his fingers over her cheek, moving her hair from her eyes.

"No, I came for the most perfect boy I ever knew, the bravest, handsomest, and kindest..."

He stopped her there, his lips pressing tenderly to hers, his fingers caressing her cheeks. There, upon the uppermost deck of the *Stenox*, he kissed the only woman he would ever love.

CHAPTER 11

Macon Empire
Twelve leagues east of the Borin Gap

The Torry 1st Army set camp along the western ridge of the Denpar Valley; its narrow stream flowing north to the Nila. They held position for two days, delayed by torrential rain and the return of their scouts and outriders. Lorn stood at the entrance of his pavilion, gazing east, where the far ridge was obscured by the waning rain. Upon concluding his command briefing and dismissing the Telnic commanders, he conferred with General Lewins on the order of march. The general feared they would be ensnared by the endless rain for the foreseeable future, turning the countryside into an endless road of mud. Lorn felt otherwise, believing it an isolated storm. The rainy season was still two moons off, perhaps longer. Yah did not lead them here to flounder in a sea of sludge. Rain or not, they would break camp tomorrow, continuing their march east.

The Lady Ilesa lay fast asleep upon a cot in the back corner of the pavilion, taking advantage of this brief respite, with few wounded to attend. She spent the last day dealing with common injuries and ailments afflicting an army on the march—twisted ankles and sprained knees among the severest. It was a welcome change from the countless casualties suffered at the Horns of Borin. Lorn allowed the matrons the use of his command pavilion to treat the wounded, after their own pavilion suffered a large tear across its roof. It was being repaired as fast as the tailors could mend it, but he wouldn't have wounded men suffering the elements while being treated.

He looked over his opposite shoulder, where Galen sat, tuning his mandolin, the minstrel his constant companion on this campaign. A stirring from the opposite corner indicated Ilesa had awoken, sitting up to stretch her tired legs.

"Play us a song, Minstrel, something lively to counter this foul weather," Lorn said.

> The fall of our king in domains far away
> With enemies surrounding our lands
> Hopeless was our cause
> Victory granted by the merest of strands
> By the fickle winds of fate
> To Mosar marched our brave prince
> Into hostile lands did he ride
> To smite the legions of Yonig the Cruel
> Master of all he surveyed
> Upon the walls of Mosar they fell
> Struck down by the hammer of Lorn
> Leading his men through fire and din
> Battle-scarred, soiled, and torn
> Driving their foes to the far north
> Saving the Yatin domain
> To victory he leads us once more
> Upon these far southern shores
> The Horns of Borin the Macons fled
> Forsaking courage and pride
> Onward again, our armies he leads
> To victory that shan't be denied.

Galen finished with a practiced bow, awaiting Lorn's critique.

"I am touched by your adulation, Galen, and my younger self would revel in such glory, but I dare not fatten my pride while seeking Yah's favor." Lorn's easy smile softened his rebuke.

"Is there a subject your God would find agreeable, my prince?"

"Perhaps. We are often entertained by retelling the feats of kings and generals of great renown, but as we spoke of before, the greatest deeds are oft forgotten, particularly those by common foot soldiers and laborers. Those who provision our army contribute more to our victory than I. Write a ballad lauding these brave fellows and ladies serving in quiet solitude. Their efforts are vital to our cause. Posterity will remember kings, princes, and queens. It falls to our bards to bring glory to the common warriors and people. You have no shortage of brave subjects to draw from, especially in this grand company." Lorn let his gaze drift through the open flaps of the pavilion, where the soldiers were camped all around them.

With that, Galen drew on his thick cloak, stepping toward the entrance.

"Where are you going?" Lorn asked.

"To find a story worthy of song, my prince. The camp is rife with such tales from our battles, stories that are still fresh in their minds." Galen smiled, inspired by Lorn's suggestion, before stepping into the gentle rain.

"Where are my sisters, my prince?" Ilesa asked, wondering where the other matrons had gone.

"They went to eat, not wanting to wake you," Lorn said, looking her over. She was still early in her pregnancy but couldn't hide the weariness in her pale-purple eyes.

"My apologies for sleeping in your pavilion, my prince. I—"

"You needn't apologize for taking rest, Ilesa. You and your sister matrons are always welcome to rest here. It is the least I can offer for your valued service. How fares you this fine day?"

"I am well, my prince, just weary, as all of us are," she sighed.

"I insist you do not partake any strenuous tasks, Ilesa. I owe it to Kato to watch over his widow and unborn child." He touched a hand to her shoulder.

"Kato would wish me here, continuing his legacy and healing our brave soldiers. There is no greater purpose I aspire."

"Not at the risk or your child, Ilesa. I allow you here as long as you are safe, not only from enemy spears but your own obstinance."

"I am in good health, Your Highness, and if that should change, I will return to Cagan."

"There is more than your health that concerns me."

"Have I been remiss in my duties, Your Highness?" she asked, wondering his concern.

"No. As always, your devotion to duty and deft skill are beyond reproach. Your mind, however, is suffering from your loss."

"I…" She closed her mouth, a loss for words.

"I have never been blessed as you, Ilesa, blessed with finding your true love. I can only imagine the glorious rapture that feeling invokes and to have it taken away." He shook his head sadly. "Kato's loss troubles me deeply, tormenting me for failing him, and your feelings are magnified many times my own. You are speaking his name in your sleep, calling out to him with heartbreaking anguish that rends the hearts of all who hear you. I can offer nothing but a sympathetic ear and friendly embrace to assuage your grief, wishing I could wipe away your pain."

"I am grieved if I have disturbed you, my prince. I will recommit—"

"Ilesa, I am not disturbed or offended by your grief, nor are the others. I simply want you to know that we care about you and wish to shield you from any pain but are frustrated by our inability to do so."

She turned away, wiping a tear from her eye. She felt lost, as if she was torn in half, the best of her cast by the wayside. Part of her wished she never knew Kato, allowing her to live ignorant of him, ignorant of his kindness, his charm, and his gentle touch. How could any other compare to him? He was perfect, and he was hers, and now he was gone.

"Ilesa?"

"If I close my eyes, he is there. If I open them, I am reminded of him by whatever I see. When I sleep, he is there, smiling back at me or dying in my arms." She lowered her head, refusing to cry, her voice breaking with emotion.

Lorn turned her around, pulling her into his embrace. He said nothing more, just holding her for a time. He thought of Corry at that moment, wishing he could embrace her for Terin's loss, holding her tight and never letting go. Once again, he failed her, leaving her to face the duties of the realm by her lonesome. He couldn't comfort Corry, but he could Ilesa. All he could do is what he could, and let the rest fall as it may.

"You may stay as long as you wish, and are able, Ilesa. And know this, you and your child have a place at Court, always and forever."

"Thank you, Highness."

* * *

Three days hence

Bright sunshine broke the gray sky, warming his face as he walked alongside the column of infantry, his ocran's reins in his hand. Lorn gazed at the morning sky, giving thanks to Yah for the good weather the past two days, allowing them to march unhindered into the Macon heartland. The way ahead was an endless sea of open pastures and shallow valleys. The locals fled before them, fearful of the *warmongering* Torries, the Macon Army spreading fearful rumors of their brutal tactics. Lorn spread the word that pillaging and looting were prohibited. They would seize only a tenth of any Macon farmers' yield, though the stores would be running thin at the end of winter. Rapists would be gelded if caught, and Lorn assured them that they would be caught. He insisted that the Macons be treated gently and emphasized it repeatedly, to the dismay of his men.

Lorn would spend time each day walking alongside the men, asking where they were from and their plans after the war. Most asked about the Yatin Campaign, listening attentively as he told of the bravery of the 4th Army and the battles at Mosar and the march to Maeii. No one failed to ask of Terin, hearing the rumors of his fell deeds at Fera and Corell and lamenting his fall. He knew morale was as fickle as a shifting wind, and Terin's loss weighed heavy on their minds. He had to balance the need for his brave acts to be told with reassurance that they could win without him, their victory at Borin going far to prove that.

It was midday when he again took to the saddle, ordering Dadeus Ciyon to accompany him. The Macon General's hands were bound to the pommel of his slower mount as he rode beside him, several Royal Elite surrounding them, amidst columns of infantry snaking their way across open farmlands.

"My offer remains, Dadeus, should you reconsider," Lorn said, their mounts maintaining an easy gait.

"Betray my oaths to spare my life? I'd rather die with my honor intact than live in shame," Dadeus spat.

"Your loyalty is commendable, General. I lament the loss of such a brave man, for I would have need of you in the battles to come, the true battles far in the north," Lorn said.

"I wish you well, for all the good my wishes can bring," Ciyon snorted.

"Truly? You would wish me well though I condemn you to death?"

"As much as I despise you and your Torry Realm, even I know the gargoyles are far worse. Not every eye in Macon is blind to this fact."

"And yet you choose death over fighting said gargoyles," Lorn pointed out Ciyon's contradiction.

"My oath is my bond, and I shall not break it, no matter the threat in far-off lands," Ciyon affirmed.

"You would place honor above the survival of mankind? Is that not dishonorable as well?"

"Cleverly used words will not sway me."

"Indeed, which further proves your resolve, more the pity. But I wonder, is it honor that guides you or pride?"

"Is there a difference?" Ciyon asked, not caring the opinion of a man who courted traitors to his ranks.

"The proud boast their own value, lauding their deeds for all the world to see. Honor is doing what you know is right when no one can witness it. The former is hated by Yah, and the latter, rewarded."

"Yah again? Your God favoring you proves he is false, for what God would bless a man rewarding traitors while condemning men that hold to their oaths?" he spat.

THE CHRONICLES OF ARAX

"You cannot hope to know Yah unless you diminish yourself in your own eyes. Humility is the true path to honor, not pride, Dadeus."

"Humility sounds eerily similar to cowardice, not honor, oh Prince." Ciyon shook his head.

"False humility breeds cowardice, and true humility breeds courage. When you are wise enough to know the difference, then you will begin to truly understand Yah."

With that, they rode in silence for much of the day. Scouts reported to Lorn on occasion, relaying the lay of the land up ahead and the movement of Macon forces. Ciyon was curious why Lorn allowed him to overhear such information, questioning if it was a ruse to feed him false tidings or a crude reminder that his knowing made no difference in the grander scheme of things. He was no fool and would not reveal whatever his thoughts on the matter were, listening in with a veil of indifference. He learned the surviving elements of his shattered army had withdrawn to Fleace, numbering over two full telnics. They were joined by the garrison of Cesa, whose five telnics commanded by Commander Clyvo successfully withdrew to Fleace. A few Macon outriders harried the Torry advance, but there was now nothing between Lorn's army and the Macon capital. The campaign and war would be decided before the walls of Fleace, a battle he was confident his king would win. Lorn's army was not large enough to lay siege to the combined strength of both the Cesa and Fleace garrisons, as well as the telnics of his battered army. At least, not before the Macon 1st and 2nd Armies came to the city's relief.

"Packaww!"

The sound of magantors broke the stillness of Ciyon's musings. Looking up, he found the sky filled with magantors, nearly twenty in all, each bearing a fire munition dangling from their saddles. Even from afar, he discerned the riders' gold mail and purple tunics, marking them Macon magantor riders. Several already released their loads; fires erupting along the columns ahead.

"Spread out!" Lorn commanded. Men broke from their columns to either side of the path, avoiding clustering together. Lorn's guards fanned out; their mounts grew uneasy with a munition striking just to their east, igniting men into flames. The poor wretches ran from the scene, flailing their limbs.

Ciyon looked on with dread as a Macon magantor broke from the others, its eyes focused keenly in their direction.

"Move!" Lorn barked in his ear, kicking his heels, his mount galloping off sharply to their right.

Ciyon was slow to react, debating whether this was his chance to escape. That decision was quickly made for him with the warbird bearing down. He turned, following Lorn southward, when his world burst in pain. A fire munition erupted behind him, caking his ocran in flames, fire sweeping over his back. The beast threw him, bounding off, engulfed in flames before stumbling into the ground, igniting the grass around it. Ciyon lay on the ground. Fire was encroaching through the grass, with him unable to move his legs with his broken spine. He screamed in utter torment; a patch of skin was seared across his back from the deadly blast. His eyes went in and out of focus, fixing on the flames encroaching through the dry grass. He tried to beat away the flames, a foolish, desperate act of a helpless cripple. The flames swept over his right arm, and pain shot up his shoulder.

"Stay with me, Dadeus," Lorn's calming voice called out from above. The Torry prince drew him over his shoulders, carrying him to safety, flames licking Lorn's feet, setting them ablaze.

* * *

"Treat him first." Ciyon heard Lorn say as he lay on the ground, his vision going in and out staring at the clouds above.

"What of your legs, Your Highness? You need attention first," Ilesa argued, kneeling between them, with dozens of wounded men gathered around.

"Do as I ask, my lady. General Ciyon must live." Lorn winced. Severe burns blistered both legs, knees to ankles, sending waves of unbearable pain through his shaking body.

"As you command, Your Highness," she relented, setting the tissue regenerator on Ciyon's chest.

Ciyon gasped, his pain quickly abating, tendrils of healing sweeping over his body, regenerating his scorched flesh, and mending his broken spine. It was the most wonderful sensation he ever felt, and then it was gone, Ilesa removing the device to treat Lorn. He lay there for a time, before sitting up, staring dumbstruck. He felt the balmy air on his now naked back, most of his tunic burned away. His hands were now free, but any plan to escape was quashed, finding himself surrounded by Torries. He felt a hand on his shoulder, turning to see Lorn healed and standing over him.

"Are you well, Dadeus?" he asked, genuine concern in his tone.

Dadeus looked at him strangely, wondering why he would care. He then recalled Lorn saving him, causing himself to burn in the process. "Why?" he coughed; his throat was parched from his ordeal.

"Why did I spare you?" Lorn asked.

"Yes. You still plan to execute me upon attaining Fleace, I assume. Is my planned death so grand that you would risk your own life to see it through?"

"I plan no great theater for your death, Dadeus. I saved your life because Yah told me to, for that reason and no other."

"Yah? I assume he has a grand purpose for my life then? Should I submit myself to him, proclaim him my God? Why doesn't he speak to me if he finds me so interesting? Perhaps then I would freely follow his will." He shook his head.

"You remind me of myself, so long ago. You can't hear Yah if your heart is filled with yourself, Dadeus." Lorn smiled sadly.

"Filled with myself? Aren't all men filled so? What must one do to rectify our nature?" he asked mockingly.

"Die," Lorn said.

"Die?" Dadeus nearly laughed.

"Die in here." Lorn tapped Dadeus's heart. "Kill the old Dadeus and let the new man arise, a man filled with Yah's glory."

With that, Lorn stepped away, leaving him to contemplate what the Torry prince meant, before the guards escorted him away.

General Lewins sought out Lorn, relaying the events of the Macon attack. They counted forty-two dead from the magantor raid; another thirty were wounded still waiting to be healed. The army would be ready to march within the hour. Their own magantors chased off the Macon warbirds, felling two of them in battle.

* * *

Two days hence

"My prince!" The rider drew his lathered mount alongside Lorn, after galloping with purpose from the east, skirting the column of infantry that disappeared into the horizon.

"Commander Delis, what tidings have you?" Lorn asked, the cavalry commander of unit appearing to burst, waiting with anticipation to speak.

"Our magantor scouts have returned. They have spotted a large contingent of infantry marching north from Cesa, two days ride to our south, bearing the sigil of the Torry 1st Army," Commander Delis reported.

"Our own sigil?" Lorn asked curiously.

"Yes, Your Highness. It is the Cagan Garrison bearing our sigil. Several warbirds from the garrison contingent joined with our own scouts and await just ahead. King's Elite Kenti is among them, Your Highness," Delis said excitedly.

"Cronus! Lead the way, Commander!" Lorn broke from the column, his guards following in his wake.

* * *

Lorn rode apace, following Delis a short distance where a dozen magantors stood in an open field being tended by a small army of handlers. Their riders were standing off to the side, with columns of infantry passing around them to either flank. Lorn was quick to spot Cronus standing among the others, set apart by his silver armor and blue tunic.

"Prince Lorn." Cronus saluted with a fist to his heart; the others followed in kind as Lorn drew nigh.

"Cronus, it is good to see you well. We received word of the victory at the strait of Cesa, but it was thin on detail. Perhaps you can enlighten me and give a full accounting of our actions south of here," Lorn said.

"May we walk, Your Highness? Much of what I say should be for your ears only, until you decide otherwise," Cronus asked, careful not to divulge Raven's involvement in destroying the Macon Fleet. The entire countryside was abuzz with fright over the Torries' secret weapon, a mysterious sea beast that no one need know was in fact the Earthers' submersible.

"Gentlemen." Lorn excused himself from the others, drawing Cronus aside. "I see the blood staining your cuirass and a fresh dent to your left greave," Lorn pointed out as they drew away.

"We encountered a few skirmishes north of Cesa. I slew two warbirds in the exchange," Cronus explained.

"I expect no less from a warrior of your renown, Cronus."

"My renown is worth spittle in the air. Terin's sword allowed me to do impossible feats no other magantor rider could, like gutting a warbird with a simple strike. Any other blade would have bounced off their thick underbellies."

"The blade is powerful but even more so in the hands of a capable warrior, now, what tidings have you?"

"The first information you should know is that Jentra is leading three telnics of the Cagan Garrison northward. They are currently two days south of here," Cronus began once they were beyond earshot of the others.

"Jentra leads them? What of Commander Corvis?" Lorn asked.

"He holds Cesa with the remaining troops, awaiting reinforcements." Cronus referred to the eminent arrival of the Torry 4th Army once they were extracted from Faust and redeployed to Cesa.

"Just as well, Corvis is more suited holding a defensive position than open battle. Now how fares our fleets? The report I received spoke little to our losses or the nature of the battle. In fact, it was quite sparse, as if some things were purposely omitted."

"That is why I needed to speak with you in private, Your Highness. Our navy suffered minimal damage, a few ships to the entire Macon 4th Fleet."

"A striking imbalance. We have heard rumors spread from the locals on our mysterious weapon, a sea beast that we control to explain the destruction of the Macon Fleet. Is this what you speak of?"

"It was no beast, Your Highness. It was Raven and the Earthers. I watched from the back of Wind Racer, looking down as one Macon vessel after another slipped beneath the waves, able to see one of the Earthers' underwater ships just below the surface. I was unable to follow them back to the *Stenox* while being drawn off by attacking magantors."

"So you spread the rumors of a mysterious sea beast to strike uncertainty and terror in the Macons?" Lorn surmised.

"That was Jentra's clever trick, in the event we could not find the *Stenox* to determine the cause of their helpful intervention. The ruse worked well. The remaining Macon Fleets drew away, and the Cesa Garrison abandoned their city to us freely."

"Once again, an Earther aids our cause." Lorn smiled wanly, lost in thought.

"Yes, but I wonder what provoked them? Raven was adamant of their neutrality. I am curious if they have learned of Kato's demise?" Cronus sighed.

"No. We have kept that information from leaking, lest our allies and foes learn of our sudden weakness. The news will eventually be known. May Yah protect us when it does," Lorn said.

"The Earthers always have a way of knowing things that we think they couldn't," Cronus reminded him.

"True, but not in this," Lorn said.

"How do you know?"

"Yah assures me this is so."

"Yah takes interest in the Earthers?" Cronus made a face.

"Yah's dominion does not end at the firmament of Arax, Cronus, or even at the edge of the starry night sky but the infinite beyond that extends far past our comprehension. All things are within his purview, including your Earth friends. There is more to this than I dare say at this time. Put your faith in that reassurance."

"I am becoming like Jentra, learning to accept your strange counsel as truth, though I shall never understand it."

"Once you open your mind to the possibilities, your vision will clarify, Cronus Kenti." He smiled.

"I don't know, Your Highness. I was raised to trust what I can see over what I feel. Either way, Raven should know what happened to Kato from a friend, not drunken rumors spread from port to port."

"You wish to seek him out," Lorn stated, guessing his intent.

"I would, Your Highness. I would leave you Terin's sword to aid this campaign before seeking Raven out."

"The sword is trusted to you, Cronus. I'll not see it in the hand of any other."

"You will have need of it here," he protested.

"Though it would always be useful, Yah has shown me the path forward. You have done your part in this campaign. Besides, your Earther friends have dealt the Macons a blow they will not recover from before my true plan bears the sweetest fruit. You have my leave to seek out Raven come sunrise on the morrow. I would not have you go alone, so take Galen with you."

"My gratitude, my prince." Cronus bowed gratefully.

"It is I who is grateful, my friend. Now tell me, how has Jentra fared without me?" Lorn smiled.

"Grumpy and full of curses, but I think he misses you." Cronus grinned.

"I would have him no other way. Even if Yah claims his heart, I doubt he would change much on the surface." Lorn shook his head.

"He will be eager to see you, Your Highness."

"And I, him, and his three telnics will be most welcome. My scouts tell me the way to Fleace is open and still no reports of the Macon 1st or 2nd Armies moving to its relief."

"Perhaps, but when they do, you shall be outnumbered unless the Torry 4th Army can be moved with greater haste," Cronus said.

"I have a few contingencies left to play, Cronus. You need only safeguard your sword and seek out Raven. Do you know where to begin your search?"

"The Ape Empire would be my first guess."

"Perhaps a stopover at Corell would be a wiser first move. I suggest you head west before angling north, skirting the Macon Empire entirely."

"I will do so, Your Highness, come first light."

CHAPTER 12

The Northern Sea
One hundred leagues north by northwest of Mordicay

Raven raised the jug to his lips, taking another generous gulp, standing on the 3rd deck of the *Stenox*, staring absently at the open sea. The waning sun dipped in the southwestern sky, casting his shadow on the calm waters ahead. His mind swam in a thousand directions, contrasting his intolerable outer shell, thoughts of her consuming him. He spent all these months pining for her, only to say goodbye so soon. He wondered how he let her worm her way into his brain, rendering him a miserable wreck. He ran the gambit of emotions—lust, desire, anger, passion, contentment, sadness, and joy—circling the pan of feelings while emptying the jug of Regoan ale he had been saving. The more he thought of his and Tosha's situation, the angrier he became; all his thoughts and emotions summed up in one word…

"Shit!" he growled, taking another gulp.

Terin found Raven in his current state, clearing the ladder to join him on the lookout deck.

"Are you well?' he asked, never having seen Raven in such a state.

"I'm all right, Champ," Raven said, still looking over the low wall at the sea ahead.

"You shouldn't drink so much, Raven. It is unhealthy." Terin came to his side, resting his forearms on the wall, with Raven letting out a foul belch.

"I haven't drank this much in a looonngg time. I'm due."

"Is it Tosha?"

"Don't say her name. We're trying to forget her," Raven said, steadying himself with a hand on Terin's shoulder.

"We?" Terin made a face.

"Me and this jug," Raven said, looking at Terin out of the corner of his eye, noticing his new wardrobe, decked out in black trousers, shirt, and jacket. Terin looked strange in Kato's old clothes, even stranger with the pistol and holster hanging off his hip.

"Kato's clothes fit you pretty good," Raven said approvingly.

"It is comfortable." Terin smiled, running his hand over his jacket.

"Looks better than that getup those wenches had you wearing on that island." Raven jerked a thumb over his shoulder, in whatever direction he thought Bansoch might be. Though Terin was in rags when they rescued him, Raven saw enough images from Darna's estate to know how the household servants were normally attired.

Terin burned with shame. Any mention of the Sisterhood brought to mind the humiliations he suffered there. Even his good treatment in the palace could not assuage the indignity of what Darna did to him. He could barely look at Corry at times, wondering how she could respect him after what he endured. It was silly, of course, for he had no choice in the matter, but once a man is forced to grovel in subservience, he might never feel like a man again, at least not the man he was before.

Pride, the voice reminded him, warning him of its corrupting influence. Was that not the lesson Yah was instilling? Whatever plan Yah had for him, he had to learn to trust it. Meanwhile, he adjusted to life on the *Stenox.* If he couldn't wield a sword yet, each attempt a miserable failure, he would learn to use a pistol. For some strange reason, Yah didn't inhibit him in this regard.

"We'll make an Earther out of you yet," Raven said, draining the jug.

"I would like that, though Corry doesn't favor my attire." He smiled.

318

"I hate to break it to you, Champ, but on Earth, only women wear dresses or tunics as you call them. If I were you, I'd keep wearing what you got on. Corry will come around. She's got you on her brain twenty-four seven."

"Twenty-four seven?"

"Just an expression. Means, all the time."

"Oh. I still cannot believe she came for me, that you all came for me. Thank you, Raven. I..." He struggled putting it in words, even after several days.

"Relax, Champ, you say that every time we talk. Don't worry about it. We don't leave our friends in places like that if we can do something about it. Besides, you warned us about Darna's rotten scheme. I mighta been killed back there if her plan unfolded the way she wanted it to. The rest of her plan woulda failed though. She's dumber than a bag of hammers if she thought the rest of our crew wouldn't figure out what she's done. It would've taken Brokov about five minutes to level her estate, and Zem would have had a bunch of fun going through the palace, snapping her neck."

"Zem really enjoys doing that, doesn't he?"

"Yep, it's his second favorite thing to do, tearing things apart with his bare hands."

"What is his first favorite thing?" Terin asked.

"Talkin' about himself." Raven shook his head.

"It appears Ujurak likes listening to him talk." Terin smiled. Raven's son took a strange liking to Zem, constantly fussing unless he held him. It was the oddest thing Terin ever saw, and he saw many peculiar things in his brief life.

"He'll be calling him Uncle Zem as soon as he can talk." Raven shook his head, wondering where it all went wrong. Tosha was going to kill him when she finds out what's become of her boys.

"Jake will too." Terin laughed, picturing it in his brain.

"Probably. Right now, he won't leave poor Ivessa alone." He thought about their tired wet nurse, who constantly tended the two voracious boys. Corry and Kendra helped her as much as they could, with Zem and Ular lending a helpful hand as well. Ular was surprisingly good with the infants, which wasn't surprising considering he was good at just about everything he tried, and he was patient too, a trait very useful in dealing with children.

"He does have a healthy appetite." Terin laughed. "Both of them."

"Yep, in one end and out the other." Raven made a face, thinking about the awful smell.

"Didn't you consider that when you brought them aboard?"

"Not really. I figured they were just babies, what trouble could they be?" Raven lifted the now empty jug, trying to collect the last few drops in his mouth before tossing it in the sea.

Terin shook his head, laughing at his friend's antics. He forgot how much he missed the big Earther. No matter how dire their situation, it always seemed trivial in the Earthers' presence. Who but them would even think of going into Fera and free Cronus, like it was just a small affair? Who but them could rescue him from Darna and destroy her power in a few moments? She spent a lifetime gathering great power and influence, and they destroyed her and all her allies with ease.

"Listen, Champ, you're goin' to forget 'bout everything that happened back there. I know those bitches did things to screw with your brain. Don't worry 'bout it. That's what women do, always messin' with yer head. Tosha always tries that crap with me, but I don't listen to her. It drives her nuts too." Raven smiled, letting out another belch. "We're gonna get yer mind off all that. Tomorrow, I'm gonna get back at Tyro for sending Draken and his goons after me back on the island. Going straight into Mordicay with the *Spectre* and sink some ships." Raven whistled, mimicking a vessel sinking with his left hand.

Terin laughed, shaking his head.

"How about it, Champ, you in?"

"Yes."

* * *

The following morn

Lorken pressed the Detach switch, the *Spectre* easing below the hull of the *Stenox*, the light blue of the ocean stretching out before them through the slanted forward portal. He began at five knots, running just below the surface until Raven set the course adjustments into the navigation computer.

"That should about do it," Raven said, sitting the captain's seat, with Corry looking over his shoulder, standing behind him, and Terin sitting the weapon's seat.

"I'd have a seat back there, Corry, but if you want to stand, better hold on tight," Lorken advised, increasing velocity, with the sea passing swiftly before them.

"I'll stand," Corry said, transfixed by the ship's awesome power, recalling her last ride on a submersible during her rescue from Molten Isle.

"All right," Lorken said, increasing speed to twenty knots, tapping the display screen where Mordicay was indicated on the map where they could all see.

"Are you ready, Terin?" Raven asked, leaning forward over his shoulder.

"I believe I am," he said.

"He's ready. He's a fast learner, and after the hours we spent training him the last few days, it's time to test his weapons-handling skill on a real target," Lorken said.

"One last practice target couldn't hurt," Raven said, depressing the target release switch, which deployed a holographic disc 1 hundred meters off the starboard bow, hovering just above the surface.

"Fire away, Terin," Lorken said.

Terin manipulated the controls of the forward lasers, narrow bursts of green light flowing above the target, disappearing in the sky above.

"Relax, Terin," Lorken advised, easing the sub's velocity. "Now close your eyes. Take a deep breath. Visualize your target. All right, open your eyes and calmly fire."

Terin focused on the target and fired, his blasts striking its outer edge.

"Much better. Let's try a couple more before we advance to Mordicay," Lorken said.

* * *

The *Spectre* passed unseen into Mordicay, the cool northern port, which seemed eerily calm with only a few merchant ships traversing its peaceful waters. The city fanned out from the mouth of the Reguh River. Most of its wharves were built along the banks of the river, with the warships of the 1st Benotrist Fleet moored nearest the sea. Towering edifices were silhouetted against the northern sky, aligned to either bank, with lesser structures spreading out around them. Each of them found it an impressive sight, seeing the large port city for the first time. Mordicay was centrally located in the Benotrist Empire, with nearly all east-west trade passing through it.

"Move a little closer, Lorken," Raven said, pointing out a large warship moored amidst several lesser vessels, with the sigil of the 1st Benotrist Fleet gracing its forward mast, a black catapult and claw upon a field of red.

"That's a big bastard," Lorken whistled, eyeing the three rows of oars jutting from its sides.

"A trioar." Terin recognized its size.

"Let's start with that one then. Aim just below the waterline, Terin," Raven said, pointing out the hull of the *Gorga's Hammer*, as Lorken eased closer, keeping well below the surface.

Terin steadied his aim, releasing a narrow beam below the *Gorga's* hull.

"Don't let the beam rise above the surface," Lorken added.

Terin patiently eased the beam higher until it cut into the hull.

"Good, now widen the beam and slide it to the left," Lorken instructed.

The ocean poured through the fissure opening along the *Gorga Hammer's* portside hull. The screams of the few crewmen aboard echoed dully through the bowels of the ship as it suddenly listed.

Most of the crew and oar slaves were presently ashore, reducing casualties, which meant fewer to witness what ailed the ship. Terin stopped the laser, leaving a gash running two thirds the length of the ship. Lorken eased the *Spectre* away as the warship's list increased. Men clambered over its starboard side, trying to jump onto the pier; many lost the battle against gravity, the listing ship throwing them hard to port. Some jumped into the water off port, trying to swim away before the ship took them under; the cold water stinging their breath. The *Gorga's* tall masts slapped the surface as it keeled onto its side, holding there briefly before capsizing.

The harbor stirred with activity, those nearby thrown into panic. Crews of other warships hurried toward their vessels, fearing the *Gorga's* ailment might strike them in turn.

"Nice work, Terin. Let's find another," Raven said, pointing out a bioar resting by its lonesome a quarter mile away, moored at a small pier with a few crewmembers visible above deck.

"One more, then we best be going," Lorken cautioned, moving into position.

"All right, but Tyro deserves a lot worse after pulling that crap in Bansoch," Raven snorted.

"Two warships will have to do. Boy, your family reunions should be a little testy after this. You have to be the worst son-in-law poor old Tyro could've had." Lorken shook his head.

"I'm not the only family member he has problems with. His grandson here killed thousands of his soldiers and ruined two campaigns." Raven slapped Terin on the shoulder. "Not to mention his niece sitting behind me, being a thorn in his side." He jerked a thumb over his shoulder.

"Niece?" Corry asked darkly.

"By marriage. Letha was his second wife. That makes you related, sport." Raven smiled, enjoying the reaction on her displeased face.

"Just one big happy family." Lorken shook his head as Terin fired away.

* * *

Orlom jumped up and down, elated with his marksmanship.

"Hah!" he taunted Grigg, standing on the 3rd deck, lowering his rifle. "You see that my aim is better than yours."

"I move the markers easier than you!" Grigg protested.

"You do not! I move them slower for you!"

"No, you don't. Even fatty moves them slower than you," Grigg snarled, dropping the target projector on the deck, balling his fists.

"Are you challenging my better aim?" Orlom set his rifle down, puffing his chest.

"Yes!" Grigg pushed him.

* * *

The bridge of the Stenox

"That ought to do it," Brokov said, plugging the coordinates to Torn Harbor into the helm.

"You place great trust in such small things." Argos regarded the size of the information screen, standing over his shoulder.

"Size isn't the determining factor when it comes to trusting things, Arg. Some of the smallest things are very dependable," Brokov pointed out just as a loud thud sounded off the deck above.

Argos looked up, his nostrils curiously flaring.

"What's going on up there?" Brokov made a face, as Argos cleared the door, stepping onto the stern of the 2nd deck, when Grigg dropped at his feet.

"Why are you jumping off the upper deck?" Argos growled. The young gorilla ignored him; he was gaining his feet, hurrying back up the ladder where Orlom greeted him with a kick to the face, before clearing the top. Grigg's head reeled from the blow but pressed on, climbing over the edge, diving for Orlom's feet, sinking his teeth in Orlom's left leg.

"Enough!" Argos growled, stepping onto the third deck, swatting Grigg's head, lifting him by the scruff of the neck with his right hand, and gripping Orlom's throat with the other.

"This isn't your fight!" Orlom said hoarsely, his throat constricting in Argos's grip.

"It's between us, fatty!" Grigg added, swinging futilely at Orlom while dangling in the air.

"Fatty?" Argos's nostrils flared dangerously, tossing Grigg over the side of the ship.

"Agghh!" Grigg's screams died with a violent splash off the starboard bow.

Orlom managed to twist free during the distraction, biting Argos's hand before jumping to the 2nd deck, with an irate Argos giving chase. Brokov wasted little time descending to the 1st deck, looking off starboard where Grigg flailed in the water, his head repeatedly going under the surf. He retrieved a rescue line from the diving room, before stripping off his jacket, holster, and boots, jumping into the frigid water to save Grigg.

* * *

The Spectre

"Still no response," Raven said upon final approach, with the *Stenox* just coming into view.

"The interference must be on their end," Lorken said.

"No, everything checks out, just no one is answering."

"You want to hold here?" Lorken asked.

"Move a little closer, and we'll have a look."

No sooner did the image break their viewscreen, they discovered the problem.

"You've got to be kidding?" Raven shook his head.

"Oh boy," Lorken added, accelerating toward the *Stenox*.

* * *

Upon docking, the *Spectre* crew hurried to the stern, finding Brokov lying face up on his back, out cold. Argos was to their immediate left, choking Grigg against the ladder running to the upper decks. Orlom was pinned underneath Argos's right foot; the young gorilla pounding his fists uselessly against his thick boot and leg. Kendra and Ular clung to Argos's back, struggling to break his grip on the choking Grigg, each trying to wrap their arms around Argos's thick neck, to little effect. Lucas knelt several steps behind the chaotic scene, nursing a bloody face, looking about to collapse at any moment. Most strange of all was Zem, who stood at the extreme end of the stern with his arms folded, observing the chaos, refusing to take action. There was no sign of Councilor Guloz or the Lady Ivessa and the children, wisely remaining inside, no doubt.

"Arg, let him go!" Raven shouted.

Argos continued to choke and crush his fellow apes.

"Get that side!" Raven said, pulling back on Argos's left arm while Terin and Lorken circled around taking hold of the other. After a long agonizing minute, they managed to pry Argos's arms from Grigg's throat; the young gorilla slipped to his rump, gasping for air. Before they could let go and work on lifting his foot off Orlom, Argos growled a fearsome roar.

"Agghh!" Argos roared, throwing them off him.

Lorken flew against the starboard rail, his shoulder striking its unforgiving steel. Terin's back slammed just beside him, passing over the top, splashing into the sea. Raven stumbled against the portside rail, passing overhead and into the water. Zem caught Kendra and Ular in midair, one in each hand, sparing them a cold bath, setting them down on the deck.

Terin struggled to the surface, encumbered by his heavy jacket and boots. The cold ocean water cut like a thousand knives tearing his flesh and constricting his lungs. Breaking the surface, he took a shallow breath, sucking fresh air into his pained lungs.

"Here, kid!" Lorken shouted, stretching his hand over the side of the ship. Terin reached out, his head briefly dipping below the surface until Lorken wrapped his hand around his wrist, yanking him up. Terin coughed as Lorken pulled him over the portside rail, Corry rushing to his side.

"Thank you," he gasped, his lips turning blue, finding the water much colder than at Carapis. Everyone seemed relatively calm as he looked around. Kendra, Grigg, Ular, Lucas, and Orlom rested on the starboard rail, nursing their bruises, and rubbing their necks. Zem stood motionless; his arms were again crossed, as he stared stoically as if he were posing for a sculpture. Brokov still lay on the deck, but now his eyes were open, staring absently at the sky above as if dead. Argos stood opposite Zem, near the entrance to the 1st deck, his heavy breath the loudest thing Terin could hear.

"Where's Rav?" Lorken asked, not finding him anywhere on the deck.

It was only then they noticed a large hand grasping the portside rail. After a long pause, a second hand reached over the side of the ship. Raven's head followed after; water dripping from his nose, chin, and ears.

"Don't everyone help me at once!" he growled, slowly pulling himself over the rail, flopping onto the deck.

"You all right?" Lorken asked, now standing over him as he lay beside Brokov, who was now blinking his eyes.

"I'm just fine. Why do you ask," he said before coughing up water, spitting it on the deck.

Lorken helped him to his feet. After several moments of each of them staring at each other, Raven decided to ask the obvious question.

"Why?" He looked at Argos for an explanation.

"They required discipline!" Argos snorted, giving his fellow apes a cold look.

"That's it? That's why I almost drowned? What did they do?" Raven threw up his hands.

Argos crossed his arms, refusing to answer.

"Orlom and Grigg were fighting," Kendra said.

"Over what?" Raven growled, giving each of the young gorillas a look.

"I shoot better than Grigg. He's a sore loser," Orlom blurted.

"You cheated!" Grigg shot back, giving him a shove.

"All right, knock it off you two!" Raven growled, stepping between them, pushing Orlom away before he could land a hit on Grigg.

"I better take a look at Lucas," Lorken said, shaking his head after looking at Lucas's misshapen nose, reminding him of their playing days at the academy when their starting running back had his nose broken, his nostrils pointing in the wrong direction. This one looked worse.

"Did Arg do that?" Raven asked, looking at Lucas, who was barely able to walk.

"An unfortunate accident during his altercation with Orlom and Grigg," Zem stated in Argos's defense, as Lorken helped Lucas inside.

"Why didn't you help break it up? Were you too busy charging your batteries?" Raven growled.

"Batteries? *My* power cells have a life span exceeding two thousand Earth years. I don't have batteries!" Zem said, insulted by such an insinuation.

"Then why didn't you break up the fight?" Raven shot back.

"Argos was justified. It is a matter for the apes to settle without our misguided interference," Zem stated.

"Thanks for lookin' out for Arg's feelings, Zem. Next time you might want to reconsider before someone gets killed. Grigg and Orlom, you two got yourselves five days of diaper duty. Ivessa could use your help."

"All right, Boss," they both mumbled.

"And can somebody wake up Brokov? It looks like he has a concussion," Raven said, before going inside for some dry clothes. One thing was clear; it was going to be a long trip to Torn Harbor.

* * *

The *Stenox* continued at a steady pace through the night, stopping late in the next morning for the crew to rest and for anyone needing to stretch their legs in the fresh air. Ular and Lucas took full advantage of these times to spar on the stern of the 1st deck, either hand to hand or with various weapons. Grigg and Orlom were always eager to join in, though each struggling to match Ular's speed and dexterity. Terin and Corry observed them from the stern of the 2nd deck, watching as Lucas forced Ular to submit with a joint manipulation, after several failed attempts. The Enoructans' joints and pressure points were slightly different from Araxan humans, and Ular helped explain the differences to Lucas, which aided him in their grappling.

"Let me try!" Grigg eagerly stepped forth to challenge Ular, hoping to repeat Lucas's success.

Ular politely agreed, calling Grigg forth. Terin marveled watching Ular sweep Grigg's feet in a blink of an eye. He was upon Grigg so quick that it made his head spin. The young gorilla held on long enough to make a showing, managing to throw Ular off before the Enoructan maneuvered him into a submission hold.

"Hah!" Orlom taunted the defeated gorilla, pointing a mocking finger at his comrade and jumping up and down excitedly.

"Don't laugh, dumb, dumb. I am better than you!" Grigg snorted.

"Are not!" Orlom shook his head.

Before anyone knew it, the two gorillas were wrestling on the deck, nearly taking Ular and Lucas's feet from under them, before they managed to drag them apart.

"Enough!" Lucas shouted, pulling Orlom off his friend.

"You must never taunt each other in training bouts, Orlom. Each of us is a student, and each of us a master. We all must teach what we know and learn what we don't," Ular sagely advised, his watery voice echoing in the morning air.

"Listen to Ular, dumb, dumb!" Grigg said, breaking free of Ular's grip.

"You should not disparage each other, either, Grigg. Nor should you become angry with one another. Anger clouds reason, which dulls your senses and narrows your thoughts. A warrior must be above such things," Ular expounded.

"Let us begin again. Grigg, how about you and I in the next match?" Lucas offered, which Grigg happily agreed.

Corry felt Terin's tension as she placed her hand in his, watching the activity below. "You should join them," she said.

Terin spent the past days exclusively mastering the Earthers' weapons and equipment, avoiding the martial skills he was accustomed to.

"I...I don't know," he sighed. Yah had humbled him so severely he doubted he could even lift a training blade.

"You will never know unless you try," she pointed out.

"I would just embarrass myself," he voiced his true fear.

"If that is true, then pride still masters your heart," she said.

"Very well," he sighed, knowing she spoke true.

"If you must humble your spirit for Yah to restore your power, then there is no better time than now. Come, I will embarrass myself as well." She drew him toward the ladder. The others stopped what they were doing, backing a step, welcoming Terin into their midst. They all knew what he endured and understood his power was bound up within him by Yah's mysterious omnipotence. They were honored that they might have a part in unlocking his power, restoring the Torry champion to his rightful state.

"What is your pleasure, Terin, grappling or weapons?" Lucas smiled, encouraging his friend.

"Well...I..." He couldn't decide.

"Perhaps the basics to begin with, and we can proceed from there," Corry interjected.

"Of course, Your Highness. You might even demonstrate what Ular taught you," Lucas grinned.

"What did he teach you?" Terin asked, looking to Ular and then Corry.

"Princess," Ular said, offering her a blunted training knife, which she took in hand, rolling it over her fingers. Terin's eyebrows grew with surprise as she picked up speed, manipulating the blade with surprising efficiency before tossing it behind her, catching it with effortless motion. He knew enough about knives to notice her using the thumb and middle finger to control the blade and her index finger to toss it. It was a basic maneuver that took some time to master. She finished with a vicious throw, striking Lucas's shield in its center.

Terin thought it impressive until Ular tossed her two daggers, which she began to flip simultaneously, concluding with separate strikes to Lucas and Ular's shields.

"Well?" Lucas asked him, a stupid grin painting his face.

"It must be her Tarelian blood. My father instructed me at length on using knives, but never more than one at a time," Terin admitted, impressed by her quick learning.

"Ular is a fountain of knowledge in the martial skills, and I was wise enough to learn from his instruction." Corry gave the Enoructan a grateful smile.

"As have I. He has taught me as much as Kato and has humbled me much the same," Lucas grinned. "I look forward to the two of them meeting one day. I would love to watch them spar."

"You are my superior when weapons are not used, Lucas," Ular admitted, having lost more than he won in grappling the Torry Elite.

"Only with rules not to use killing moves, Ular. You could kill me many times over if we allowed such," Lucas countered.

"As could you, Lucas," Ular said.

"Teach us so we can beat fatty," Orlom begged. If he hoped to ever gain advantage over Argos, he and Grigg needed to rely on skill and speed to counter the disparity in size and strength.

"The first lesson is to not disparage Argos with such a moniker, Orlom. Humility is the foundation of any warrior," Ular reminded him, harboring great respect for Argos.

"Argos is Matuzak's champion. Ular is the Enoructan champion, and Terin is the champion of the Torry Realm. Perhaps we could have a melee." Lucas smiled at the thought.

"The power that made me champion is no longer with me, Lucas," Terin confessed, feeling unworthy of the comparison.

"Then let us fix it." Lucas slapped his shoulder, mimicking the gesture the Earthers oft used.

Terin removed his holster and jacket, taking up a grappling stance as Lucas and he began. He pinned Terin to the deck with a swift movement. Ular had them repeat the bout; Terin fared little better the second time. Lucas could sense his friend holding back, as if crippled by his own mind. Ular saw this as well, calling Terin out on it. Much like Torg, Ular would not relent, pushing Terin to continue. Corry looked on, her heart breaking for him but knowing he needed to push through. And so it went for some time. Terin finally held his own and even won a bout. Before his capture, he was often able to best Lucas in nearly half their matches, which was no small feat considering Lucas's prowess as the finest grappler in the Torry Realm.

"Let us move on to blades!" Ular said, handing Terin a blunted sword.

Terin could barely raise it; the blade was shaking in his hand before slipping from his fingers, clanging on the deck. Corry stepped forth, returning it to his hand with similar result. Orlom and Grigg remained curiously quiet, finding the scene entirely strange. Lucas cringed internally, concerned for his friend.

"Perhaps we should be less ambitious to begin with," Ular said, replacing the sword with a dagger. And so, it went, with Terin able to handle the weapon with little more than novice ability, practicing time and again, repetition building his confidence. By the session's end, he was much improved, handling a knife with adequate skill, but still lacking his once impressive ability.

* * *

The late evening found Terin and Corry again on the 3rd deck, staring at the darkening horizon, the sun setting behind their right shoulders, its waning light reflecting off the cold watery surface. He was torn between hope and hopelessness, wondering if he should celebrate his progress or lament how far he had to go. Terin recalled the effect Darna's sword had on him when he first entered the throne room, its power driving him painfully to his knees. After he showed Deva mercy, he was at least able to suffer its presence, though couldn't lift it off the floor. When he started today, he couldn't match Lucas's grappling ability but finished their bouts with a victory. Then the knife-wielding proceeded with him advancing his skill before finishing with a sword in his hand, which he could only hold for a brief time, before dropping it again.

"In time, Terin. Have faith, my love," Corry assuaged, resting her hand over his, upon the low wall that circled the forward section of the deck.

"Time is no longer our friend, Corry. I must restore my power, or we are lost. And I cannot do that until Yah is appeased. I asked him what he demands of me but cannot hear him."

"He spoke to you in the throne room," she reminded him, recalling his call for *mercy*.

"And I obeyed, and I haven't heard him speak since. Lorn often said Yah cannot dwell in a proud heart, and I am routinely expunging it from my soul, but it does not appease him. I have so much to be grateful for, Corry. I am free, sailing the ocean in the company of my friends, standing beside the woman I love. All I could have dreamed has been given me, and yet I am denied the one thing that might prevent the loss of all these gifts. I need the power of my blood to stand against Tyro's legions. Without it, I do not know what I can do." He left unsaid his fear of losing her, having her die by his failure.

"You have already done enough to balance the scales. Let others share in the burden, for it is too much for any one man, even the heir of Kal."

"Perhaps that is what Yah intends, but I know the enemy's strength, and it is still many times our own."

"We have come this far, and I trust we will see it to the end. I need look no further than into your beautiful eyes to know that nothing is impossible." She smiled, touching a hand to his face.

"I can claim the same." He returned the gesture, losing himself in her eyes.

"Then we are equally blessed."

"A part of me wishes I could speak with Tyro, try to reason with him to end this war," he voiced his thoughts.

"That can never be." She turned away, recalling what Jonas had told her about their Kalinian blood.

"Corry?" he asked, knowing there was more to what she said.

"You can never speak with him without risking your life, or so your father claimed," she said, looking at him once again.

"How so?"

"The power of your blood would reverse itself. Yah would alter its power, invoking bloodlust and hatred over fear and weakness in the gargoyles. They would tear you to pieces. This would come to pass should you waver in your cause, aligning with them in any way, even showing them sympathy could invoke this. That is why your grandmother and father fled, seeking shelter in Torry North. It is why your father never returned, for he loved his father, and that love might invoke Yah's judgment," she said, revealing Jonas's bitter confession.

"His love could do that?"

"Yes, but there is more. Despite the power of your blood, there is a weakness, a counter if you will," she said.

"What sort of weakness?"

"The blood invokes great power in you to destroy your enemies, driving them before you with terrible resolve. It is something incredible to behold when observing from afar. I assure you."

"It doesn't feel that way when I am fighting. I feel as if every enemy sword is trained on me. It is overwhelming and surreal, a constant whirlwind that dulls my senses."

"If you could only see what you are doing through my eyes, you would believe differently. You have turned certain defeats into victories throughout the siege of Corell and in Yatin, as I have been told. But with this power, there is a weakness. You are able to destroy those you hate but are helpless against those you love and therein lies your weakness."

"Why would that be a weakness? I don't want to hurt those I love, but it doesn't mean I can't," he said, not making sense of what she was saying.

"Can you?" she challenged.

"What do you mean?"

"You cannot hurt me because you love me. Nor can you hurt your friends or even your brother Elite in the training yard."

"That's not true. I have inflicted defeats on all of them, even besting Lucas in grappling, which is his greatest strength."

"You are very impressive in the training yard, and I have observed you there more than anyone, save Torg. But you never hurt anyone, not even by accident. You are restrained, though you see it not. In combat, you have no such hinderance."

"Training is different. No one wants to hurt their comrades."

"True, but you are even more restrained, struggling with men who you could easily best in warfare. It goes to the heart of the matter. You cannot harm those you love, and neither can your father. Despite what Tyro has done or what he supports. Jonas is helpless against him, and so are you."

"I don't love Tyro, so I would have no difficulty running him through if it came to that."

"No, you couldn't. Your father loves him, and you could not hurt anyone that he loves. It is this paradox that would doom you should you ever meet. Tyro would simply disarm you and try to bend you to his will. And should you falter in the slightest, your power would be inverted, bringing about your destruction. Tyro wouldn't mean to do this but couldn't help himself."

"My father told you this?" he asked, wondering why he didn't share it with him when he revealed the awful truth when they last parted.

"He did and would have told you if you weren't already burdened with everything that he had revealed to you. Your hasty departure played a role in that decision, as you were preparing to leave for Yatin."

"I remember," he sighed.

"Perhaps you can understand why he held back this last piece of information," she said.

"I can. But if I can't reason with my grandfather, I must regain my power. Even if Lorn is victorious in the south, we are hopelessly outnumbered. I cannot simply match Morac. I have to beat him to balance the scales."

"No, you only have to improve your skills, day by day, step by step. Do not think on the whole, only the small detail that you must address tomorrow. We still have several days before we reach Torn. Use them to improve and trust Yah with the rest. He did not bring you this far without reason. I never believed in Lorn's God, thinking him an excuse for Lorn to shirk his duty, chasing after whatever fairy tale his God had conjured to occupy his fancy. How wrong I was," she confessed her changing heart.

"And now?" he asked.

"And now…I know he is true because he gave me what I thought was gone forever."

"What did he give you?" he asked, knowing full well the answer.

"You." She smiled, pressing her lips to his as he took her into his arms.

CHAPTER 13

Tro Harbor
Estate of House Maiyan

Orvis Maiyan looked out across the Troan Bay from the terrace of his private chamber, one hand resting upon the palisade circling the rich stone outcropping and the other holding a goblet of wine. The late evening found him lost in thought, staring out across the tranquil water, watching several galleys traversing the harbor. He could see the lights on the opposite shore reflecting off the surface, and the outline of the *Moorn* against the northern sky. He looked to the day that wretched establishment was torn from its foundation. Sweeping his gaze to the west, he found the quiet remains of his own sorry investment, the former *Lady's Favor*, standing like an abandoned relic. It required a substantial investment to repair, funds his father refused to give him after the damnable Earthers visited such ruin upon it.

Orvis contemplated his fortunes, both good and ill. As the eldest son of one of Tro's ruling families, he would inherit immense wealth and power, once his father passed. He was young and handsome, drawing the attention of the noble ladies of Tro, who constantly sought his favor. He was the envy of every man in the city, yet his one failure consumed him, the betrayal of Jenna Talana, who chose an Earther over him. Vengeance consumed him, haunting his waking thoughts and tormenting his dreams. The offense could not go unpunished, though his first attempt to bring the Earthers to justice met with ruin, as the pitiful state of the *Lady's Favor* could attest.

The unfortunate incident brought to his father's attention—Orvis's dalliance with Tyro's agents, especially Hossen Grell—causing the patriarch of House Maiyan to sever all ties to Tyro's Empire. Any negotiations with Tyro would have to be overseen by the ruling council and magistrate Adine.

Orvis stewed, upset with his father's harsh rebuke. The ruling families were fools if they believed Tyro would cower before their steep demands, charging ridiculous sums to unload provisions to supply their legions at Notsu. To strengthen their position in negotiating with Tyro, they invited the Ape Republic into an alliance, which would be formally signed once all the diplomats arrived. A small advance flotilla recently arrived from the Ape Republic bringing several tribal elders and an official ambassador from Matuzak's court. The entire 1st Ape Fleet would soon follow, providing a visible show of force, giving teeth to their union. Rumors were already swirling that the Enoructans might join this military and trade alliance, further strengthening Tro's hand when dealing with Tyro. The apes were far away, however, and should Tyro push the issue, they would be too far afield to lend aid before Tyro's might fell upon the city.

"Master?" a female slave called out from the entrance of his chamber, her soft voice carrying to the outer terrace.

"Come hither, Danella," Orvis ordered, not bothering to look at her, his eyes fixed to the center of the harbor governing district below, where it's stone edifices towered impressively above the stone wharves running the length of the southern shore of the bay.

The young girl hurried forth; her slipper-clad feet echoed softly over the stone terrace, once she stepped off his carpeted chamber. She quickly knelt at his feet, pressing her head to the floor.

"Speak, girl," he ordered, now looking at her. She was lovely to look upon; her shapely features and comely face were easy on the eye, especially with the brevity of her garment and the silver collar adorning her slender neck.

"A visitor, Master. He waits in the front atrium and asks to speak with you," she said, not lifting her head from the floor.

"Did he give a name?"

"Rolis, Master."

"Bring him here," he said, sending the girl off, before setting down his goblet and smoothing the folds of his robes, awaiting his acquaintance.

After a painfully dull wait, Rolis appeared, the man regarding Orvis with a knowing glance. Orvis dismissed Danella, inviting Rolis onto the terrace.

"I told you to never seek me here," Orvis growled.

"Your father is at the city forum with the other patriarchs, and your brothers are with him," Rolis answered dryly, his gaze wandering across the bay, admiring the view from the rich hillside that the manse of House Maiyan was perched.

"He has ears and eyes across the harbor, especially his own house," Orvis warned.

"Of course, and should he grow suspicious, I am officially a wine merchant bearing vintage stock from Stapero, pressed on my vast estate on the northern shore of Lake Veneba."

"And unofficially, an agent of the Benotrist Empire, acting as Hossen Grell's second," Orvis whispered, not caring for that information to be overheard.

"Yes, and with our mutual acquaintance presently away, I stand as Tyro's authority in this fair city."

"Hossen chooses a poor time to be absent. If you haven't noticed, the ape delegation has started to arrive. I can smell the creatures from here, their odor carrying above the wharves like a foul wind."

"Yes, a most disagreeable scent but not unexpected." Rolis shrugged.

"What brings you here at this hour? It surely isn't to share in our mutual dislike of our southern guests," Orvis asked.

"As you know, our plans are moving apace. Soon you will assume your rightful place as regent of Tro and overseer of its surrounding tributaries. Subject to the Benotrist throne, of course."

"Of course," Orvis concurred, relishing the day when the other families were removed and his father with them, leaving him and, him alone, as the last patriarch standing. In that moment of duress, the city would turn to him and be amenable to Benotrist inclusion. He would be regent of all the lands south and east of Lake Veneba and along the coast from Bedo in the north to the ape coast in the south. He would head a powerful house within the Benotrist Empire and would take a bride from a noble Benotrist family, perhaps even a daughter from the regent of Nisin.

"And to bring all these plans to fruition, you must do your part," Rolis continued, drawing Orvis from his flights of fancy.

"I have replaced the ship inspectors with men of your choosing," Orvis reminded him.

"Yes, that is very helpful, but you must do a great deal more for our plans to succeed."

"Since Hossen's failure, my father has limited my influence. Until that changes, I…"

"Your father will be incapacitated after tomorrow, if only for a short while but long enough for you to oversee the affairs of House Maiyan," Rolis assured him.

"How?"

"A certain poison that will put him in a state of delusion for a time. Be assured he shall recover in time to play the part appointed him," Rolis said dryly, as if it were a small affair.

Since the head of House Maiyan would be required to attend the official signing ceremony, Orvis needed to be far removed from that fated venue. "And how do you plan for the pirate raiders to slip into the harbor to assassinate the entirety of the council? Even I cannot get enough foreign galleys access to the southern wharves without raising suspicion."

"Patience, Orvis. You need only assume the mantel as head of House Maiyan for a time and effect the changes we require. There are many ways for us to smuggle enough *pirates* into striking distance of the city forum. Be assured, no one shall escape that gathering alive. And the blame will fall entirely upon pirates, who are opposed to this treaty. And further blame will fall upon the Ape Republic. I doubt the good people of Tro would have faith in their ability to protect the harbor from Tyro, when they could not protect them from a band of *pirates*." Rolis smiled evilly.

"And I shall be there to pick up the pieces." Orvis nodded, visions of glory repeating in his brain.

"Yes, the last surviving patriarch of Tro, stepping forth to lead the city in its time of need. Welcome to the Benotrist Empire, my friend." Rolis smiled.

* * *

Notsu

Ben Thorton entered the former estate of Tevlan Nosuc, with his small retinue. The estate acted as Morac's private residence and headquarters, after Councilor Nosuc, the wealthiest merchant of Notsu, surrendered it to Morac upon his return from Corell, including its rich furnishings and small army of servants. Much of Tevlan's private wealth was moved from the city before the Benotrists fell upon it, as well as his children and nearest kin.

Emperor's Elite Daylas, the acting governor of Notsu, escorted Thorton through the wide halls of the vast estate, having sent a steward ahead to inform Lord Morac of their arrival. Morac received them in his private sanctum, with Kriton, the steward, and Hossen Grell standing beside him; the latter recently arrived from Tro, apprising Morac on tidings in the eastern port.

"Thorton," Morac greeted, regarding his fellow Elite carefully. The two men rarely spoke. Tyro often sent them in different directions. He recognized the gargoyle Zelo standing to Thorton's right, wearing a holster and weapon similar to the big Earther. It was the other two accompanying him that drew Morac's eye. One was a man with a distinguished air about him, as if he held or once held great importance. The other was a woman of striking beauty with rich black hair and stormy gray eyes. He wondered her purpose. She was wearing brown leather trousers and blouse fit for riding, and her hair was secured tightly to her head in a high bun.

"Morac, Kriton, and I assume, you are Hossen," Ben said, noticing Grell's distinct beard and portly midsection, rarities in Arax, indicating his Lone Hills ancestry.

"Correct." Hossen nodded.

"And your companions?" Morac asked, regarding the others with interest, especially the woman who kept suspiciously close to Ben's side.

"The Lady Ella is my guest. If your steward can see her to her chambers," Ben introduced her.

Morac ordered his steward to attend to her, escorting her from the chamber.

"A lovely find, Thorton. You have taken a concubine? I am surprised," Morac said approvingly.

"She is my guest, not my concubine or whore, if that is what you mean," Ben said dryly, setting Morac straight on that matter before introducing Monsoon, which drew even greater surprise from the others.

"Monsoon? The fates favor you, standing before us unblemished considering your crimes against the emperor," Morac said, regarding Monsoon overseeing the abduction of Princess Tosha.

"Our emperor has found a need of my unique knowledge and services, Lord Morac," Monsoon said, revealing his new allegiance.

"Your presence here indicates that the unique knowledge you possess that drew the emperor's interest involves a certain eastern port," Hossen surmised.

"Very perceptive, Hossen. Monsoon will help you plan your upcoming assault and will help coordinate with the pirate factions you have contracted," Thorton said.

"I can help you determine which are good to their word and which cannot be trusted, among other things, such as their strengths and weaknesses," Monsoon offered, trying to read the room, determining where he stood in this dangerous company.

"Will you oversee the operation in Tro?" Morac asked Ben, guessing his purpose here.

"I was going to see to it personally, but matters to our north require my attention," Ben said, before moving to a table along the side of the chamber. The others followed him, gathering around it as Ben searched through the dozen furled maps set off to the side. Eventually he found the one he was looking for, unfurling it across the wooden surface, placing stone markers to each corner to hold it flat.

"The eastern half of the empire," Kriton hissed, his eyes flaring with recognition, the map detailing Nisin Palace and its surrounding tributaries.

"Aye. The emperor tasked me with overseeing the situation at Tro and dealing with the rebellion springing up in the east. When I departed Fera, the emperor received the news of the sack of Nivek Castle and the murder of governor Culn. Upon arriving at Nisin on our journey here, I was met with even more troubling news. Three holdfasts were sacked and burned along the upper Tur, as well as uprisings throughout all the lands between Pagan and Nisin. Other troublesome reports surfaced of the chaos spreading southeast of Nisin, threatening your overland supply routes. The emperor stated that a spreading rebellion took precedence over the Troan operation," Ben explained.

The others looked on with disgust and alarm.

"What are your intentions?" Morac asked. His legion's fate rested on tenuous lines of communication.

"I will be returning to Nisin at first light. Unfortunately, some of the reinforcements you were depending on will be needed to quash this rebellion. I came here to escort Monsoon and to give you a special weapon you can use in your raid." Thorton directed Zelo to unsling the rifle hung over his shoulder.

"One of your weapons—this will be most useful," Hossen quipped.

"Perhaps, but not like you think. This was mine. It was damaged at Mosar and will not work, and I cannot repair it. It can be used in another way but only once, so you must use it judiciously," Ben said. Luckily for him, he was able to secure Kato's rifle for himself and his pistol for Zelo.

"How did you come about your extra weapons?" Morac asked, regarding Zelo's pistol and the second rifle slung over Thorton's shoulder.

"They belonged to Kato" was all Ben would say.

"Was he the Earther that attacked my legions at Corell?" Morac asked.

"The same," Zelo answered. If they wanted any details of Kato's demise, neither Zelo or Thorton would be forthcoming.

"Excellent, one less thorn in our saddle. How does this work?" Morac said, regarding the Earther's weapon.

"I'll demonstrate how that works before I leave. Just remember, it can only be used once," Ben pointed at the broken rifle.

"We will make good use of it," Hossen mused.

"Now why don't you go over your plans for Tro?" Ben said, giving Hossen a stern look.

And so, Hossen Grell detailed the plans he arranged for the assault on Tro, including the role of the faux pirates they recruited and the mercenaries they planned to sneak into the city. He revealed even the most remote details of the operation at Ben's insistence, including the raid on the city forum and their plans to decapitate Tro's ruling oligarchy in one fell swoop. He went on to discuss recent events in the city, including the Earthers' assault on the *Lady's Favor* and the sinking of the *Lady Talana*.

"It seems your former friends deal harshly with the ladies," Morac quipped.

"If it keeps them away from Tro, I count it as a blessing," Ben snorted.

"It matters not, for they shall have to be dealt with at some point," Kriton hissed, recalling their many interferences in the affairs of the empire.

"No point in stirring up trouble. The last thing we need is to involve them while the Torries are still standing. Should they appear in Tro, you will delay the operation until they leave. Is that understood?" Ben gave Hossen a hard look.

"A delay might risk discovery," Hossen argued.

"And an attack on the harbor is doomed if the *Stenox* intervenes," Ben countered.

"You place much faith in your former comrades," Morac sneered.

"Faith has nothing to do with cold facts, Morac. The *Stenox* is more than capable of sinking the empire's entire navy and leveling every city within a hundred leagues of the coast. Not to mention that any one of them could decimate a legion, let alone if they came ashore in a group. If they are present in Tro, leave them be," Ben ordered.

"Very well." Morac knew when not to push the matter when dealing with the ornery Earther.

"What is the status of your recent resupply caravans?" Ben shifted to the more pressing matter at hand—their shaky logistical position.

"We are receiving two of every three shipments as of late. We were down to less than a half some time ago," Governor Daylas dryly stated.

"That is because the raiders moved north into Nivek and are now spreading their revolt across the eastern half of the empire," Zelo explained, giving Daylas a hard look.

Zelo and Thorton were of one mind on strategic matters, and each found Morac's handling of the Torry Campaign lacking. Neither of them would've assailed Corell in the manner in which he did. They would have surrounded it with one legion before advancing into the Torry heartland, razing the country to the ground, preventing their forces from converging on them. Morac was drunk on the easy victories at Kregmarin and Bacel, which clouded his judgment. Thorton knew history was replete with examples of victorious generals meeting with terrible defeats, forgetting that the next battle is different from the last.

"How could peasant farmers move so swiftly?" Hossen asked in disbelief.

"They have help," Zelo said.

"Help?" Morac lifted a brow.

"Jenaii warriors are advising them, aiding their ability to assemble, coordinate, and disassemble before we can bring them to battle," Ben said.

"We knew Jenaii warriors were involved with the raids on our caravans but to infiltrate our homeland…" Daylas's voice trailed.

345

"There aren't many of them, but the few they sent are doing enough damage. I can deal with them, but that takes me away from other vital duties. Morac and Kriton need to plan the invasion of Torry North and let Daylas see to securing your supply caravans. Hossen and Monsoon will oversee the Troan operation, and Zelo and I will take care of our northern problem. Before I departed Nisin, I ordered the governor to assemble a large cavalry contingent to send to you. Your lack of cavalry during the siege proved fatal to your supply efforts and scouting," Ben added. The cavalry would complement the mounted units they had already gathered.

Morac bristled with the recommendation, not appreciating being second-guessed.

"Pride clouds judgment, Morac, and has betrayed the greatest generals time and again," Ben warned, recognizing the look in Morac's haughty eyes.

Morac thought to say something but stewed in silence, staring daggers at his counterpart. As first among Tyro's Elite, he held rank over Thorton, but the Earther acted outside the normal chain of command, holding the emperor's trust on the direction of the empire. If Raven was a wild tempest, unpredictable, and dangerous, Thorton was a quiet breeze waiting to erupt into deadly whirlwind. Of all the men in the world, he was the only one to give Morac pause.

"If you want my advice, Morac, forget about your victories. We learn from our failures, so start from there when planning your invasion. Now if you will excuse me, I would like to clean up after spending the past days in a magantor saddle," Ben said, turning to leave.

"Blast the spirits!" Morac cursed, staring at the map as Ben disappeared through the archway. Victory was all but assured after Kregmarin but now hung by the barest of threads. If their supply routes weren't fully restored, he could only renew his attack on Corell with the forces on hand. He needed reinforcements, and that required even more logistical support, and that meant he needed Thorton to secure it.

"Who is the woman?" Hossen voiced what they were all thinking, regarding Thorton's companion.

"He discovered her in Tenin. She sings and dances," Zelo said.

"A Yatin dancer, and his collar does not grace her throat?" Morac asked curiously.

"She is no slave. The last men to treat her so met a deadly end," Zelo warned.

"He favors her then?" Hossen asked.

"I am not certain," Zelo shrugged.

"Has he touched her?" Morac asked.

"Not that I know, and I advise you not to ask him. He protects her."

"Let a pet?" Hossen sneered.

"No. She sings for him," Zelo said.

"Perhaps she could sing for us," Morac mused.

"If you ask her kindly, she may do so," Zelo said, before warning each of them to tread carefully and to treat her with utmost respect.

Hossen would be certain to tread carefully after dealing with Raven. He picked up the rifle off the table, wondering how he would employ it in his raid. The possibilities appeared endless.

CHAPTER 14

Torn Harbor

The *Stenox* dropped anchor along the wharf lining the western bank of the lower Torn River, greeted by thousands of cheering apes spilling out onto the docks as word of their arrival spread. Terin stood upon the lookout deck, standing between Grigg and Orlom, each hooting excitedly, pointing at the crowd. Terin marveled, staring out at the cheering throngs lining the riverfront of the eastern port, each apparently pleased with their arrival. He only knew three gorillas in his time and thought well of them, but to see thousands gathered in one place was a sight he would never forget. The sea of faces was a strange mix of black furred males, with wide flaring nostrils, and white and light-pink furred females, with narrow, exotic faces. The males were clad in thin linen shirts over thick trousers, contrasting the females in flowing linen gowns. Unlike their Araxan human counterparts, the male apes towered over their females, outweighing them nearly two or three to one.

As soon as the *Stenox* docked, the throngs of apes broke out into the strangest melody Terin ever heard, which Brokov would later explain was their own version of an Earther fight song from a place called Notre Dame, wherever that was. Zem took a particular dislike to the refrain, considering it an affront to his own alma mater, a place called Annapolis, which Raven and Lorken said didn't count since he only spent a few weeks there, completing the entire curriculum with ridiculous speed.

"Once a midshipman, always a midshipman," Zem would say, proud that he was the fastest cadet to ever gain his commission.

No sooner had the crowd finished their song, they parted, making way for a large gorilla clad in leather mail over thick trousers, leading a sizable entourage toward the *Stenox*.

"Who is that?" Terin asked, noting the gorilla's large stature that nearly rivaled Argos.

"General Matuzak," Grigg answered with admiration.

"*President* Matuzak," Orlom corrected him.

"He was a general first," Grigg growled.

"President is better," Orlom said, regarding the newly created post as the head of the republic.

"General is better," Grigg reached across Terin's chest to slap Orlom.

"No, it isn't!" Orlom struck him back, brushing Terin aside. The two of them immediately went to the deck, furry fists flying with Terin struggling to keep his feet as they rolled about.

"Knock it off, you two, everyone's watching!" Raven shouted out from the stern of the second deck, just stepping from the bridge with Lorken and Ular following him through the door.

"Sorry, Boss!" they said almost simultaneously, Terin helping them to their feet. They immediately felt a thousand pairs of eyes on them, including Matuzak, who simply grinned, shaking his head.

"Come on, Terin. There's someone I want you to meet," Raven called him down as they descended the ladder to join the rest of the crew spilling out onto the stern of the first deck. Just about everyone, save for Ivessa and the children, gathered on the stern of the ship as they decided who would go ashore. It almost didn't matter as Matuzak was nearly upon them, showing no sign of slowing down. Before he could climb aboard, Raven stepped onto the wharf, exchanging a hug with the ape president. That, in itself was the strangest thing Terin had ever seen. No sooner had the two of them parted that they started slapping each other on the back like a pair of drunken friends in a tavern.

"Raven, my boy, were you successful?" Matuzak's booming voice echoed with hundreds of gorillas looking on, each waiting to greet the Earthers.

"Yep, we found him," Raven said, jerking a thumb in Terin's direction, where he stood between Corry and Lucas. Raven waved him on and Corry also before inviting Ular as well.

"Come," Corry reassured him, offering her hand as they climbed onto the wharf. She met the famous Matuzak only once, when first arriving at Gregok in search of Raven, finding Lorken instead. The ape president was not what she was expecting, a loud, boisterous gorilla who lacked any sense of formality. She recalled her entrance to his court at Gregok, where she dipped into a formal bow as a visiting dignitary, only for Matuzak to say "We don't do things like that here." He immediately offered her a tankard of ale and had her recount the siege of Corell while addressing the chieftains gathered in the great hall. When she explained what happened to Terin, Matuzak offered her escort to Torn, where the *Stenox* was at the time, and called for a great feast to honor the Torry princess who was a friend of the Earthers. She didn't correct him on his false belief of her friendship with the Earthers, and when Lorken suddenly appeared, he only reinforced their kinship by receiving her warmly like a long-lost friend, for which she was grateful. Now here she was again, meeting Matuzak, taken aback with how the famed general interacted with Raven, ruffling his hair like Raven was his son. It was almost endearing if it wasn't so odd.

"Ah, the lovely Corry returns triumphant!" Matuzak boomed, taking her into his arms, swinging her around like a toy doll before setting her back down.

"President Matuzak," she greeted as formally as she dared, considering the ape's animosity for frivolous protocol.

"Let's have a look at you, lad," Matuzak said, ruffling Terin's hair before slapping his shoulder. "You look healthy, lad, and I admire your choice in attire." He regarded Terin's Earth garb.

"Thank you, President Matuzak." Terin bowed stiffly, unsure how to address the large gorilla.

"None of that here, lad. No one bows to apes, and we don't bow to anyone else, especially friends." Matuzak slapped his shoulder again, the friendly gesture nearly knocking him from his feet.

Terin and Corry shared a look, doing their best from bursting in laughter. No wonder the Earthers took such a liking to the apes. They were so much alike.

"Was he where you thought he was?" Matuzak asked, recalling what she first told him about Jonas's vision.

"Yes, Jonas was true to his word." She smiled, again taking Terin's hand, squeezing it tightly.

"Then he is blessed by the Creator. Any man like that has my respect," he said, before again looking at Terin with a sense of awe. "I've heard many good things about you, lad. I look forward to hearing everything when we dine tonight. You have a pretty lass here who thinks quite highly of you. You need to wed her. She has the fiery temperament of an ape lass. I can tell that by the look in her eyes, spirited and strong." Matuzak now ruffled Corry hair, like she was a wee tot.

Lucas stood on the stern of the *Stenox*, shaking his head. As a Royal Elite, he was trained to guard the royal family from anyone even touching them, but such things were hardly relevant when dealing with the Earthers, let alone the apes. It was all strangely surreal.

"I speak for the Torry Realm and offer our deepest gratitude for helping us retrieve Terin," Corry thanked the large gorilla.

"Bah, think nothing of it. Any friend of Raven's is a friend of mine." Matuzak slapped Raven on the back. "I sent a messenger to fetch your soldiers. We garrisoned them just south of the city. From what I've been told, they have been scouting the coastline for us. Their magantors come in quite handy," he said, regarding her escort she was forced to leave behind.

"Maybe it's time the republic built up its own magantor squadron," Raven said.

"I've already suggested it to the Onam since all funding starts with them," Matuzak referenced the lower legislative body, where tribes were represented based on population size.

"If we were not at war, I would send you a few of our own warbirds to begin your stables," Cory offered, but the Torry Realm needed every magantor they currently had.

"A kind offer, Corry. I now see why Raven considers you a friend." Matuzak grinned before turning his attention to Ular. "Now this is a grand sight, indeed, the mighty Ular. You represent your people well, lad." He rubbed Ular's scaly head.

"President Matuzak, my chieftains send their deepest regards," Ular stated proudly, not visibly bothered by the large ape's rubbing his head.

"A delegation from Linkortis arrived after you departed and are presently with our delegation at Tro, to negotiate our new trade alliance. As for you, I'd wager a keg of ale you played no small part in rescuing young Terin over here," Matuzak said, jerking a thumb at the Torry champion.

"They both did, along with Lucas and Lorken," Raven added, pointing out Corry and Ular.

"We will hear the tale, every detail. We will have the grandest feast the harbor has seen since our victory over the Casians. It appears like your ship is overflowing with new recruits, by the looks of it, lad," Matuzak said, regarding the crew crowding the stern of the ship.

"Afraid most are temporary. Lucas will be returning with Terin, and the woman standing next to Zem is Dejara Guloz, an ambassador sent here from my mother-in-law," Raven pointed out.

"An official ambassador from the far west? What are you waiting for? Call her over," Matuzak said.

And so, Councilor Guloz began her ambassadorship with the president of the Ape Republic greeting her with a monstrous hug, inviting her to drink with him at his table during the grand feast. To say she was taken aback would greatly understate her shock. One by one, the other crewmembers disembarked; Matuzak greeted them in kind. Brokov and Kendra remained aboard to secure the ship while the others followed Matuzak to the grand feasting hall, where preparations were being made. Grigg and Orlom trailed Argos, sharing the crowd's adulation for Matuzak's champion. Zem received the loudest cheers. Everyone in the crowd marveled at his towering presence, recalling his powerful deeds during their revolution when he came ashore, tearing apart Casian formations with pitiful ease. Raven had Ivessa remain with the children aboard the *Stenox* before deciding where they could be housed. Lorken was pleased to discover that Jenna and his children were currently housed in Matuzak's villa outside the city and hurried off with a small escort to visit her there.

* * *

> In the halls of the apes
> Where we raise out tankards high
> Cheering our place
> Beneath the southern sky…

Terin sat at the high table, seated between Matuzak and Corry, listening as the great hall erupted in song, with no voice louder than Matuzak, whose booming baritone echoed above the crowd. It was all so surreal sitting in this place of honor, surrounded by friends, and sitting beside the woman he loved. He thought of how a short time ago, he was enslaved and alone, suffering at Darna's hand, before all his worries were swept away. When all hope seemed lost, Yah delivered him, returning Corry from her apparent grave and freeing him from slavery. His power still wasn't fully restored, but he was now able to wield a sword, though still weak in strength and skill. He came to trust that Yah would restore him in his own good time and resolved himself to that fact. Meanwhile, he would appreciate all that life offered. He thanked Yah for his friends, the brave fellows that joined him in this crowded hall, and those still aboard the ship. The only ones missing were Cronus and Kato, causing him to wonder what each was doing at this time.

"You are doing it again." Corry smiled, placing her hand in his beneath the table.

"Doing what?" he asked curiously.

"Your mind is elsewhere."

"Yes and no. I was thinking of how grateful I am for all of you, for saving me. I was also thinking of Cronus and Kato, wondering where they are and how they are faring."

"They are probably with my brother in Macon if the rumors are true. We will find out soon enough once we return home. Your grandfather will be certain to put you through your paces for worrying him so." She lightly laughed, reminding him of the torture awaiting him in the training yard at Torg's hand.

"I hadn't thought of that," he bemoaned, thinking of the grueling tasks Torg would subject him to.

"It is what you deserve for worrying him and me as well. I will be certain to observe your training from the comforts above the arena." She smiled, not able to help herself.

"Thanks." He shook his head.

"I am certain your father will help in your instruction."

"It is unbecoming for a princess of the realm to revel in the torment of her loyal subject," he reminded her.

"True, but not for your future wife to watch you interact with the patriarchs of your family," she teased, enjoying their banter.

He couldn't help smiling at the thought of her as his bride, willing to suffer anything Torg or his father threw at him for that to come to pass. He caught sight of Lucas and Ular sitting farther along the table, deep in conversation with several of their host, a gorilla merchant of some sort, and his wife.

"They are becoming fast friends," he said, observing the Torry Elite and Enoructan champion.

"Yes, another strange pairing. They have been constant companions since we first stepped aboard the *Stenox*," Corry said.

"Truly?" he asked.

"Truly. As have those two," she sighed, pointing out Orlom and Grigg standing in the middle of the open area below, in lively banter with several other apes, each with a tankard in hand, taking turns belching.

"They seem to be having fun." Terin smiled.

"Too much fun. They are always having too much fun, which gets them into trouble." She rolled her eyes.

"There is nothing wrong with too much fun," he said. There was no place more unlike the hell he suffered than the *Stenox* and its collection of characters. He loved every moment with his friends, his wonderful friends.

"Perhaps not," she agreed, squeezing his hand. She could see him looking fondly at the two young apes and Lucas and Ular. She followed his eyes across the chamber where Argos was dancing with one of Matuzak's many daughters, a fiery white furred lass that he towered over. Lorken finally made an appearance with his lovely wife, the Lady Jenna, who shared heartfelt greetings with Terin and Corry a short while ago. Raven and Matuzak were deep into their cups, each trying to drink the other under the table, with a mortified Dejara Guloz looking on. Zem stood along the far wall amid a small crowd of gorilla warriors, sharing some boring tale that they found entertaining for some reason. It was obvious to her how much Terin cared for his friends, and they, him. "You are fond of them, aren't you?"

"Grigg and Orlom?" he asked.

"Not just them, but *all* of them—the Earthers, Ular, Argos…" she rattled off their names.

"I love them. They are my brothers, the brothers I never had," he said, giving her the most beautiful smile she ever saw.

"My father once told me that it spoke well for a man such as Cronus that so many would risk so much for his freedom. He said only a man of high character could invoke such loyalty from such a diverse group. You are very much like him, for so many of us went to such lengths to see you free," she caressed his cheek.

"Your father said that about Cronus?"

"Yes, just before he departed for Notsu. Cronus said he told him the same thing when he attained Notsu before returning to Corell. You are no different. Do you know that every member of the Elite begged to join the mission to seek you, and every member of my magantor escort wanted to be the one that I brought along on the *Stenox*? Every man in our detachment wanted to partake in your rescue, to save the hero of Corell, each envious of Lucas for the chance to return the favor you gave each of them by your brave deeds."

"If I only knew," he sighed, recalling the loneliness he felt in Darna's manse, thinking everyone thought him dead, wondering if he would ever escape.

"So many love you," she said, the look in her eyes saying so much more.

"And I them," he said, returning her gaze, just as a commotion was heard at the entrance to the great hall, where the Torry contingent Corry left behind finally arrived. Matuzak was first to acknowledge them, raising his tankard into the air, fresh ale spilling its rim.

"Ah, our Torry friends have finally shown themselves! Come in, lads. The food is excellent and ale lively!" Matuzak's baritone voice boomed.

"We are grateful, Your Majesty!" Commander Velis, commander of the princess's escort greeted.

"None of this *majesty* talk, lad. The only title I hold is president, and that doesn't warrant royal treatment, and no ape worth his salt would offer it. To all my brave apes gathered here, let us give our Torry brothers a welcome cheer!" Matuzak declared, the crowd erupting in thunderous approval, many slapping the Torries on the back as they made their way to the head table to greet their host and their princess. They exchanged greetings with Matuzak, Corry, and especially Terin before taking their places at a table set aside specifically for them, partaking food and drink.

Terin noticed other humans seated at the opposite end of the high table, a pair of men in their 5th or 6th decade, dressed in rich robes with a superior air about them. Corry told him they were delegates recently arrived from Teris, envoys of the Casian League. It seemed Raven's stopover in the Casian port was more successful than they first believed, with the Casians open to negotiate with the emerging Ape Republic.

As the late afternoon bled into night, Matuzak again stood from his seat to address the increasingly inebriated assemblage.

"The time has come for curious ears to be rewarded for their enduring patience. I know all of you are as eager as I to hear the tale of Terin Caleph. Since he is a shy lad who refuses to boast his fell deeds, one of his brave comrades will tell his tale. Lucas!" Matuzak called the Torry Elite to the center of the open space in the center of the hall, which was surrounded by long tables and a sea of cheering faces.

"This tale began long before I came to know Terin, before the start of the war, when he lived a humble life on his father's farm," Lucas began. The assemblage hung upon his every word as he relayed the tale from the events at Rego to their rescue of Terin from Darna's dungeon, concluding with the battle at the queen's palace.

Terin felt so many eyes drifting to him as Lucas spoke, offering looks of wonder, awe, and sympathy. He never favored such attention but wasn't embarrassed as he often was, overcome by their genuine affection. Whether it was the apes gathered in the great hall, the Earthers, Ular, or his Torry brethren, he felt one unifying emotion binding them as one—love. He felt pimples raise across his flesh, tingling with rapture, like a comforting embrace. Though he felt it before at Corell, his home, and the times he shared with Cronus and Raven before he was captured, only now could he see it so clearly. Only dwelling in darkness provided him a stark contrast to appreciate this feeling. The darkness of Darna's estate made this moment shine all the brighter.

It suddenly struck him, like a bolt of lightning in a starless sky. He looked at one face after another in that sea of friends, examining each in its individual glory. Each was special in its creation, crafted by the hand of Yah for a great purpose; whether that purpose was small or large, each was significant. The truth was that the Creator loved his creation and wanted his creations to love one another. The more he loved each of them, the more he felt Yah fill him with overwhelming joy. He was so overcome he could barely breath, his voice failing him when Corry squeezed his hand, asking if he was well.

He turned, staring longingly into her blue eyes; a tear of joy ran the length of his cheek, his unspoken words easing her concern. Ever since his rescue, he couldn't stop hugging his friends or stop saying how fond he was of them, but it was so much more. He loved them, all of them, especially Corry, whose love was of deeper intimacy, but it was love, all the same. This is what King Kal must have felt, wanting to share this outpouring with the world, wanting to erase the hurts of the afflicted and lift the burdens of the laden. He wanted everyone to feel what he was feeling.

There in the feasting hall of the apes, Terin's heart mended a little more; the spark of Yah was igniting a slender flame in his soul, a flame that would grow into a great conflagration if he nurtured it.

* * *

The late evening found Raven and Matuzak sharing one last tankard in the president's private sanctum on his unofficial estate just outside the city. Zem retired to the ship, helping Brokov and Kendra, while the rest of their party enjoyed Matuzak's hospitality; each assigned spacious rooms on this estate. Matuzak welcomed Ivessa and Raven's sons to share a nursery with Jenna and Lorken's children. The ape president's eldest daughter, Malva, a buxom white furred lass, warmly received the children, taking them under her wing, doting on them like a favored aunt.

"Good evening, Father." Malva kissed her towering father on the cheek, bidding him good night.

"How fares our little guests?" Matuzak asked as she kissed Raven's cheek before retiring to her chambers.

"They are as ravenous as Lorken's boy but are resting finally. Bless poor Ivessa. The poor nurse has the patience of a stone," Malva said before stepping without, leaving the two of them alone.

"Hungry sons just like their mighty sire." Matuzak lifted his tankard toward Raven, boasting his friend's prowess.

"They sure like to eat. I'll give them that. They aren't too shy about sending stuff out their other end either." Raven made a face, already weary of the smell.

"Welcome to fatherhood, my boy. Ain't it grand?"

"Not so much without their mother to mind them." Raven shook his head.

"From what I hear, she'd be expecting you to mind them. If she has as much fire in her belly as the Torry princess, I'd say you have your hands full."

"Corry's a gentle bird next to Tosha. I might as well have married a gragglogg with how much she's bitten me," he grumbled.

"Taking her children won't win you any favors."

"She's made peace with that, and if not, she can put the blame on dear old dad for sending mercenaries to snatch his grandsons," Raven pointed out.

"Lad, you have much to learn about females. No matter whose fault anything is, it is also your fault. I've had enough bumps on the back of my head to prove it, courtesy of my fair Lanisa." He grinned, referring to his late wife.

"Now that, I'd like to have seen," Raven said, emptying his tankard into the waste basin beside Matuzak's desk. The gorilla did likewise before reaching for a jug of ale to replace the water they had been drinking all night.

"She was quite a lass—fearsome, strong, and a mite quick-tempered, the kind of female to make an ornery old cuss like me a happy male." Matuzak topped off their tankards, finally able to sate their palate with actual ale.

"Finally, the good stuff," Raven said, downing a large gulp.

"Aye, lad, I've been looking forward to this all night. It ain't much fun watching everyone else drink and be merry while pretending we are doing the same, but I managed to build our revolution by pretending I'm strong where I'm weak and weak where I'm strong," Matuzak said. It was an old trick he learned in his youth, a way to flush out conspirators or false friends, who revealed their true nature when drunk or when they thought you were.

"I think Sun Tzu had a similar saying," Raven tried to recall the exact quote but was never good at remembering such things. If Ben were here, he'd have the correct quote and philosopher and maybe even a date to go with it. He sorely missed his friend, wondering how he could be working with Tyro.

"Sun Tzu? One of your famous generals, I assume?" Matuzak downed another generous gulp.

"Yep. He had a book of military advice, things he learned as a general. Most of it is common sense, but it's like my father used to say, "Common sense ain't so common.""

"A wise man, your father. I would like to meet him one day, if your people ever find us."

"You two would get along like two lions on a sheep farm or two hogs in a mud pond."

"I never know what the blazes you're saying but always catch the meaning. We are pretty similar, is what you're saying."

"Like brothers joined at the hip." Raven took another gulp, the ale hitting the spot.

"I'll take it as a compliment. How are young Grigg and Orlom working out for you? I had my reservations about their suitability."

"I couldn't ask for better recruits. Brokov has taken a particular shine to them." Raven tried to claim in all seriousness.

"Hah! Don't lie to me, Raven. I can see that stupid grin about to break across your face," Matuzak pointed at the corner of Raven's mouth.

"All right, they are a couple of rascals, but they're not bad. Let's say they are an acquired taste."

"Do you want them replaced? I have many young warriors wiling to supplement your crew if you need them."

"We'll keep them. We don't cast off crewmates. They still have a lot to learn, but they are loyal, and as you know, that's something you only discover during combat."

"I'm pleased to hear it. Argos says he will stay on as well. He seems quite content with his assignment."

"Really? Arg always seems disgruntled, especially with Grigg and Orlom," Raven pointed out.

"I've never seen him happier, despite sharing a ship with those two," Matuzak said.

"We are glad to have him even if he's a big bully." Raven rubbed his jaw, recalling the incident in the northern sea when he threw half the crew overboard fighting the two rascals.

"So are you, if half the rumors I heard tell are true." Matuzak grinned.

"I have had a few scrapes over the years," he confessed.

"Tavern brawls, beating slavers, and your courtship test at Fera. I hear tell you killed several of Tyro's pit champions with your bare hands?"

"Hardly my fault they had weak necks." He shrugged.

"Lorken said you smashed one in the head with a shield."

"That might have happened."

"Hah! Wish I could've seen it."

"Wish I had Arg or Zem with me. It would've been a lot easier."

"Aye, I heard what they did at Bansoch. Lady Guloz spoke glowingly of their exploits. Argos made a good impression on the Federation, well representing our new republic."

"I noticed many of them taking a shine to Argos and Zem. The two of them are quite popular in Enoructa as well."

"Argos speaks well of him."

"Yep, the two are as thick as thieves, a couple of big bullies."

"I gathered such. What of Ular? How has he fit in?"

"Good. I wish we had ten more like him. He is everything that—"

"That Grigg and Orlom aren't?"

"That's not a fair comparison. Ular is the Enoructan champion. You can only compare one champion to another, and that would be Arg. And you well know, there is no one on Arax tougher than Arg except—"

"Zem."

"Yep, his good buddy." Raven shook his head.

"Well, it seems your crew situation is finally taking shape."

"Yep. Kendra is learning her way around the ship. Now if only Kato would come back, we'd be nearly perfect."

"That might take awhile from what I have heard tell. He has fought bravely for the Torry cause. He is a smart and brave lad. I'll salute him for that." Matuzak took another gulp.

"He is," Raven sighed, wondering where his friend was exactly.

"Now that you're sorted out. Let's get down to business. As you know, we have the emissaries from the Casian League here. Their ruling forum has agreed to proceed with a peaceful resolution to our differences and would like to formerly join our trade alliance with Tro.

Our legislature has deferred such matters to me, and I have agreed to send them on to Tro to help facilitate the agreement. The Enoructans have also sent delegates on ahead with Admiral Zorgon. His fleet should drop anchor any day now at Tro."

"Let me guess, you would like us to deliver the Casians so they arrive on time?"

"If you would be so kind." Matuzak gave him a toothy grin, his prominent incisors jutting severely below his lips.

"All right, we best get underway tomorrow."

"Yes, that would be best, but there is one other matter."

"I figured."

"Our Casian friends would like a third party to oversee the signing, one above reproach with no apparent interest in any of the signee's affairs."

"Good luck with that. We hardly count, considering—"

"Not you, lunkhead, everyone one, including Admiral Zorgon's aunt Becta, knows you are with us."

"Aunt Becta again? I really need to meet her," Raven quipped.

"Maybe you can fix her eyes. She has them going in two different directions, and I never know which one I'm supposed to look at. Never mind that. What we need is a third party that meets the criteria they're looking for, and I can only think of one."

"Who?"

"Come now, lad, even you can guess."

"Corry? She's hell bent on getting home. I don't think she wants to make a lengthy detour."

"The Torry Realm has much to gain from this alliance if for nothing else than guaranteeing Tro does not fall under Tyro's sway. A few days of her time should be worth it. Besides, she does owe you a favor."

"We can ask her," Raven said, imagining how that would go.

"And your boys, they can stay here where they will be safe. You have my word of honor on that, Raven. My daughters will take a liking to them as they have with Lorken's brood, I'm certain."

"I'll drink to that. You can be the grandfather they deserve, not the one they got on this planet."

"Sounds good." Matuzak finished off his drink, with Raven pouring them another.

* * *

The next day found them on the wharf beside the *Stenox*, where Matuzak saw them off. It took little persuading for Corry to agree to overseeing the treaty, aware of the strategic importance of Tro's neutrality. Her escort resigned themselves to having to wait a little longer before returning home but appreciated the apes' friendly hospitality. Of course, Lucas would be going with her to Tro, as well as Terin, who she would not let out of her sight. Councilor Guloz was torn between her invitation as well and her need to remain by the young princes, who only had poor Ivessa to watch over them, other than their ape host. As soon as it could be arranged, Queen Letha would send along a formal guard to watch over her grandsons, as many as would be acceptable by their ape host.

After Matuzak gave his farewells, he drew Terin aside, walking the boy out of earshot of the others, stopping along an empty pier overlooking the harbor.

"I don't often speak of such things, lad, but I can see the Creator's spark in you. It's almost blinding for those who recognize it. The others spoke of your troubles and your unique heritage. I can't know the will of the Creator or his plan for you. I don't know if he will restore you as you once were, but even I can see a great purpose in you. Keep faith in that." The large gorilla slapped his back. The blow nearly took him from his feet.

"You know of the Creator? Of Yah?" Terin made a face.

"My people may not have been made in his glorious image, but we honor him all the same, and his faithful servants, like you. We have been plagued by war with humans through much of our history. Only three times have humans reached out to us in friendship, and each time, the Creator has blessed my people for accepting their friendship. The first was in the days of Kal, your mighty forebear. Kal fought beside my ancient kin, protecting our autonomy and aiding us against our gargoyle foes. The second time was ancient Tarelia,

363

who aided the Jenaii in helping us construct Gregok, and permanently expelling the gargoyles from the ape hills. The third was the Earthers, who are not even Araxan humans. I don't need to explain what they helped us accomplish."

"No, you don't. You are not the only one who owes them a debt," Terin said fondly.

"No debt. As Raven often reminds me, there is no debt owed in friendship, only bonds of brotherhood, and as my brother's brother, you are my brother as well."

"I am honored you think of me as such, General," Terin said, not able to think of the legendary general in any other way than with the appellation he was famed for.

"Kal was our friend, and you are his descendant. Ancient Tarelia was our friend, and you serve their last surviving colony on the continent. The Earthers are our friends, and you are as well. You are bound to all three through blood, loyalty, and friendship. Beyond this, you are a servant of the Creator, our Creator, the Creator that raised Kal, rose up Tarelia, and brought the Earthers to our shores."

"Raven says they were brought here by accident," Terin pointed out.

"Do you believe it was a mishap? They are here by the will of the Creator. I am certain of it. It is something I have spoken with them about, but they do not believe me, though are too polite to voice it."

"That is because they have great respect for you," Terin said.

"Aye, and I, them, but it doesn't change the fact that their purpose is interwoven with your own. Now if you would be so kind—" Matuzak drew his dagger, running it lightly across his palm, raising a thin line of blood. He took his hand, rubbing it on Terin's jaw, before handing his blade to Terin. Terin drew it across his own hand, rubbing his blood on the former general's jaw.

"Now we are brothers of blood, Terin Caleph," Matuzak said, before embracing him and sending him on his way.

The others waved farewell as Terin climbed aboard the *Stenox*, pulling away from it mooring, heading north for Tro.

CHAPTER 15

Cronus soared through the firmament, coursing above the Torry heartland, the western edge of the Zaronan Forest gracing the horizon before them. A late-winter wind pressed upon his face, Wind Racer gliding effortlessly through the crisp air. Cronus's heart beat soundly in his breast with Corell resting on the other side of the forest, the east-west road below, guiding their path, before bleeding into the tree line. He thought of nothing but holding Leanna in his arms and never letting go. She waited beyond the horizon; the promise of her lips consuming his thoughts.

Galen rode off his left, his magantor responding as well as could be expected with his awkward grace. After traveling to sawyer, then Cagan, Mosar, Maeii, back to Cagan, then on to Macon, the bird was growing accustom to him. Torg would be certain to recover the magnificent warbird for the royal stables upon his attaining Corell, but Galen would be loathe to do so. If there was one vocation he would favor over being a minstrel, it was a magantor rider. Perhaps in another life, he might have been so blessed.

Trailing them were two more companions they acquired during their stopover at Central City, each a member of General Valen's vaunted magantor corps, assigned courier duty, ferrying messages between Central City and Corell. Cronus briefly visited Jarvis and Rehya Celen, Leanna's parents, during their brief stay in the Torry capital, who received him with conflicting emotions. They were pleased he was rescued from Fera but torn with the quick nuptials he shared with their Leanna. The fact they were formally joined by

Princess Corry during the great celebration of their victory at Corell went far to assuage their misgivings. They were both honorable people, and Cronus respected them deeply. It was with heavy heart he relayed the grim tale of his fated unit and the death of all his men, including Arsenc. Though neither of them knew Terin personally, the were grieved by the loss of the hero of Corell and the boy who befriended their dear Leanna and Cronus. When Cronus finally bid his farewell, they exchanged a tearful embrace.

General Fonis greeted him at Leltic Hall, the royal palace at Central City, eager to hear events unfolding in the Macon Campaign. Everyone had learned of Terin's fall and were sorely grieved by the loss, but almost no one heard of Kato's fate, the tidings striking Fonis like a bolt to the chest. Cronus relayed the awful news and the urgency of his quest to attain Corell before proceeding to find Raven.

And so they continued on, following the east-west road to Corell, the endless stretch of Torry farmland giving way to the Zaronan Forest, before slivers of white and gold graced the horizon in the far distance. The slivers quickly took shape beyond the eastern edge of the forest, the towers of Corell rising above its massive walls, like a mountain of white upon a brown sea, the once surrounding greenery giving way to dead grass and blackened fields scarred by war. He could make out small winged forms circling the highest reaches of the palace, taking shape as Jenaii warriors, who constantly patrolled Corell's skies since the breaking of the siege.

Cronus pointed a gloved hand toward the *Golden Tower*, the prominent citadel spiraling above the upper palace, making a circle with his hand, signaling Galen on their protocol of approach. They sped forth, angling south of Corell's inner keep before circling the upper palace, exposing their heads and backs to the lookouts perched on the upmost platforms. They circled the palace three times before setting down on the western facing magantor platforms jutting from the inner keep, where they were greeted by an armed flax of garrison troops who ushered them to the throne room.

* * *

Cronus was surprised to find Master Vantel presiding over the realm upon entering the throne room. The craggy master of arms stood before the king's empty throne, his muscled forearms crossed over his chest. Even more surprising was Jonas standing to Torg's right, appearing as if he was expecting them.

"Master Vantel," Cronus began to kneel upon stopping at the base of the dais, his companions following his gesture.

"Keep your feet, Cronus, and report!" Torg cared little for the pomp of his present authority, eager for Corry or Lorn to return and relieve him of his current regency.

"I return with urgent news on matters of the realm," Cronus said, his lack of detail indicating the delicate nature of the tidings.

"And your companions? I see the minstrel has returned, and Minister Antillius has not," Torg observed.

"Minister Antillius remains at his post in Sawyer, where we delivered him," Cronus said.

"I see," Torg said, knowing there was more to this than was appropriate to discuss in the throne room. "I recognize your other companions and the large bundle they carry. Have we truly earned so much correspondence in a few days?" He noted the heavy satchel one of them bore, bearing messages from Central City and the lesser satchel the second one bore, bearing official parchment, and correspondence for officials and commanders of telnic and above.

"Most are messages for soldiers in 3rd Army, from their kin, Master Vantel," one of the magantor scouts explained. Prior to this, only a trickling of messages were sent from Central City, with many families lacking writing skills to send word to their husbands, sons, or fathers, serving in 3rd Army. Royal scribes were posted at Leltic Hall to transcribe messages on behalf of soldiers' families. With so many casualties breaking the siege, many were fearful that their missives would go unanswered.

"Very well. Galen, the palace steward will see to your lodging and escort you to Lady Leanna, who is eager to receive whatever news you have while we speak with her husband. Leave the correspondence with Commander Nevias. Cronus, come with us!" Torg bluntly ordered, wasting no more words than necessary. He and Jonas led him to an inner sanctum behind the throne room.

* * *

"Speak!" Torg ordered, cutting to the bone of it, upon the three of them entering the secluded sanctum.

"I come with news from our Macon Campaign and—" Cronus began, uncertain how much they were apprised of the situation in the west, before Torg cut him off.

"We received a messenger three days ago, detailing Prince Lorn's victory at Borin and the naval engagement at Cesa. Are these the tidings you bear?"

"Yes, but there is one more delicate matter that requires my personal attention, explaining the urgency of my quest," Cronus added.

"And I am guessing it has something to do with your Earther friend, the one called Raven," Torg snorted, causing Cronus's eyebrows to rise in surprise.

"How—" He tried to ask before Torg interrupted.

"How did I know? Ask him," Torg pointed at Jonas, stepping back with a shake of his head.

"How did you know?" Cronus asked Jonas, regarding Terin's father with an odd mix of respect, wonder, and pity, wondering how he received news of Terin's fall.

"You will find Raven at Tro. Terin should be with him." Jonas might as well have grown a second head with the absurdity of that statement.

"If you are wondering how he knows, you won't believe it. Just take it as fact," Torg grunted, crossing his arms, adjusting to the strangeness of it all.

"Terin's alive?" Cronus didn't believe it.

"So he claims. If you're wondering why I am sitting the throne and not Corry, it's because she isn't here," Torg added.

"She isn't?"

"When we learned of Terin, she was quite upset until my son by marriage here"—Torg jerked a thumb toward Jonas—"revealed his unique gift of visions, informing her that he survived and where he was taken. She promptly departed, seeking out the only men who could rescue him."

"Where is he? Who did she seek? Why…" He had more questions than he could think to ask.

"Terin survived the battle, washed ashore, and was taken by slavers at Carapis, who delivered him to market at Bansoch. He was purchased by a commander of high rank. Our princess sought out your Earther friends to effect his rescue, which was successful as my visions have shone. They are currently en route to Tro," Jonas explained.

"He lives!" Cronus couldn't stop smiling, pimples raising across his flesh in euphoric splendor.

"Kato is dead. That's why you seek Raven," Torg said, his words feeling like a bucket of ice on his head.

"Yes," he sighed, his smile dying on his lips.

"And you wish to tell him personally," Jonas said, admiring Cronus's loyalty to his friends.

"It is the least I could do. My friends deserve to learn this from us rather than the rumors whispered from port to port."

"I needn't remind you that Morac's legions separate us from Tro," Torg grunted.

"I will have to angle south before turning back north to Tro," Cronus said.

"It is still a perilous journey," Jonas said.

"Every road is fraught with danger as late, but I must do this. And if Terin is there, I can return this blade to its rightful master." He slapped the hilt of the Sword of the Moon.

"As much as I would like to see Terin again wield his blade, I don't think it wise to risk its loss with you traveling perilously near Morac's legions," Torg reasoned.

"He won't be traveling alone or blindly in the wilderness," Jonas said cryptically.

"Another damn fool idea," Torg snorted with a most disagreeable look on his weathered face, far exceeding his usual disgruntled disposition.

"Galen has followed me this far. A little further should not be an issue," Cronus said.

"The minstrel stays. Jonas has someone else in mind, despite my misgivings, as well as nearly every commander of rank that he has approached with this." Torg shook his head.

"It is within your authority to deny my suggestion, Master Vantel," Jonas pointed out.

"It's one thing to question the sanity of your visions, but another to deny them when they keep coming true. No, I won't stop you, but I won't keep silent about how crazy it all sounds," Torg said, his doubts surrounding Yah and Jonas' visions ever present in his thoughts, much like Cronus and Jentra.

"Who are you sending with me? I won't bring anyone who doesn't want to go," Cronus said.

"It was Elos who recommended himself for this journey. He is only recently returned from the far north, where he helped Alen ignite a revolt within the Benotrist Empire," Jonas said.

"Elos wishes to go with me? That would risk both our Swords of Light." Cronus didn't favor that idea.

"True, but it also better protects your blade with his nearby to help guard it," Jonas countered.

"I will guard him with my life, as he guards mine," Cronus said.

"Very good. I have shared with Elos all of Terin's unique heritage, a heritage you should be aware of," Jonas said.

"Prince Lorn alluded to some great mystery concerning his origin, but we never spoke again on the matter," Cronus said.

"The full tale requires some time in its full telling. If we do not have time to speak of it before you leave on the morn, then Elos can share what he knows during your journey," Jonas sighed tiredly.

"Can you speak of it now?" Cronus asked.

"You can speak with him later. I know that anxious look in your eye, the one that wants this discussion ended so you can see your beloved wife. Get on with it, lad. She's waiting to see you," Torg said, pushing him out the door, knowing Leanna had wondrous news to share.

* * *

He stopped short of the door to their chamber, his steel helm resting in his left arm, while his right hand raked his black mane. He was saddle weary and smelled of magantor but knew she wouldn't forgive him if he tarried any longer to clean himself. The door was open, and he could hear Leanna and Galen's voices echoing from within, Galen's usual flowery banter replaced with a serious tone while recalling their journeys. Their discussion ended once Cronus entered, with Leanna springing to her feet, rushing into his arms.

"I should see myself out and allow you to share the company of your lovely wife, my friend." Galen smiled, excusing himself, drawing the door closed behind him as he left.

Cronus wrapped his arms around her, crushing his lips to hers with a savage hunger. She returned his fervor, digging her hands into his back, squeezing possessively, lest a foul wind lift him from her arms. Their kiss was long and breathless, an intimate dance neither wished to end. They relented briefly, brushing their lips across the others, before again diving in, losing themselves in their embrace. They briefly parted, opening their eyes, staring longingly into the other's, their breath hanging in the air like a pregnant tempest about to break.

"I love you," she whispered.

He smiled, sweeping her into his arms, carrying her to their bed, her light gasp giving him pause.

"Leanna?" he asked, cradling her in his arms, his face painted with worry.

"We must talk." She gifted him the most beautiful smile, her left hand touching a bulge in her stomach.

Cronus's eyes drew wide with wonder, carrying her to their bed and easing her down as if she might break.

"I am not a frail flower, my love," she whispered as he lay her down, sitting himself on the edge of the bed, fearing to touch her.

371

"A child?" he asked, joyous breath caught in the narrows of his throat.

"Yes," she sighed, loving the wondrous look transfixing his face.

"When?"

"Soon, the matrons say late spring," she said, reaching her hand to touch his face but only able to graze his chin before ordering him to shift closer, running her hand over his cheek. Oh, how she loved him, losing herself in his soulful green eyes that stared at her with such intensity to raise pimples across her flesh.

"Leanna." He smiled, overcome with elation, lowering his head, pressing his forehead to hers.

She ran her fingers through his hair, closing her eyes, drinking in his masculine scent. They remained there for an eternal moment, radiating in each other's love, until a lonely joyful tear squeezed from his eye, running down his cheek before dropping to her face.

In that moment, she never loved him more.

* * *

Torg and Jonas remained in heated discussion long after Cronus stepped without, weighing their options and the dangers surrounding them on all fronts. Of greatest concern was the coming spring, and Morac's inevitable return weighed against Lorn's campaign in Macon. Though Torg was loathe to do so, he already ordered General Valen to aid Lorn at Fleace, with strict orders to return with all haste, limiting his time there to a fortnight. Jonas reluctantly agreed, understanding the need to concentrate their forces when possible, bringing as much force to bear upon the enemy at the critical moments, just as they did when sending Terin and Kato to aid Lorn. It was their only hope to survive while hopelessly outnumbered.

"We can agree on that much," Torg sighed, wondering how the fate of the realm came to rest on their tired shoulders, which neither could guess. Jonas planned to leave after the siege was broken, returning to his dear Valera, but Yah kept him here, first for Corry and then for Cronus, giving them the information that they needed.

Now he was free to go home, but Torg insisted he stay until Terin returned safely to Corell.

"Valera needs me. I have never left her side all these years until now. I dare not tarry," Jonas said.

"Until Terin is here, you are the only one with Kalinian blood. Morac's legions will begin their march at the first sign of spring, maybe before. As much as it pains me for my dearest Valera to be alone, the fate of the realm may rest with you. Would you risk all our lives and hers as well just to be by her side?" Torg asked sternly, hating himself for putting the realm before his daughter, but such was the burden of duty.

"Terin will be here when you need him. His destiny is linked to our realm, and mine is linked to Valera. Her life and safety are my highest priorities," Jonas said, placing a gentle hand to Torg's shoulder.

"Blast it, lad! Only you could put me in such a bind, debating against protecting my own daughter. You can leave at first light but only to retrieve Valera and return her here, where she can be protected and where you can do your duty. The time of your exile is at its end," Torg ordered.

"I made a vow to King Lore, to live in isolation," Jonas began.

"To live away from court to raise Terin into manhood, which you have accomplished. He has performed beyond even Lore's grandest expectations. Your isolation is no longer required and, in fact, works against the needs of the realm. I will send a flax of magantors with you to fetch Valera and return here posthaste."

"Very well." Jonas smiled, seeing the light in Torg's eyes at the prospect of seeing Valera once again.

The door creaked slowly open with Commander Nevias stepping within, carrying a sealed parchment. The castle commander closed the door behind him, before giving the parchment to Jonas.

"This was among the missives sent from Central City," Nevias said.

"Who sent it?" Torg asked as Jonas broke the seal, opening the square folded parchment.

"The messengers don't know. It was delivered to Leltic Palace and placed with the other messages allotted for Corell."

"Jonas?" Torg noticed his trembling hands. Jonas's eyes moved rapidly back and forth over the parchment as if searching for something or not believing what he was reading. Torg had never seen Jonas so disturbed as if shaken to his core, not even on the day he confessed his love for Valera to King Lore, all those years ago.

Jonas shook his head; disbelief and anguish vying for dominion in his mind.

"Blast it, lad, what ails you?" Torg growled, taking the missive from Jonas's trembling hands, his own eyes drawing painfully wide as he read.

Jonas Caleph,

I hope this message finds you well. I apologize for failing to make your acquaintance upon visiting your fine home, where I was received by your beloved wife, Lady Valera. My benefactor has contracted me to seek you out and bring you and your kin to treat with him. He is most eager for your company and to learn where you have spent these many years since he last saw you.

Lady Valera will accompany my small party to treat with my benefactor in your stead. Be assured that her safety is foremost in our minds and that of our benefactor, the man you once knew as Taleron, just as he knew you as Joriah. He will be most pleased to greet her at his palace and welcome her into his keeping. He will also be pleased with her current condition and will offer her great care throughout her pregnancy. Lady Valera revealed that you are likely unaware of her quickening, discovering it herself after your departure. Your presence is requested at his palace, at his seat of power. He has instructed all his border garrisons to lookout for your coming. You must turn yourself over to them under the guise of Joriah Taleron, whereupon they shall escort you to his palace.

Your friend,
Hutis Vlenok

"They have Valera!" Torg growled, barely containing his rage.

"She is with child," Jonas whispered, his haunted voice sending a chill up Nevias's spine.

"Your visions did not see this?" Torg snarled.

"If they had, I would have been there," Jonas said, stepping toward the door.

"Where are you going?" Torg asked.

"To find my wife."

Nevias looked on as Jonas stepped without, leaving Torg holding the foul parchment, the craggy warrior reading it over for any detail they might have overlooked before handing it to Nevias.

"Who is Joriah?" Nevias asked.

"I believe it is Jonas's true name, though he never spoke of it."

"And Taleron?"

"Tyro." Torg shook his head, disgusted by the entire affair. What sort of man steals his son's wife and with child no less and uses her to bait him?

"Tyro?" Nevias made a face, wondering the connection and why Jonas would abandon them and surrender himself to their enemy.

"You best sit down, Nevias. This will be a lengthy tale," Torg sighed, figuring it time for the garrison commander to know the full truth.

* * *

They found Elos upon Zar Crest; his gray white-wings enveloped his shoulders, shielding him from the early evening chill. His back was to them, his black mane blowing freely in the gentle breeze.

"Welcome home, King's Elite Kenti," Elos greeted, not turning around, staring off to the northeast as if searching for something in the distant darkness.

"I am welcomed, Elos, champion of the Jenaii," Cronus formally greeted him, he and Leanna stepping to his side.

"Jonas foretold your coming, bearing grave tidings of Kato and bearing the Sword of the Moon. I see this is so." Elos turned, his silver eyes staring intently into Cronus's green.

"He spoke true," Cronus said, holding the warrior's gaze, nearly overwhelmed by his stoic presence.

"He is in harmony with Yah and possesses the blood of Kal. His visions are beyond the prophetic gift. They are windows to reality past, present, and future and as reliable as the world we see with our own eyes," Elos explained.

"Yah." Cronus shook his head. The deity was making it very difficult for him to not believe in him, the skeptic in him dying a little with every passing revelation.

"Yah is all-knowing, all-seeing, all-powerful. His gifts are to be revered and given the highest esteem. The sword you carry is proof of this truth." Elos regarded the Sword of the Moon that hung on Cronus's hip.

"Its power is from Yah?" he asked.

"More than its power. The very materials that the swords were forged from were gifted to my people by the Creator, a *divine gift* flung from the heavens in wondrous glory, striking the temple of Yah in our native homeland across the sea. It was there our ancient mystics discovered the unique properties imbued in the fallen star that destroyed our temple, determining their divine origin and purpose. Thus, we gathered a great host and armada, sailing across the sea to the southern shores of Arax, where the Elaris empties into the sea, building great holdfasts before seeking out the Tarelian order, bestowing them the *divine gift*. It was they who were given the gift of smithcraft by Yah to use the materials from the fallen star to forge the Swords of Light, swords intended for the blood of Kal. Jonas's gift of visions is even greater than the gifts of smithcraft and fallen stars, a direct conduit to Yah's will that would shatter lesser men. Thus, when he spoke of your coming, I knew it to be true."

"He also spoke of you joining me as I continue my journey," Cronus said.

"Yes, a vision we both shared, and one of the reasons for hastening my return from the north. Yah desires that I accompany you to Tro."

"The north? You were with Alen?" Cronus asked.

"Yes. He is fulfilling his appointed role, a role that has shaken Tyro's realm from within, forcing him to alter his plans and perhaps compromise Morac's legions at Notsu," Elos said.

"Is he well?" Cronus asked, marveling at his friend's transformation from timid slave to revolutionary.

"He grows stronger every day, his mind growing sharper, demonstrating a unique cunning. Slaves and serfs are rallying to his side. You would be proud to see his accomplishments," Elos stated with a rare passion unlike his usual indifferent tone.

Cronus smiled, pleased with Alen's progress. He was fond of his young friend, appreciating what he suffered after his own time in Fera's dungeon. Alen's lifetime of servitude dwarfed his brief time in that foul place.

"I worry for both of you traveling to Tro, passing so near Morac's legions," Leanna reflected sadly.

"Fret not, my lady Leanna, for Yah guides our path and will see us return. It is here at Corell where our concerns should rest. Morac shall return with whatever strength his logistics will allow, and when he does, we must meet him with decisive force. General El Tuvo's 1st Battle Group will remain to bolster Corell's garrison," Elos reassured her.

General El Tuvo's battle group was much reduced from the breaking of the siege, the battles that followed, and pilfering its ranks to replenish the 2nd Battle Group to full strength, reducing it to ten telnics. Along with the Bode's 3rd Army, they would greatly strengthen Corell compared to the first siege, but with them accounted for, there were few other forces to call upon to lift the siege.

"I hate to see you both leave after just arriving, but you go with my blessing. I only ask that you complete the task and hasten back," Leanna said.

"I promise, my love." Cronus ran a comforting hand over her back.

Their attention was soon drawn to Jonas stepping onto the platform, his usually gentle countenance replaced with a terrible intensity, causing them alarm, except Elos, who looked on impassively.

"Jonas." Cronus regarded him with utmost respect but wary of his strange demeanor.

"I will not be here when you return, Cronus. There is a delicate matter I must attend. There is a chance I will not see any of you ever again unless Yah wills it," Jonas said cryptically.

"What troubles you?" Cronus asked in alarm, wondering the sudden change that came over him.

"Something has arisen that requires me elsewhere. Torg knows what it is and will tell you upon your return. After Terin learns where I have gone, you must promise me, both you and Elos, that Terin will not follow. It is imperative that he remain and defend the realm!" Jonas said intently.

"I swear to it upon my brother's grave, Jonas," Cronus affirmed.

"My word is my bond," Elos seconded.

"Very good, but I must warn you that Terin is much changed since you last saw him. His power is changed and not all to our benefit, but it serves the will of Yah and his plan for our peoples. Hold faith in that and in each other. Tell him, above all else, to not follow me, no matter the anguish conflicting his heart. Warn him of the last time he defied Yah's will and the cost of such disobedience. I will be gone come sunup. Fare thee well, my friends."

And with that, Jonas stepped away, disappearing down the ramp into the darkness.

* * *

The following morn

Cronus took her into his arms one last time, each holding tight to the other, overcome with emotion. They stood upon the outcropping of the west-facing magantor platform. The wind swirled about, lifting their hair in the breeze. They barely slept the night, hating to waste precious time in slumber, cherishing every moment, not wanting the sun to rise.

"Promise me you will return," she said, pressing her head to his chest.

"Have I failed you yet?" He smiled, savoring the feel of her warmth in his embrace.

"The first time required a great deal of help bringing you home," she sighed, the awful memory of his capture causing her to hold him tighter.

"But I still returned, and I returned from Yatin, and I shall return from Tro," he assured her.

"Nothing is certain in this awful war, not even the promises of true love. Death is the enemy of all, and our love is no different," she whispered sadly, a sudden shudder coursing her heart.

"We haven't endured all this to falter now, my love. If Jonas claims I shall return, then I shall return."

"I shall hold you to that, Cronus Kenti." She smiled, pulling briefly away to look into his beautiful green eyes that melted her heart every time she looked into them.

"Leanna, I am only a mortal man who has no power to defy a face as lovely as yours," he teased, running his hand through her hair, smoothing it behind her left ear.

"Yes, and don't you forget that." She tried to swallow the smile twisting her lips and failing miserably.

With that, he kissed her, lifting her in his arms and spinning her around.

"Ahem!" Elos's calm voice caused him to stop, placing her back to the floor of the platform. The Jenaii warrior stood at the entrance; his stoic countenance masked even the slightest emotion.

"Are you ready, my friend?" Cronus greeted him, just as Leanna's feet touched the floor, expecting the Jenaii warrior to question his spinning his wife around so close to a perilous drop, but Elos said nothing.

"Yes. My magantor is saddled," Elos said. An attendant drew it from its stall behind him.

Cronus gave Leanna one last embrace before mounting Wind Racer when Galen and Torg appeared to send them off. Elos's bird strutted across the platform, bounding off the lip of the outcropping. His mount dropped briefly from sight before lifting, gliding over the battlements, angling southwest. Cronus gave each of them one last farewell, waving briefly before following Elos. The others watched until their magantors were but specks in the distance, disappearing into the southern sky. Jonas departed just before them, furthering the loneliness each felt standing there on the windswept platform.

"Take heart, my fair Leanna. A great omnipotence watches over Cronus and shall guide him safely back to your waiting arms," Galen said.

"I can do naught but trust in that, but I feel lonely, so very lonely," she sighed, running her hands over her growing womb.

"So do I," Torg grunted, wrapping a protective arm about her shoulders before she embraced him, holding tight to his grandfatherly embrace.

* * *

Notsu

The smell of burning flesh permeated the air; billows of black smoke drifted skyward with the citizens of that despairing city cowering in their dwellings. Morac's legions ravaged the city for two full days, rampaging unchecked through the streets. Their long winter encampment, cramped living conditions, and strained logistics fueled their impatience. The looting began over a comely Notsuan maiden shopping in the market square, being set upon by three lust-starved soldiers. Others quickly interceded, vying to claim the prize for themselves, igniting a riot. Benotrist soldiers ravaged the city, dragging women from their homes to rape, slaughtering their menfolk who tried to stop them or killing them for no reason at all. Food stores were plundered; shops, stripped bare; and fires set throughout the boroughs of the east districts. The bodies of slain civilians and soldiers littered the streets, with overturned wagons and slaughtered ocran rotting where they fell. Near the end of the carnage, even old women and children were made sport of.

Lord Morac paced the city square. His red cape fluttered in the breeze; his displeasure apparent in his vicious scowl while surveying the solemn faces of his men gathered before him. Every telnic and unit commander gathered in the city square; their soldiers were assembled in the surrounding streets, standing at attention to receive his judgment. It took him two days to regain control of his legions, killing many of his own men to douse their reckless fervor. He ordered his men to draw lots, picking one man of every hundred rioters for punishment. Three hundred and six men were brought forward of his assembled commanders, bound and knelt. The surrounding streets effused a foul smell, choking the breath of those congregated to witness the spectacle. Many of Notsu's citizens were assembled opposite Morac's commanders, watching with trembling knees as they suffered the stares of their Benotrist masters.

Before addressing his men, Morac cast a contemptuous eye to the Notsuan citizens gathered opposite them. They were a pitiful example of manly virtue, trembling before him with quivering knees. They barely raised a hand in defense of their women until the threat was at their door, and even then, most did nothing. The brave were slaughtered; the weak survived to stand in his presence. And his men wished to sire their get from this poor stock? Even his own collared girls were chosen from powerful bloodlines, far greater than these wretches' offspring. He cared not for their suffering or the actions of his men. Only his men's disobedience kindled his wrath, and their wanton destruction of vital stores needed to feed their legions.

"Two days!" Morac began, addressing his men; his stern countenance sent waves of apprehension through the kneeling ranks of the bound prisoners and the commanders arrayed behind them. "For two days, you roamed freely through my city, taking liberties of the locals' excess, as well as our own provisions. Did you not trust me to grant you such bounty when the time was right? This war is not yet won, and you allow the flesh of women to distract you from the task ahead. The women of this city are not worthy of Benotrist seed. Their wombs yield cowards and weaklings. Look to the west, where the Torries are rich in wealth and women. Fix your eyes on prizes such as those. When my banner flies above the towers of Corell, I shall reward your patience with wealth, slaves, and women worthy of your seed, brave wenches who shall wear your collars well. Look to that day with heady zeal and loyalty to our cause. I could have ordered each of you slain for your disobedience, but I had you choose one of each hundred by the drawing of lots. Three hundred and six of your fellows kneel before me, chosen by lots to pay for the transgressions of the whole. Any of you could now kneel in their place, your lives only spared by mere chance. Remember that it was your defiance that condemns them, not I!" Morac declared as Kriton dragged the first bound prisoner before the crowd. The man's rich attire and three braided cords adorning his shoulders indicated him a commander of telnic and the ranking soldier of all those condemned.

Kriton pushed him to his knees, forcing his head to the ground as Morac drew his sword. Sunlight danced along its blade like a morning flame before igniting with otherworldly light. The assembled host gasped in awe, spellbound by the sword's mysterious power; every eye following its swift descent. The telnic commander's head rolled upon the ground, his dying eyes staring briefly at the faces in his line of vision before fading, unnerving those who witnessed it. Morac sheathed his blade lifting his steely gaze to the surrounding host.

"Commander Fortis was blindly selected from the ranks of my telnic commanders, his lot selected randomly as were each of you. Let him be an example to his peers to control their charges. You may proceed!" He signaled the prisoners' comrades to perform the executions, further shaming them for their rebellion.

Morac looked on as his men executed the selected mutineers, unfazed by their grim punishment. Every man beheading his fellow soldier knew it could just as easily be himself receiving the blow, and therein lay the ugly truth that their brothers paid for their transgressions. It was a brutal but effective tactic that Morac learned from Tyro, the emperor who mentored him since childhood to be a great warrior and general. A great general must be feared and respected by his men. Despite his brutal tactics when dealing with his enemies, Morac was often magnanimous with his own men, but this wanton destruction could not go unpunished.

He turned away once they finished; his aides and fellow Elite following him to his headquarters to fully assess their logistical situation. With winter nearly over and spring soon to come, he would renew his invasion of Torry North, with massive reinforcements to see it through to the bitter end. Morac paused briefly, noting the lack of pain or discomfort in his left leg for the first time since Kregmarin. He smiled knowing when the battle was joined, he would lead his men into the fray.

CHAPTER 16

Fleace, capital of the Macon Empire

Lorn's colors blew proudly in the breeze before his pavilion, a golden crown upon a field of white, the sigil of the House of Lore. He stood beside his standard, upon a hillside overlooking the Fleacen vale, with the Macon capital in the distance to his north. Fleace straddled the banks of the Monata River, with glimmering citadels dotting its skyline and a tall curtain wall circling its perimeter. Rising in the center of the city was the imperial palace, a massive golden-hued structure with towering minarets spiraling above its highest battlements, with the royal standard rippling in the wind, a golden crown upon a field of black. He regarded the city's majestic beauty, admiring its ancient splendor. He could make out the slender silhouettes of soldiers lining its walls and battlements, their faces obscured by distance. What were these men thinking? Did they look to the coming siege with optimism or dread? To which emotion was he leaning?

Neither, he thought miserably. The task before him was merely that…a task. There was no glory in war and no true victory in killing your fellow humans. He resigned himself to the fact that Yah brought him here for a purpose and hoped the Macon king would see reason, choosing it over the fruitless slaughter of both their peoples.

Lorn surveyed the task before him. The Macons deployed no forward units, withdrawing to the safety of the city's walls. He guessed their strength between twelve and twenty telnics, the garrisons of Fleace and Cesa numbering five apiece, and two telnics of Ciyon's

384

army joining them after escaping the battle of Borin. He received conflicting reports of the 1st Macon Army, with some placing them at Sawyer, and others here at Fleace. Cronus attested that their banners graced the battlefield at Sawyer, the distinct green sword on a field of gold, the sigil of the 1st Macon Army. More recent accounts placed them here or at least part of them. Did General Noivi split his command, lending half his strength to the siege of Sawyer and the other half here? It was a question that gnawed at him, affecting much of his planning.

Lorn deployed most of the 1st Torry Army upon the hillsides circling the southern half of the city, using the banks of the Monata to guard their flanks. To his relief, his scouts reported a sizable contingent marching south from the Nila, bearing the sigils of Teso and Zulon, their kings bringing nearly five telnics to join the siege. He looked forward to treating with King Sargov of Zulon, his maternal uncle by way of his sister being Lorn's mother. He had met the man several times since the death of his mother, passing through the small kingdom on his travels between Torry North and Torry South. His father's marriage to the Princess Erella also joined him to the kingdom of Teso, as Sargov and Erella's mother was a princess of Teso.

The Teso and Zulon Armies were complemented by five units of infantry from the garrison of Tuk, along with two hundred cavalry, led by General Avliam, who hurried from Maeii, bringing his fastest mounts to hasten his arrival, leaving most of his strength still making their way from Yatin. These reinforcements managed to circumvent the Macon forces guarding the northern approaches of Fleace, catching the Macon capital by surprise. He ordered the three telnics of the Cagan garrison that Jentra brought north from Cesa, across the Monata to reinforce the arriving forces of Teso and Zulon, strengthening the northern half of the siege.

To Lorn's relief, couriers reported that nearly half the 4th Torry Army was returned to Cagan, preparing to make their way here as soon as they were able. He hoped they were not needed, but one never knew the fickle winds of war, especially if King Mortus proved obstinate. The most advantageous arrival was that of General Dar Valen, commander of all Torry magantors, bringing nearly thirty of his vaunted warbirds from Torry North to aid in the siege. He was joined by his younger brother, Denton Valen, who commanded the Cagan contingent of the Torry Magantor Corp. Lorn knew well that he couldn't keep Dar Valen here for long, with spring soon upon them, when Morac was certain to return. Torg left the commander with explicit instructions to return within a fortnight, with the safety of Corell resting on a knife's edge.

"Your Highness," General Valen greeted, approaching from the magantor pens resting west of his pavilion, donning the uniform of a Torry magantor rider with gray mail and silver tunic, and his helm resting in his left hand.

"General, how fares you this fine morning?" Lorn greeted, sparing a cursory glance skyward, appreciating the clear weather and agreeable climate.

"I am well, Your Highness. The siege is progressing ahead of my expectations. You are to be commended," Dar said, sparing a glance to their surroundings, noting the entrenchments and fortifications along the surrounding hillsides. The prince made good use of the terrain, securing vital watering sites along the approaches of the city, as well as upstream.

"I am in good company, General. The Torry Realm is well-served by their commanders. General Lewins and Admirals Horikor and Morita have conducted this campaign with great skill," Lorn praised the commander of the 1st Army and the admirals of the 2nd and 5th Fleets.

"You are most gracious, Your Highness. We are equally served by a brave monarch. Your exploits in Yatin are impressive. Your father would be very proud," Dar said proudly, masking the pain of Lore's death that haunted him still.

"Now you are being gracious, General. You were with him before he met his fate, I am told."

"I was," Dar sighed. "It was the last counsel of war he held before I departed. By then, we were surrounded and hopelessly outnumbered, but he stayed and fought to the end. I witnessed much of the battle from afar, battling in the skies above Kregmarin such carnage."

"Many brave men fell with him, brave men who are sorely needed."

"Yes, but they bled the enemy dearly on those hillsides. Their sacrifice was not in vain. I was told to give you this by Master Vantel." Dar retrieved a sealed scroll from his satchel, gifting it to Lorn.

"I would have given it to you last night when I first arrived, but Master Vantel instructed me to give it to you the morning after I arrived. Why he ordered it so is a mystery," Dar said as Lorn opened it.

Dar could see the prince's visible reaction as he read the parchment.

"Your Highness?" Dar asked, taken aback by his prince's sudden mirth.

"Do you know the contents of this missive, General?" Lorn asked excitedly.

"I do not, Your Highness. I was at Central City when it was delivered to me. But If I were to guess, it pertains to Princess Corry's absence from court. She departed Corell with a dozen of my finest riders some time ago," Dar said, though he was not privy to her destination or purpose.

"She believes Terin lives." Lorn's words struck Dar like a thunderbolt.

Dar's grave silence gave Lorn pause; the general looked deathly pale.

"General?"

"Our couriers arrived a short while ago from Cagan, Your Highness, with two men claiming to have seen Terin alive. My men are further interrogating them before bringing them here," Dar explained.

"Men? Who are they and from where do they hail?"

"It seems a fancify yarn, which I doubted very much. One is named Guilen and hails from the Sisterhood. The second is a Torry sailor named Criose."

"Bring them here!" Lorn commanded.

* * *

Criose released a nervous breath, tugging at the collar of his new tunic as they stood before the Torry prince in his pavilion. Guilen appeared all too comfortable standing beside him, seemingly unaffected by their prestigious company. Their arrival at Cagan was rather innocuous, reaching the safety of the port in obscurity, though wary of anyone who might be agents of Darna sent to find them. They were fortunate to gain audience with Regent Ornovis after presenting their claims to his steward at Soren Palace. Regent Ornovis was skeptical of their claims but decided to send them on to Lorn for him to determine the verity of their story. And so here they stood before the Torry crown prince in the middle of a war, awaiting to answer the many questions sure to follow.

"Stand at rest, gentlemen, there is nothing to fear," Lorn reassured them. Jentra and Dar flanked their prince, with two more guards posted at the flaps of the door.

"We are honored to be received, oh Prince." Guilen gave a practiced bow.

"You are welcomed. You are Guilen of House Estaran. Is this so?" Lorn asked. If this was so, the man was a distant cousin.

"I am, oh Prince." He again bowed.

"One bow is enough, Guilen. Be at rest. And you are Criose, a sailor upon the Torry warship *Vengeance*?" he asked, looking to the second man.

"I am, Your Highness," Criose said, stopping mid bow upon the look Lorn gave him.

"Very good. You each claim Terin is alive and have information detailing what transpired after Carapis?" Lorn asked.

"We do, oh Prince. Perhaps Criose should begin, for he was first to encounter Terin upon the slaver's ship," Guilen said.

"Criose?" Lorn looked to him to begin.

And so they relayed the tale from Terin awaking upon the *Queen's Dagger* and his sale at Bansoch, continuing with his ordeal on Darna's estate and their escape. Their mention of Terin finding another Sword of Light, one in Darna's keeping, was of equal interest and concern. They concluded where Terin was captured with the others managing to flee. The more they spoke of all he endured, the angrier Jentra became.

"And that was the last you saw him?" Jentra growled after they spoke of his capture on the street of Caltera as they sailed away.

"Yes." Criose lowered his head in shame.

"You left him there while you escaped?" Jentra growled, taking a step toward the two.

"Easy, old friend. There was nothing they could do. We know well what Terin is like when afflicted by such madness," Lorn said.

"The captain of our ship would not entertain such notion of going back to shore with my mother's soldiers flooding the streets. The only reasonable choice left to us was to escape and inform His Highness of Terin's whereabouts," Guilen explained.

"A difficult but logical decision," Lorn conceded while Jentra snorted derisively, stepping back beside him.

"How can we be certain that the man you spoke of was truly Terin?" Dar asked.

"He was clad in the uniform of a Torry Elite when he was captured, General," Criose said.

"His fighting prowess and the strange effect he has on gargoyles were quite convincing, as well as his finding my mother's sword," Guilen added.

"They speak true. I am sure of it. And if I had any doubts, Torg's missive removed them," Lorn said, still holding the parchment in his hand, speaking of Jonas's visions of Terin in captivity in Bansoch and Corry's plan to seek out Raven to rescue him.

"Then what are we waiting for? Give me leave, Your Highness, and I will lead our fleet there, demand his release, and exact justice from Guardian Darna!" Jentra growled.

"Little need of that, old friend." Lorn smiled knowingly, handing him the missive.

Jentra read the parchment thrice over, his mind a whirlwind with news of Jonas's visions, Corry's boldness and talk of the Earthers' intervention. "This is madness," he said, looking to Lorn and then General Valen.

"Madness? Or simply the times we are living? Either way, we must trust the evidence before us," Lorn said.

"Trust the evidence before us?" Jentra wanted to laugh. Their evidence was the testimony of two fools and the prophetic visions of Terin's father. Either would be worth chancing a journey to Bansoch, but what guarantee had Corry of enlisting the Earthers' help? That is, if she could find them to begin with.

"I trust more than the evidence before us, Jentra. The word of Yah stands above everything," Lorn said knowingly.

"Yah, again? What divine wisdom has your God bestowed this time?" Jentra snorted.

"Jentra, you of little faith. How many times must his words to me prove true before you believe?" Lorn smiled wanly, touching a hand to his friend's shoulder.

"Fair enough, Your Highness. I humbly ask once more, What divine foresight has he bestowed upon you?"

"He said when I came to this place, I was not to proceed until given a sign, a sign of hope. Here we stand, receiving separate confirmations that Terin lives at the same time. Such coincidences are not happenstance. It is a sign from Yah. Terin lives," Lorn declared.

"A sign to do what? Are we to attack now?" Jentra asked.

"Gather our commanders while I speak with our friends here," Lorn ordered Dar and Jentra, leaving him alone with Guilen and Criose.

"Wine?" Lorn offered the two men, stepping toward the small table beside his cot, where a pitcher and goblets rested.

"I would be delighted, Your Highness." Guilen smiled, not at all shy to partake, where Criose felt quite differently in the presence of royalty.

"Here," Lorn offered each of them a goblet, forcing Criose to accept the hospitality. "There is much to your tale still to tell. I am certain. Perhaps in the coming days you might relay more of it. Since you have fulfilled your duty to Terin by informing me of his whereabouts, what are your plans?"

"I was fortunate to relieve my mother of some of her gold, just compensation for my rightful inheritance. I thought to establish my own merchant exchange, perhaps even purchase a ship to begin a fleet. Cagan would be an excellent place to establish a new house, if the harbor regent or yourself are in agreement, of course, Your Highness," Guilen said.

"I would be in agreement, Guilen. Any friend of Terin's is most welcome in the Torry Realm. Perhaps if Guardian Darna ever visited Cagan, you could be my honored guest during her stay," Lorn said, drawing a mischievous smile from the impish Guilen. "And you, Criose?" Lorn asked.

"I served as a ballistae crew chief before my ship sunk at Carapis, Your Highness. I would serve wherever you have need of me," Criose said proudly.

"Can you handle a sword?" Lorn asked.

"Fairly so, Your Highness, though after seeing Terin wield a blade, that assessment would be overstated," Criose stated honestly.

"You are not alone in your humility, Criose. We have all been humbled by his prowess with a sword and his fell deeds in battle. Guardian Darna is quite ambitious to believe she can hold him." Lorn shook his head.

"Ambition and foolishness share a delicate line of distinction, Your Highness," Guilen said, unable to curb his flippant tongue where his mother was concerned.

"True, there are many positive and negative traits that straddle a thin line. Courage and stupidity are oft assigned to the same act, as are cowardice and wisdom. As for what I am to do with Criose's offer, I have just the place for you, if you are so willing?" Lorn asked.

"Wherever you have need of me, Your Highness, I am your man," Criose said.

"Then take a knee," Lorn ordered, drawing his sword, touching the flat of the blade to Criose's head. "Do you vow to serve the Torry Realm with leal service?"

"I so avow," Criose said, repeating the vows he swore to when he first served the Torry Navy.

"Do you vow to guard the agents of the throne with your life, unto your dying breath?"

"I so avow."

"As regent of the realm, I so place you in my service. Arise, Criose, warrior of the crown and guardian of your prince," Lorn declared.

"I am honored, Your Highness." Criose bowed as he rose.

"I am honored to have you. As your first assignment, I am placing you with Jentra as his personal guard. He will not like it, and he will not like you at first but give him time. He needs someone guarding his side, especially with him across the river."

* * *

King Mortus gazed out the window of his private sanctum atop the tower of Mortun, the citadel bearing the namesake of the first Macon king. Observing the Torry Armies gathered to his south, he wondered if he might be the last king of greater Maconia. He rested his palm against the stone wall beside the window, lost in his thoughts and plagued by his dreams. All his ambitions and fears brought him to this critical place, the fate of his realm resting in the balance. His dreams were more visions than passing thoughts, repeating themselves over and again for many years. In one, he sat his throne, with a great conqueror kneeling before him, symbolizing his victory. In the other, he placed his own crown upon the head of a future Torry king. Which vision was true? This question plagued his waking hours and visited him again while he slept, driving him to madness. And now a great conqueror was at his doorstep, in the guise of a future Torry king. He had met Prince Lorn many years ago, and he was the conqueror in his vision but not the Torry king upon whose head he set his own crown. Did this portend his victory here at Fleace? Or would Lorn decimate his capital and armies but leave him to be conquered by his future heir?

Madness, he thought miserably to himself.

"Father?" His eldest daughter's voice drew him from his maddened thoughts, turning to find her lingering at his doorway.

"Deliea." He smiled, taking in her lovely form, her rich black hair framing her sharply feminine face. Her long lashes accentuated her fierce emerald eyes, deep and intelligent like her late mother. Of his four daughters, she held a special place in his heart, reminding him of his fair Demetra, who died birthing his fourth and last daughter. She was the one voice that calmed his spirit, much like his own mother, who currently held court in his name while he dealt with military matters at hand. A king with no sons but only having four daughters was looked down by some as vulnerable, further fueling Mortus's insecurities, driving him to expand his realm, and no prize consumed him like Sawyer. The acquisition of Sawyer would solidify his hold of the Monata River and secure his northeastern flank.

"Are you well, Father? My sisters and I worry for you, as does Grandmother," Deliea asked, stepping into his embrace.

"Do not fret, my lovely flower. We hold a strong position behind thick walls with relief armies underway to lift this siege. The Torry prince will rue raising his sword against me."

"Is there no path for peace, Father? Should we not be friends with our Torry neighbors?" she asked, briefly pulling away to look up into his fierce green eyes that matched her own.

"Peace? It is they who attack us, my child."

"Because we attacked Sawyer, Father. Could we not compromise? Perhaps Prince Lorn might listen. The House of Lore is reputably honorable. They did arrange my rescue at Molten Isle," she reasoned.

"They arranged their own princess's recue, not yours. That was the Earthers' doing if my sources are accurate. No, there shall be no peace between us until one has beaten the other. There are two paths before us—one dark and the other light. It is here at the walls of Fleace that the fate of greater Maconia lies."

* * *

"We have spotted columns of infantry along the river road here and here, bearing the sigil of the 1st Macon Army, a green sword upon a field of gold," General Valen pointed out on the map, some 150 leagues to their east.

That information was not unexpected from the commanders gathered in Lorn's pavilion around the map table.

"What of Sawyer? Does the city still hold, or is Mortus recalling his army because it has fallen?" Jentra asked.

"It still holds as of four days ago, if my scouts' reports are true," Dar said. His warbirds skirmished with Macon magantors along the northern approaches of Sawyer, each side losing a single avian in the exchange.

"Any sign of the 2nd Macon Army?" Lorn asked. Cronus told of the 2nd making up the majority of the besieging forces at Sawyer.

"Still at Sawyer, as far as we know, Your Highness," Dar said.

"What of the areas south and east of us?" General Lewins, commander of the 1st Torry Army, asked, wary of his rear flank.

"Nothing of note. The roads east are clogged with civilians fleeing the conflict. Our hold on Cesa appears secure, as does our position in the straits," Denton Valen reported. His magantors were tasked with scouting those regions.

"It appears your strategy has proven correct, Prince Lorn," General Zubarro, commander of the 2nd Zulon Army, praised. His three telnics were camped on the north side of the Monata River, just beyond the city walls, along with the two telnics of General Velen's 2nd Teso Army. General Velen remained with their command, with General Zubarro speaking on his behalf, along with the king of Zulon and Lorn's uncle, King Sargov V, who stood at Lorn's right.

"Indeed," King Sargov agreed, admiring Lorn's strategic brilliance conducting this campaign, especially his maneuvering General Ciyon to attack at Borin while landing a force in his rear at Cesa. Those victories brought the bulk of Lorn's strength to the southern side of Fleace, where its walls were weakest, with the remaining Macon Armies far afield. "It seems your objective of lifting the siege of Sawyer has been achieved without having to go there to do so. If King Mortus has ordered his 1st Army back to Fleace, be certain the 2nd will soon follow."

"That was the objective as we originally planned it, but even I did not see our victories so easily gained," General Lewins said.

"Aye, but we are still facing a heavily guarded city with anywhere between twelve to twenty telnics guarding it, with a relief army perhaps four to five days off," Jentra said, knowing any attacking force required a three-to-one advantage, which they currently lacked, unless they could draw the Macons out of their city.

"How goes the movement of your men across the river, Jentra?" Lorn asked, looking at the point on the map downstream of the city where he ordered the Cagan garrison troops to cross out of sight of the city walls.

"More than half have crossed over. They should complete the crossing by nightfall," Jentra said.

"Very good. I want them in position by morning, bearing the standard of the 2nd Torry Army," Lorn pointed out the banners stacked neatly in the corner of his pavilion.

"The 2nd? I thought we were pretending to be the 4th, after feigning to be the 1st?" Jentra wasn't sure who they were supposed to be.

"I have plans for the 4th, which will be positioned to our east, with the 1st here," Lorn pointed out each position along the perimeter, where the 1st Army would take up the guise of two armies instead of one.

"A clever trick, Your Highness, but the real 4th Torry Army is still in Cagan and Yatin, far from here. The Macons will not see forty telnics outside their walls no matter how many banners we present to them," General Lewins pointed out.

"Come now, General, you forget the 2nd Torry Army under General Fonis here." Lorn regarded Jentra. "He commands twenty telnics as well."

"I do?" Jentra shook his head. No magic trick could increase his meager three telnics to twenty unless the Macons were blind.

"Play the part, Jentra, and you would be surprised by who believes it." Lorn smiled.

Jentra threw his hands up, knowing no one could talk Lorn out of his half-brained ideas once he was committed.

"So we attack on the morrow?" General Zubarro asked, trying to follow what was going on.

"No, General. Tomorrow, we talk," Lorn's smile widened even further.

* * *

The following morn, the Macon defenders looked to their north in horror as the banners of the Torry 2nd Army appeared in the distance, along with the 2nd Teso and 2nd Zulon, though the terrain masked their true strength. With the sigils of the Torry 4th and 1st Armies gracing the siege lines to the south of Fleace, panic rippled through the Macon capital. By midday, an envoy from the Macon king was brought to Lorn, asking for parlay.

"Prince Lorn, I am Minister Hulan of King Mortus's council." The envoy bowed, greeting Lorn upon being brought to his pavilion. His rich flowing robes were a stark contrast to Lorn's warrior garb, soiled from use and battle.

"Speak, Councilor!" Lorn commanded sternly, flanked by General Lewins and King Sargov.

"My king, the great Mortus of Macon seeks an audience between his ministers and yourself to discuss a truce, Your Highness." Hulan again bowed, with his heavily perfumed scent stifling in the confines of the pavilion.

"I will not discuss such matters of importance with your king's ministers or servants. Tell your master that I shall treat with him face-to-face under the flag of truce halfway between your city's south gate and our siege lines," Lorn said.

"Of course, Your Highness, but there are many delicate matters to address, and…" Hulan tried to explain.

"You know my terms. Return to your master with my conditions," Lorn declared, sending him from his sight.

* * *

The late day found Lorn siting his mount beneath the blue flag of truce, mid distance between his lines and the south gate of the city, with King Sargov upon his right and General Dadeus Ciyon to his left, and a flax of Royal Elite forming a half circle behind him. Ciyon wondered his purpose here, with nothing preventing him from fleeing to the safety of the city. He sat a spirited gray ocran, dressed in his colorful golden armor and tunic, his polished helm shining even under the gray-clad sky.

"Something troubles you, General?" Lorn asked, dressed in his resplendent silver mail and blue tunic, but with no other adornments befitting his regal station.

"Curious, Your Highness," he replied, watching as the gates of the city drew open, followed by King Mortus's standard bearer, a golden crown on a field of black emblazoned upon its sigil.

"Curious? You think me daft allowing you such liberty within the shadow of your capital?" He guessed the Macon general's thoughts.

"Yes. You have made it clear that I am to die if I do not disavow my oaths to my king. Yet here I sit upon a healthy mount with the gates of my city open to receive me. I am not bound. What prevents me from fleeing?" Dadeus asked.

"Nothing. You are free to go if you choose. I'll not keep you, though I suspect you shall stay for a time, as your curiosity shall hold you where I will not." Lorn shrugged.

"Are you touched?" Dadeus asked, wondering what game the Torry prince was playing.

"No, though Jentra might disagree." Lorn smiled.

"I am free to leave? After all the times you declared my life forfeit?"

"Free. The way is open, Dadeus." Lorn waved an open hand to the gates of Fleace.

"Fine, I shall leave with my king when this farce of a parlay is ended. Enjoy the company of traitors. May they serve you as well as they have betrayed me," Dadeus said, referencing his three commanders of telnic who foreswore their oaths.

"You have a sharp tongue, boy. Perhaps a little grace is warranted for the man who spares your life," King Sargov reproached the youthful Ciyon.

"A sharp tongue perhaps, but I still have my honor. Aye, I'll stay until this parlay is ended. I am curious as to what you shall say to my king, Your Highness." Dadeus gave a mock bow, his ocran shifting beneath him.

They looked on as King Mortus approached, riding a beautiful golden ocran, cantering with practiced grace as it drew nigh. The king was dressed in bright golden armor over a scarlet tunic, as if arrayed for battle, his very visage befitting a warrior king of old. Ciyon was taken aback by his liege's disposition. He did not recall seeing the king in anything other than flowing robes and fanciful vestments befitting his regal station. He led a procession of royal guards, attendants and ministers of the court.

King Mortus drew ahead of his standard bearer, his cold green eyes fixed to Lorn as he stopped several paces before him, sparing Ciyon a brief glance before returning his fierce gaze to the Torry Prince, his men taking up position behind him. With Lorn's helm in his left hand, Mortus removed his own, allowing his dark mane to cool in the breeze. Lorn discerned much from studying the king through the years, taking his measure again at this critical juncture. King Mortus spent his many years yearning for what he lacked, never satisfied with what he had. Nothing satisfied him, not the expansion of his empire or the birth of his daughters or the growing wealth of his merchant cities. If all the world was given him, he would thirst for more with an insatiable hunger, never content, never fulfilled, never joyous. Now he faced a young Torry prince who conquered more in a few moons than Mortus had in his lifetime. The more he looked upon Lorn, the harder he scowled; bitterness twisted his innards, further driving his hatred. For years, he planned the seizure of Sawyer, the crown jewel of Lake Monata, and the one necessary piece to secure his realm. Offers of political union and overtures of acquisition were refused, forcing his hand in conquest. All he needed was the opportune moment, and the Torry-Benotrist war gifted him that moment. With the Torries occupied in the north and in Yatin, Sawyer hung like low hanging fruit to be plucked. But alas, all his plans went horribly awry, foiled by the Torry prince.

"Greetings, King Mortus," Lorn politely welcomed the Macon monarch.

"Spare me your pleasantries, Prince Lorn. They cannot mask our mutual dislike." Mortus was never one for such pretense.

"I am not here to trade barbs and insults, King Mortus. You wished to treat with me, and here I am," Lorn calmly replied.

"You may think you hold the advantage, considering the forces you have managed to assemble, but I am not one to easily frighten. Consider your own precarious position, my young prince. While you wreak havoc in my lands, you leave yourself open in the north. Spring is nearly here, and with it, Tyro shall renew his attack upon your northern kingdom. Do you wish to drag out this siege with your kingdom at stake? I remind you that I am well fortified within the city walls. My soldiers are motivated, well supplied, and eager to defend their homeland. You could storm the walls, but how many Torry sons are you willing to sacrifice in the exchange? More than you can spare, I surmise. And what of your southern realm? You have emptied Torry South of its defenses. Can you fully trust your new Yatin allies? I know Yangu's addled mind enough to also know that even a fool wouldn't trust him, and you are no fool, Prince Lorn. Is my city worth such risk to both of your kingdoms?" Mortus was almost smiling stating Lorn's dilemma.

Mortus continued. "And I see you have called upon General Fonis and the 2nd Torry Army. Having them march from Central City to my capital is a masterful stroke, but is it truly wise? Yes, you have me surrounded, but at what cost? Your northern kingdom's western flank is naked. A single legion could sweep over your homeland, conquering everything this side of Corell, and there is naught you can do to stop it."

"What you say is true, King Mortus. I am vulnerable in the north, and a single legion could sweep across my heartland to the very walls of Corell. Perhaps I am equally weak in the south should Yangu betray me, but none of these facts matter here and now. All that truly matters is that I will not leave your land with an enemy at my back. I will storm your city if required, slaying your army to the man. With Fonis' arrival I have more than fifty-two telnics at my command, more than enough to destroy you," Lorn stated flatly, driving this point forcefully.

Mortus stirred uneasily in the saddle, knowing Lorn could do as he boasted.

Lorn continued. "I will seize your city, if necessary, oh King, even though it may cost me dearly elsewhere. And if I do suffer from it, you will not live to see it."

A long silence passed between them, each looking to the other in serene silence.

"But"—Lorn strung out his next utterance for effect—"there is an alternative."

"Speak of it," Mortus growled.

Lorn quietly dismounted, taking a step toward the Macon monarch, urging Mortus to do the same. There they stood, face-to-face between their armies with thousands of eyes fixed upon them.

"Do we not breathe the same air, oh King? Does the same blood not flow in your veins as mine? Are we not each human? We are much alike, oh King. We both desire security for our realms and people. Look to your people and then to mine. What separates them but the banners they follow into battle? Our people are much the same. They have lived side by side for thousands of years," Lorn said.

"You speak of similarities that any people share. They are pointless." Mortus disliked his patronizing tone.

"I cannot leave an enemy to my back, oh King. And attacking one another will doom us both. What our people share is greater than what divides us. You have not faced gargoyles in battle, your good fortune of geography sparing you that...for now. But what shall Tyro do if he overtakes the Torry Realm? Do you think he will gladly leave you to your own volition? You know what he shall do, oh King. We have countered Tyro at Tuft's Mountain, Corell, and Mosar, but have bled ourselves doing so. The Yatin Armies are nearly spent. The Torry 5th Army has been destroyed to the man. The 3rd and 4th Torry armies are greatly reduced. Bacel has been destroyed. If humanity is to survive, you must come to her aid, King Mortus. If our two peoples are to survive, we must become one. One people, one vision, one kingdom, and eventually...one king," Lorn declared, his voice heard by no one but Mortus.

"One king? And you would be that king, I suppose," Mortus snorted, ready to draw steel and be done with this farce.

"No," Lorn sighed, taking Mortus aback.

"You would bend to me?" Mortus didn't believe that.

"No," Lorn said with equal emotion.

"Speak sense, boy!"

"Only united can we stand."

"So you have repeatedly said, but you will not bend to me, or I to you."

"I cannot leave an enemy to my back but would welcome a friend at my side," Lorn said.

"Friend?" Mortus sneered. "You've destroyed one of my armies, sunk one of my fleets, and overran half my realm. Speak not of friendship to me, boy! I'd rather die than hand you my kingdom. There is but one way to settle this!"

"What would you propose, oh King?" Lorn asked knowingly.

"If you've the nerve, boy, I challenge you man to man, here, before the city's walls in full view of our men. Your sword against my own, to the death. I win, and your armies leave this land, never to return, and Sawyer is mine. If you kill me, you can have my empire, what's left of it." Mortus had many faults, but cowardice wasn't one of them.

"I could do as you ask, and I would kill you, oh King. Your empire would be mine. I have foreseen this as Yah has shown me. But hear me well, oh King. Yah is allowing you one reprieve, one chance, if you will. I know the dreams that confound you, dreams that have tormented you for many years, the very ones you dare not speak to any other," Lorn said, his voice barely above a whisper.

Mortus's silence was deafening, unable to form words of rebuke.

"Two dreams you have, oh King," Lorn continued, Mortus's breath quickening with anticipation. "One is of you upon your throne, with a great conqueror kneeling humbly at your feet. That conqueror is me. It is I that kneels at your feet, oh King. Your second dream is what troubles you. It is of you placing your crown upon the head of a Torry king."

"How…how can you know this?" Mortus felt his heart pounding emphatically in his chest as if to burst from his ribs.

"Oh, great King, it is Yah that has revealed this to me. It is Yah that has guided my every step in your land, bringing my armies safely to your doorstep, sweeping your armies and ships from our path. Your own visions speak truth to my own, for they come not from your fevered imaginings but the mind of Yah."

"Which is true? Shall you kneel to me or I to a future Torry king, for the man's head I set my crown was not you," Mortus asked, his voice laced with apprehension.

"They are not separate, oh King. Each dream is joined to the other. Yah is giving you this one choice, this last reprieve before judgment falls upon your realm. You may choose war and with it your destruction, or you can choose the path of your visions," Lorn said.

"My dreams are in conflict. One disproves the other unless you bend to me and your future heir takes my throne for himself."

"Yes," Lorn affirmed.

"What madness do you speak?"

"Your choice is war and destruction or unity through your visions. As to what you must do, you must first lift the siege of Sawyer. Two, your eldest daughter and heir, the Princess Deliea, shall be my bride. With our union, our two peoples will be one. Three, your remaining three daughters shall wed the heirs of Teso, Zulon, and the widowed Vintor Ornovis, regent of Cagan. In turn, you shall wed the only daughter of Regent Ornovis, the Lady Illana. Fourth, all unwed maidens of our two lands shall be wed to unwed soldiers of our two armies. Fifth, you shall release General Ciyon of his oath of loyalty, allowing him to swear loyalty to our union and lead a joint Torry-Macon Army into battle in the north. Lastly, you shall march with me, side by side into battle against our true foe, Tyro."

Ciyon sat speechless, overhearing Lorn's demands in disbelief. The terms were drastic yet fair, seeming no harsher on Macon than on the Torry Realm.

Mortus was dumbstruck, his mind trying to work out all that Lorn had said. This was unprecedented, two nations at war suddenly dropping hostilities and joining in union.

"I do not seek your defeat, oh King, and I cannot accept my own. I desire union, King Mortus. Look to your dreams for the answer. Your vision of my kneeling before your throne is of me and Princess Deliea submitting to you as the overseer of our marital union. It is you that shall place my hand in hers. It is from her that a son shall be born, who shall one day be my heir and yours. On that day, you shall happily give him your crown, as I shall gift him mine. True union doesn't grow from a victor imposing his will upon the vanquished, but when two enemies can look into each other's eyes and learn to love the other as a brother or a father or a son. This is Yah's gift to mankind. You have received his visions. Now take up his cause and receive his blessing, oh King," Lorn added, his gentle smile touching his eyes.

Mortus was beguiled, searching Lorn's eyes for deceit and finding only truth. A sudden break in the clouds cast blinding sunlight upon them, bathing the two men in its brilliance. Those gathered to either side gasped for surely this was a sign of something greater. Mortus staggered before Lorn steadied him, touching a hand to his shoulder.

"What say you, oh King?" Lorn asked.

"What of my empire?"

"Your empire remains yours until our mutual heir is born. Until that day, brides and grooms shall be exchanged between our peoples, and your realm shall never know defeat or come to ruin, lest the gargoyles overrun us all and throw down our kingdoms. Stand with me, and we can stop that from happening," Lorn said.

"So be it!" Mortus declared, clasping Lorn's hand to seal their union.

"Dadeus Ciyon!" Lorn called out to the Macon general.

"Yes, Your Highness?" Ciyon replied.

"Shall you swear loyalty to this union and lead a joint army of Macons and Torries into battle?" Lorn asked.

"I shall avow it!" Ciyon declared.

"Very good. Your first order is to deliver telnic commanders Gaiv Lucen, Fen Zaden, and Coln Vladek to King Mortus for judgment," Lorn said, calling out the three commanders that betrayed their oaths.

"With pleasure, Your Highness." Ciyon bowed, taken aback by Lorn's honor, an honor the prince did so well to hide, playing a part to test his own virtue. It was never Lorn's honor that was disputed but his own, and he passed the test.

CHAPTER 17

Tro

Terin drew in his breath as he beheld the *Sentinel of Tro* greeting them upon entering the port, its jeweled eyes casting a guarded stare to the entrance of the bay, as if standing watch in eternal vigilance. Standing the height of fifteen men, it towered over the ships passing below its face, its massive sword outstretched toward the sea, warning any who dare assail the eastern port. He recalled Cronus's speaking of its wonder, wishing to see it for himself one day, and here he stood upon the 3rd deck of the *Stenox*, viewing this wonder with breathless awe.

"The Sentinel of Tro," Corry whispered in his ear, equally impressed by its majesty, resting her hand in his, a gentle breeze pressing her face.

"I still cannot believe any of this is real." He shook his head, still haunted by Darna, his mind a constant battleground of chaos and peace vying for dominion.

"Can you not feel the wind upon your face? Can you not see the wonder of the bay? Can you not hear the sound of my voice? Does your heart not pound when my hand touches yours?" she asked, looking over to him, a beautiful smile upon her lips.

"I must learn to trust my senses again, as if I am an infant learning to crawl." He returned her smile, losing himself in her eyes.

"You are free, Terin, free to begin the world anew."

"Freedom is only a reward if I share it with you." He lifted his free hand, caressing her cheek.

"What are you waiting for?" She lifted an expectant eyebrow.

"Waiting?" He looked confused.

"Boys." She shook her head, grabbing his chin, pressing her lips to his.

Oh, he thought, realizing what she meant, returning her fervor. There, they kissed, with the *Stenox* skirting the face of the *Sentinel,* passing below its watchful gaze.

* * *

"A lot of activity on the docks ahead," Lorken said, sitting the helm, observing the harbor garrison assembling along the wharves of the southern shore of the bay, with the massive stone edifices of the city forum and magistrate towering in the foreground.

"Another welcoming party just happy to see us," Raven growled, scanning the expanding images of soldiers' scowls.

"You would think they would show a little respect for citizens of the new Ape Republic, especially with their new alliance." Lorken pointed out.

"They might've if you hadn't sunk the pride and joy of Marcus Talana's trade fleet," Raven reminded him of their last visit when he destroyed the *Lady Talana.*

"He deserved worse than I gave him."

"True, but it doesn't change our situation any. Might as well pull in and have a talk with Klen. Just park it there," Raven said, eyeing a long stretch of open piers near the magistrate where most of the garrison troops were gathering.

"You sure that's a good idea?" Lorken didn't like the looks they were getting from the crowd.

"Might as well face this head on. Besides, what are they going to do?"

"Beat us up." Lorken shrugged.

"Maybe you, the most sacked quarterback in academy history. How many times did you go down in that game against Egypt College? Fourteen or fifteen times," Raven goaded him.

"Egypt College? You mean Assiut University. It was established in 1957 and is the most prestigious institution of advanced learning in the eastern hemisphere, ranking 1st or 2nd in academic excellence for the last fifty years," Lorken said indignantly.

"That's good, Lorken. So how many times did they sack you?"

"Seventeen," he mumbled under his breath.

"Seventeen in one game? Did you ever hear of throwing the ball away?" Raven shook his head.

"They had a good D line," he mumbled, picking up the ship's speed to end this conversation.

"Not that good," Raven said as the ship lurched forward. "You might want to take it easy, or we'll lose our lovebirds up top," he added, half expecting Corry and Terin doing a Peter Pan off the top deck.

* * *

Klen Adine stood forward of his soldiers, awaiting the *Stenox* with a heavy sigh. Of course, they would have to appear just as negotiations were proceeding so well, like an obnoxious relative inviting themselves to dinner. Klen smoothed his long burgundy robes and lifted his chin, presenting the air of indifference he practiced with natural ease. As magistrate of the largest city state of Arax, he wielded incredible power, as long as he appeased the mercurial personalities of the ruling families of Tro, a delicate balance that his predecessors were woefully inept in achieving, but that he demonstrated with remarkable skill. Despite his ability in balancing their varied interests, he was severely tested by the sudden reappearance of the *Stenox* whose nefarious crew drew the ire of two of the ruling patriarchs from Houses Talana and Maiyan. They would be certain to demand that the Earthers immediately depart, but that might offend their ape allies, upon whom Tro was desperately dependent with Tyro's legions a stone's throw from the city walls.

Klen ordered Commandant Balkar, commander of the city garrison, to keep his men far to his rear with spears at attention. There was no reason to greet their guests with leveled weapons at this time, where a simple show of force sufficed to begin their discourse. And so he waited with the patience of a stone as the *Stenox* drew near, pulling up to the wharf before him with all the subtlety of a starving *moglo*. He was surprised to see a young Araxan man clad in Earther garb atop the 3rd deck, standing beside a beautiful woman dressed in warrior's tunic with silver breastplate, her golden hair blowing freely in the breeze. The two quickly descended to the 1st deck as Raven emerged from the bridge and several others from the 1st deck. He would have been taken aback if he was prone to such a response, by the odd gaggle of individuals spilling out onto the stern, including three apes, an Enoructan, a Torry Elite, and two finely dressed diplomats adorned in rich Calnesian robes to match his own.

It was no surprise that Raven was the first to step onto the pier, with all the grace of mangy *lanzar*. If he was shy about showing his face after his antics during his last visit, he didn't act it, approaching Klen like he was an old drinking buddy.

"You didn't need to greet us with such a grand welcoming party, Klen, but we appreciate the gesture," Raven said, slapping him on the shoulder.

"Indeed," he sighed, shaking his head, wondering if the Earthers ever took a hint that they were not welcome.

"It's been a long time since our last visit—"

"Not that long, I assure you," Klen interrupted.

"I hope Lorken's misunderstanding with Marcus Talana hasn't soured our welcome, but I'm sure they can overlook that."

"They?" Klen raised a skeptical brow.

"The ruling families. We are here on business after all, and personal differences can be put aside until later."

"Personal differences? You sunk the pride of the Talana fleet. That is considered an act of *war*. Since any confrontation with you is almost pointless, considering the power you wield, you could have at least had the decency to stay away from this port for a far longer time than you have," Klen explained as the others stepped off the ship, overhearing their conversation.

"No reason to be upset by little things like that, Klen." Raven shrugged.

Klen rolled his eyes with the Earther's nonchalance, preparing to refute his idiotic statement when the beautiful woman clad in warrior garb stepped forth to address him.

"Magistrate Adine, I am told?" she asked, stopping at Raven's side.

"I am he. And you are, my lady?"

"I am Princess Corry, acting regent of Torry North," Corry introduced, catching Klen by surprise, which he managed to suppress.

"Your Highness, I am honored to receive you but must ask the purpose of your visit considering the state of things to our west."

"A fair question, Magistrate. I was asked by President Matuzak to act as an intermediary to facilitate the signing of your treaty. Our Casian passengers proposed a neutral third party for this role and the former ape general asked if I could intercede," she explained.

"Casian passengers?" Klen asked, looking just beyond her shoulder where the two regally attired men approached from the ship.

"Yes, may I introduce Pors Vitara, the archon of Teris, and Porlin Galba, the vice archon of Port West," Corry introduced the Casian delegation.

"Gentlemen, we are honored to receive you." Klen bowed, acknowledging them properly, impressed that the Casian League would send representatives of such rank.

"We are honored to be received, Magistrate Adine. We hope we are not too late to participate in the negotiations," Pors Vitara said, his discerning green eyes drifting subtly to the city forum gracing the skyline behind him.

"Fortune shines upon you, Archon Vitara. Negotiations have only just begun. I confess, I am surprised by your appearance. I was not aware that you would be partaking of this treaty," Klen said.

"Our ruling forum decided it was wiser to join your trade alliance than initiate a blockade of all east-west trade, bringing ruin to us all," Pors said.

"Very well. If you would follow my steward to the city forum, I shall formally introduce you to the heads of our ruling families and the representatives of Enoructa and the Ape Republic. Several lesser city-states have also sent representatives to contemplate joining our new alliance. I will be sure to introduce each to you," Klen called his aide forth to guide the Casians. Once they were away, he returned his attention to Corry and the young Torry now standing protectively beside her along with the Araxan youth in earth garb.

"I would offer a full escort for you, Your Highness, but I assume you did not venture here without adequate protection. These two men are your guardians, I presume?" Klen regarded Terin and Lucas.

"Yes, I present Lucas of the Torry Elite and Terin, the champion of the realm," she introduced them.

"My sources must be remiss, for last I heard, the Torry champion was lost at sea. But here he stands dressed like an Earther and very much alive." Klen lifted a curious brow.

"We discovered he was…detained." Corry left much unsaid.

"Whereupon you enlisted the aid of Captain Raven to retrieve him, I surmise." Klen regarded Raven briefly. The stupid look on his face confirmed his summation.

"Perhaps, but the details are best left unsaid, for now, Magistrate," Corry said.

"Very well. As your good captain has likely told you, discretion is a necessary attribute for my position." Klen bowed.

"I was told this but not by Raven. He merely said you were good friends, and that he would buy you a round of drinks at the *Moorn* upon our arrival to celebrate their return," she said, giving Raven a roll of her eyes.

"Indeed," he said dryly, not at all surprised by Raven's complete lack of preparation for this meeting, especially considering the nature of their last visit.

"Lighten up, Klen, you could use a few brews. I bet if I stuck a piece of coal up your—" Raven retorted before Corry wisely interceded.

"If you would be so kind, Magistrate Adine, to lead me to the city forum. Terin and Lucas shall accompany me, along with Argos and Ular, the champions of their respective peoples," she said.

"Of course, Your Highness. As for the rest of the crew, I expect them to confine themselves to the *Stenox* until given leave to come ashore," he said, giving Raven a stern look. He doubted he would be granting such leave anytime soon.

* * *

Corry was met by the patriarchs of the five ruling families of Tro upon entering the forum, along with Admiral Zorgon who commanded the 1st Ape Fleet. They were all pleasantly surprised by her overseeing the negotiations, though Marcus Talana and Ortus Maiyan cast suspicious gazes toward Terin, wary of his Earth attire. The Casian delegates were joined by the representatives of the Ape Republic and Enoructa, with ambassadors from the city-states of Bedo, Gotto, and Terse in attendance. The apes were represented by Chief Hukor of the Narsus tribe, and Chief Gargos of the Manglar tribe. Chief Ilen was the lone representative of Enoructa, his aqua-blue scaly skin contrasting the apes' black fur.

Corry noticed a disagreeable look upon Ortus Maiyan's disposition, as if he were ill. The patriarch recently suffered a strange ailment, forcing his son Orvis to attend the affairs of House Maiyan, in particularly overseeing harbor inspections for visiting ships.

"Shall we continue, gentlemen?" Klen addressed the prestigious assembly, inviting Corry to stand at the periphery of the circled floor upon which the forum was centered, with rows of benches circling above in the usual bowl shape that most Araxan forums were built.

Terin, Lucas, Ular, and Argos stood behind Corry, listening on as the delegates debated the most inane details involving everything from the territorial rights of fishing grounds to the uniformity of cargo inspections. Little did they know that this was actually the third day of negotiations, and they had yet to begin the important topics of military cooperation and protection of trade routes. Argos snorted lightly, already bored with the conversation, wondering why he must suffer so while Grigg and Orlom remained aboard the ship.

Because they are nitwits, he cursed to himself. For some reason, being idiots was rewarded, while he suffered this nonsense. He also had Lorken to blame, his sinking of the *Lady Talana* soured the Troans' tolerance for any of the original Earthers' presence. A slight movement along the domed ceiling above drew his eye, spotting the tiny disc hovering in the shadows above, meaning his crewmates were watching this tedious affair back on the ship, and taking delight in his misery, no doubt. If he discovered any of them laughing at his misfortune, he would be certain to toss them overboard upon his return.

* * *

Weapon's room of the Stenox

"This shit is painful. I can't watch anymore," Raven complained, looking over Brokov's shoulder as he monitored the negotiations through disc number 2.

"It's important to know what they are discussing, Rav. Some of this might pertain to us at some point," Brokov said, zooming the lens to the face of Lubion Tobian, the Troan patriarch of House Tobian and Klen's most ardent supporter. Lubion had just put forth a proposed compromise on the fishing boundaries dividing Enoructa and the Casian port of Milito. Since each party favored different types of fish, he proposed joint operations where they would split their catches by preference while sharing their fishing grounds. It was logical and well thought-out and, of course, tabled for later consideration.

"It all sounds a little fishy to me, so have fun with that." Raven patted him on the shoulder and walked out, leaving Brokov and Kendra to watch the video feed by themselves.

"Idiot." Brokov shook his head with Raven's impatience.

"Where is disc 1?" Kendra asked, sitting to his right, staring at the other screens.

"At the *Moorn,* checking in on Kaly. It's a good place to start before we expand our search," he explained.

"Expand where?" she asked.

"West. We will start at Gotto and work our way to Notsu and then look north and east."

"What of the harbor?"

"It looks relatively peaceful for now. Everyone looks well-behaved with the bulk of the Ape Fleet here," he said, looking through disc 3 hovering two hundred meters above the *Stenox,* giving him a panoramic view of the bay. From those airy heights, he could see most of the 1st Ape Fleet moored along the north side of the harbor, their sigil blowing strongly upon their mast poles, a black furry fist wrapped around the neck of a scrawny soren bird upon a field of white. He wondered if the sigil was an attempt at humor but doubted it knowing the apes as he did. They probably thought it tasteful. Most of the Troan Navy was berthed across the bay along the southern piers to their immediate west, most of their crews milling about their decks as if ready to launch at a moment's notice. It was all for show, Brokov knew, to impress upon their new allies their worth and readiness.

"Where is the rest of the Troan Navy? I only count forty vessels," Kendra said, knowing their full strength to be fifty war galleys.

"Probably patrolling the waters north of here. We didn't see any sign of them on our southern approach. It is something we can look into later," Brokov said, tuning up the volume on disc 2 just as Klen was about to say something, which turned out to be nothing important. Brokov shook his head, wishing Zem had taken this task from him. He'd probably find it interesting and think it a privilege to sort through the forum's ramblings.

* * *

Twenty-eight leagues north by northeast of Tro

Commodore Darelis stood upon the prow of the *Flen Raider,* the flagship of his small squadron, staring north with the southerly wind at his back. They were nearing the end of their patrol before returning back to Tro when their lookouts spotted a pirate vessel to their immediate north, the ship turning to evade as they gave chase.

"Full sails!" The order went out as the ten ships of the Troan squadron broke off into two separate columns, each angling to either side of the fleeing vessel, the pirate valley losing ground with its slower hull. Darelis's squadron was built of sleeker hulls than its sister warships, designed to overtake most pirate galleys threatening the eastern port. They were gaining ground steadily, closing distance to within seven hundred meters as the pirate vessel angled toward the shore, with rocky cliffs jutting above the coastline. Darelis knew this area well, knowing there was no place to put ashore for another three leagues, which their prey could not hope to attain before they overtook them.

"Ready crews!" The order went out as men ignited the braziers of their catapults and swiveled their giant crossbows into position. The Troan seamen waited with bated breath as the lead ships closed to within three hundred meters, dressed in aqua-boiled leather mail over gray tunics and gold helms.

The squadron's two columns angled west and east of the labored vessel, trapping it between them, the left column drawing dangerously near the towering cliffs of the shoreline off their portside. Darelis's flagship headed the right column, staring off his portside bow as they nearly drew even with the pirate vessel, trapping it between his columns.

"Hard to port!" he commanded his helmsman. The pirate vessel a mere hundred meters to their west, and his far column an equal distance further.

"Commodore!" the captain of the *Flen Raider* shouted, pointing to the cliffs looming ominously behind their left column.

Darelis looked on in horror as thousands of winged forms spewed from the cliffs, sweeping down upon the Troan warships forming the left column. Most of the crews were caught unawares, their eyes fixed to the pirate galley to their east while the gargoyles descended into their midst.

"All hands, on deck! Prepare to be boarded!" Darelis ordered, knowing they had little time to withdraw the five ships in his right column before the gargoyles were upon them.

"Hard to starboard! Turn out to sea!" His follow command seemed wishful thinking at this point, but what choice had he but to hope some of his ships could escape this ambush. The appearance of gargoyles meant one thing...*war.*

The *Fallen Legend* was the center ship in the left column, sailing within the shadow of the cliffs of the shoreline. It was first to feel the full brunt of the gargoyles. Archers along its port and stern took sudden aim; their hasty shots fluttered awry in the wind. Several creatures set down upon the masts above, clinging to the guide ropes before dropping into their midst. Others angled lower, setting down astern, scimitars slashing as crewmen drove them back with leveled spears. Others dropped behind crewmen, slashing blows taking men across the back or neck. A Troan archer struck one target in the throat; the creature dropped short of the stern, its body striking the surf. That small victory was short-lived with more gargoyles dropping all around, hacking the archer to pieces. The captain lost all order, unable to coordinate any organized defense, fighting for his own life with gargoyles to his flanks and front, before going under the swarming creatures.

Fires erupted across the midships of the *Troan Anchor*, the lead vessel in the left column, its braziers spilling their contents across its deck.

Commodore Darelis looked helplessly on as all the ships of the left column were overcome, with gargoyles swarming their decks. His right column braced for the onslaught, given precious little time to prepare before the enemy was upon them. A separate wave of gargoyles swept over the left column, angling for the right column en masse, thousands of gargoyles darkening the sky, wingtip to wingtip, chanting their foul war cry, "Kai-Shorum!"

They swept over the lone pirate galley, its crew waving them on like giddy spectators. They were obvious in league with one another, the pirates' loyalties bought by Tyro's gold. Catapults hurled balls of flame into the encroaching foes, striking those who couldn't evade the crowded air; the projectiles ignited several in flames, knocking many others from the sky, sending them disoriented to the surf. Archers released volleys into the enemy host. Dozens fell from formation; many others continued on with shafts feathering their bodies. The archers' efforts did little to stem the tide. Darelis cursed his folly as the creatures approached, beginning to set down astern, the southerly wind doing them little favor to draw quickly away. The damnable wind afforded the wretched creatures greater lift, allowing them to assail them from above, while others angled lower, their wings working just above the waves.

"Commodore!" a seaman shouted, pointing north where a small armada emerged along the horizon. A closer examination would show a bloodred flag with black X upon its field, adorning their crests, the favored sigil of the eastern pirates who raided Troan shipping.

* * *

Monsoon stood at the prow of the *Troan Bane*, the aptly named flagship of his new armada, gazing south with tempered glee, watching as the Troan ships were overtaken one by one. He doubted many prisoners were taken as he requested, but he didn't truly need them as long as he had their ships. He only hoped his new allies were not foolish enough to kill the Troan oar slaves, but gargoyles were never known to curb their bloodlust once bestirred.

"Your orders, Admiral?" the captain of the *Troan Bane* asked, standing at his side.

Monsoon smiled at the honorary title. Should this operation prove successful, he would gladly exchange it for a place among Darkhon's Elite.

"Onward, Captain, let us speak with our gargoyle friends and inspect our new ships."

* * *

One day hence
Tro harbor, the Maiyan estate

"I told you not to visit me here," Orvis Maiyan sneered as Rolis joined him upon his terrace, looking out across the bay, the morning sun reflecting off its watery surface. Looking across the bay, he spotted a small flotilla of Benotrist merchant vessels making their way to their wharves, each paying a heavy toll to disembark their provisions for Morac's legions. They would dock along the northern piers, awaiting inspection by men chosen by him. It was the third such flotilla in as many days, and they were piling up, awaiting approval, with more ships arriving daily.

"Your father is in attendance at the ruling forum and will be there most of the day, Orvis. Hossen thought it prudent to coordinate our efforts."

"To what end? We can do naught while the Earthers are present, else they shall ruin our plans," Orvis lamented, casting a wary glance at the damnable *Stenox* moored near the magistrate below. It was a shameless display of their flaunting the wishes of the ruling families.

"Hossen disagrees. We have been given a great boon that will accomplish our goals and place the blame fully at the Earthers' feet." Rolis left unsaid that Thorton told them to postpone any attack if the Earthers suddenly appeared.

"A boon?" Orvis lifted a curious brow.

"Yes, a special weapon that can destroy the forum in one fell strike," Rolis enticed.

"Speak clearly, Rolis. I have no time for innuendos."

"We have an Earther weapon that can be used to great effect. Imagine the forum being destroyed by such sorcery. Where do you think the blame will fall? Add to this our pirate assault upon your own fleet and the blame that will fall on the ape fleet for failing to protect them. Your people will run the apes and Earthers out of the harbor and name you regent."

"You truly have such a weapon?"

"Yes, but your assistance is required to use it to its full effect."

"What do you require from me?"

417

"Now that is the question," Rolis said dryly, casting a knowing glance to the magantor stable beside the spacious estate, where House Maiyan quartered their two warbirds, a rare asset reserved for only the wealthiest of estates.

* * *

One day hence

They soared through the sky, the rising sun greeting them full in the face, with the endless expanse of the eastern sea breaking the horizon. Elos drew his magantor up alongside his, pointing out the beacon tower overlooking the coast, one of many along the shoreline guiding ships along Tro's southern approaches. Cronus acknowledged the landmark, turning Wind Racer north, hoping to find the harbor before too long. They spent many days circumventing the crossroads at Notsu, traveling far to the south before crossing over the headwaters of the Flen, following its course northward. They broke east before reaching the confluence of the Veneba and Flen Rivers, where the city of Gotto lay, coming upon the coastline here, some untold distance from Tro.

Their magantors sped through the morning air with graceful ease, coursing above the jagged coastline, with flocks of soren passing below them. Cronus spied several dorsal fins crest the surf off his right, before dipping below the water. The clear sky and gentle air made for a scenic end to their long journey. He only hoped Raven would be at Tro as Jonas had predicated. Any doubts were met with Elos's undying faith in Terin's father. Even Torg believed it, and who was he to question it until it was proven false. Either way, he would know soon enough as the outer walls of Tro took shape along the horizon, before the whole city came boldly into view.

He looked over to Elos, who simply nodded his acknowledgment with no more emotion than a planted tree. Drawing closer, he made out the Sentinel of Tro rising above its small rocky isle, guarding the mouth of the bay, and the towering edifices of the forum and magistrate dominating the southern shore of the harbor. The palatial estates of the ruling families ringed the hillsides south of the bay, overlooking the harbor proper. He couldn't miss the Troan warships moored along the southwestern bend of the bay and the larger ape armada berthed along the north. Cronus grinned like a fool when his eyes finally found the *Stenox* docked near the magistrate, its bluish silver hull unlike anything else around it.

* * *

The bridge of the Stenox

"Another day of this nonsense, and I might just put my pistol to my head and pull the trigger," Raven mumbled with his left leg hanging over the side of his chair, leaning back, bored out of his skull.

"They have a lot to discuss," Lorken said, tapping his viewscreen excitedly.

"What are you doing over there?" Raven asked.

"Breaking your best score, that's what." Lorken grinned.

"What?" Raven sprang from his seat to see what he was doing, finding Lorken tallying up a mighty score on *Planet Smasher*, Raven's favorite game.

"Sitting here for three days has paid dividends." Lorken smiled as he broke Raven's top score, receiving a slap across the back of his head for his success.

"Tough break, Rav." He grinned, continuing to pile on the points as Brokov stepped onto the bridge.

"What are you two arguing about now?" Brokov asked while checking the monitor on the captain's chair, performing the daily diagnostics, making sure all their systems were working in sync.

"Nothing," Raven mumbled.

"He's just a sore loser. I finally beat his top score on *Planet Smasher*."

"Who cares about his top score? Zem beat that a year ago," Brokov said, touching the viewscreen.

"What do you mean a year ago? The high score is right there at the top of the screen," Raven said.

"That is the top score for the bridge monitors, not the weapons and engineering monitors. You might know that if either of you did anything other than talk about your playing days back at the academy." Brokov shook his head, looking out across the bay where Commodore Darelis's squadron cleared the mouth of the harbor, returning from their long patrol. They appeared to be two ships short, with three captured pirate vessels in tow.

Before either of them could respond to that, Grigg came rushing through the door.

"Boss, come outside and look!"

They quickly stepped onto the stern of the second deck as two magantors circled overhead, before setting down upon the wharf where they were moored, drawing the attention of the harbor guards posted to watch over the *Stenox*. They didn't recognize the Jenaii warrior sitting the gray-white magantor, but the human upon the black-beaked white magantor was another matter.

"Cronus!" Raven shouted as his old friend dismounted from the great avian.

Cronus looked up with a strange look upon his weary face, a mix of dread and joy but mostly relief. Orlom met the others upon the 1st deck as they welcomed Elos and Cronus aboard while Kendra hurried off to reassure the harbor garrison troops of their friends' peaceful intentions. A pair of garrison magantors had followed them upon their entrance to the harbor, circling overhead before passing on once the guards below met the intruders.

"You are a sight for sore eyes!" Raven lifted Cronus off the deck in a crushing hug, squeezing the air from his lungs.

"Rav, you are breaking my ribs," he coughed, smiling as his friend set him back down.

"Cronus," Lorken greeted him next.

"Lorken," he barely said before he, too, lifted him in the air.

Brokov politely just shook his hand once he was returned to the deck, but Orlom and Grigg quickly repeated Raven and Lorken's gesture forgoing any formal introductions and proceeding to do likewise with Elos. To his credit, Elos did not take offense, quietly letting them lift him off the deck like a long-lost relative. Cronus cringed watching the awkward exchange, half expecting the Jenaii champion to lop their heads once his feet touched the deck and breathed a relieved sigh when he didn't. Cronus quickly introduced his companion, emphasizing his esteemed rank, which didn't impress any of them. The fact that Elos was his friend was all that mattered to the Earthers and their ape friends. He was heartened when Kendra returned from calming the harbor guards, exchanging a warm embrace with him.

"It is wonderful to see you all," Cronus said, unable to stop the smile spreading across his face. "I witnessed your handiwork at the straits of Cesa, whichever of you was piloting your underwater vessel," he said, watching their reaction to see which one it was.

"You were there?" Lorken asked.

"Yes. I was upon Wind Racer, flying above where I saw the exchange, watching you sink one Macon ship after another," he pointed out the magantor's name.

"How did we miss that?" Brokov wondered.

"All three of us were aboard the *Specter* during that maneuver. We thought your people could use a little help, and it made your princess happy," Raven said, the mention of Corry causing Cronus's eyes to alit.

"Is she here now?" Cronus dared venture, seeking confirmation of Jonas's vision. If she was here, then Terin might be as well.

"Yep, over in the forum, overseeing the negotiations, along with Lucas, Arg, Ular, and *Terin*," Raven emphasized.

"Then it is true. He lives." Cronus felt like weeping with joy.

"We found him, just like his father predicted, though we still don't know how he managed to dream all of it." Raven shook his head.

"I need to see him. This sword needs its rightful master," Cronus said, slapping the hilt of the Sword of the Moon, sheathed upon his left hip.

"You will brighten his day, and he could use it after suffering in that place for the past few days, guarding your princess," Raven said.

"Whatever he is suffering is a sweet reward after all he has been through. Thank you for rescuing him. I know what it means to suffer in bondage without hope and to be delivered by the finest friends any man has ever had." Cronus grasped Raven and Lorken's shoulders fondly and Brokov's thereafter.

"We owed a couple favors, so now we are even," Raven said.

"True friends stop counting their favors owed to one another. As I have said many times, old friend, we shall always be even. I may have lost a brother in Cordi and another in Arsenc, but I have gained many more with each of you and Elos." Cronus regarded the Jenaii warrior fondly before looking to Grigg and Orlom. "And you two, I look forward to hearing of your adventures with my friends here. As they may have told you, any friends of theirs are friends of mine, just go gently with your hugs, for my poor ribs cannot endure it."

"The great Cronus Kenti is our friend!" they both chorused happily.

Cronus had become something of legend in many parts of Arax, especially in the Ape Republic, not for Tuft's Mountain but for his unique friendship with the Earthers.

"I am not great. I simply travel in the company of those who are." Cronus smiled wanly, remembering why he was truly here.

"Don't be so humble, pal. You're one of the bravest men I've ever known," Raven said.

"I am honored you believe so, Rav." He smiled wanly.

"Would you like to see Terin and Corry now? We can escort you to them if you'd like." Brokov asked.

"Yes, but there is something I first need to share with you, with all of you. It was the purpose for this journey, and you needed to hear it from my lips, if you have not learned of it already," Cronus said, looking into their eyes to see if they already knew, but their good humor seemed to indicate that they had not.

"What's on your mind, Cronus?" Raven asked, starting to feel like a hammer was about to fall by the odd look painting Cronus's face.

None of them could miss the pained look twisting his mouth, like he swallowed a hive of bees. Even Grigg and Orlom noticed he had some awful news to share.

"Perhaps Zem should be here as well before I tell you." Cronus didn't want to repeat what he had to say.

Lorken raised Zem on the comm, calling him outside. The giant automaton greeted Cronus with his characteristic metallic voice, happy to see his old friend.

"By the look on your face, this has to be very bad news, especially to bring you all the way here," Raven said, suspecting what he was about to say.

"Yes. Kato is…dead," Cronus sighed, closing his eyes, unable to look at any of them.

Nothing but silence followed for a painfully long time. When Cronus finally opened his eyes, most of them were looking down, barely able to speak. It was Zem that asked the obvious question that was foremost on their minds.

"How did he die?"

"I only know what the men who were there told Prince Lorn. They claim he and Thorton stumbled upon each other somewhere northwest of Maeii, where Thorton struck him down. They claim Thorton was grieved by what happened, if that is any consolation. He was honorable enough to return Kato's body and a parchment Kato had written for his wife. Prince Lorn ordered his body to be taken to Cagan where he shall be entombed with great honor and remembered for all he has done for our cause," Cronus said, keeping his voice even, lest he break down in tears.

They continued to stand there; no one spoke a word. Everyone was looking down or staring aimlessly across the harbor. Raven felt as if his heart was torn out and stomped on the ground. In one moment, he lost two of his best friends—one dead and the other… dead as well, at least in his mind. There was no coming back from this. Ben made his choice. He chose Tyro over his brothers. When next they met, he would have to kill him. If Jenny was somewhere up there looking down on him, he only hoped she could forgive him for what he will have to do.

"Raven, why is the returning squadron preparing to fire on the ape fleet?" Zem asked curiously, his keen eye looking north across the bay where Darelis's ships closed rapidly upon the moored ape fleet.

"What?" More than one of them asked, their eyes drawn to where Zem was looking. There, across the bay, fire munitions erupted across several ape galleys, flames sweeping their decks. Small dark forms poured out of the holds of the Troan vessels, taking flight with awkward grace…*gargoyles*.

"Battle stations!" Raven ordered hurrying up the ladder to the 2nd deck; Lorken following close behind.

Harroom!

Horns sounded to the west, causing Raven to pause upon clearing the ladder, looking over his shoulder where fires erupted along the Troan ships docked further along the shoreline from their position. He could make out men spilling onto the wharves brandishing spears and sword, assailing the vessels, with Troan seamen fending them off with mixed results. The sounds of clashing steel echoed south and west, drawing dangerously near the city forum.

"Cronus, go to the city forum and get Terin and the others out of there! Orlom will show you the way!" Raven ordered before rushing onto the bridge.

CHAPTER 18

Harroom!

Horns sounded to the west, causing Raven to pause upon clearing the ladder, looking over his shoulder where fires erupted along the Troan ships docked further along the shoreline from their position. He could make out men spilling onto the wharves brandishing spears and sword, assailing the vessels. Troan seamen fended them off with mixed results. The sounds of clashing steel echoed south and west, drawing dangerously near the city forum.

"Cronus, go to the city forum and get Terin and the others out of there! Orlom will show you the way! Brokov, fire up the engines. Zem, post up in the weapon's room, prepare for anything!" Raven ordered before stepping onto the bridge; Lorken already ahead of him, manning the helm.

"Fire up the engines? This isn't the 21st century." Brokov shook his head, following Zem inside the 1st deck.

Cronus and Orlom were already off the ship, climbing onto Wind Racer's saddle, racing toward the city forum. Elos hurried after them, gaining his mount; the garrison troops guarding the *Stenox* followed them into battle.

"Come along, Grigg, let's take up position!" Kendra said, climbing the ladders to the 3rd deck, with laser rifle in hand as the *Stenox* pulled away from the pier, a grinning Grigg happily following her.

* * *

425

Monsoon couldn't hide the smile twisting his lips with Tro's ruination playing out before him. He stood the prow of the *Flen Raider*, Commodore Darelis' former flagship now his own; its Troan crew chained to the oars below. They had taken the squadron nearly intact, losing two to fires sweeping their decks; the rest requiring only superficial repairs. They entered the bay unchallenged; the ruse working with pitiful ease. Halfway across the bay, they turned sharply north, where most of the ape fleet was peacefully moored, with few crew members upon their quiet decks to oppose them. They approached swiftly, with no alarms raising to warn their helpless prey. His only real concern was the *Stenox*, which Hossen Grell assured him would be taken care of. That didn't put Monsoon at ease, casting a watchful glance to where the Earthers' ship rested along the south shore of the bay.

"Fire!" the ship's ballista commander ordered as they drew in range. Fire munitions arced over the calm waters, breaking the stillness of the day. Several ballistae fell short, splashing harmlessly into the sea. One struck true off Monsoon's left; the rear mast of *Gregok's Arm* bursting in flames. Several others off his right struck amidship *Garm's Anvil*, fires sweeping the warship's deck.

"Prepare to ram!" Monsoon warned; his eyes fixed to the massive ram affixed to the bow, cresting the surf like a dorun's fin, a colossal slab of tempered steel meant to wreck an enemy hull.

"Kai-shorum!" the cries of gargoyles echoed behind him. The foul creatures emptied out of the lower hold, bounding over the ship's sides, their dark wings taking flight above the watery surface. The scene repeated itself all across his small fleet, his warships driving for the helpless ape vessels, gargoyles spewing from their holds as they drew near.

The ape galley ahead barely registered a response. A few of its crew drew swords to receive them, with no archers above deck to do them harm. Monsoon could see men and apes scurrying along the wharves beyond, running to and fro without direction. The *Flen Raider* continued apace, its ram slicing the surf, closing the final distance, the stern of the *Broken Skull* resting in its path.

Crash!

The ship struck true; the force nearly taking Monsoon from his feet. He struggled holding on to the ship's rail; broken timbers from the *Broken Skull* showering the helm. The emphatic blow caved the stern of the ape vessel, twisting it from its mooring. Monsoon ordered reverse oars; his ship struggling to untangle itself from the stricken ape warship. Finally pulling free, the *Flen Raider* drew away, the stern of the *Broken Skull* dipping severely, water pouring through its fatal wound.

Drawing further away, Monsoon could see the other ships' success. Several ape galleys listed; fires igniting across their decks. Monsoon's three pirate vessels that pretended to be captives took up rear guard duties; their heady crews preparing for any counterattack that appeared more unlikely as the moments passed. Further east along the wharves, gargoyles were spilling out of the Benotrist merchant ships that had waited in port for days to unload. Thousands of the creatures swarmed onto the piers or attacked ape ships moored nearby, dropping fire munitions upon the hapless vessels. The smell of burning fur and flesh permeated the air, choking the surviving crew members with its ghastly fumes. The gargoyles had great success dropping their munitions from afar but struggled with the apes in close engagements, where the gorillas' fierce strength took hold. Unlike most human navies, the apes used warriors as oarsmen, which acted as infantry at sea. Few were below deck at the outset of the battle, with some housed in the harbor, and others enjoying the ale and hospitality of local taverns. Soon, these apes heard the call to arms, rushing toward the docks where their fleet lay with broad swords raised high and shouting their own war cries.

Monsoon knew they had little time to withdraw far enough to regain ramming speed before the enemy was prepared to receive them. Instead, he ordered his ships to shadow the docked ape ships, firing munitions into their midst. The nearest untouched vessels of the ape fleet were already beset by gargoyles swarming their decks, though their initial success gave way to stubborn resistance; the more powerful gorillas required many gargoyles to overcome them. Several gargoyles set down upon the bow of *Matuzak's Hammer*, when an ape warrior met the first with an ax to its skull, driving the creature to the deck. A follow strike took another in the breast, nearly halving it; the gargoyle dropping like a weighted sack. A third gargoyle sprang for the gorilla's head; the ape released its grip on the ax to grab hold of the creature's arms, snapping them at the elbows, tossing it aside, its fangs snapping in defiance. A fourth managed to circle behind the gorilla, slashing its scimitar across its knee. The ape faltered as others rushed it, slashing at it from all sides.

"Fire at will!" Monsoon ordered as his ships drew past the *Gackor's Fist*; the vessel's crew now swarmed its top deck, preparing to return fire when fire ballistae rained upon them. Flames spread across its stern and mast poles. Gargoyles set down amidst the festering flames, striking at any ape standing to meet them.

Monsoon looked beyond the stricken vessels where gargoyles swarmed the piers, pouring into the city proper. Inhuman screams echoed hauntingly above the din. They caught Tro unprepared, taking it apart from the inside out with such ease. Another ape vessel went up in flames to his west, one of its munition stores likely struck, spouting fire high above its center mast. The *Grakon* and the *Pogar* were listing to port, each ablaze and set adrift from their moorings. The *Tempav*, *Mondar*, and *Volran* were sinking. A dozen other ape warships were abandoned; their crews unable to combat the fires spreading across their decks. Some poured water upon the festering flames, but to no avail, the fluid only spreading the gelatinous material. Monsoon was guardedly optimistic he could finish the bulk of the ape fleet in quick order.

Boom!

The *Fallen Legend* exploded into a million fragments just behind them; a massive laser blast struck the captured Troan vessel, spewing body parts and debris across the *Flen Raider*, the force of the blast lifting the ship's stern high into the air, knocking Monsoon from his feet. The pirate admiral struggled to stand; his body again thrown into the air when the ship settled. He reached up to grasp the rail, pulling himself to his feet just as another of his ships burst apart to his east, blasted into a hundred million particles. The ships nearest it were showered with debris, tearing holes in their masts. Dozens of smaller laser blasts passed overhead, striking gargoyles swarming over the ape ships.

Boom! Boom! Boom!

All three of Monsoon's pirate vessels guarding their flank blew apart in quick succession. He chanced a peek over his portside, watching in horror the carnage the Earthers wrought. There in the center of the harbor was the offending vessel, laser fire spewing from its bow and sides, striking targets across the north side of the harbor, Hossen Grell's reassurances counting for naught.

* * *

The bridge of the Stenox

"Shift aim to that big one on the end!" Raven said in the comm, pointing out the lead ship in Monsoon's flotilla, its ballistae crew wreaking havoc on another ape vessel.

"Which end, the east or the west?" Zem answered back through the comm.

"East! Blow it out of the water!" Raven barked. Another intense beam of energy burst from the bow, striking the vessel amidship.

"We got activity all across the bay, Rav," Lorken said, sweeping their viewscreen 360, bringing the full harbor into view. Benotrist merchant galleys moored along the north shore were spewing gargoyles; the foul creatures emptying from their lower holds. There had to be nearly a hundred merchant vessels involved with this treachery, berthed peacefully for days before unleashing their deadly cargo. How they passed the harbor inspections, one could likely guess. The wharves along the southwest corner of the harbor were crowded with groups of men clashing. Lorken was unable to determine who was fighting who. Small armed groups appeared across the streets to their immediate south, dressed in nondescript armor and tunics, with unknown loyalties. Fires erupted all across the city; whether they were the work of armed bands or individual arsonists, one could only guess. Smoke drifted above the estate of House Corbin, overlooking the harbor from its hillside southeast of the Flen River. Considering that each of the ruling families employed small armies to guard their estates, this portended poorly for the fate of Tro altogether.

Boom!

Zem sent another blast to the ship farthest east in Monsoon's shrinking flotilla.

"What do you want to do first, Rav?" Lorken asked, sifting through their myriad of targets.

"Concentrate on the gargoyles, the Benotrist merchant ships, and the returning squadron, what's left of it. At least with them, we can sort the good guys from the bad," he said, relaying the information to Zem, who responded by shifting the heavy laser batteries to the Benotrist merchant fleet.

"Looks like trouble brewing at the *Moorn*," Lorken said, pointing out Kaly's famed establishment resting just west of the ape fleet, where a band of gargoyles began flooding through its front doors.

"Zem, Kaly could use a hand," Raven said into the comm.

"Who doesn't need a hand?" Zem snorted in reply, redirecting the smaller lasers to target.

Zip! Zip! Zip! Zip! Zip!

Laser fire showered the entrance to the *Moorn*, dropping dozens of gargoyles in as many seconds, half dead, the others crawling or staggering forward or away. Once Kaly's men recovered, they hurried forth across the barroom floor, dispatching the wounded and slaying the strays, preparing for the next onslaught.

* * *

"There!" Orlom shouted in Cronus's ear, pointing out the city forum. Massive stone pillars lined each side, making it difficult to miss. A small stone wall circled the perimeter, which Cronus and Elos bypassed, setting down before the main entrance, with forum guards rushing to challenge them.

Cronus dismounted as Wind Racer's talons touched the stone courtyard. Orlom followed in kind while Elos remained atop his mount, his silver eyes sweeping the sky above for any threats.

"Hold!" a forum commander of flax challenged, drawing his sword as Cronus took a step toward the bottom step of the entrance, the stair rising five meters to the entryway above. Men were already spilling out of the prodigious landmark, news of the attack already spreading to its prestigious halls.

"I am Cronus of the Torry Elite. I seek Princess Corry and Terin Caleph!" he declared with authority.

Before the commander could reply, Cronus caught sight of Argos's familiar form emerging between the pillars above, quickly followed by Ular, Lucas, and finally Terin and Corry. Upon seeing Orlom and then Cronus, they wasted little time racing down the steps. Cronus's heart nearly leaped from his chest, affording Terin a brief embrace before drawing the Sword of the Moon, setting it in his hands.

"This blade cries out for its master." He smiled.

Terin froze, overwhelmed by seeing his friend and feeling the sword again in his hands. There were so many things he wanted to say, so many questions to ask, but there was no time. Sparing a cursory glance across the bay revealed the dire straits they were in. Countless ships had listed or sunk, smoke billowing across the harbor, masking even greater carnage wrought throughout the city.

"We must bring Admiral Zorgon to his fleet!" Lucas said, just as the ape admiral hurried down the steps, followed by the ape and Enoructan delegations, each brandishing swords, ready to give battle.

Cronus shook his head. "Impossible. Most of the fleet is under direct assault."

"His command squadron rests along the south shore to our direct west. It should still be intact," Lucas explained.

"I will take him!" Elos said, still sitting his mount, his eyes scanning the sky for threats.

"I will go with you," Terin said, his heart leaping at the sight of Wind Racer, who stared knowingly back at him, reasserting their bond. Terin lifted his sword briefly, testing its weight. It felt both light and heavy, a beguiling mix of strength and weakness, which was alien to its nature. No azure light emitted along its silver blade, but an eerie dull aura that permeated his soul. If Terin had time to reflect or pray, he might be hesitant, overcome with doubt, but there was no time for anything but a subtle, hasty prayer. *Yah, guide my hand. Your will be done.*

With that, Terin gave Cronus his pistol, exchanging one fell weapon for another. Cronus knew well its operation, nudging him toward his waiting mount.

"Go with all haste. We shall safeguard the princess," Cronus said.

Admiral Zorgon followed Argos's direction to Elos's warbird, climbing into the saddle. Within moments, Elos and Terin took to the skies, skirting the shoreline west toward Zorgon's flagship.

"Where should we go?" Lucas asked the question on all their minds, with no direction looking entirely safe.

"To the wharf where the *Stenox* was moored and will likely return. The forum is a primary target, and its defenses are lacking," Cronus explained.

"Then what are we waiting for? Lead the way!" Chief Hukor of the Narsus tribe said.

* * *

"I got one!" Grigg shouted excitedly, lowering his rifle while pointing out his handiwork, his laser taking a Gargoyle standing at the prow of *Matuzak's Hammer*, through the back, the creature flopping off the side of the ship.

"Keep shooting and brag later!" Kendra scolded him, focusing her aim on another gargoyle circling the upper mast of *Lorgan's Flame*, the vessel drawing away from its mooring, trying to get underway despite the creatures assailing it.

Zip!

Her blast struck its left wing; the creature dipped briefly before flying off awkwardly.

Zip! Zip!

Her follow blasts went awry, grazing the gargoyle's feet, hastening its departure.

Boom!

Another direct beam from the ship's heavy batteries burst from the bow below them, striking a Benotrist merchant vessel along the northeast shore of the bay, sending debris a thousand feet into the air. Kendra marveled at the *Stenox*'s power, like a giant lanzar swatting gnats, standing in the middle of the harbor unchallenged. Amid all the carnage, the *Stenox* was resolute, striking down the enemy in detail. The north shore was a hopeless inferno of sinking wrecks with men and apes caught up in the flames, hundreds of corpses bobbing in the surf, and many more wounded lying across broken decks and bloody piers. To the southwest, fires ran unchecked. Flames spread building to building, sending spirals of black smoke high into the air. Armed groups seemed to contest every street of the southern harbor, from the forum in the east to the Flen River Bridge in the west. Kendra couldn't make sense of the activity throughout the southern half of Tro, with armed insurgents dressed like local militias or Tro garrison troops. It was chaos. Even the estates of the ruling families were under assault, with flames encroaching the gates of houses Fixus, Corbin, and Talana. Several magantors took to the air from the hillside estates, escaping the carnage or sending for aid. Kendra wondered what aid could be rendered with uncertainty in each direction and unable to determine friend from foe.

Kendra's next blast found purchase in the skull of a man attempting to board the ape warship *Morning Blood*, slashing his sword at the ape warriors defending the vessel. The man's lifeless corpse fell on the gangplank before rolling into the water. Countless wounded men, gargoyles, and apes bobbed in the water around the sinking wrecks, panicked by the dorsal fins of hungry versks circling them, drawn by the blood of the stricken. Kendra caught sight of many being dragged under by the vicious predators, disappearing from sight. Grigg didn't bother noticing, moving happily from target to target, with improving accuracy.

A strange sensation coursed Kendra's flesh, like the tingling feeling running north of your legs while standing upon a precipice.

"Packaww!"

She looked suddenly up; one of the Troan magantors dove headlong toward the ship, its beak drawn open as she stared into its open mouth. Preparing to lift her rifle, she froze as its rider released a strangely bright item. A terrible humming sound erupted from the object as she felt Grigg's arms wrap around her forcing her off the side of the ship. She hit the water just as the world seemed to explode. *Boom!*

* * *

The *Stenox* lifted out of the water, before slamming back to the surface, the powerful energy burst sending rippling waves to each direction. The magantor from House Maiyan that delivered the blow, lifted with the energy wave, nearly throwing its rider before flying off. Orvis Maiyan looked on from the terrace of his chambers, horrified by the ruin of his city. It was not to be this way. The Earthers had to leave before the attack commenced, and the broken laser rifle was to be dropped on the forum, killing everyone within. Nor was the city to be sacked and its fleet destroyed, but he looked on as one Troan vessel after another went up in flame or dipped below the sea. Was he to be the regent of ash and debris?

"You look displeased," Rolis observed, standing at his side.

"My city." Orvis lifted his open palms to the carnage below, giving Tyro's agent a dangerous look.

"Yes, an unfortunate necessity. Hossen felt targeting the Earthers' vessel took priority over the fools in the forum. We might never have had this opportunity again to use their own weapons against them," Rolis recalled the conversation he had with Hossen Grell upon his return from Notsu. Hossen would have stuck with Thorton's original plan to destroy the forum and blame the entire affair on pirates, discrediting the ape alliance, but Morac wanted the harbor destroyed, arranging the gargoyle attack, smuggling them into the port in the holds of their merchant ships. Once the *Stenox* appeared, Hossen decided to commence the attack, using the broken laser rifle given them from Thorton to target the Earthers' ship. Once they were removed, the forum could be attacked after. Looking at the result, Rolis had to agree. The *Stenox* sat dead in the water, drifting aimlessly in the center of the harbor, no sound coming from it. He doubted anyone survived that explosion, Thorton's warning about incurring his old friends' wrath obviously overstated.

"I care not of the Earthers, fool! What of my city? Why would you bring gargoyles here? All will know that Tyro is responsible for this. They will not agree to an alliance after this! And what would I be regent of but smoke and ruin!" Orvis growled, looking once again to the harbor below.

Rolis deftly drew a dagger concealed in his robes, driving it into Orvis's back, the heir of House Maiyan's eyes drawing wide in shock, unable to cry out from the pain. Rolis twisted the dagger free before running it across his throat, easing Orvis's dying body to the floor, whispering in his ear.

"We have no need of alliance from a man who would betray his own. After this day, your people will accept any terms we give them, whatever few remain," Rolis whispered, before slipping away, few guards remaining on the estate to question him.

* * *

A disquieting calm settled over the harbor, swords lowered and eyes drawn to the *Stenox* as the blast reverberated across the bay. The hearts of apes and men of Tro failed them, as those of their Benotrist and gargoyle foe rejoiced. There in the middle of the bay sat the stricken ship, hopelessly adrift in a deathly quiet. The faces of those looking on suddenly erupted into a terrible mix of joy and anger. Terin felt his heart leap in his throat. A knowing dread washed over him as he looked on; his magantor circling Admiral Zorgon's flagship, the *Tempest Wind*, looking for a place to set down when the *Stenox* was struck. He was torn between helping Elos deliver the admiral to his ship and flying to check on his friends. The docks below were a maelstrom of chaos; men in dark leather mail tried to board the vessel, with ape sailors holding them at bay. The dozen men with crossbows took up position along the nearest wharf, targeting ape sailors at will. The bodies of apes that guarded the ships littered the adjoining piers; most taken by surprise at the outset. Terin still felt no pull of the sword, no divine instinct giving him direction. He had to make his own decision, and time was fleeting.

"So be it," he sighed, his words lost in the wind. He flew south, away from the ship, before circling back, urging Wind Racer into a steep dive, coming upon the crossbows from behind. Wind Racer set down amidst the crossbowmen's ranks, crushing two of them in his talons upon landing. Terin sprang from his back, sword in hand, taking the first man he came upon across the crossbow in his hands, slicing the weapon in half and the left arm with it. He moved on, leaving that foe writhing in pain, before taking the next across the throat, lifting head from neck. Terin spun away as the severed crown tumbled in the air, thrusting his sword in the next man's back, twisting it free through breaking ribs, blood spattering from the tip of his blade before moving on. He couldn't see the bewildered stares of the remaining men; their eyes wondering what was befalling them. Another looked past Terin before he lopped his head, taking the easy kill, finding another across his back, halving the wretch above the hip. Terin caught sight of Elos's blade flashing nearby, an emerald glow emitting along its length, Admiral Zorgon beside him, sword in hand. Within moments, they slew the last crossbowmen, moving on toward the men attempting to board the *Tempest Wind*, striking them down from behind while the ape sailors charged down from the ship, trapping them between them. Zorgon released a terrible roar, hacking the last of them, head from neck, kicking the fallen crown off the wharf.

"Ready the ship!" Zorgon bellowed, marching up the gangplank, his sailors scurrying across the deck to obey. He stopped at the top, giving Terin and Elos an appreciative snort, acknowledging their aid, before seeing to his ship.

"I must see to my friends," Terin said to Elos, unable to see the *Stenox* with Zorgon's flagship obstructing his view.

"There are enemies here that require our attention," Elos reminded him, pointing out the other ape vessels under assault along the wharves as the *Tempest Wind* prepared to push off.

Terin froze, unable to choose a course of action, to fight the enemy here or see to his friends there, when Admiral Zorgon looked over the side of his flagship, overhearing their discourse as his ship began moving from its mooring.

"Secure my ships here, and I will see to our friends!" Zorgon bellowed, directing his crew to the *Stenox*.

With that, Terin followed Elos into battle, moving along the wharves to the next skirmish, where a unit sixed element of hired mercenaries battled the crew of *Garn's Vengeance*.

* * *

The bridge of the Stenox

Raven pushed himself off the floor, blood running down his skull, struggling to gain his feet. He managed to grab hold of the arm of the captain's seat, pulling himself up, a terrible ringing in his ears. The blast threw him into the ceiling, knocking him senseless.

"Ugh!" Lorken moaned off his left, his friend managing to work himself into a sitting position, nursing broken ribs by the way he was holding his chest.

"You all right?" Raven asked.

"Why are you shouting?" Lorken growled, trying to gain his feet but grimacing from the pain.

"I'm not. Why are you whispering?" Raven made a face, feeling like he bruised every bone and muscle in his body.

"Check your head, Rav!" Lorken shouted loud enough for his friend to hear as Raven helped him to his feet, his every movement feeling like torture. Even speaking more than an utterance or breathing deeply caused him pain.

"We don't have time for this," Raven said after wiping the blood from his face, rubbing it off on his jacket, the ringing in his ears subsiding slightly.

"Try and raise Brokov or Zem!" Lorken winced, hobbling gingerly toward the helm to check for damage.

"Brokov, you all right down th—" Raven stopped midsentence. "Comms are down."

"Emergency lighting is on too," Lorken said, finding all instruments dead.

"What hit us?" Raven wondered, slapping his seat monitor, hoping rough treatment would straighten it out.

"It looked like a laser rifle set on self-destruct, but I only got a glimpse on the sensor before it hit." Lorken shook his head, unable to bring any system back online.

"Shit!" Raven growled, heading toward the door, pressing the manual override to open it.

Lorken suddenly realized what he was thinking…Kendra and Grigg were up top when it hit.

Stepping onto the open stern of the 2nd deck, they were greeted by the harbor in flames. Chaos ran the circumference of the shoreline while they drifted with the current's ebb and flow. Raven looked up to the 3rd deck, finding no sign of their friends.

"There!" Lorken shouted, pointing off the portside bow, his voice paining his ribs whenever he raised it.

Raven saw what he was pointing at—Kendra holding tight to what looked like Grigg, struggling to keep him afloat, her head bobbing below the surface. He jumped to the 1st deck, stripping off his boots, holster, and jacket before jumping in while Lorken made his way down the ladder, entering the forward section of the 1st deck to check on Zem and Brokov, and fetch a towline.

Lorken stepped through the doorway, the backup lights flickering through the central hallway, indicating the dire situation with the ship. The door to the weapons control room was ajar at the end of the corridor, red light from within bleeding through the entrance, hurting his eyes with the flickering lights above. Lorken hobbled as quickly as he could, spotting Brokov pushing the door fully open as he neared the end of the corridor.

"You're alive," Brokov greeted him, his right arm hanging useless at his side, obviously broken, the pain evident on his face.

"We are a matched pair by the looks of it. Where is Zem?"

"Just sitting there. He seems out of it." Brokov jerked a thumb over his shoulder to where Zem sat at the control seat in the weapons control room, staring blankly at the viewscreen.

"We need to revive him."

"How?"

Lorken's silence about summed up their dilemma.

"Where's Kendra, Grigg, and Rav?"

"Raven's swimming out to grab them" was all Lorken could say before Brokov hurried past him, grabbing his right arm with his left hand, ignoring the pain shooting through him.

Lorken followed him onto the open stern, after snatching a towline from the diving room. Brokov's heart went to his throat finding Kendra struggling in the water holding desperately to Grigg as Raven tugged her back to the ship by the collar of her leather shirt. Lorken fastened the towline, tossing the rescue disc into the water near Raven's head. Lorken managed the best he could with his broken ribs and Brokov with only his left hand, each pulling their friends aboard. Raven hoisted Grigg up first, the young gorilla not breathing, his back scorched, the back of his jacket and fur burned away. Kendra followed, flash burns covering the right side of her head, her eyes dilated severely. No sooner had they hoisted Raven aboard then Lorken went to fetch a tissue regenerator, the others huddling over Grigg's still form, with Raven desperately trying to resuscitate him.

Lorken hobbled through the hallway, the flashing lights paining his eyes, making his way back to the weapon's room where their regenerators were stored, along with their extra rifles and pistols, most set in their charging stations. Of the three regenerators they still had, two were cradled in their charging stations, completely drained by the explosion, the other resting on the floor, with very little power left in its energy containment.

"It will have to do," he grumbled, snatching it off the floor.

No sooner had he stepped onto the stern, they positioned it on Grigg's chest, initiating the device.

Nothing.

"Try again!" Raven growled, looking helplessly at Grigg's lifeless eyes staring at the sky.

Lorken reset the regenerator, his second attempt faring no better.

"He's gone." Brokov lowered his head.

"He saved me," Kendra cried, tears falling on Grigg's chest.

"We have to use what power is left to fix ourselves," Lorken said, making the difficult choice.

"What about the other devices?" Raven asked.

"They are drained. The explosion drained everything that was in the charging stations," Lorken explained, setting the device on Brokov's broken arm, initiating the healing sequence. He moved on to Kendra, repairing her damaged tissue, relief washing over her. Brokov took hold of the regenerator, fixing Lorken's ribs, before trying to do the same for Raven's skull where a bloody patch rested on his scalp.

"I'm all right," Raven tried pushing it away.

"You don't have enough brains to spare any," Brokov scolded him, healing him as the device began to falter. Whatever happened next, they had no means to heal anyone, at least not until they could recharge it.

"Let's get this ship operational," Raven growled, sparing a glance to the chaos circling them, as they drifted freely with the current, moving dangerously close to the north shore, where they were drawing the attention of the gargoyles and Benotrist merchant vessels moored there.

"I'll do what I can." Brokov shook his head, stepping back inside.

"Where are your and Grigg's rifles? We might need them," Raven asked Kendra.

"I don't know." She looked over the side of the ship.

"There's one of them," Lorken pointed out a rifle a few meters off the stern, the flotations built into its grip and stock keeping it from sinking.

"And there's the other." Raven found the other just off starboard amidship, jumping back in after them.

"Rav, you best hurry!" Lorken shouted, spotting several Benotrist merchant ships heading their way, masts full with the wind.

* * *

No sooner had Cronus led their small group from the forum, they were set upon by a two flax of mercenaries dressed in dark mail over black leathers, their fore ranks coming at them with swords drawn, with crossbows taking up position behind them.

Zip! Zip! Zip!

Cronus, Argos, Ular, and Orlom quickly fired into their ranks, with Corry, Lucas, and their ape and Enoructan chieftains coming quickly to their sides, blades, and axes raised, one crossbow bolt finding purchase in the shoulder of Chief Hukor. The ornery ape ripped it out with his free hand, ignoring the pain and blood, rushing forth to bury his ax in one fellow's head, jerking it free.

"Argos!" Corry shouted, pointing out an archer upon the roof of the amphitheater, directly to their west.

Zip! Zip! Zip!

Argos sprayed laser fire along the edge of the structure's roof, chunks of stone breaking off where he struck, the archer dropping below the parapet circling the upper reaches of the edifice. Whether he was hit or not, they couldn't tell. Lucas kept to Corry's side throughout while the others finished their attackers.

They continued north, using the upper columns of the magistrate building resting near the shoreline to guide them, when the explosion erupted above the *Stenox*. Cronus caught sight of the disaster as they cleared the last corner, stepping onto the stone wharves, the open moorings giving them a clear view of the ship. A light breeze pressed his face, fed by the shock wave reverberating from the blast. Knowing dread washed over them, briefly freezing them in place, before the realization hit them.

"What ails the *Stenox*?" Ular asked calmly, his watery voice belying his troubled heart.

"I don't know." Cronus shook his head.

"Grigg would have been on the top deck," Orlom said, his eyes wide as saucers, fearing for his friend.

"Who would dare such a thing?" Lucas wondered.

"We have to help them," Corry said.

"We'll need a ship," Cronus said, looking along the wharves. West of their position was a maelstrom of chaos and battle, but the east had few offerings. Few but not none. "Follow me and stay together," Cronus ordered, racing east, skirting the shore.

* * *

Southwest shore of Tro

A column of infantry closed on the *Blazing Forge*, the ape warship still berthed at its mooring, half its crew ashore or dead, with precious few to hold the gangplank. A number still held position along the pier, buying time for the crew to make way with the enemy pressing upon them. The mercenary infantry drove the apes back with lowered spears, sweeping them toward the ship in a disciplined phalanx, skewering many, driving their bloody bodies off the wharf. The crew raised the gangplank, trying to push the ship off the pier, with crossbow bolts and arrows whizzing past. Two canny crewmates managed to ready a catapult, firing a load of fist-sized rocks into the crowded wharf, cutting a hole in the mercenary's ranks. Mercenary archers struck the ship's center mast with fire arrows, flames taking grudging hold in the gentle wind.

Captain Norgar stood amidship of his beleaguered vessel, dark nostrils flaring with tempered rage. The ape warrior wanted nothing more than to lead his sailors into the fray, but they were too few, and he needed to be underway to protect his ship. With Admiral Zorgon's flagship already underway to his immediate east, he needed to join him. Such plans were in doubt with the enemy already leaping upon the side of his ship, with nary three meters separating the hull from the wharf. One fellow sprang off the pier, grabbing hold of the bulwark off his right. Norgar made quick work of him, driving his short sword into his face, twisting it free as the man fell backward, splashing in the bloody water. Norgar ducked his head, an arrow grazing the top of his skull. He cursed, crouching below the bulwark, stealing a glance from time to time as the ship inched further off the pier.

Crunch!

A loud crash sounded off his left where the foul mercenaries managed to drop a boarding ramp onto the stern, breaking the timbers of the side rail. The men sent a party of skirmishers first, with a more organized phalanx to follow. His brave warriors cut down the bravely stupid men leading the charge, greeting them with axes and sword thrusts, their corpses cluttering the ramp as the ship drew a little further away. Another three meters and the ramp would fall free, ending this last desperate attempt to board. Another arrow drove Norgar to the deck, ducking as the shaft embedded in the wall of the inner deck behind him.

"Agghh!" The sound of dying men drew the ape captain's ear. Stealing another glance, he saw the mercenaries scattering, witless and without direction. There, in their midst, was the Torry champion, with blade in hand, cutting men down like a divine tempest, darting from one man to the next, limbs and blood flying off the tip of his murky silver sword, its blade dimming with every blow, as if bewitched. He would catch men from front or behind, each oblivious of his approach, like blind men grasping at the wind. Further behind him was a Jenaii warrior wielding an equally beguiling sword, cutting men to pieces with practiced skill, but each at least standing to fight him.

Norgar stood erect as the mercenary archers and crossbowmen were slaughtered or fled, the air clear of their threat. He briefly regarded his skeletal crew, knowing they were too few to battle another vessel but could make a difference following in Terin's wake.

"Put ashore!" he bellowed, ordering his ship back to the pier. Within moments, his crew followed him down the gangplank, chasing after Terin and Elos as they raced west along the shoreline, clearing the wharves of mercenaries attacking the next ape vessel, the *Night Roar*, its beleaguered crew faring little better than the *Blazing Forge* had before Terin's arrival.

Terin moved among the mercenaries, cutting them down as if unseen. He moved along the wharves striking one man across the ribs; the fellow looked surprised as his chest lifted freely from his body, his eyes staring beyond Terin for some strange reason. Terin spun around the stricken warrior, taking the next man at the left knee, moving on before he toppled over, his screams echoing in his wake. Elos trailed him, dozens of warriors rushing toward him, and bypassing Terin for some reason.

Split! Thrust! Slice!

Elos made quick work of two more, shifting to engage the others as Terin spun around, charging them from behind after they passed him by. His silver eyes narrowed with focus, a sharp slice breaking the next man's shield. Elos shifted as a second attempted to circle wide to his left. He drove forward, a hurried thrust taking the first man through the breast, withdrawing before the second could come behind him. The second man paused, transfixed by the emerald glow of his fell blade. Elos took quick advantage, driving toward the man with a surprising burst, driving his sword through his chest, kicking it free. Before he could take stock of his surroundings, a wave of dark fur and boiled leather mail rushed past him.

"Come, friend, we have a battle to win!" Captain Norgar gave Elos a toothy grin. His crew rushed to help Terin, who just cut down three more men; his sword growing darker by the moment.

* * *

Southwest barracks of Tro

The harbor garrison was housed in a series of barracks circling the city proper, just within its curtain walls. The troops billeted in the southwest barracks were caught unaware at the outset. Mercenaries flooded through their open gates, moving from chamber to chamber, slaughtering everyone within, setting it ablaze upon their exit. Many of the soldiers were elsewhere at the time, forced to link up with other elements or fighting in small groups on their own.

The west barracks fared better; its guards managed to sound the alarm and bar the gate before the mercenary army battered it down. They held off the attack long enough for reinforcements to arrive from the west wall and the surrounding precincts and the garrison guarding the southern half of the Flen River Bridge. From there, the commander of the west wall reorganized his troops and advanced east through the city, clearing the enemy street by street, gathering more stray units as they went.

The south barracks was beset by poisoned food at the outset, many barely able to wield a sword when the enemy struck in force. The gate was barred, however, affording the few unaffected to hold long enough for reinforcements to arrive. Unfortunately, none did, with the garrison eventually put to the sword. The attackers fared little better, losing 60 percent of their strength storming the citadel. They were soon put upon by various local militia and private armies employed throughout the rich southern districts and hillside estates of the ruling families.

The southeast barracks met the attack fully prepared and provisioned, stopping the enemy at the gates and crushing them with a powerful counterattack.

The northeast barracks was untouched, eventually sending reinforcements west to secure the next barracks and another force to the shore, to counter activity from the gargoyles swarming into the city from the Benotrist merchant fleet.

The north barracks was breached at the outset; gargoyles swarmed through the adjoining streets using the nearby edifices to bound over their walls. Fighting raged there throughout the battle, men and gargoyles contesting every space in the stronghold.

The northwest barracks was beset by poisoning, fire, and gargoyles, yet held long enough to blunt a sizable contingent of attackers. With only gargoyles attacking the northern half of Tro, it was easy for the people to determine friend from foe, lending their strength to the garrisons.

Once it was determined that no threat presented outside Tro's walls, the commanders began to dispatch more and more men to the city interior to join the fray.

The *Moorn* suffered a similar assault as the barracks, only spared destruction by the *Stenox's* timely intervention at the outset, laser fire tearing the heart out of the gargoyle attackers. Kaly led his remaining men onto the wharves, losing count of the dead gargoyles littering the front of his establishment. He stood upon the empty piers, looking out across the bay where the *Stenox* now drifted like a lifeless tomb, wondering their fate. Hundreds of apes were now spilling out onto the wharves from adjoining streets, enjoying shore leave when the attack commenced, leaving their ships undermanned and easy prey. They were joined by hundreds if not thousands of Troan seamen and citizens seeking out gargoyles wherever they could find them. Most of the creatures were still coming ashore to their direct east, spilling into the city from the holds of the Benotrist merchant fleet. The Earthers managed to sink two dozen of the vessels, as well as most of the captured squadron that commenced the attack, but many ships remained in the fight. Looking south across the bay, Kaly could make out several Troan warships underway, the sigil of the harbor, five swords crossed upon a field of gray, lifting above their forward masts. They were joined by several ape galleys pushing off from their moorings. Looking east, dozens of Benotrist merchant ships abandoned the attack on the city, driving south into the middle of the harbor. Gargoyles crowded their decks with their feral gaze fixed to their prey. The remaining gargoyles were now returning to their ships, withdrawing from the northern half of Tro like a foul tide receding from the shore, drawn to a greater prize. Kaly suddenly realized where they were headed…the *Stenox*.

"We must get to a ship," Kaly said to Vade Cavelle, his most trusted lieutenant and capable enforcer.

"The *Maiden's Purse* appears untouched," Vade pointed out Kaly's personal vessel resting to their west. It was more fit for pleasure than giving battle, with only one catapult, and no ram to speak of.

"It will have to do." Kaly resigned himself to what they must do.

* * *

Raven tossed both rifles onto the deck before climbing aboard, barely gaining his breath as he looked off their portside at the encroaching ships. There had to be forty vessels, their masts full with the wind; gargoyles crowding their decks. Lorken stepped back onto the stern, having secured Grigg's body inside, moving freely with his restored ribs.

"Better buckle up. It's going to be a rough ride." Lorken tossed him his holster.

"You any good with a pistol?" Raven asked Kendra, fastening his pistol belt, tying off the holster to his right thigh.

"Better with a rifle, but I might be able—" She tried to answer.

"Take your rifle back." He shoved it into her arms, offering the other to Lorken. They were down to the two rifles and the pistols on their holsters; their remaining weapons presently drained.

"I'll take the high ground," Lorken said, climbing the ladder to the 2nd deck.

Raven cautioned him not to advance to the 3rd deck in case he was forced to retreat inside. Raven went inside to fetch Grigg's pistol from his holster, giving each of them two guns. He returned to the stern, finding Kendra already targeting the approaching ships, firing off several hurried blasts.

"Settle down, killer. We need to make every shot count so we don't drain our lasers," Raven said, taking careful aim with Grigg's pistol. He trained his sights on the nearest merchant vessel, a Benotrist ship, two hundred meters out, ignoring the ugly gargoyles crowding the bow, sending his first blast through the forward hull. He couldn't quickly see what damage he inflicted before sending another blast. The laser sliced through the ship's hull, punching a fist-sized hole through its keel, water pouring in. A second and third blast opened more holes, slowing the vessel's pace, its prow dipping lower in the surf.

Lorken took aim at another Benotrist merchant ship, trailing fifty meters of the first. His first blast brained a gargoyle leaning over the bow; the laser passed through several others crowded behind him before ending astern. He shifted left to the next creature, sending a salvo through its breast, the course of the laser passing through several others before ending amidship.

Zip! Zip! Zip!

Lorken continued thinning the deck of gargoyles, ignoring the mechanics of the vessel; whereas, Raven was already trying to slow or sink his next target, one just beyond Lorken's, sending seven blasts through its portside bow. Kendra concentrated on the ship furthest left in their view, sending blast after blast through the center of the top deck. She took satisfaction with gargoyles dropping along the length of her blast, gutting their ranks with terrible efficiency.

Raven shifted aim with his second target's bow dipping severely in the water, gargoyles springing off its deck to escape a watery death. A few hurried blasts along the upper rigging dropped several fleeing gargoyles tumbling upon their comrades, entangling them in the ship's ropes and netting.

"Enjoy the swim," he mumbled, firing at his next target.

Lorken moved on as well, leaving his first target to continue on toward them with few creatures left to attack with. Lorken wondered what they planned to do. Perhaps ram them or use their human crew to board the *Stenox*. Either way, they would make quick work of them should they attempt it. Meanwhile, he had too many other targets looming, choosing a light galley drawing within 120 meters. His first shot took the helmsman through the nose, dropping him like a sack of grain; the ship turning hard to port with his dead hand. A second blast took the man trying to correct the wheel; the ship turned into the path of a galley trailing portside, its bow striking amidship. The sound of snapping timbers echoed over the surf, ocean water spilling into the stricken ship's hull.

"Beat that, Rav." Lorken grinned, shifting aim elsewhere.

"A little humility wouldn't kill you," Raven growled back. His blasts crippled a third vessel. The second was already floundering, its stern slipping beneath the waves.

* * *

"Wake up, Zem!" Brokov slapped his friend on the head before taking a seat beside him, working the console feverishly. Zem sat his seat, staring blankly ahead, his luminous blue eyes dim as if dead. Brokov fought the fear creeping in his brain that his friend was truly gone but didn't have time to dwell on it. He needed to turn the ship back on somehow. All overrides were useless with their power core exhausted. The backup core was down as well. Racking his brain, he resorted to one final idea, the only idea to come to mind. He crawled under the console, finding the manual reset switch, the one failsafe Thorton ironically insisted the *Stenox* have in the event of a solar burst or flare disabling the ship.

"Here goes nothing or everything." He closed his eyes and flipped the switch. He opened his eyes to expected silence, not knowing if he was successful until he looked at the console. Retaking his seat, he looked dejectedly at the blank screen, all hope seeming lost. He lowered his head, defeated. There was nothing more for him to do than help his friends outside. Brokov stood up, taking one foot toward the door.

Beep!

He turned quickly back, his eyes finding those glorious words flashing at the bottom of the screen—*power storage 0.001 percent.* The solar recharge was enabled. All they needed now was time, time they might not have.

* * *

"Oh, come on!" Raven growled after sinking his fifth ship when another maneuvered around it, bearing down upon them, drawing nearer than the last. They were perilously close at eighty-five meters, their gargoyles already springing over the side of the ship, joining the survivors from his earlier victims, their winged forms nearly upon them.

Zip! Zip! Zip!

Kendra shifted aim to those approaching portside, their dark forms splashing into the water just shy of the ship. Lorken shifted as well, forsaking the ships in the distance for the pressing threat upon them. He could hardly miss at this range, dropping four in quick succession approaching the bow, with three managing to set down on the 3rd deck.

Zip! Zip! Zip!

His hurried blasts struck all three, leaving two flailing on the deck and a third lunging at him on the 2nd deck.

Zip! Zip!

He brained the creature, its scimitar grazing his shoulder.

Raven dropped several more approaching the portside stern, one hitting the railing before slipping into the water.

"Don't know how long we can keep this up!" Lorken said, standing the deck above them, dropping another short of the bow, with several passing from sight across the prow, circling to attack starboard.

"It's getting ridiculous!" Raven growled, firing continuously, dropping one after another, each a head shot to make certain of them. Kendra aimed center mass, lacking the skill to accurately hit the head of her targets with any measurable speed. She took the nearest through the stomach, the creature continuing on, adrenaline fueling its dying body. It grazed the rail, forcing her back a step, jaws snapping feverishly before she blasted a hole through its neck. It slipped into the sea as others swarmed over the rail, Raven dropping them as they tumbled upon the deck.

Lorken turned his eyes briefly from the danger portside to the few circling low, around the ship to attack starboard, dropping several short of the ship. There were too many to catch them all, three sweeping over the starboard rail of the 1st deck.

"Agghh!" Kendra cried out. A gargoyle slammed into her back, face-planting her to the deck, sinking its fangs into her shoulder. Raven brained the creature after finishing the others before turning back to portside where countless others drew near.

Zip! Zip! Zip! Zip!

Raven and Lorken fired with abandon, all precision thrown out the window with the enemy now fully upon them. Raven could hear Kendra's painful moans lying beside him but couldn't spare her a glance with every moment occupied with another threat.

"Kai-Shorum!" a creature screamed, approaching the stern, bloodred eyes aflame with rage.

Zip!

Raven sent a blast through its skull; the gargoyle slamming into the rail of the stern, the sound of breaking bones echoing over the din.

Zip!

His next blast passed through the open throat of another gliding over the portside rail; the blast exited its lower back, its outstretched wings carrying its dead carcass across the deck, impacting the surface off starboard. Two more dropped portside, their wings crippled as they flailed about in the surf.

Whoosh!

A versk snatched another out of the air in its razored jaws; the giant fish shooting from the water before splashing into the sea with its prey. Raven counted a dozen dorsal fins circling the ship, drawn by the gargoyles' bloody corpses littering the surrounding waters.

Brokov stepped onto the stern, firing quickly into the cluttered sky, standing protectively over Kendra's writhing form.

"What's with the ship?" Raven grunted, firing off more hurried shots, stepping to Kendra's other side. Gargoyles were now setting down on the deck before being blasted.

"Reboot worked, but it'll be a while to store enough power to help us." Brokov sent several blasts through a gargoyle's chest, the creature dropping dead at his feet.

"Take her inside and see if you can hurry it along." Raven dropped another landing portside stern, it crotch landing painfully on the rail before leaning over the side and falling into the water.

"What about you? You can't stay out here." Brokov kept firing into the sky, unable to miss as the dark mass drew ominously close.

"I'm right behind you. Lorken, take cover!" Raven shouted above, where Lorken fended off another near-miss, a scimitar grazing his scalp before braining the creature, its blade clattering off the deck.

"Aye!" he shouted back, withdrawing to the bridge.

"Go help him. This deck has the double doors. They won't get in anytime soon," Brokov said, dragging Kendra through the door by the collar with his free hand, his gun hand firing as he went.

Raven waited until the door closed before climbing the ladder, joining Lorken on the 2nd deck. Gargoyles landed unhindered behind him, one trying to reach for his leg before he fired under his opposite arm, blasting its face. He cleared the doorway to the bridge, closing it behind him. Lorken took up position behind the helm while he knelt behind the captain's chair, their pistols leveled on the doorway. They heard clawed feet scraping on the deck above, and the sound of swords striking against the door.

"We'll see how long the door lasts," Lorken said.

* * *

Southwest Tro

Slice! Thrust!

Terin moved across the westernmost wharf, cutting men down like stalks of dead grass, coming upon them unawares with Elos struggling to keep pace. Men turned, drawn fearfully to the emerald glow of Elos's fell blade, looking past Terin as if he were unseen. He spared them little thought, cutting down men where they stood; only their surprised looks registering a response. He spun from one foe who flailed helplessly as if blind, drawing his blade across the back of another mercenary, the pitiful wretch's torso slipping from his hips.

Slash!

A wide arc took two above the shoulders, their heads flying off his darkening blade. Terin moved on, dropping men as he went. Elos gathered a force of Troans and apes, following in his wake, slaying those he left to them. He no longer lost himself to the blade, strangely conscious of his every action. He could not move beyond exhaustion, limited by his labored breath. The more he immersed himself in the power of the sword, the darker it became; its once silver luster dimming like a turbid sky.

He pushed on to the end of the last wharf, driving the last of his foes before him, each blindly swinging their swords in his general direction. He slipped to the right, skirting the edge of the empty moorings, lopping the arm of one fellow, before slipping behind him, stopping at the end of the stone lip at the water's edge. Spinning about, he struck at his last foes from behind. Most were facing away from him, their eyes fixed to Elos and the mob of men and apes following at his heels.

Lop! Lop! Lop!

He sent three heads into the air, before stopping, with Elos finishing those standing between them. He spared a glance around them. The sound of battle was waning in the adjoining streets south and west of them. The nearest wharves were littered with dead and dying men. Apes and Troans finished off those that lingered, showing no mercy for the vanquished. Most of Admiral Zorgon's squadron pushed off their moorings, joining the remaining Troan ships toward the center of the bay where the enemy was concentrating on the *Stenox*. Three of Zorgon's vessels succumbed to the attack, burning at their piers. Smoke from their burning wrecks choked the air, leaving only Captain Norgar's ship at its mooring. The grizzled ape sailor led the growing crowd that followed Terin's mad charge along the wharves.

"You are a greedy lad. I'll give you that!" Norgar grinned, joining Elos and Terin at the wharf's edge, catching his breath. "You might have left a few more for us to kill but took most for yourself."

"Your help was most welcome, Captain." Elos regarded Norgar respectfully as a Troan commander of rank, stepping forth from the crowd that followed them.

"As was yours, whoever you are," the Troan commander greeted them. His silver mail was marred, and the white tunic, bloodstained.

"I am Elos of the Jenaii, and my friend is Terin, champion of the Torry Realm."

"Torry and Jenaii! We are not alone at least. I am commander of Unit Daytov," he said proudly.

"Our friends need our help, Commander. If you and the good captain could secure the area, we can be on our way," Terin said, looking to Daytov and Norgar.

"Aye," they chorused. With the wharves clear, they could take the fight to the adjoining streets where the sounds of battle still rang.

Terin looked around one last time, standing in the shadow of the Flen River Bridge to his northwest, where men could be seen running across it to its southern end. "I would start in that direction," he advised them before racing back east where their magantors were waiting.

* * *

Thud!

The Corbin's *Glory* struck the *Stenox*'s bow head on, its ram buckling. The force of the blow nearly tore it from its prow. The impact jarred the *Stenox*, driving it briefly back, but also severely damaged the captured Troan warship, with water pouring through the broken fissures spreading from its bow. Monsoon stood amidship the *Flen Raider*, the two vessels all that remained of his captured squadron, the *Raider* trailing the *Glory* some one hundred meters. He cursed, the blow doing naught to the Earthers' damnable vessel. It simply stood there unmarred and unbroken, with gargoyles swarming over its hull like ants crawling over a nest. Thousands more filled the sky, circling the *Stenox* like carrion to be plundered, searching for a place to set down upon its serried decks. Dozens of Benotrist merchant vessels surrounded the stricken vessel, feeding more gargoyles to the battle. Further south and west, he descried the small flotilla of Troan and ape vessels drawing near, the pitiful remains of once proud fleets, ready to give battle. He dismissed them out of hand, their numbers precious few, as they drove below the deadly mass of gargoyles overhead. Several ape vessels drew from the northwest, the few that survived the ambush, with whatever crews they could assemble. Staring across the bay north and south, he looked on with mild satisfaction at the burning city, smoke twisting into the sky in spirals of gray and black, including one of the estates of the ruling families, their hilltop manse engulfed in flame.

Monsoon looked to the east, where the rest of his pirate flotilla passed through the mouth of the bay; their timely arrival a welcome sight. They trailed his captured squadron some distance, entering the harbor to join the battle, nearly twelve ships in all, eight armed with rams and all with munitions. He would order them to converge on the *Stenox*, striking its hull from all sides until it cracked like an egg.

The ship showed little sign of life, and the Earthers could be dead for all he knew, but he needed to make certain of it before withdrawing.

"Kai-Shorum!" Gargoyle chants echoed above the din, their haunting war cries reverberating across the water in a deathly chorus. Even from afar, he could hear the clanging of their axes and scimitars upon the ship's hull.

"Soon," Monsoon whispered to himself, "it has to be soon."

* * *

Zem was struck by a memory, standing beside Raven's father as the Mekiana family gathered around the fireplace singing Christmas carols in their log home high in the Rocky Mountains. He reveled in their warm acceptance, especially Raven's father, Nukilik, who fondly called him his favorite son, much to Raven's annoyance. Raven's mother, Analisa, was no less endearing, offering him homemade cookies and hot chocolate, which his taste sensors allowed him to enjoy, depositing the remains later as food was for pleasure not necessity. It was Raven's brother Matt who helped develop Zem during his research in New Zealand, bringing him home with him for the holidays, imprinting in his new brain a sense of belonging to the large clan. The large brood included five sons and two daughters, with their maternal grandparents, Jake and Maria Evans, along with their uncles and Raven's friend Thorton, who was wedded to Raven's sister, the lovely Jennifer.

"Welcome to the family, son," Raven's father said, slapping Zem's thick metallic shoulder as Jennifer stood before the fireplace singing "The Yellow Rose of Texas," for her beloved Ben, who looked on from the far side of the room with adoring eyes, smitten by the girl. Raven had to smack his friend up alongside the head from time to time to snap him out of it. Zem found the humans' emotions of romantic love an odd curiosity, thankfully one he was not afflicted with. He did, however, enjoy the familial bonds he shared with his creator and his creator's kin. It was a sense of belonging that strangely affected him, setting him apart from other artificial life forms. He could think independently and care for others with a bond most similarly shared between brothers or even parents. He enjoyed his time in the Mekiana home, where they even gave him his

own bedroom, not that he had any need for sleep, but he appreciated it all the same.

"I've reviewed your application to Space Fleet, Zem, and sent along my recommendations to the fleet applicant review board. You should have little problem receiving a direct commission," Raven's grandfather said, standing at his opposite shoulder. As a retired admiral in Space Fleet, Jake Evans still held incredible influence within the service. A recommendation from him went far. He was a tall man with a commanding presence and piercing blue eyes. His wife, Maria, stood at his side, a black-haired beauty with the light-brown skin of her Tejano heritage, smiling as she looked on to her grandchildren circling the fireplace.

"I am grateful, Admiral. I will justify your recommendation with an exemplary performance of my duties," Zem answered.

"None of that admiral talk, Zem. Around here, you can call me Grandpa." Jake smiled, slapping his other shoulder.

Zem returned the gesture with a gentle pat on Jake's shoulder.

It was then the memory changed to a dream, with Jennifer finishing "The Yellow Rose of Texas," and starting anew with "Daydream Believer," a song hundreds of years old sung by musicians sharing a name with primitive primates called monkeys. What struck him as odd was that Jennifer never sang that particular song, only Kato.

* * *

Kato, Zem suddenly remembered. Kato was dead, killed by Thorton, as Cronus told them. Why was that so important now? Why did his dream transform into a memory? Why couldn't he wake up? He felt trapped, his eyes unable to see or his fingers move. Was he dead? No, he couldn't be, for he was aware. He needed to wake, but how?

"You can do this, Zem, just as we discussed. Remember your contingencies should your primary power source drain?" He heard Matt's voice echo in his brain, Raven's brother and his beloved creator.

"They need you, Zem," Matt added. "Awake."

System Restore.

The words flashed before his eyes with "Daydream Believer" repeating in his brain, to his utter annoyance, wishing it was "Anchors Aweigh" instead, but it was a reminder of Kato and the sacrifice he made for others and the friendship he shared with them all.

Zem's luminous blue eyes suddenly alit.

* * *

"That's about enough of this nonsense. Let's open the door before they break it," Raven said.

"You sure about that, Rav?" Lorken didn't look convinced of that plan, holding position behind the helm, his rifle slung over his shoulder and pistol trained on the doorway. The gargoyles outside were hacking away with axes, swords, and even claws, their nails scratching at the door.

Thud!

The ship jerked; another ship rammed its hull, this time from portside.

"You want to wait until they punch through our hull?" Raven asked.

"It's made of Trundusium. They aren't punching through that," Lorken reminded him. If they could see the effects of the strike, they would know the pirate ship's ram snapped off its prow and was taking on water, its bow listing.

"Our pistols are near fully charged, and I'm tired of sitting here, taking their shit," Raven growled.

"All right, Rav, go ahead."

* * *

"Send two this time, one from each side!" Monsoon ordered from the deck of the *Flen Raider*, watching with disgust as the bow of the *Maiden's Virtue* dipped severely into the surf off the portside of the *Stenox*, the second ship he lost trying to ram it. If one could not breach it, then he would try two, much to the misgivings of his reluctant captains.

"Their hull is too strong, Admiral. Perhaps we should pummel her with ballistae first," his own captain advised.

"Their decks are crawling with gargoyles. We'd only be killing them and drawing their ire. No, we must ram them again!" Monsoon commanded.

Zip! Zip! Zip! Zip!

Monsoon winced as laser fire erupted from the door of the bridge, spraying through its opening from within. Gargoyles drew briefly away from the portal, laser cutting down a dozen of the creatures. Some flew off, holes burned through their torsos; a few faltering before crashing to the surf. Others escaped unscathed, clambering over port and starboard, while the unfortunate lay dead or dying, flopping upon the deck like fish thrown upon the shore.

"Ram them with every ship we have!" Monsoon shouted, knowing their fate rested on finishing the Earthers here and now. Given the signal, three ships circled into position to the *Stenox*'s starboard—one to sternand two to port. Behind them rested the Benotrist merchant fleet, with gargoyles still launching from their serried decks. Desperation drove Monsoon to end the Earthers before the small enemy fleets drew in range, one from the north and the other from the southwest, a collection of ape and Troan warships, looking to give battle. At five hundred meters, they were still far enough off to give him time to finish this before they arrived.

The gargoyles recovered from the deadly volley, hundreds descending upon the *Stenox* from all sides, their feral eyes fixed to the open door of the bridge while screaming their war cries.

"Kai-Shorum!" echoed hauntingly over the din, kindling their courage as they threw themselves upon the open doorway, with laser blasts spitting from that deadly space.

* * *

Zip! Zip! Zip!

Raven fired away, unable to miss with the creatures filling the doorway, his blasts dropping them like puppets with their strings cut, all head shots. They learned their lesson after blasting one creature through the abdomen and chest, only for it to crawl through the doorway, making it halfway to the helm before Raven brained it. Gargoyle corpses were collecting in the doorway, blocking those without from storming freely through. Other gargoyles dragged their fallen away, clearing the door for the next to rush through. The next group fared little better; Lorken and Raven dropped the first in quick succession, their corpses blocking the doorway and the others trying to clammer over the growing pile.

Zip!

Lorken took another through its open mouth, the laser exiting at the base of its skull, striking another behind it through the chest, and another behind it in the right wing; its squeals drowned in the din.

Zip!

Raven took another through the side of the ear, its body dropping upon the pile, limbs flailing as its fellows stepped over him.

Zip! Zip! Zip!

They continued to fire, corpses piling to the top of the door frame, as those without again dragged the corpses away from the side of the door, keeping out of Raven and Lorken's line of sight.

"Persistent little bastards, aren't they?" Raven grunted, waiting for them to clear away the dead and try entering again.

"Unfortunately, I'm sick of hearing their annoying war cry too, Kai-shrub, or whatever they call it," Lorken lamented.

"I don't know. It sounds kind of catchy. It can't be worse than the academy fight song," Raven said, blasting the next gargoyle to enter, through the brain.

Zip! Zip! Zip!

"You might have a point," Lorken said after firing three quick bursts, recalling *The Pride of Brussels* playing in his brain over and over again, the dorky fight song that the Space Fleet Academy refused to change.

"How long can they keep this up? They have to run out of gargoyles at some point," Raven said, blasting the next creature through the nose as it tried squeezing over the pile of corpses, its wings scraping the top of the door. Within moments, those without began clearing this pile of dead, preparing to charge through again.

"Either that, or our pistols will drain first."

"Good luck to them. We've got plenty of juice left," Raven said.

"Maybe, unless they get creative," Lorken said warily, getting a clear shot at a gargoyle flying above the stern after the corpse pile was cleared, taking it through its middle, the creature dropping to the surf. The next wave was immediately upon them storming through the doorway, the first to enter dropping just beyond the entry, a deeper incursion than their last efforts. Raven and Lorken dropped the next at the doorway, the others charging overtop their comrades.

Thud! Thud!

The ship rocked, struck portside and starboard by pirate rams, its hull integrity withstanding the blows but nearly taking Raven and Lorken from their feet, allowing two of the creatures to squeeze fully through the doorway, each lunging for the helm. Lorken recovered taking one through the breast, and Raven dropped the other with a blast through the right ear before shifting aim to the door.

* * *

Weapons control room of the Stenox

Brokov grew frustrated with the ship's slow recharging, removing every pistol, rifle, and tissue regenerator from their charging stations to help the process along. The small maneuver only helped a little, the storage restoration only reading 0.1 percent on the console readout.

"Come on, hurry up!" Brokov growled at the screen, desperate to restore the ship's power. They needed to win the battle and restore power to the tissue regenerators if he had any hope of treating Kendra, who lay upon her bunk in her crew cabin or set them in the sun to recharge them, which was impossible with the battle raging outside.

"The ship isn't programmed to respond to such urgings, Brokov." Zem's metallic voice drew him from the console, looking to his left where his comrade showed the first sign of life, turning his large metallic head toward him.

"Zem! You're back!" Brokov could've kissed him, never so happy to see those luminous lights he calls eyes come to life.

"Aye. What is our status?" Zem asked.

"Power banks drained. Grigg dead. Kendra wounded. Raven and Lorken defending the bridge unless their dead. We are blind until we can restore enough energy to power our sensors. We're currently surrounded by anywhere between thirty to fifty enemy vessels and thousands of gargoyles."

"That is unacceptable," Zem stated dryly, plugging in audio program 2187 into the ship's external amplifier.

"What are you doing? That will use a lot of the power I've restored!" Brokov asked in alarm.

"True. But this is for Kato." Zem stood from his chair, patting Brokov on the back before heading down the hall.

"What are you doing?"

Zem paused at the end of the corridor, looking back at Brokov while pounding his right fist into his left hand. "It's time to kick some ass," Zem said in all seriousness. Brokov would've laughed at the outburst if their situation wasn't so dire. Zem unholstered his pistol, tossing it to Brokov.

"You'll need this more than I," Zem added, before opening the door, greeted by the surprised faces of the creatures trying to break it down.

* * *

Hundreds of gargoyles clung to the *Stenox*, swarming over its decks like insects trying to enter the bridge time and again. Raven and Lorken desperately repulsed them with each attempt. The pirate ship *Galbon* rested off its portside, its bow cracked, taking on water. The *Night Whore* sat astern, its ram still attached, struggling to back away and ram again. The *Vixen's Wrath* and the *Bounty Bosom* sat starboard; their bows crippled but still afloat to feed gargoyles into the fray. Thousands of gargoyles circled lazily above, waiting their turn to set down, kept in the air by the gentle breeze lifting their wings.

Monsoon observed the battle some distance off portside, nervously waiting for the gargoyles to finally breach the bridge. He ordered others to deliver fire munitions to the gargoyles. All they need do was toss them through the doorway of the bridge, and Raven would be finished, but communicating with the creatures when their bloodlust was roused was nearly impossible. Only those that haven't yet launched from their decks could be reasoned with. He was keenly aware of the approaching enemy ships from the northwest and southwest, keeping many of his gargoyles in reserve to unleash them upon the encroaching ships.

All his plans rested upon the brink, his eyes furtively scanning the Earthers' vessel for any sign of success when a great commotion erupted on the stern of the 1st deck, several creatures thrown clear, while others swarmed over a lone figure hidden beneath the sea of gargoyle flesh. Another creature was thrown clear of the *Stenox*, its broken body flying ten meters off portside, falling amid swarming versks, which made quick work of him. Another was thrown into the deck of the *Night Whore*, smashing into its forward mast, snapping it in two. Knowing dread dampened Monsoon's spirit, for only one creature was capable of such power…Zem.

But what is that awful music blasting from the ship? Monsoon made a face.

* * *

Greeted by stunned faces upon clearing the doorway, Zem grabbed the first gargoyle he could grasp, snapping its right arm, tossing it over the side of the ship, its body hitting several others in its path. He punched the next straight through its face, ripping its skull free with his other hand, before tossing it starboard.

"Kai-Shorum!" the gargoyles screamed, recovering from the surprise, rushing him from all sides.

Zem dug his fingers into one of the creatures pressing upon him, tearing away his guts, its innards spilling onto the deck. His other hand grasped a wing, tearing it from a creature's back, using it to bash another upside the head. Another clung to his shoulders, sinking its fangs into his face. Zem threw several off him, reaching up to dislodge his attacker, ripping its wings from its back. The creature slipped away, its screams lifting above the din.

Music started blaring from the external amplifier, the words of "Daydream Believer" echoing through the air as Zem terrorized the gargoyles. They swarmed over him, hacking away at exposed parts with their scimitars or biting wherever they could reach, all too little effect. Blades snapped, and fangs broke upon his impenetrable skin. Zem kicked several off his left leg, sending three over the starboard rail. One trying to pin his right arm to his side was lifted overhead, tossed into the mast of the *Night Whore*, trailing astern. His fists started flying, smashing gargoyles left, right, and forward, with bones snapping with every blow. Zem tore heads from necks and arms from shoulders. Corpses piled on the deck and littered the surrounding waters. The pirate ships surrounding the *Stenox* held fire, lest they strike their gargoyle comrades, but that restraint was quickly waning with Zem's reign of terror.

Harroom!

Horns sounded from afar. The gargoyles and pirates looked on with growing dread as the squadron of ape ships drew from the north, and the larger force of Troan and ape ships closed from the south. Monsoon ordered all gargoyles launching from his pirate fleet to attack the southern force. Many carried fire munitions in the first wave, converging on the lead ships in the flotilla. Zem grew angry as the gargoyles began drawing away, with the sky clearing overhead, though hundreds remained, assailing him from each direction.

* * *

Troan Fleet, southwest of the Stenox

Admiral Purvis stood at the prow of his flagship, the *Tro Champion*, leading the remnant of the Troan Fleet, twenty-three warships, toward the enemy surrounding the *Stenox*. The trioar *Tro*

Champion was the pride of the Troan Fleet, with eight catapults and a dozen large crossbows lining her upper decks. The crew braced for battle as a thousand gargoyles filled the air, drawing ominously nigh. Off her starboard sailed the *Tempest Wind*, Admiral Zorgon's flagship, leading the remnant of the ape squadron berthed on the southern wharves of the harbor, converging on the enemy ahead.

Admiral Purvis withdrew to the inner deck issuing commands as the enemy drew nigh. His archers took aim at the gargoyles bearing munitions; the pouches of gelatinous materials dangled from their weak hands, with torches alit in their strong hands.

"Fire at will!" The order went out as the gargoyles passed over the bow, arrows filling the air.

Most of the shafts fluttered awry or failed to reach the higher altitudes of the fire bearers. A few struck true dropping some creatures short of the bow, splashing to the surf. Others set their pouches ablaze, dropping them before veering off. A few struck true; others missed the deck altogether, landing harmlessly in the sea. Many more set torch to their pouches after breaking into a steep dive, depositing them across the serried deck of the Troan flagship while others passed on for the ships trailing her.

Purvis jumped aside, a munition striking the catapult crew beside him. Some were killed on impact; others lingering, engulfed in flames. Two men ran past him, flames pouring off their backs before jumping into the sea. He winced with another munition striking amidship, taking an archer with its explosion. Another hit the center bow, flames spreading portside to starboard, engulfing several crewmen there. Crossbows dropped several circling portside; their giant shafts impaling their targets midflight. The orders rang out to prepare for boarding, the following waves of gargoyles angling to land, their wingtips kissing the waves as they drew nigh.

Purvis drew his shortsword, stepping toward portside to receive a gargoyle flying over the bulkhead, driving his sword upward as it passed. A screech indicated he cut something, but the foul creature continued on toward the upper inner deck, taking an archer from behind. He backed toward the stern, cutting down another, setting down with its back to him, slashing its scimitar at a sailor while Purvis lopped its head.

Admiral Zorgon fared little better, the *Tempest Wind* taking three hits to starboard. Flames spread across amidship before hundreds of gargoyles began setting down portside; his crew fending them off, the gargoyles faring poorly against apes in close combat. Unlike most human navies, the apes used warriors as oarsmen, doubling as infantry at sea. The *Tempest Wind* slowed, allowing her warriors to spill onto the deck to fight the flames and repel their boarders. Admiral Zorgon was heartened by his reinforcements. Apes were filling in around him, with swords and axes in hand, cutting down the creatures as they landed.

"Kai-sho—" a gargoyle's scream was cut short with Zorgon's blade driven through its throat. He twisted the sword free, another setting down to take its place on the bulkhead. The gorilla to his right rent the creature's left wing, cutting into its ribs, its jaws snapping at Zorgon's sword arm, before he finished it.

"Thanks, lad." Zorgon gave the young warrior a toothy grin. The thrill of battle was restoring his youthful vigor. Gazing skyward, he spied a dozen warbirds passing overhead, half breaking for the Troan fleet and the others toward his trailing vessels, each bearing fire munitions, one heading directly for his flagship. Below them soared many more gargoyles armed with munitions; some were assailing the *Tempest Wind*; the others were heading to finish his fleet.

"Admiral!" one sailor shouted, pointing skyward.

Whoosh!

A great white magantor swept over the enemy magantor, plucking its rider from its saddle, releasing him after; his limbs flailing before impacting the surf. Hearty cheers rang out across the serried deck as Terin passed overhead.

Wind Racer soared through the firmament bearing Terin into the fray; his powerful wings thrusting with effortless grace. He swept over the *Tempest Wind* depositing his first kill to a watery fate before circling Zorgon's flagship; his razored talons slicing several gargoyles from above. The creatures fell with their wings rent or spines severed, their screams dying in the surf below. Terin guided his warbird across the bow of the *Tempest Wind* before banking sharply astern, driving for the next Benotrist magantor speeding toward the second ship in Zorgon's squadron.

* * *

Elos circled above the *Stenox*, watching as Zem tore gargoyles apart with his bare hands, ripping wings from backs, limbs from sockets, and heads from necks, tossing the grizzly trophies overboard while a strangely calm melody issued from the ship. The macabre scene drew hundreds of versks to the surrounding waters, their dorsal fins swarming the bloody surf. He waited patiently as most of the gargoyles drew away, drawn to the approaching Troan and ape ships. More sprang from the Benotrist and pirate galleys, following their comrades to the new threat, as well as several magantors joining the fray from the north, an obvious Benotrist squadron late to the battle. After the enemy thinned, he swept down toward the *Stenox*; his magantor plucked a gargoyle from the 3rd deck, crushing it in its mighty talons before setting down. Elos dismounted in a fluid bound, slashing the only remaining creature upon the observation deck. The creature crumbled to the deck, cut in half above the chest.

Elos sprang to the deck below, slashing another across the back, a third raising a scimitar in its right hand before Elos took the arm at the elbow and a foot as it turned to flee, bounding over the side of the ship.

Zip! Zip!

Laser flashed behind him from inside the bridge, striking another creature approaching the stern, its body tumbling to the bloody surf.

"This deck is clear, my friends!" Elos shouted, holding beside the door, caring not to expose himself to their fire.

"Who said that?" Raven asked, holding position behind the captain's chair, his pistol trained on the door.

"It is I, Elos of the Jenaii. Terin sent me to aid you!" Elos said, his voice rippling like the wind.

"Elos?" Lorken made a face looking at Raven.

"Cronus's bird buddy," Raven said.

"Let's have a look," Lorken said, coming out from behind the helm.

"And see who is playing that awful music," Raven growled with "Daydream Believer" repeating in his brain.

Stepping onto the stern of the 2nd deck, they were met with Elos's stoic face staring back, standing at the starboard rail. Several ships surrounded them, their crews scurrying across their decks, readying their munitions.

"Greetings." Elos regarded them, his eyes sharply turning to the threats surrounding them. An audible crunching sound echoed below where Zem snapped a gargoyle's spine, holding the creature overhead, before tossing him over the stern into the bloody water.

Raven already took aim, blasting the catapult crew aboard *Vixen's Wrath* as they readied a munition. Lorken covered portside, spraying the deck of the pirate bioar *Glade*, preventing its crew from retuning fire, the sinking wreck of *Galbon*, separating the ship from the *Stenox*. Zem kept the ship resting off their stern busy, throwing gargoyle corpses at it with deadly effect.

"Can either of you see what Zem is doing?" Raven grunted, shifting fire to the other ships resting starboard, the *Bounty Bosom* and the *Dorun Slayer*. They kept their crews in check, dropping any who dared stick their nose above a bulwark.

"Looks like he's playing pitcher for the Yankees by the looks of it." Lorken shook his head, stealing a glance as Zem drilled an archer standing at the prow of the *Night Whore* in the chest with a gargoyle's head, taking him from his feet.

"What's that supposed to mean?" Raven asked, unable to take his eyes from the fight at hand, blasting a commander of rank standing amidship of the *Bounty Bosom*.

"You don't want to know." Lorken shook his head, blasting the supports from under a heated brazier on the bow of the *Glade*, spilling its coals across its deck.

"Inside!" Elos shouted in alarm, looking skyward as a munition arced from the *Dorun Slayer*. Lorken and Raven followed him through the doorway of the bridge as the ballistae splashed across the 2nd deck, setting the gargoyle corpses piled there afire.

The lucky blast bought time for the other crews to man their catapults, releasing their volleys upon the *Stenox*, with several showering Zem, who finally cleared the last gargoyle from the 1st deck. Flames erupted all around him, setting his jacket and trousers ablaze but causing him no harm. He stepped back within before more ballistae fell.

"Well, this sucks!" Raven growled, unable to close the door with several gargoyle corpses blocking it, with the flames outside warming his face.

Elos took up position on the other side of the door, hacking away at the corpses, allowing Raven to push half the grizzly remains out of the way to close the door. Several more munitions splashed across all the decks, keeping them from stepping out and returning fire.

"Hope Zem is all right," Lorken said, again taking up position behind the helm as Elos and Raven waited beside either side of the door.

"He should be fine if all they throw at him is fire. Problem we have is, we can't see what's on the other side of this door to know if it's safe to open it," Raven said, looking out the forward viewport where another pirate galley rested off the bow. Its crews were hurling ballistae; another, splashing across the hull.

"Maybe but what was he doing with that song blaring from the external amplifier?"

"Don't know, but if we have enough juice for that, then why isn't Brokov blasting those ships?" Raven growled.

Thud!

The ship lurched forward, another pirate ram striking astern.

* * *

Monsoon looked on with growing angst as his fleet bombarded the *Stenox* with every munition at their disposal; fires igniting every corpse littering its decks. The magantor perched atop the 3rd deck took to flight when the first munition fell, its winged form circling above as if waiting for the battle to turn.

"Cease fire! Prepare to board!" Monsoon ordered his ships closer. If the Earthers wouldn't come out to fight, he would force their hand. Within moments of relaying the command, the *Vixen's Wrath* lowered its boarding ramp, her crew racing onto the stern of the 1st deck of the *Stenox*. The *Glade*, *Bounty Bosom*, and *the Night Whore* did the same, their crews climbing over the decks of the *Stenox* armed with rams and fire munitions.

* * *

Explosions erupted off Terin's right, where Benotrist magantors landed three hits to the *Fairer Maiden*, two to the *Falling Star*, and one to the *Blazing Torch*—all three Troan bioars' decks engulfed in flames. Just ahead, a fire munition splashed against the forward mast of the ape galley *Angry Fist*, igniting its sail. Terin pressed on. Wind Racer lifted high into the air, closing upon the next magantor in his line of sight. A Troan warship farther afield brought down another magantor, its crews driving a giant crossbow shaft through its breast, the bird splashing off its starboard bow.

Wind Racer sped apace, rapidly closing the distance to the magantor approaching *Garm's Roar*, the avian preparing to release its munition when Wind Racer swept underneath, breaking east as Terin sliced its wing. Terin swept back across the *Roar's* bow; the Benotrist magantor dipping hard left, tossing its rider before crashing into the sea. Terin flew west toward the Troan column of ships, leaving behind cheering apes crowding the deck of *Garm's Roar*.

* * *

"Forward!" Admiral Zorgon commanded, standing amidship of the *Tempest Wind*, losing sight of the *Stenox* amid the chaos ahead. Pirate galleys surrounded the stricken vessel, and pirates crowded its decks, beating on the doors of the 1st two decks with heavy iron hand-held rams. Others pounded the doors with axes or hammers.

Approaching starboard, he was greeted by three pirate galleys, the one nearest the *Stenox* with few crews left to man their catapults while the others greeted them with fire munitions splashing off their portside bow. Gargoyles still circled overhead, trying to set down wherever they could. Some found space upon the ship's upper rigging, hissing demonically at the apes below. Archers took careful aim, several striking true; their targets falling to the deck or caught in the rigging.

Zip!

Blue laser struck a gargoyle circling the forward mast, piercing its right wing, sending it spinning to the surf.

Zorgon followed the source of the laser to his west, where a merchant galley drew nigh, bearing a golden coin on a field of green upon its forward mast, the sigil of House Fixus. There, upon the deck stood several figures he was unable to identify from afar but likely Argos and his companions.

"Hard to starboard! Ready munitions!" Zorgon ordered, forgoing ramming the pirate vessel, choosing to strike en masse from his broadside, trusting the *Tempest Wind*'s veteran crew's aim unlike most of his fleet's green recruits.

The *Tempest Wind* swept east behind the pirate vessels aligned along the *Stenox*'s starboard, delivering hits to the *Dorun Slayer* and *Bounty Bosom*, fires erupting across their sterns. Zorgon signaled the following vessels to ram the stricken vessels now that their catapult crews were otherwise occupied while hundreds of gargoyles trailed them, circling above like *carka* birds chasing carrion.

* * *

Zip!

Argos cursed, his blast missing its mark, grazing a gargoyle's foot trailing the *Tempest Wind*.

"Aim smaller, fatty," Orlom teased, standing at his side upon the prow of *Fixus Glory*, the personal flagship of Farbo Fixus, patriarch of House Fixus. Argos gave Orlom a not-so-gentle shove, nearly taking him from his feet.

"Easy, Arg," Cronus said, standing his other side, fixing aim on a catapult crew upon the *Bounty Bosom*, firing several blasts into their midst. Ular stood to Cronus's other shoulder, targeting the gargoyles nearest Zorgon's flagship, taking many midflight. Corry and Lucas stood behind them, waiting to come near enough to draw swords, looking nervously upon the unfolding battle. The apes and Troan flotillas were now fully engaged with the remains of the pirate fleet while the dozens of Benotrist merchant vessels waited to their north, hundreds of gargoyles still crowding their decks, springing into the air to join the attack on the *Stenox*. Corry kept a watchful eye to the southern end of the ape and Troan columns of ships, catching sight of Terin downing another Benotrist magantor, sending bird and rider to a watery grave.

"Fool!" Corry hissed as Wind Racer banked hard left, nearly tossing Terin from his back before snatching a gargoyle from the air in his talons. The warbird was obedient to Terin's orders, no doubt. She would be certain to have words with the boy when this was over. He was no longer spellbound by the blade, thus negating its beguiling excuse. No, this was all Terin.

"The lad has courage!" Chief Gargos of the Manglar tribe said, standing beside her, along with his fellow ape delegate and Chief Ilen of Enoructa.

"The good it will do us if he dies." Corry shook her head.

"Such is war, Princess, but we are not dead yet. Tyro hasn't tasted ape steel, and I intend to give him his fill!" The ape chieftain grinned, lifting his battle ax proudly in the air.

* * *

The bridge of the Stenox

"A lot of activity outside," Lorken said, sparing a glance over his shoulder to the forward viewport as Zorgon's flagship crossed behind the *Bounty Bosom*, scoring several hits. Laser fire from another vessel further east drew his attention.

"Is that what I think it is?" Raven asked, still holding at the doorway.

"Probably Arg and the others," Lorken said, unable to expand the magnification to get a proper identification.

"Looks like the cavalry has arrived. What do you say we open this door and start blasting?" Raven said.

"Cavalry?" Elos made an uncharacteristic face, wondering what cavalry he was referring.

"Figure of speech, Elon. It means our relief is here," Raven explained.

"I am *Elos*," he corrected him.

"Sorry, Etos, I'm not good with names," Raven said.

"*Elos*," he again corrected him, as Raven gave Lorken a look, signaling him to be ready.

"Shoot quick before they lob a fire munition in here," Raven said, before opening the door, the sound of the ram and axes pounding on it still ringing in their ears.

Once again, they were greeted with stunned looks when the door opened; one fellow was face-planting in the entryway when the force of his ax swing met empty air.

Zip! Zip! Zip!

Lorken sprayed the opening, dropping those holding the small ram where they stood. He continued firing, finding several standing further back, including the unfortunate wretch holding a fire munition, which exploded in his hand, covering him in flames. Elos lopped the head of the fellow who fell between him and Raven while the big Earther aimed around the corner of the doorway, shooting several more standing to either side of the 2nd deck's stern. Lorken held fire as Raven looked to Elos, signaling him to button hook around the door. They both moved as one. Elos exited the bridge before turning to his right, attacking those standing portside, while Raven went to starboard, making quick work of their opponents.

Raven took a step toward the stern before turning around, sweeping the 3rd deck with his pistol, blasting two men standing there—one falling dead, the other clambering over the forward lookout parapet before Raven sent a laser up his rear. His screams echoed over the din as he slid down the bridge viewport, smearing blood across it as he went.

Elos rushed to the stern of the 2nd deck, driving his blade into the breast of a pirate just clearing the ladder, sending him falling to the 1st deck, where dozens of men crowded that small space. Suddenly, the door to the 1st deck opened. Zem again rushed out to meet them. Elos watched as the large metallic Earther drove into them, tossing men aside like straw dolls. Elos prepared to spring down to aid him when Raven grabbed his arm.

"Zem's got it. No point in ruining his fun," Raven advised.

"Fun?" Elos raised a curious brow, his stoic countenance nearly breaking, watching as Zem drove his hand through one fellow's chest, exiting his back to grasp another by the throat.

"I know. It's a little much." Raven winced as Zem crushed the man's throat in his grip before tossing both over the starboard stern into the waiting jaws of a hungry versk. He couldn't help notice Zem's missing trousers, the material burned away, leaving him exposed. The scene made him chuckle, which he would remind his friend of for the rest of their lives. Raven's gaze swept the surrounding sea for immediate threats. The *Night Whore* rested off their stern, the lead ship in the Troan column ramming its starboard stern; the sound of breaking timbers echoing in their ears. The *Dorun Slayer* and *Bounty Bosom* sat off starboard, both listing severely at the stern, their bows rising prominently into the air, victims of ape rams and catapults, fires raging across their decks. The *Vixen's Wrath* separated the sinking wrecks from the *Stenox*, its top nearly empty with most of its crew dead from assailing the *Stenox*. A column of ape ships passed behind the sinking pirate galleys, circling east around the *Stenox* to assail the Benotrist merchant fleet waiting north and east of their position. The Troan warships circled west of the *Stenox*, engaging the *Glade*, the pirate bioar desperately trying to draw away off their portside. Several other pirate warships were in full retreat, sailing for the mouth of the bay. Another column of ape warships closed from the northwest, the pitiful remnant of the once mighty 1st Fleet, most of their sister ships sunk or burning along the north side of the bay.

Lorken exited the bridge, taking up position portside, leveling his rifle on the retreating *Glade*, spreading laser fire across its decks before zeroing in on the helm, blasting the crewmate manning it through the back. The ship lurched hard to port, allowing the pursuing Troan warships to close within ballistae range, sandwiching the stricken vessel between the Troans and the ape column drawing from the north.

Raven quickly scaled the ladder to the 3rd deck, taking aim at the gargoyles still hounding the ape fleet crossing east of the *Stenox's* bow. Elos's magantor set down beside him, the bird giving him a knowing look, which took him aback.

"Easy there, big fella, I'm on your side," Raven reminded the warbird before taking aim on a gargoyle clinging to the upper rigging of *Motar's Rage*, the ape warship running alongside Zorgon's flagship, pursuing the fleeing pirate fleet.

Laser fire erupting from the bow of *Fixus Glory* east of the ape column caught his eye; their fire was directed on the trailing pirate vessel sailing northeast toward the mouth of the harbor. Many of the Benotrist merchant fleet followed in their wake. A quick scan of the *Glory's* deck found his friends alive and well, with Cronus, Argos, Orlom, and Ular making good use of their lasers. Wind Racer passed across the bow of the *Stenox*, some two hundred meters east, pursuing a Benotrist magantor fleeing north. Raven used his pistol's scope to zero in on the Benotrist rider flying the smaller avian.

Zip!

His blast took the rider through the head. The fellow slumped in the saddle, and the bird drifted off as Terin looked over his shoulder, raising a hand in the air before turning east toward the fleeing pirate vessels.

"Where's he going?" Raven growled, wondering if the kid took one too many hits to the head. He looked around frantically, feeling helpless with the *Stenox* sitting stationary in the water, before feeling Elos's magantor breathing hot air on his neck.

"Hey, Esos! If your bird can carry two, why don't you give me a ride!" Raven shouted below, where the Jenaii warrior was preparing to jump upon the *Vixen's Wrath*, to finish any crew members lingering there. The pirate vessel was sitting dangerously near the ship's starboard, drifting aimless amid the bloody surf.

"His name is *Elos*, Rav!" Lorken said over his shoulder, keeping his eyes and rifle trained on the *Glade* as the Troan and ape ships were about to engage the pirate vessel.

"Where do you wish to go, Raven of Earth?" Elos asked, his silver eyes looking up at him from the 2nd deck.

"Terin might need some help. Thought we could give the kid a hand."

"Go on, Elos, we got things covered here," Lorken said, turning his attention from portside where the *Glade* was being overrun in the distance.

"The ship is secure. We need only wait for a full power restoration to return to full capability!" Zem added from the 1st deck, crushing the last breathing pirate's head with his foot, the sound of his cracking skull echoing sickeningly.

"Thanks and put some trousers on, Zem." Raven grinned, joining Elos in the saddle.

With that, Raven and Elos took to the air, following Terin toward the fleeing pirate vessels.

"Idiot." Zem shook his head as they sped away.

* * *

The remaining Benotrist merchant ships were slowly overcome, squeezed by Admiral Zorgon's force approaching from their southwest, the northern ape column from the northwest, and the Troan fleet form the west. From their south came the *Fixus Glory*, where Argos, Cronus, Orlom, and Ular struck from afar, targeting the lead vessels. Wind Racer swept past the Benotrist merchant ships, his keen eye fixed to Monsoon's remaining pirate vessels further east, nearing the mouth of the bay.

Terin kept Wind Racer above ballistae range, closing on the trailing vessel of the escaping ships. He counted four ships in all, including the *Flen Raider*, the captured Troan warship acting as

Monsoon's flagship. Terin observed little activity on the deck of the trailing vessel, the *Maiden's Price*, as if they were blind to his approach.

"Yah, my life is in your keeping," he whispered in the wind, taking a deep breath before the plunge. Wind Racer swept low, diving for the stern of the pirate warship, setting down astern. Terin jumped upon the deck, catching a pirate unawares. He cut the man down from behind; the wretch looking starboard for some reason. Terin moved on, letting him fall where he died, taking the next man unaware as well, severing him shoulder to shoulder. He moved on to the helmsman, taking his head and splitting the wheel in half. He hastily withdrew before the ship veered to port, falling away from its sister ships. Springing atop his saddle, Terin watched the crew scramble to right their course as Wind Racer lifted into the air.

Do they not see me? he wondered. Even the gargoyles clinging to the rigging above didn't seem to notice him. He sped off, skimming the white caps cresting the waves, his gaze fixed to the next ship in line.

* * *

Stenox, *weapons room*

"Come on!" Brokov growled as the power meter lingered at 1.94 percent for what felt like an eternity. He finally cut the feed to the outside amplifier, saving that energy to hasten storage restoration.

Power storage 2 percent.

Brokov smiled with the words bursting across the bottom of the screen. The screen suddenly came alive, readouts playing across it in all their glory. He looked down to the comm, holding his breath before activating it.

"Rav, do you copy?"

"Brokov?" Lorken answered after a long pause.

"Lorken, where's Rav?"

"Somewhere across the bay with Elos. We got comms back?"

"Obviously. Go man the helm. We got work to do."

"It's about time. Let's start blasting away with our big guns," Lorken said into his comm, clearing the doorway to the bridge.

"Maybe our smaller guns for now. We are only at 2 percent," Brokov said. That was enough to provide base functions and limited movement and perhaps a few long-range laser bursts but just a few.

Zem staggered on the stern of the 1st deck as the ship lumbered forth, catching him by surprise as he finished tossing bodies overboard. An uncharacteristic smile played across his metallic face as he stepped back inside.

* * *

"He's doing it again!" Raven shouted in Elos's ear, watching as Terin set down on another pirate vessel.

"Yah be with him," Elos said, hastening his mount over the waves, circling south of the trailing vessel, which appeared to be circling, unable to right its course.

"Move up alongside it but keep out of their range!" Raven said, training his pistol amidship, the crew staring nervously at him before he unloaded.

Zip! Zip! Zip!

He cut into their serried ranks, before lifting his aim, targeting the gargoyles clinging to the rigging above, dropping them in quick order. Several were caught in the rigging; others sprang free, fleeing portside, hoping to reach the north shore of the bay, just a short distance north. Raven continued firing, shifting toward the bow as Terin raced along the deck, dispatching pirates as he went.

"He's an idiot!" Raven growled as Terin continued across the deck, already disabling the helm, refusing to relent.

"He can be brash, so I have observed," Elos politely replied, his magantor crossing the bow of the vessel, cutting back along its portside.

"He was that way at Fera during our escape, so Cronus told me, but it wasn't this bad," Raven snorted, targeting anyone he could with their second pass. Terin finally stopped halfway to the bow before turning back for Wind Racer.

"He was much worse at Corell, Mosar, and Carapis, if truth be told," Elos said. If the Jenaii was prone to smile, he would be doing so now, but all Raven saw was his nondescript face.

Zip!

A burst of green light flashed below them, shooting across the bay, striking the two remaining ships further east. Several more bursts of light followed, breaking most of the starboard oars of either vessels. Follow strikes struck the masts, dropping them in quick succession.

"That came from the *Stenox*," Raven shouted, pointing out the beautiful ship in the distance, making its way to the Benotrist merchant ships between them, where it seemed every other ship in the bay was now converging.

"Your friend has repaired it," Elos stated flatly.

"Yep. He may be an idiot, but he is a smart idiot. We're back, baby!" Raven grinned like an idiot before blasting the deck of the ship below in front of Terin's feet, causing him to stop in place, looking up at them as they circled above. Raven pointed his hand toward the activity to their direct west, where everyone seemed to be converging, signaling him to proceed there.

Smart idiot? Elos wondered how Cronus or Terin understood anything Raven said.

"Terin can help out with those jerks. Let's circle the cripples ahead and break their crutches!" Raven added.

* * *

Monsoon stood at the prow of the *Flen Raider*, staring desperately at the mouth of the harbor so teasingly close, but oh, so far away. The *Stenox* managed to recover in time, destroying all the oars starboard and blasting the rear and amidship masts, their sails and rigging dangling over the sides of the ship. He ordered half the oars moved from portside to starboard to balance the two and try to continue on their way, desperate to flee before they were overtaken. How far they could get with only half their oars and one sail, he could only guess. He couldn't fathom falling captive again with the Troans, apes, and Earthers out for blood, his blood.

"Admiral, we should be ready to continue in a few moments," the *Flen*'s captain informed him.

"Make haste! I care not to get caught in the nets they will be soon throwing," Monsoon said.

"Aye, Admiral. There seems to be activity on the shores ahead," the captain pointed out the two arcs of land mass jutting into the bay ahead, forming the mouth of the harbor. The Troans placed watchtowers at the rocky tips of each protrusion, armed with heavy trebuchets upon their upmost battlements, though neither could cover the vast ranges between them. The towers were mostly quiet when they entered the bay, but now were alive with activity.

"Yes, the watchers are awake this time, but it will matter not if we set course between them. Magantors on the other hand could be troublesome if they positioned any there to compensate for their obvious weakness," Monsoon mused. He didn't expect any to be there, for Orvis Maiyan removed them elsewhere at Hossen Grell's request. The only magantors that might trouble them were the two plaguing the ships to his rear. His hopes that they might be satisfied with those kills quickly soured once Elos's warbird flew alongside the *Raider*'s starboard, and Raven started targeting his remaining oars.

Monsoon stood unmoving upon the deck, looking skyward as the magantor circled his vessel, sealing his fate. Raven blasted away at his remaining mast pole, the stricken beam falling behind him, before blasting several oars along their portside. Raven did the same to his other remaining vessel, the *Wanton Temptress*, the vessel trailing his by three ship's lengths. The damnable Earther circled two more times, destroying every oar in sight and sending several blasts into each hull for good measure. The holes were not enough to quickly sink them, just filling them with enough water to prevent them from drifting far. Raven kept out of range of their ballistae, gifting him a crude gesture with his middle finger, whatever that was supposed to mean, before flying back west, where his comrades where converging upon the remains of the Benotrist merchant fleet. It would've been a kinder mercy if Raven had just blasted him where he stood, instead of leaving him here, helplessly adrift, waiting to be captured.

"Your orders, Admiral?" the captain asked.

Monsoon gave him a look before lifting his tunic, running his dagger across the inside of his thigh, the deep gash draining him, his blood spilling across the deck.

* * *

The Benotrist merchant ships were reduced to an ever-shrinking pocket, assailed from each direction by the remaining Troan and ape fleets, along with a motley collection of other vessels hostile to their actions, most notably the *Stenox*. Even Kaly arrived upon the *Maiden's Purse*, leading a small squadron of like-minded free swords, closing from the north. Cronus and those aboard *Fixus Glory* drew from the southeast, keeping a safe distance from the Benotrist ships, sending volley after volley of laser fire into any ship trying to break east to escape the bay.

The *Stenox* managed to recover enough energy for Brokov to send another beam into the Benotrists' midst, gutting the hull of the centermost galley; the ship went down by the keel, slipping from sight into the unforgiving sea. After that strike, Lorken and Zem went above deck, taking aim with their pistols, targeting any gargoyles attempting to spring from their ships bearing munitions.

Admiral Purvis's Troan fleet drew within ballistae range, firing at will at the nearest galley, munitions striking true across the ship's starboard stern. He kept a watchful eye on the gargoyles circling above the enemy ships, wary of their threat. Any attempt to ram their ships would bring his own vessels under their umbrella. It was one thing for the creatures to attack from afar, expending their strength to reach you, and another to come underneath them while rested, incurring their full measure.

Admiral Zorgon held no such compunction with the threat of the gargoyles, ordering his remaining ships to ramming speed, closing on the Benotrist merchant ships with all haste.

"Kai-Shorum!" gargoyles hissed demonically, springing from the rigging and masts of the Benotrist ships as the apes drew close, their guttural chants carrying upon the waves.

"Prepare for battle! Send the bastards to a watery grave!" Zorgon bellowed, drawing his helm over his furry head, thick shield in his left hand and sword in his right.

"Harumph!" his crew roared, pounding their shields with their axes and swords, the pressing wind rippling their furry arms.

Zip! Zip! Zip!

Laser fire swept before them, courtesy of Argos and his companions to their right, and the *Stenox* crew to their left, blunting the gargoyles' fury. The other ships in his column fanned out to port and starboard closing on the enemy. Gargoyles sprang from the Benotrist ships, their bloodred eyes alive with rage, their winged form filling the sky. Others circling above dove upon the advancing warships. Ape archers let loose as they drew close, dropping dozens short of the fleet. Those bearing fire munitions drew laser fire, dropping most well short of the ape fleet. The surviving gargoyles swarmed over the bows of the ape ships, crashing into walls of shields or setting down upon the decks where they could. The ships were a flurry of slashing steel and flailing limbs. Blood and chaos reigned upon their foredecks as they drove onward. The ape ships met the merchant galleys like hammers to clay, their sturdy rams breaking their hulls, fissures spreading from their broken timbers. The apes reversed oars, drawing away, allowing the sea to pour cleanly through their fatal wounds.

To the north, the other ape column charged, fueled by rage at the destruction visited upon their fleet, greeting the gargoyles filling the sky with toothy grins and hungry blades.

Amidst the chaos, Wind Racer swept over the enemy flotilla, before diving into their midst. Corry's heart rose to her throat as Terin disappeared from sight. No arrow rose to meet him or ballistae targeted him as he set down astern the centermost ship, springing from Wind Racer's back in a flourish, cutting down gargoyles and men with apparent ease. He split upraised blades, catching foes by surprise, their eyes wide, searching blindly for whatever afflicted them, seeing naught but a shadow moving in their midst. Terin moved with economy toward the nearest brazier, slashing its supports, spilling its fire upon the deck, before proceeding to the helm, crippling it with two hasty strikes. Turning back to Wind Racer, he met an onrushing warrior.

Split!

Terin cut him down, shoulder to opposite hip, spinning around his flailing corpse, catching another across the throat, the man's head flying off his blade. Others came upon him from behind, following him as if he were a glimmer, an apparition that was there but not there, disappearing and reappearing with every movement. Terin moved among them, splitting swords and limbs, his blade growing murkier with every cut, darker with every kill. The darker his blade became, the harder to see he became, moving among them as if they were blind. Terin fought his way to Wind Racer, mounting his warbird and taking to the sky, arrows fluttering in his wake, and then not following at all, as if he disappeared from their sight.

Corry's heart lifted seeing Terin emerge above the fray but dropped when he again slipped from sight.

"Take heart, Your Highness. His God guides him as we have seen him do time and again," Lucas said into her ear, standing upon the foredeck of *Fixus Glory*, with Cronus and the others standing along the bulkhead before them, firing at will, with no shortage of targets.

"His God," she sighed, wondering what to make of it. "Is it the God who led me to him or the one that has forsaken him?"

"He is a God, or *the* God, if what Prince Lorn claims is true. Who can know his will or intent? All I know is what I see with my eyes, and my eyes tell me he is again with him," Lucas said, watching as Wind Racer swept behind a Benotrist bioar, again passing from view.

"The enemy do not flee his blade or fear his coming. Yah no longer illuminates his path," she said. She hated standing there helpless to do anything. She knew Lucas felt the same, forced to watch as their friends used the Earthers' weapons and their advantageous range to great effect, which meant they needed to remain out of swords' reach. Whenever an occasional gargoyle strayed near, their friends made quick work of them. Just as she thought that, Ular blasted a gargoyle off their starboard bow, dropping it several ship lengths away.

"The enemy may no longer flee his presence, Your Highness, but they seem to be faring rather poorly against him, all the same," Lucas observed.

"So it seems," she sighed.

"Nor does he lack in friends." Lucas smiled as Elos's warbird passed over the shrinking enemy flotilla, with Raven sitting behind him, targeting gargoyles anywhere near Terin.

* * *

"Do we have enough power for another blast from the big guns, Brokov?" Lorken said into his comm, standing upon the 3rd deck with Zem, dropping gargoyles with painfully slow precision.

"Not yet," Brokov answered from the weapons control room, looking at the readout barely showing 2.1 percent. Any blast now might lower it below the critical threshold. He was lucky with the first salvos but didn't want to risk it a second time. He wanted a clear 3 percent.

"Most unfortunate," Zem stated, blasting a gargoyle flying off Wind Racer's right, piercing its midsection, the creature faltering, splashing between two Benotrist ships.

"Is there anything else you can do down there?" Lorken barked into the comm.

"There is only one thing I can think of, but you two best get in the bridge and buckle up! It's going to be a hell of a ride!" Brokov warned.

* * *

Wind Racer soared over the enemy fleet, dodging errant shafts and zealous archers, sweeping between ships, snatching gargoyles in flight in his deadly talons, depositing them into the sea. Elos's magantor followed close behind, Raven blasting any threat fixing on Terin. Terin's hair lifted in the breeze, Wind Racer cutting across the bow of the stricken galley. Fires spread across its upper decks, an archer upon its prow taking aim as he passed.

Zip!

Raven blasted the archer following close on Terin's trail. Terin leaned with Wind Racer's turn, catching sight of another Benotrist galley going under off his left, its stern high into the air before slipping beneath the waves. To his right, the ape bioar *Harkor* listed severely to port, fires ravaging her bow. Wind Racer plucked another gargoyle from the air, snatching him in his talons, crushing its wings before releasing it into the sea. Laser flashed off his left; Raven riddled the serried deck of *Nisin's Bride*, dropping gargoyles and men crowding its decks.

Crash!

The sound of breaking timbers echoed over the wind. Terin circled about as a Benotrist galley to his west shattered; debris showering the surf all around it. Terin looked on as a familiar shape emerged from the wreckage, the nose of the *Stenox* passing through the wooden galley like a hammer through stale bread. Hearty cheers rang out from ape, Troan, and allied vessels. The Earthers' ship turned hard to port, aligning with the nearest galley, smashing into it amidship before passing through, the ship cracking in half, bow and stern lifting into the air before settling into the surf; the *Stenox* cut it in two.

And so it went, the *Stenox* smashing ship after ship, using its impenetrable hull as a ram, crushing the remaining Benotrist vessels. The battle continued for hours, with the Troans and apes hunting down the surviving gargoyles and fishing enemy survivors from the wreckage. Versks moved among the debris field, snatching easy prey from the bloody waters. The battle in the northern streets of Tro quickly quieted with most of the gargoyles caught up in the attack on the *Stenox*. The battles in the southern streets of the harbor continued throughout the day and into the night, with citizens and local militias battling the mercenaries running rampant through the streets.

* * *

"It is time," Hossen Grell said, staring off across the harbor from a hillside beside the Maiyan estate, eyeing the carnage he wrought across the city.

"A great victory," Rolis congratulated, standing at his side. Their magantor was saddled and waiting behind them.

"Yes, a grand victory," Hossen proclaimed, though believed it naught. Though they destroyed most of the ape and Troan fleets and decimated the harbor's defenses, the *Stenox* was still afloat. He could only hope that it suffered permanent damage with a substantial loss of crew.

"Tro would be wise to seek terms, especially with the force we can bring against her," Rolis added.

"Wisdom doesn't always guide the powerful. Pride is often their greater master. We shall leave the matter for them to debate. Perhaps wiser counsel will prevail now that their ape friends can no longer help them. Let us be off," Hossen Grell said calmly, before taking to the skies, taking flight to Notsu, leaving Tro in ruin.

CHAPTER 19

The forum of Tro

They gathered in the great forum after most of the fighting was finished; the weary faces of the ruling patriarchs pallid and forlorn. The
Casian emissaries looked worse. Pors Vitara, the archon of Teris, was
nursing a burned hand and face, with a noticeable limp in his right
leg. Chief Ilen of Enoructa stood stoically beside his ape brethren,
chiefs Hukor and Gargos. They saw most of the battle upon *Fixus
Glory*, which denied them much action with Argos and the others'
weapon more effective at greater range. All three hungered for blood
and were forced to watch others land the decisive blows. Klen Adine
presided over the hastily called assembly, looking uncharacteristically
disheveled, the blood of his men staining his raiment, holding many
a dying man in his arms, saying farewell. The emissaries from Gotto
and Bedo looked little better, each bloodstained and battle-weary.
The emissary from Terse was noticeably absent, suffering an arrow
to his throat, expiring thereafter. Admiral Purvis and Commander
Balkar were elsewhere reordering the defense of the harbor. Raven
came on behalf the Earthers at Zorgon's insistence. He stood off to
the side, leaning against the wall with his arms crossed, eager to get
back to his ship, which the others were trying desperately to repair.

"What is the state of our city?" Varin Corbin began, patriarch
of House Corbin.

"What city? We lay in ruin!" Marcus Talana snorted, looking at
Raven with pure loathing.

"We suffered a serious blow, but we still stand. Take stock in that, old friend," Lubion Tobian replied. As patriarch of House Lubion, he was the elder statesman of Tro and Klen's greatest supporter.

"Do we? And how long will Tyro let us stand? A day, ten days, twenty? Our fleet is smashed. Our garrison reduced, and our allies… destroyed." Marcus shook his head.

"Destroyed? We still stand, Troan! The Ape Republic will not suffer this insult!" Chief Hukor growled.

"The Ape Republic is far away, and your fleet is reduced to a pitiful squadron. When Tyro comes to us, you will still be far afield," Varin Corbin reasoned.

"And what of you, Earther? Where do you stand in all this madness?" Marcus Talana called out Raven.

"Where do I stand?" Raven's intense stare sent a shiver down Klen's spine as he came off the wall, stepping into the chamber's center. "Tyro just made the worst mistake in his sorry life. You all can decide whatever you like, but as for me and my crew, this is war!" Raven turned and left, leaving them that grim declaration.

"What is there to decide? The answer is clear"—Admiral Zorgon stepped to the center, driving his war ax into the stone floor, the sound of cracking rock echoing through the chamber—"WAR!"

Chief Ilen of Enoructa, stepped forth, raising his sword before his face, sweeping it formally to his side. "WAR!" His voiced rippled like running water. Once his fellow chieftains in Linkortis learned of this attack, the cries for war would be shouted throughout the land.

To everyone's surprise, Pors Vitara, the archon of Teris and emissary of the Casian League, stepped forth, the right side of his face scarred and blistered. "I cannot say what my people shall do, but my voice carries more weight than any other. I shall not forgive Tyro this!" He pointed to his burnt face, courtesy of a fire munition dropped in their midst. "This treachery cannot stand. I will vote WAR!"

"As shall I, upon our return!" Porlin Galba, vice archon of Port West, seconded.

"Gentlemen?" Klen looked to the ruling patriarchs of Tro, who all nodded in agreement.

"Then war it is. What do you require from us, Klen?" Lubion Tobian asked.

"I will present my recommendations on the morrow. We should reconvene then," Klen advised.

* * *

Brokov initiated the tissue regenerator, hoping the charge was enough to do the job, kneeling beside Kendra's trembling body, where she lay upon the lower bunk in the 2nd crew cabin. She was barely breathing, with pale clammy skin. A bloody bandage pressed against the side of her neck, where the damnable creature tore into her, snapping her collar bone, tearing a good portion of flesh with it. He held his breath as her flesh began to mend, hoping there was enough power to finish before it was drained. They only had a short period of sunlight left after the battle concluded for him to recharge the device and only partially at that. Once it was again drained, they would have to wait for sunrise to recharge it and the other devices. That would be little comfort to the many wounded that would die this night.

"Agghh," Kendra gasped, her eyes fluttering before opening fully. Confusion gave way to joy upon seeing Brokov looking back at her.

"Good." He smiled, removing the device from her chest, her wound fully healed.

"Thank you," she said, returning his smile.

"You had me worried."

"Did I now?" She raised a skeptical brow, fighting back her grin.

"Yes. No more volunteering to be a gargoyle's lunch. Is that understood, Sailor?" he asked sharply.

"Aye, aye, sir!" She gave him a mock salute, mimicking the Earthers' formal gesture.

"All right. Now you be a good girl and get some rest while I see who else I can help with this thing."

"I have one request before you go running off," she said.

"What is that?"

THE CHRONICLES OF ARAX

"Kiss me."

"I can do that." Brokov smiled, reaching down as she lifted her lips to his, devouring him with long restrained passion. He returned her fervor, savoring the rapturous joy coursing their flesh.

* * *

Raven returned from the city forum, finding Argos, Ular, Lucas, Lorken, Cronus, and Orlom bringing Grigg's body off the *Stenox*, setting it down at the end of their pier. Other apes gathered around to offer their help preparing it for burial. Raven stepped among them, squatting beside his fallen friend, his elbows resting on his knees.

"You were a brave warrior and a good friend," he said, placing his hand to Grigg's chest, the gesture causing the gorillas around him to pound their fists to chests, honoring Raven's words.

"A brave friend," Cronus said.

"A brave warrior," Lucas said.

"A brave warrior," Ular acknowledged proudly.

"A brave warrior and a better friend," Lorken added, pounding his fist to his chest.

"A brave warrior and better friend," Argos declared, pounding fist to chest.

"A brave warrior and my brother," Orlom said bitterly, a lone tear squeezing from his eye.

Raven gained his feet, placing a hand to Orlom's head, ruffling his fur, as Argos, Ular, Lucas, and Lorken placed their hands to his shoulder, supporting their friend and brother. At that moment, Zem and Elos stepped onto the pier, with "Daydream Believer" sounding off the ship's amplifier, the ancient melody strangely uniting them in their grief.

"For Kato and for Grigg," Zem declared, looking to his friends gathered around with a sense of belonging that he didn't know he could ever feel.

"For Kato and Grigg," Cronus agreed, the others bringing Zem and Elos into their circle.

* * *

He felt so alone staring out across the bay; the fires of crippled ships alighting the night sky marred its natural beauty. Corry found him standing upon the empty stone wharf away from the others, lost in his thoughts. She spoke not a word, simply standing beside him, wondering how the world turned so horrid. Would every land in Arax suffer such ruin? The great loss of life and physical destruction felt small to one's own personal loss, and no loss felt so heavy as Kato's and Grigg's. The body of the young ape was taken ashore to prepare for burial. Orlom stood over his comrade like a stone sentinel; his once mischievous grin was replaced with cold anger. Terin could barely look at him, torn by the tragedy of it all. Hearing of Kato was a blow none expected and affected them all so deeply, especially Terin. Despite all he suffered at Darna's hands, he took solace that Kato lived and stood by Lorn's side. It was all false hope. He could not imagine the burden their combined loss put upon Prince Lorn when news reached him of their deaths. Kato was so much more than a warrior aiding their cause; he was a constant encouragement when things looked dire. He was a fountain of sage advice and a kind ear. He was good and kind, and now…he was gone.

"You were very brave today, Terin," Corry said, finding no other words she dare utter.

"The sword masked my fear. Without it…" his voice trailed, words failing him.

"The power of the sword no longer guides you. It no longer illuminates the battlefield, portending its awesome power. Nor does it drive the enemy to madness and flight, driving them before you. Despite this, you struck at the enemy time and again, dispatching hundreds as they held their ground. That was you, my love." She looked over to him.

"Those powers of the sword may not be there anymore, but different powers have replaced them, powers that greatly aided me this day, powers that frighten me, Corry." He turned to her, a tortured look crossing his beautiful eyes, rending her heart.

"What do you mean?"

"A great shadow has replaced the sword's brilliance, fueled by my anger or a secret darkness kindled within me. This is not of Yah, and I fear what I have become," he confessed, her heart breaking with his sad eyes.

"A shadow?"

He pulled the sword from its scabbard, holding it aloft, not a hint of its former glory emitting from its ancient blade.

"It is much lighter now than it was earlier, at the height of the battle. It was nearly black as the moonless night sky, growing darker with every kill."

"I don't understand? You slew so many, and none could touch you. Surely the sword's power protects you?" she asked.

"I don't know. The darker the blade became, the harder it was for the enemy to see me. That was all the advantage it provided."

"They were blind to you?"

"Maybe." He shrugged.

"Perhaps partially," he added, recalling the times men saw him briefly before losing sight of him during the battle.

"Must you look for ill tidings in all your blessings? This power may be different, but it still carried you safely through your perils. Yah still guides you. Why do you not believe this to be another test he has placed before you?"

"But the darkness…"

"There is no darkness in you, Terin. You are as bright as the sunrise. Even a blind man could see it."

"There is darkness in all men. Your brother showed me that, and he is the best man I know."

"So," she said. "What is darkness before the sun? Does not a single flame illuminate the night all around it? Any darkness you carry from Tyro shrinks before Kal's majesty and Torg's light. Now quit moping," she reproached him.

"As you command." He gifted her a smile, taking her in his arms, holding her in his embrace, the sound of lapping waves echoing in the night air.

She didn't wait for him to act, taking him in her embrace, crushing her lips to his. Despite all the death and chaos around them, they had each other, holding tight to each other, lest the fates sweep them away.

CHAPTER 20

Fleace, the Macon capital

The gates of the city were drawn open, welcoming the royal procession, led by Prince Lorn and Princess Zevana, second daughter of King Mortus and betrothed of the prince of Zulon, Artus III. They were followed by General Ciyon and Jentra and Lorn's Royal Elite, their silver helms and cuirass resplendent in the midday sun. Trailing them were Guilen, Criose, and long columns of Torry, Macon, Zulon, and Teso soldiers bearing standards of their respective commands. Lorn rode at the head of the procession, clad in bright-silver armor over his sea-blue tunic, without his helm, so the people of Fleace could look upon his face.

The citizenry lined the wide stone avenues, throwing voli petals in the air, greeting them and celebrating the new peace.

"Hail, Prince Lorn! Hail King Mortus!" the crowds cheered as they passed.

"A momentous day, oh Prince," Princess Zevana said, observing the festive crowd.

"Peace and friendship in place of war and hatred is joyous indeed, oh Princess." He smiled in kind, regarding her dark beauty. She was as lovely as her sister, if his memory served him, her deep olive skin without blemish, radiating her feminine charm.

"Our people agree. You seem to have won them to your cause, just as you have my father," she returned his smile.

"My cause is his cause as well, and when we next ride to war, it shall be by each other's side. And what of you, Zevana? You shall be leaving your homeland for Zulon and the arms of Prince Artus," Lorn asked.

"It is unexpected but pleasantly so. I am told he is handsome and intelligent—two traits I favor in a mate. It appears my eldest sister is equally favored in her match," she complimented, expecting him to blush, which he did not.

"We shall see if she is in agreement," he said in good humor, regarding the throngs gathered to either side of the avenue with genuine charm. He noticed a young urchin peeking behind two well-dressed merchants up ahead along his left, a dirty-faced young boy who looked no older than five years but could be older, his true age masked by his malnourished state. Lorn summoned one of his Macon escorts to draw the boy from the crowd.

Zevana looked on as the soldier drew the young boy into the street, as the column came to a halt. She was further surprised as Lorn dismounted, walking ahead to speak with the child, kneeling to look him in the eye.

"Do not be frightened, my young friend. What is your name?" Lorn asked. The child's eyes were drawn as wide as saucers, looking nervously around as the surrounding crowds of people stared at him.

"D-D-Dougar, sir," he squeaked, lowering his eyes.

"He is a prince. You shall address him as Your Highness!" the soldier standing over him barked.

"He is fine." Lorn raised his open hand, staying the soldier's temper. "Tell me, Dougar, where are your kin?"

"I...I am alone, Your Highness. Momma died of fever last winter. Poppa drowned on his ship the winter before," the boy said with the saddest brown eyes Lorn had ever seen. He was poorly dressed in a long woolen tunic and a ragged cloak, with bare, dirt-covered feet.

"That is sad, Dougar. My father and mother are gone also." Lorn smiled, touching a hand to the boy's shoulder.

The child started to tear up; memories of his mother and father reminding him of happier times.

"Are you hungry, Dougar?" Lorn asked, his heart breaking at the sight of this poor child.

A simple nod of his head was enough for Lorn to scoop him into his arms, setting him on his saddle. He took the reins, leading his ocran on foot. The crowd grew silent as he walked. Zevana was taken aback by the kind act, giving the child an encouraging smile.

They continued along the broad avenues of the city, passing massive stone edifices lining either side of the streets, each growing larger and more elaborate than the last. The largest of the structures outside the king's palace were the city forum and the amphitheater, each circled by towering columns, resting at opposite ends of the city square. Richly tended gardens circled much of the city square, with a massive dais and throne erected in its center. There upon the dais sat King Mortus, clad in rich Calnesian robes in hues of silver and gold. Upon his head rode a golden crown with sapphires, rubies, and diamonds embedded along its circumference. Standing upon the dais to either side of the king were the ministers of the realm, commanders of rank, and the princesses Bedela and Portencia. Standing at a position of prominence at Mortus's right was King Sargov of Zulon, Princess Zevana's future father by marriage. Beside Sargov stood the Lady Ilesa, given this prestigious place as the special guest of the king and Prince Lorn, having spent the days since the alliance was agreed upon, tending the ailments of the citizens of Fleace with Kato's wondrous device. Beside Ilesa stood the Queen Mother, who looked on proudly as her granddaughter drew nigh, gifting Zevana a knowing glance.

Before the dais stood hundreds of courtesans, commanders, and city officials dressed in their finery for the momentous occasion. Standing directly below the dais was Princess Deliea, dressed in a flowing silver gown with emeralds embedded around its high collar and billowing sleeves that drew taut at the shoulder. The crowd parted as the procession drew nigh, allowing her a clear view of her betrothed. Lorn's eyes found her over the sea of faces, blue eyes meeting green, causing her to take in a breath, raising the swell of her breasts within her tight bodice. He smiled; her reaction not lost on the Torry prince. She was taken aback as he helped a young boy from his saddle, whispering to the nearest guard and passing the child on but not before ruffling the child's mop of brown hair. Another warrior dressed in the sea-blue tunic of a Torry Elite took the child, placing him upon his shoulders. She recognized him as Jentra, the Elite Prime, and trusted companion of the Torry prince. Lorn then helped her sister Zevana down from her ocran before advancing toward the dais. His eyes again found hers if ever so briefly before shifting to her father, who stood from his throne at Lorn's approach.

Deliea recalled the handsome prince, but his countenance had matured since she last saw him. Gone were the youthful looks of a privileged royal, replaced by the seasoned warrior who stood before her father. He was breathtakingly handsome but equally humble in his carriage, a strange contradiction that made her admire him all the more. When her father spoke of their arrangement for alliance, which centered upon her becoming Lorn's bride, she was equally thrilled and terrified. But duty to her people gave her courage. She was apprehensive upon learning of their coming nuptial, wishing not to be bound in a loveless marriage, fearful of his contempt for her as the daughter of his former foe. Looking at him now waylaid those initial fears, his gentle eyes confirming his true nature, setting her at ease.

Lorn halted at the base of the dais, with Zevana, Ciyon, and Jentra stopping behind him, with young Dougar still sitting atop Jentra's shoulders.

"Welcome, Prince Lorn. I offer the hospitality of Fleace and the Macon Realm to you and your countrymen!" Mortus declared, beginning the ceremony.

"I am welcomed, oh King!" Lorn inclined his head with deep reverence.

"As agreed upon, our two great realms are to be forever joined, unified by purpose and by blood! Let it be known henceforth that the Macon Empire and the Torry Realm will be joined one to the other, their crowns falling to an heir born from their union!" Mortus's voice carried across the city square with great authority, his eyes falling upon the face of the Torry prince before continuing.

"Prince Lorn, I present my daughter and heir, the Princess Deliea!" Mortus said, lifting an open hand to the princess, who stepped forth.

"I am honored and pleased, oh King!" Lorn declared, his gaze shifting from father to daughter, the warmest smile touching his lips.

"My prince." Deliea bobbed a curtsy, looking up at him through long lashes that drew him into the depths of her green eyes. Her lustrous black hair framed her achingly beautiful face, with a slender tiara nestled in its rich folds.

"My princess." His smile widened further, taking her hand in his, pressing his lips to her fingers.

She trembled; his touch sending a shudder across her flesh. No man ever looked at her with such passion, igniting a fire within her to match his own. His gaze was equally gentle and fierce, calming her racing heart while undressing her, as if she were naked before him in body and soul. She knew then that he desired her, that he always desired her, and came to claim her for his own.

Mortus was not blind to what was transpiring before him. A marriage for a political union was one thing, but this was something more. Only then did he surmise that Lorn's purpose in arranging this nuptial was for more than the good of both realms. He chose her because he wanted her. Lorn gently withdrew his hand from Deliea's, turning to face Mortus, as Deliea did likewise, struggling to take her eyes from her betrothed. They knelt in unison; their heads bowed to the Macon king as he addressed the assemblage.

"Let those gathered here bear witness! From this day shall our realms be joined, not only through royal blood but also that of our people. As father of Princess Deliea, I offer her hand in union with Lorn, crown prince of the Torry Realms! Prince Lorn, do you accept the Princess Deliea as your bride?"

"I accept the hand of Princess Deliea as my bride with great pleasure, oh King!" Lorn declared, his head still bowed in deep reverence.

"And you, my daughter. Do you offer yourself as the bride of Prince Lorn?"

"I offer myself to Prince Lorn as his beloved, oh King!" she declared, her head bowed with equal reverence.

Mortus descended the dais, a servant hurrying forth holding out a white Calnesian cloth, embroidered with gold stitching. Mortus leaned down, taking Lorn's right hand and setting in Deliea's left, before taking the decorative cloth, wrapping it around their wrists, binding them in union.

"As king of greater Maconia, I declare the wedded union of Prince Lorn and Princess Deliea, by royal decree!" he proclaimed.

Lorn stood, lifting Deliea with him, sweeping her into his arms. There, before his countrymen and hers, he kissed her a passionate but slow embrace, tender and full of promise. A great cheer rang out from the gathered host, heralding the union of their two peoples. In the coming days, more marriages would be performed, joining Torry and Macon soldiers with brides from the other's realm, ushering in a time of peace throughout these lands.

"Prince Lorn, he is the making of a legend," General Ciyon marveled.

"Nay," Jentra replied, standing at his side as they watched the spectacle a few paces before them, the sound of hearty cheers ringing in their ears. Jentra did not care whether Lorn was a legend or not, though he was well on his way. What he saw in his young friend was something far more significant to his native realm. Lorn led a successive campaign in Yatin, saving that empire from falling into Tyro's grasp. He defeated Yonig's legions, pushing Tyro's minions north. He then, in an unprecedented maneuver, shifted all the resources of Torry South to the relief of Sawyer. Against all conventional thinking and the opinion of his commanders, he split his forces and overwhelmed the Macon Empire. Lastly, he managed to convince the Macons they were hopelessly outnumbered, bringing Mortus into an alliance and forgoing bloodshed that would have decimated the Torry cause. When Mortus later discovered that the Torry 2nd Army was still at Central City, he did not respond with anger but laughed, his heart overtaken by the prince's audacity. Now the strength of Torry South was preserved and wedded to the might of the Macon Empire. Truly, Lorn was the master strategist, a crown prince, worthy of the name.

"Nay?" Ciyon lifted a curious brow.

"Nay. Not a legend. He is the *making of a king*!"

EPILOGUE

Fera, the Black Castle

Valera felt the eyes of everyone she passed upon her. The humans were curious, but the gargoyles drew away from her as if she was poison. She wondered how Terin felt traversing these very corridors during his visit here, though he was a guest, and she, a prisoner. She was flanked by a flax of guards to either side and another behind and in front as if she were the most dangerous individual ever brought to the ancient holdfast. She reflected on the arduous journey from her home, traveling upon ocran and eventually magantor to reach Fera. She was still dressed in her traveling dress, more leather than cloth, able to endure the lengthy time in the saddle. Upon setting down on the upper platforms of the palace, she was able to see the damage wrought by Raven, Lorken, and her son during their escape from this fell place. She smiled inwardly at Terin's courage, wondering how Tyro reacted to his many deeds against him, after learning who he truly was?

"Make way!" the voice of General Naruv barked, leading her escort through the cavernous corridors, clearing their path to the throne room, soldiers and servants scurrying from his rebuke. They met the Benotrist general at the border, where he assumed possession of her, leading their small party to Fera. As commander of all Benotrist magantor units, Naruv was informed of Terin's exploits at Corell and his feats dispatching his magantors with ease. Naruv constantly regarded her with contempt, knowing who her son was, but that was weighed favorably considering who her father by marriage was. Naruv informed her quite sternly upon their first meeting that she was not to speak of her kinship to the emperor with anyone.

Kinship? She thought at the time, *Why would she boast of it?* Considering the manacles affixed to her wrists, she understood the true nature of her kinship to Tyro. She was merely a means to lure Jonas. She doubted she would be warmly received by the emperor; that moment drew painfully nigh as they approached a massive statue where three corridors met before the large doors of the throne room. She wrinkled her nose at the sight of the statue, a grotesque amalgamation of human and gargoyle forms. Strangely, linen was wrapped around the figure's groin, covering the genital alteration Lorken conducted with his pistol, an insult Tyro would see met with measured retribution.

They circled the statue, pausing before the massive doors as General Naruv ordered them opened, before passing within, leaving her with her guards and the detestable Hotis Vlenok, the man who captured her.

"This is a momentous day, Lady Valera. The emperor shall be pleased to finally meet you," Hotis said, standing at her side.

"The pleasure shall be yours once you are paid for delivering me into his keeping," she said, gray eyes trained forward.

"My service to the emperor exceeds favors of gold and privilege, my lady. I am of the Imperial Elite," he said.

Of all the Elite, Hotis was the one Tyro placed the greatest trust, entrusting him with finding his lost heir. His travels took him across much of northern and central Arax over the years before word of Terin's exploits at Fera focused his search to Torry North, the name Jonas Caleph greatly aiding his search.

"Tell me, good sir, how many years and how many men did it take you to capture one woman, one who is with child? We shall soon see if your emperor is pleased with such little return for so many resources," she said icily, sparing him a cold glance from the corner of her eye.

"You poorly state your worth, my lady. You are worth more to him than a mountain of gold, you and especially who you carry." Hotis smiled knowingly.

"My lady? Such courtesies are meaningless to a woman in chains," she said, lifting her manacled hands.

"Chains with generous slack and padded to protect her lovely skin from chaffing, *my lady*," he said, emphasizing the last to raise her ire.

"Guard yourself well, Hotis Vlenok. My husband will not suffer these offenses to his wife and unborn child," she reminded him.

"I certainly hope he is aggrieved, my lady, aggrieved enough to answer his father's summons."

With that, they were ushered into the throne room.

* * *

Tyro sat his throne, his mind a maelstrom of emotions. Anger, apprehension, pain, and hope vied for dominion, but he felt mostly excitement. He would finally have answers to the questions that ran through his tortured mind for so many years.

"My emperor, the Lady Valera!" General Naruv declared upon her entrance.

Tyro drew up on his throne, his eyes following her as she approached. Most of the guards split off to either side of the vast chamber, leaving Hotis and two others to usher her forth. She was lovely, with piercing gray eyes that denoted a deep intelligence. His son chose well finding a woman of such beauty and intellect. The boy was no fool; he granted him that much. She was stopped before the dais; her guards forced her to her knees as she looked up at him with a cold stare. He smiled inwardly at that, admiring her courage.

Lovely, intelligent, and brave, he mused, three attributes he could admire.

Hotis knelt beside her, pressing his head to the floor before given leave to rise and report.

"My emperor, I have returned. My search led me to the home of Jonas Caleph, where I discovered that he was away at Corell, leaving

501

his wife, the Lady Valera, alone and with child. I forwarded a missive to Corell to be delivered long after we departed Torry lands, calling upon him to join her here and present himself to his rightful liege," Hotis stated.

Jonas. Tyro wanted to spit at the bastardized name his son had taken. Joriah was his true name, and he would set him to rights on that when he showed himself.

"Well done, Hotis. Your service to the throne is greatly admired. And you, my dear, may stand," Tyro said. The guards helped her to her feet.

Valera twisted her arms from their grasp once she gained her feet, making known her disgust.

Tyro rose from his throne, descending the dais before stopping in front of her, each regarding the other for a time, their silence deafening. Her eyes drew wide as he removed Terin's necklace from the folds of his sleeve, lifting it to her face, his eyes studiously comparing her face to the one carved by Jonas.

"An excellent representation, but still failing to match your full beauty, daughter." He smiled, lowering the charm.

"That doesn't belong to you," she said, keeping her eyes on his, lifting her chin in defiance.

"Its rightful owner is free to claim it. He need only ask it of me. Ironic, is it not, that I gifted this very charm to my son, who gifted it to his son, who delivered it back to me? Life is full of such mysteries, daughter, and so many questions I shall have answered."

"Jonas will not be pleased with what you have done," she said, cringing every time he referred to her as *daughter*.

"*That* is not his name. You shall refer to him rightfully as Joriah!" he said sternly.

"Fair enough. And if we are using true names, shall I call you Taleron?"

"I see where Terin inherited his ill manners, another fault I shall have to correct in both of you. That shall not be an issue with the one you now carry. I will see it raised with proper respect for its rightful liege." He touched a hand possessively to her womb.

"My son is not ill-mannered. He is kind, honorable, and just, sharing the same attributes as his father, and thankfully, none from his grandfather."

"Just and honorable? What is just and honorable in deserting one's grandfather and rightful emperor? The boy lacks respect, which is another flaw I shall have to correct, if his own recklessness has not already done so," he said knowingly.

"Courage is oft mistaken for recklessness. He has survived every battle, delivering you a bounty of defeats, and still stands in defiance." She pushed back at his rebuke.

"Stands? You have not heard, have you?" He smiled evilly, an amused tint in his golden eyes.

"Heard what?" she asked, her defiant demeanor breaking.

"He was lost at sea at Carapis and thought dead, but in truth, he was taken slave and sold at Bansoch, laboring under an ambitious mistress, who discovered his unique heritage and planned to wed him to her daughter. He was beaten upon a failed escape, only to be rescued by his Earther friends. If the rumors are true, his connection to his Kalinian blood is severed."

"That is not true!" she said. The doubt in her eyes proving otherwise.

"Oh, it is very true, child."

"Sold?" She lowered her eyes so he could not see her tears. The thought of Terin suffering so pained her more than anything she endured coming here.

"Sold and enslaved. Unfortunately, he was freed before I could retrieve him." He shrugged as if it was mere inconvenience. Had he known of Terin's whereabouts, he might've left him where he was, allowing Darna to keep him in exchange for his male heirs. Terin was far too enamored with his Torry blood to ever come to his side, but his offspring was another matter if Tyro could influence the child from birth.

"How do you know this?" she asked, her eyes dry enough to raise to his without revealing her anguish.

"I have many eyes in many courts, my dear Valera, and agents who witnessed much of what I claim." He motioned for Nels Draken to step from the shadows of the throne.

"Terin is free now?" she asked, desperately searching his eyes for the truth of it.

"For now, I shall reveal all when you dine with me this eve, and in turn, you shall answer my questions pertaining to my son's whereabouts for these many years," he said, before ordering a steward to see her to the royal apartments.

Thus ends book four of the *Chronicles of
Arax: The Making of a King.*
The saga continues with book five—*The Battle of Torry North.*

APPENDIX A

Armies of Arax

Torry Armies

Army	Location	Commander	Size
1st	Macon Border	Lewins	20 telnics
2nd	Central City	Fonis	20 telnics
3rd	Corell	Bode	12 telnics
4th	Faust	Farro	12 telnics
5th	(Destroyed at Kregmarin)		

Large Garrisons

	Location	Commander	Size
	Cropus	Torgus Vantel	5 telnics
	Corell	Nevias	3 telnics
	Central City	Torvin	5 telnics
	Cagan	Telanus	5 telnics
	(With 2nd Torry Fleet)		

Cavalry

	Location	Commander	Size
1st	Corell	Tevlin	300 mounts
2nd	Corell	Connly	700 mounts
3rd	Western Border	Meborn	500 mounts

4th	Yatin Border	Avliam	412 mounts

(100 reserve cavalry of the 4th attached to 1st Torry Army)

Navy

1st	Faust	Kilan (Grand Admiral)	31 galleys

(Includes 3 captured Benotrist warships)

2nd	Macon Border	Horikor	50 galleys
3rd	Faust	Liman	21 galleys
4th	Faust	Nylo	22 galleys
5th	Macon Border	Morita	20 galleys

Benotrist and Gargoyle Armies

Legion	Location	Commander	Size
1st (gargoyle)	Telfer	N/A	10 telnics

(Survivors of Mosar reassigned to 2nd Legion)

Legion	Location	Commander	Size
2nd (gargoyle)	Tinsay	Torab	24 telnics
3rd (gargoyle)	Destroyed at Mosar (survivors reassigned to 2nd Legion)		
4th (gargoyle)	East of Corell	Tuvukk	15 telnics
5th (gargoyle)	East of Corell	Concaka	20 telnics
6th (gargoyle)	Destroyed at Corell		
7th (gargoyle)	East of Corell	Vaginak	9 telnics
8th (Benotrist)	East of Corell	Vlesnivolk	22 telnics
9th (Benotrist)	Mordicay	Marcinia	50 telnics
10th (Benotrist)	Pagan	Gavis	50 telnics
11th (Benotrist)	Notsu	Felinaius	39 telnics
12th (gargoyle)	Eastern Border	Krakeni	50 telnics
13th (Benotrist)	Laycrom	Trinapolis	50 telnics
14th (gargoyle)	Laycrom	Trimopolak	50 telnics
15th (gargoyle)	Tuss River	Unknown	10–15 (estimated) telnics
16th (gargoyle)	Destroyed at Tuft's Mountain		
17th (gargoyle)	Destroyed at Tuft's Mountain		
18th (gargoyle)	Destroyed at Tuft's Mountain		

Garrison Forces

Fera	29 telnics (Benotrist)
Nisin	20 telnics (Benotrist)
Pagan	10 telnics (Benotrist)
Mordicay	10 telnics (Benotrist)
Tinsay	20 telnics (Benotrist)
Laycrom	20 telnics (Benotrist)
Border posts	10 telnics Benotrist)
	10 telnics (gargoyle)

Benotrist Navy

Fleet	Location	Admiral	Size
1st	Mordicay	Plesnivolk	50 galleys
2nd	Tenin	Kruson	7 galleys
3rd	Pagan	Elto (Grand Admiral)	80 galleys
4th	Pagan	Pinota	50 galleys
5th	Tenin	Unknown	32 galleys
6th	Pagan	Silniw	50 galleys
7th	Tenin	Onab	24 galleys
8th	Tinsay	Zelitov	50 galleys

Yatin Armies

Army	Location	Commander	Size
1st	Mosar	Yoria	8 telnics
		(Only 16 of 25 mustered at Mosar)	
2nd	Faust	Yitia	20 telnics
		(21 of 25 answered muster)	
3rd	Destroyed at Mosar (3 surviving telnics joined with 1st Army)		
4th	Tenin	Surrendered to Torab	

Garrison Forces

Mosar	Yakue	3 telnics
Telfer	Destroyed in Siege of Telfer	
Tenin	Surrendered to Torab	

Yatin Cavalry

1st	Telfer	Destroyed in Battle of Salamin Valley	
2nd	Mosar	Cornyana	475

Yatin Navy

Fleet	Location	Admiral	Size
1st	Tenin	Sunk in Battle of Cull's Arc	
2nd	Tenin	Sunk in Battle of Cull's Arc	
3rd	Faust	Horician	18 galleys

Jenaii Armies

Battle Group	Location	Commander	Size
1st	Corell	El Tuvo	10–12 telnics
2nd	El Orva	Ev Evorn	20 telnics
	(Casualties suffered at Corell replaced with soldiers of the 1st Battle Group)		
3rd	El Tova	En Elon	20 telnics

Garrison Forces

	El Orva	El Orta	15 telnics
	El Tova	En Vor	5 telnics

Jenaii Navy

Fleet	Location	Admiral	Size
1st	El Tova	En Atar	20 galleys
2nd	El Tova	En Ovir	20 galleys
3rd	El Tova	En Toshin	20 galleys

Naybin Armies

Army	Location	Commander	Size
1st	Northern Border	Duloc	3 telnics
	(7 detached to expeditionary force, destroyed at siege of Corell)		
2nd	Plou	Rorin	10 telnics
3rd	Non	Corivan	10 telnics
4th	Western Border	Cuss	10 telnics

Garrison Forces

	Location	Commander	Size
	Plou	Cestes	5 telnics
	Non	Rasin	7 telnics
	Naiba	Tesra	3 telnics
	Border Posts		5 telnics

Naybin Navy

Fleet	Location	Admiral	Size
1st	Naiba	Gustub	10 Galleys
2nd	Naiba	Galton	10 Galleys

Macon Empire Armies

Army	Location	Commander	Size
1st	Fleace	Noivi	10 telnics
	(5 telnics sent to siege of Sawyer, 5 remaining with General Noivi)		
2nd	Sawyer	Vecious	15 telnics
3rd	Western Border	Ciyon	10 telnics
4th	Null	Farin	8 telnics

Garrison Forces

	Location	Commander	Size
	Fleace	Novin	5 telnics
	Cesa	Clyvo	5 telnics

Macon Navy

Fleet	Location	Admiral	Size
1st	Cesa	Goren	20 galleys
2nd	Null	Vulet	20 galleys
3rd	Eastern Coast	Talmet	20 galleys
4th	Western Coast	Gara	20 galleys

Ape Empire Armies

Army	Location	Commander	Size
1st	Gregok	Cragok	20 telnics
2nd	Torn	Mocvoran	20 telnics
3rd	Talon Pass	Vorklit	10 telnics
4th	Northern Coast	Matuzon	10 telnics
5th	Southern Coast	Vonzin	10 telnics

Garrison Forces

	Location		Size
	Gregok		10 telnics
	Torn		10 telnics
	Talon Pass		10 telnics

Ape Navy

Fleet	Location	Admiral	Size
1st	Torn	Zorgon	60 galleys
2nd	Torn	Vornam	40 galleys

Casian Federation Armies

Army	Location	Commander	Size
1st	Coven	Gidvia	12 telnics
2nd	Milito	Motchi	12 telnics
3rd	Teris	Elke	7 telnics

Garrison Forces

	Location		Size
	Milito		3 telnics
	Coven		4 telnics

| | | Port West | 3 telnics |
| | | Teris | 3 telnics |

Casian Navy

Fleet	Location	Admiral	Size
1st	Coven	Voelin	100
2nd	Milito	Gylan	80
3rd	Port West	Gydar	60
4th	Teris	Eltar	60

Federation of the Sisterhood Armies

Army	Location	Commander	Size
1st	Bansoch	Na	20 telnics
2nd	Fela	Vola	20 telnics
3rd	Southern Border	Mial	20 telnics

Garrison Forces

| | Bansoch | | 10 telnics |
| | Fela | | 10 telnics |

Sisterhood Navy

Fleet	Location	Admiral	Size
1st	Bansoch	Nyla	120 galleys
2nd	Bansoch	Carel	80 galleys
3rd	Southern Coast	Daila	50 galleys

Teso Armies

| 1st Army | Southeastern border | Hovel | 4 telnics |
| 2nd Army | Central Teso | Valen | 2 telnics |

Zulon Armies

| 1st Army | Northern Border | Zarento | 2 telnics |
| 2nd Army | Western Border | Zubarro | 3 telnics |

City-State Armies

Sawyer	5 telnics	100 cavalry	
Rego	3 telnics	100 cavalry	
	(Rego garrison size fluctuates with new conscription)		
Notsu			
	(Of Notsu's 3 surviving telnics, 2 are joined with Torry forces, along with their cavalry)		
Bacel	Destroyed at Kregmarin and siege of Bacel		
Barbeario	8 telnics		
Bedo	10 telnics	100 cavalry	40 galleys
Tro Harbor	10 telnics	50 cavalry	50 galleys
Varabis	5 telnics		30 galleys

EMPIRE

PAGAN

TUR RIVER

BEDO

CORPI

TERSE

NISIN

LAKE VENEBA

BACEL

NOTSU

TRO

CROS

BESOS

CORELL

KREGARIN ISLE

TORRY

NORTH

LONE HILLS

TALON PASS

APE

TORN

GREGOK

EMPIRE

EL ORVA

IENAII

BARBEARIO

NAIBA RIVER

ELARIS RIVER

NON

PLOU

EL OVA

NAYBORIA

ENORUCTA

VARABIS

MIKUS

LINKORTIS

ROCKY SHORE

CASIAN SEA

MILITO

COVEN

TERIS

PORT WEST

CASIAN LEAGUE

STENOX

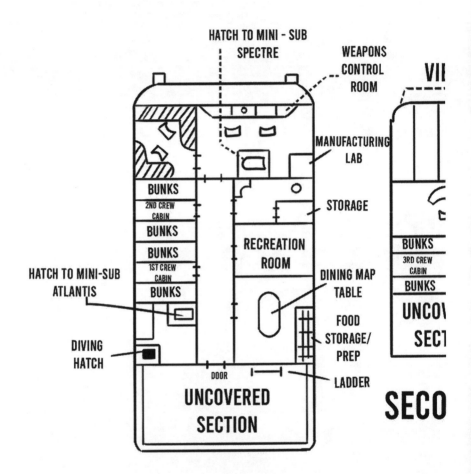

HATCH TO MINI - SUB SPECTRE

WEAPONS CONTROL ROOM

VII

MANUFACTURING LAB

STORAGE

BUNKS
2ND CREW CABIN
BUNKS
BUNKS
1ST CREW CABIN
BUNKS

RECREATION ROOM

DINING MAP TABLE

BUNKS
3RD CREW CABIN
BUNKS

UNCOV
SECT

HATCH TO MINI-SUB ATLANTIS

FOOD STORAGE/ PREP

DIVING HATCH

DOOR

LADDER

UNCOVERED SECTION

SECO

FIRST DECK

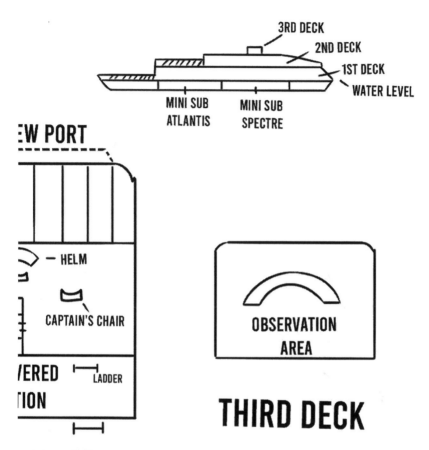

3RD DECK

2ND DECK

1ST DECK

WATER LEVEL

MINI SUB
ATLANTIS

MINI SUB
SPECTRE

:W PORT

— HELM

CAPTAIN'S CHAIR

/ERED
TION

LADDER

ND DECK

OBSERVATION
AREA

THIRD DECK

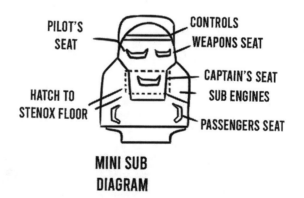

PILOT'S
SEAT

CONTROLS

WEAPONS SEAT

CAPTAIN'S SEAT

SUB ENGINES

HATCH TO
STENOX FLOOR

PASSENGERS SEAT

**MINI SUB
DIAGRAM**

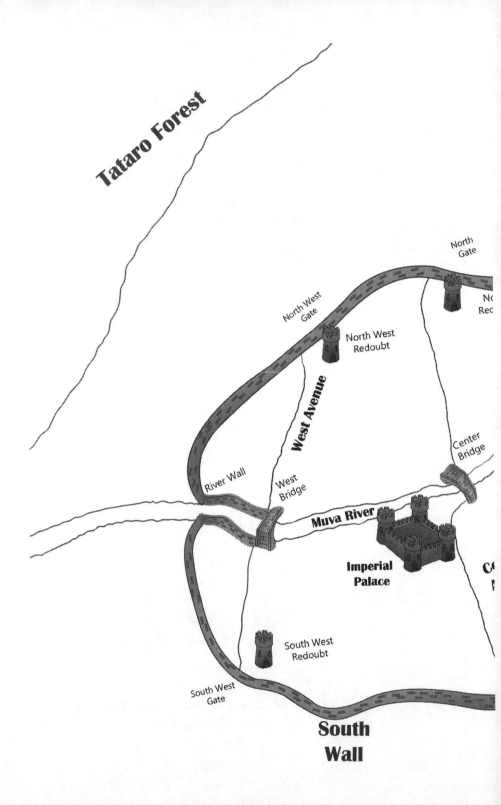

MOSAR

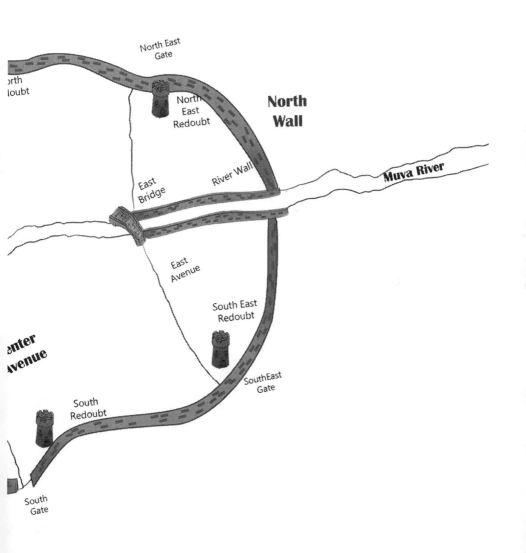

North East
Gate

North
doubt

North
East
Redoubt

North
Wall

East
Bridge

River Wall

Muva River

East
Avenue

South East
Redoubt

enter
Avenue

SouthEast
Gate

South
Redoubt

South
Gate

OTHER BOOKS BY AUTHOR

Free Born Saga

Book 1 Free Born
Book 2 Elysia coming 2023
Book 3 Dragon Wars (in production)

Chronicles of Arax

Book 1 Of War and Heroes
Book 2 The Siege of Corell
Book 3 The Battle of Yatin
Book 4 The Making of a King
Book 5 Battle of Torry North (late 2023)
Book 6 Fall of Empires (2024)

ABOUT THE AUTHOR

Ben Sanford grew up in Western New York. He spent almost twenty years as an air marshal, traveling across the United States and many parts of the world, meeting people from a broad range of cultures and backgrounds. It was from these thousands of interactions that he drew inspiration for the characters in his books. He currently resides in Maryland with his family.

Terin's Family Tree

Made in the USA
Middletown, DE
27 October 2023

41384725R00312